LEGACY

SHADOWS OF WAR

LEGACY

SHADOWS OF WAR

BOLGER BOOKS

This book is a work of fiction. Names, characters, places, and incidents are the product of the author's imagination or are used fictitiously. Any resemblance to actual events, locales, or persons, living or dead, is coincidental.

Cover Design: Vila Design
Developmental Editing: Jonathan Oliver
Copy Editing and Proofreading: Enchanted Ink Publishing
Book Design and Typesetting: Enchanted Ink Publishing

The text type was set in Minion Pro

ISBN: 99781068870774 (E-book)
ISBN: 781068870767 (Paperback)
ISBN: 9781068870781 (Audiobook)

WWW.BRADLEYELLIOTT.CA

To Jeff, Jodi, Debbie & Scott

LEGACY

SHADOWS OF WAR

BRADLEY ELLIOTT

BOOK 3 OF THE LEGACY SERIES

PROLOGUE

THE SECRET WAR

The sprawling white space station floated silently above the swirling power of the massive gas giant, a dichotomy of order against a backdrop of the unrelenting chaos, raging storms and crushing gravity.

The station buzzed with activity, small cargo ships coming and going while workers transferred goods in the massive main cargo bay. Two large refueling pods below the bay provided sublight and antimatter fuel, while two nearby orbital refinement operations worked tirelessly to meet the demands of their masters.

In the distance, a dozen warships rested, moored at another station in a higher orbit, while eight more patrolled the system in pairs, guarding the hidden installations from any that might venture into the system uninvited.

A series of explosions suddenly rocked the station, cascading from the outer wing on the upper level towards the center as plumes of fire erupted into space before being snuffed out by the vacuum. The forcefield protecting the huge cargo bay fluctuated as the main power failed across the station.

A second later, it was gone.

The sudden and deadly decompression that followed launched hundreds of bodies and dozens of ships out into the void, the rush of atmosphere pushing the station out of its orbit and down towards the planet.

Liquids jetted out from the breaches in the hull, flash-frozen in seconds as more bodies appeared from dozens of jagged tears, sucked outward at breakneck speeds, their silent screams lost in the blackness as the life drained from their eyes.

Inside the section of the station that remained intact, alarms blared, a hooded figure emerging from the chaos of a smoke-filled room, more explosions echoing behind him as he raced down the corridor, away from the devastation, his long, worn, and faded coat trailing behind him. Two small silhouettes appeared from a doorway ahead, lit by the strobing emergency lights, blocking his path. The figure raised his rifle and fired without hesitation; the bodies dropped as he continued forward without breaking his stride.

"Shen, prep the ship and meet me at the rendezvous point. I'll be there in a minute," he said, his voice rough and gravelly as more plasma fire from his rifle echoed over the comm.

"I'm on it," she replied.

"Any signs the *Ranger*'s been detected?"

"Negative. They haven't picked us up yet, but two of the cruisers docked with the station just launched half a dozen fighters each that are spreading out in a search pattern, and there's two rescue ships moving in to investigate the far end of the station. The other ships on patrol are all heading back at full sublight. So far, our cloak is holding, and I'm in position at the docking collar."

"They'll sweep the damaged sections first, trying to figure out what happened. That should buy us plenty of time," he said, firing three quick plasma bolts, taking out several more enemy targets as they appeared down a side corridor.

"Scans show the station has lost attitude control from the cargo bay decompression. It's being sucked in by the pull of the gas giant. It's going to burn up in just under five minutes. You've got to hurry!"

"I'm almost—"

He stopped in his tracks as a tall, ominous figure appeared ahead. Huge, clawed fingers twitched in the dim red of the emergency strobe lights, illuminating a sinister smile filled with razor-sharp teeth. He raised his rifle and fired, quickly switching to full auto, acutely aware that he was outclassed in a physical confrontation.

Searing hot plasma tore through the air, leaving an acrid smell in its wake as the figure moved with unnatural grace and speed, rushing towards him, evading the incoming fire while she weaved and dodged. Her shields absorbed several hits before she finally closed, clawed hands ready to tear out his throat.

He rushed forward at the last second, dropping and sliding on the floor, narrowly evading the attack. His left arm struck out as they passed one another, a wave of energy emerging from his palm, the impact throwing his attacker back several meters.

She landed on her feet, one clawed hand digging into the smooth metal floor, slowing her momentum, the sound of metal screeching as she shook off the impact of the blast.

"There's nowhere to run this time, Arkamus!" she said, venom dripping from her voice. She stood upright, her full height towered menacingly above him, and she darted forward once more.

"Who's running?" he spat defiantly, his rifle unleashing a barrage of deadly fire.

She evaded the onslaught, swiping with a large, clawed hand and knocking the rifle to the side. Arkamus pulled back, raising his arms, then bringing them down assertively as scythe-like blades of transparent blue light appeared from his wrists. A hum followed as he swept the blades towards her, going on the offensive.

She twisted, ducked, and dodged as the blades sliced through the air, narrowly missing her but forcing her back with each swipe. He flicked his wrist, deactivating one of the blades, then raised his hand, firing the shockwave gauntlet once more. The blast narrowly missed her as she leapt off the wall, bounding with the grace of a cat. She landed on the deck, and he struck out with the blade once more, grazing her in the midsection as she twisted away.

A wicked smile crept across her face as she wiped a thin trickle of blood from her armor. "I see you've learned from our last encounter," she said.

"I'll take you apart one piece at a time if I have to."

"What a lovely idea," she said, launching forward, her speed making her little more than a blur. She closed the distance between them, catching him before he could parry, claws raking across his thigh and back as he fell to one knee.

She slid across the smooth deck, spinning, then pushing off the wall and coming in for another attack. He twisted at the last second. A single razor-sharp claw gained purchase, tearing a streak of red across his cheek and up into his hairline, narrowly missing his eye.

She slid past him, turning, then stopping to lick the blood off her clawed finger. "Not as sweet as I remember. You've gotten old, Arkamus."

"At least I haven't gotten careless, Neyetta," he said, a smile crossing his lips as a thin trickle of blood ran down his chin, his hand coming up to reveal a detonator.

Her eyes widened as he pressed down on the plunger.

A small light flickered on her lower back an instant later, the charge exploding, tearing through flesh and bone alike, and launching her into the air. She landed half a dozen meters away, her body sliding across the floor.

Arkamus stood, pushing through the pain and retrieving his rifle. He towered above her prone, broken form. She looked up, blood pooling beneath her, and let out a low, defiant growl.

He stared down at her broken body, hatred filling his heart while the strobing light glinted off the metal of his cybernetic hand, remembering the agonizing pain from when she had severed it from his wrist during their last encounter.

"I'll see you in hell, Neyetta," he said, leveling his rifle.

He fired twice into her chest, a thin trail of smoke wisping up from the hole in her body.

The sounds of distant footsteps echoed down the corridor, and he got moving once more. He rounded the next corner, pushing through the pain, limping towards the airlock. The doors separated as he approached, and Shen appeared with a rifle from the inside *Ranger*, firing over his shoulder. Several small gray figures fell behind him as they entered the umbilical tunnel, followed by more still, a hail of plasma fire exchanged between the two sides.

Arkamus's shields lit up, and he turned, lashing out with the shockwave gauntlet once more, the impact throwing his attackers back. He leveled his rifle, firing several more bursts of plasma to keep them down for good.

Just as he stepped into the airlock, the sound of his name echoed down the corridor, the voice full of unbridled rage.

"Arkamus!"

He looked back, locking eyes with the huge, imposing figure who stood glaring at him, the broken body of his mate, Neyetta, cradled in one arm. The figure's other hand came up an instant later, and he fired.

Arkamus ducked, returning fire, then slammed his fist onto the airlock control, the heavy door closing as he reached into his tattered coat, retrieved a grenade, and threw it into the tunnel to destroy it.

The small sphere detonated, the tunnel shattering in an instant as the airlock on the station side snapped closed automatically.

Arkamus looked through the glass of the *Ranger*'s airlock window, meeting the eyes of his pursuer.

"Better luck next time, Lecari!" he spat, their eyes locked in mutual hatred.

"Computer, get us out of here!" he called, the sound of the engines revving up filling the ship. He turned, the sound of Shen's rifle hitting the deck startling him.

She stood just a few meters away, a perplexed look on her face as her hand lifted from her abdomen.

She held it in front of her in disbelief, turning it to show it to him. Blood stained her fingers.

"No!"

He rushed to her, his own pain forgotten, catching her just before she collapsed, cradling her in his arms, blood trickling from the corner of her mouth.

"I'm…I'm sorry," she said, her eyes glazing over, her body growing limp, her last words lost as bubbling red liquid filled her mouth. The last sliver of life slipped away, her head turning sideways, her chest falling one final time.

"No!" he screamed as he lowered his head, the ship jumping into hyperspace a moment later while the crippled station lurched ever closer to the deadly gas giant, pulled in by its immense gravity, its fate sealed.

He laid Shen's body in a cryo-tube before moving to the medical bay where the automated systems treated his own wounds. Still limping slightly, he made his way to the bridge. The lights of the hyperspace convergence illuminating the space in their soft, multicolored glow as he took a seat. He stared forward at the unoccupied helm where Shen normally sat, his eyes flickering to two other vacant stations. Waves of pain washed over him at the emptiness surrounding him. He was alone now. Truly and completely.

Perhaps not, he thought, pulling himself from his grief. *The second son is still out there. Somewhere.*

He pressed a series of controls, and a holographic display appeared before him. Arkamus pulled a chip from his coat pocket and set it on the edge of his chair. "Computer, access data chip."

"Accessing. Ularan database detected. Uploading and running analysis," the computer's voice spoke over the ship's speakers.

He watched on the viewscreen as the computer displayed several key data points, his frown deepening; the information contained lists, timetables, and comms logs. All of it confirming his worst fears.

Several minutes later, he tapped a control on the other arm of his chair and opened a holographic message window. He spoke, his words appearing as text only.

"Es'ah, I know it has been some time since we've spoken, but much has happened. And I fear that perhaps I am already too late. I've destroyed several enemy facilities over the past year; however, despite my efforts, they continue to grow closer to achieving their goals. I've discovered that they've been working with the Imperium, trading technology for intel, and are still searching for the second son. His location continues to elude me. I recovered a copy of the intel they've received from the Insectoid spies so far, and I have a lead. An admiral who I once served with long ago. I'm also sending you something else I discovered. I'm uncertain what it is, but it appears to be some kind of technical plan for a series of control centers, along with small satellites deployed in a web. I fear you may recognize it.

"I'll contact you again in a few weeks to allow for the time differential. I am…I am *alone* now. The rest of my crew are gone. I will do what I can, but it may not be enough to stop them this time. Two of the Ash'katar were there at the facility I just destroyed. But I have little doubt that one got away.

"Its destruction will set the Ularans' plans back considerably, but it is only a matter of time until they gather what they need. I fear we are losing this war…that time"—he looked back around the empty bridge—"that hope…is running out.

"I'll follow up on my lead and see what it brings, but you may need to be prepared to act soon. If they gain hold of the second son, then all will be lost. Arkamus out."

CHAPTER 1
THE PLAN

Admiral Valentyen rose and the lights in the conference room of the *Waverly* dimmed. A holo-map of the galaxy appeared above the table.

"As Admiral Thompson mentioned, over the past several years, we've led a team that's been scouring the known galaxy looking for Ancient military sites well-preserved enough to be viable for exploration. After sending probes to investigate over a hundred potential sites, we finally found three that look promising. The first is located on the third planet of the Brestin System, a small G-type star near the edge of GCH space, just six light-years from our border with the Imperium. Orbital scans indicate that there appears to be an Ancient structure buried beneath millennia of rock and sediment on the southern continent. We can't be certain it's a military structure, as something, possibly a vein of magnetic ore or other natural phenomenon, is interfering with the sensor data, but the structure appears intact from what we can tell. We've decided not to explore this site, however, unless absolutely necessary. Brestin III is a Vicara class world, and there are primitive settlements nearby we can't risk coming into contact with.

"The second site is in the Praxian System, a binary consisting of F- and K-type stars, where a civilization once flourished thousands of years ago. The fourth planet, called Praxian Prime, has been surveyed in the past with no signs of Ancient sites." The admiral looked at Jackson. "But using the data collected from the tests of the Ancient devices you did years ago, we've been able to refine our scanning parameters, and our probe in the system detected faint power readings, which we believe are Ancient in origin."

"Is it possible that the power core is Praxian?" Verris asked, drawing a look from Admiral Janus. "Uh, sir."

"Good question, Lieutenant," Admiral Valentyen replied. "We don't believe so, as the readings indicate quantum fission, far beyond anything the Praxians were known to possess. And we've had the androids triple-check the readings to ensure this isn't another trap."

Verris turned to Jackson, and he gave her an *I'll explain later* look while the admiral continued.

"The Praxian System is in the borderlands between the GCH and the Kerattan Empire. It's unclaimed, but we have detected Kerattan ships in the system on multiple occasions over the past several years, so it's possible that they are setting up a colony there. In any case, it is a promising location and one we feel is worth investigating. The planet has a heavily polluted atmosphere, but despite this, many of the lifeforms there are still thriving, and some are hazard level five or above, so it's a dangerous environment. But certainly doable.

"Which brings me to our third site, a planet called Vishnara. The Vishnara System is in an unoccupied region in one of the outer spiral arms and is beyond the edge of our space.

Several hundred years ago, one of our long-range probes traveled through the system and took detailed scans. The data showed only one planet and two small moons capable of supporting life and indicated that there were unidentified alloys present. We now know that the signatures match up with those we've found at other Ancient military sites and, therefore, we feel it's worth a look. This will be our first location. In time, we may visit all three, but for now, we'll start with Vishnara and see what we find.

"I've put together a team that I've hand selected for this operation, consisting of an engineer, an exobiologist, a tactical specialist, along with yourselves: an exceptional pilot and a covert operations operative. Our mission will be to travel to the Vishnara System, locate the Ancient structure, then recover any working technology we can salvage. Once completed, we'll take it back to our base of operations to analyze, and hopefully reverse engineer."

Jackson and Verris stared at the holo-map, the distances between the three planets considerable, the reality becoming clear to both of them that this wasn't just going to take a few days. They'd likely be gone for weeks, or possibly months.

"Two more things," the admiral continued. "First, our base of operations is a GCH black site, meaning that it's completely off the books. This will allow us to perform our analysis in a secure location, ensuring that there are no security breaches of any kind. Our enemies would do just about anything to get their hands on working Ancient technology. In fact, many of us in the intelligence and military history fields believe that's how some species may have gained their interstellar capabilities in the first place."

Jackson and Verris looked at one another, perplexed.

"I'm not surprised you haven't heard of it. It's not a well-known theory. As you likely already know, however, we believe that the Ancients' core worlds were located within what is now Insectoid and Reptilian space. This is fairly common knowledge, but what many of us believe is that based on how little both the Imperium's and the Empire's technology have changed or grown over the past several thousand years, that they may have somehow reverse engineered Ancient technology, at a basic level at least, using that knowledge to build their ships and spread out into the stars. While both have shown that they can certainly create technology, they're not particularly inventive or innovative, which has led to several theories that they didn't create what they have on their own but have been slowly reverse engineering Ancient tech instead. It's speculative and circumstantial evidence, I know, but it certainly explains how humanity has caught up to and, in many ways, surpassed them technologically in just a few thousand years. In any case, it's just a theory.

"Which brings me to our last item. I've been able to procure us a ship, the *Eritus*. She's a Perseus class reconnaissance vessel. Small, fast, and maneuverable, with a limited cargo hold, but making up for it with a class III cloaking system. She's a little light on the weapons, but she's stealthy as a ghost and should get us in and out of wherever we need to go undetected."

The lights came back up, the holo-display disappearing as the admiral turned to them. "Any questions?"

Jackson thought for a moment. He had about a million, so many that he didn't even know where to begin. He pushed them aside, knowing that the answers would come in time and excited by the prospect of finally getting past this challenge that had hung over him like a storm on the horizon for years. A tinge of guilt crept into his thoughts that he'd brought Verris into this, putting her in unnecessary danger. Knowing that if he hadn't pushed for her to attend Captain Delgado's program, the admirals may have opted for a different pilot for this mission. He also knew that this would take her away from the S&R work that she loved so much, and he wasn't sure if going back to the Fleet proper was something that she really wanted.

"I just have one question, sir," Verris said, breaking the silence, pulling Jackson from his train of thought. "When do we leave?"

Jackson looked at Verris, feeling his fears and doubts being washed away. He turned to look at Admiral Valentyen and smiled. "What she said, sir."

After the meeting, Admiral Thompson asked Jackson to stay behind for a few minutes. "Before you go, Lieutenant Commander, I'd like to upgrade Bits with the latest protocols for interfacing with and monitoring Ancient technology. We've continued to make some significant progress since the initial tests you ran for us five years ago, and they should help Bits to better access their technology and document how it works. I've got another update from my team with additional programing and a few other enhancements that we're now rolling out to our special ops that I think you'll like."

"Sounds great, sir," Jackson replied.

The admiral gestured for him to sit, placing a small device on the back of his neck while opening a case on the table with a control console inside. "Just close your eyes. This will only take a moment."

Jackson closed his eyes, a small hum filling his senses. "Sir, I noticed that Admiral Valentyen had left out of the briefing *when* I came from. Is the team he assembled aware of this, or do I still need to keep it a secret?"

"They've been briefed, yes," Admiral Thompson replied. "We discussed bringing it up during the briefing but felt that there was already a great deal of information to share. And we thought it may be best for you to inform Lieutenant Verris of this detail personally."

"Thank you, sir, I appreciate that. I think it's probably better that she hears it from me, as I'm sure she'll have a lot of questions."

"That was my thought as well. It's difficult keeping secrets from colleagues you work closely with and, in my experience, it's better for them to find out the truth firsthand, rather than having it come from someone else."

Jackson nodded slightly, careful not to shake the device from the back of his neck.

A few seconds later, the hum ceased. "There, the upgrade is complete. Just wait a moment longer with your eyes closed while your systems reboot."

Jackson waited, swearing he could feel a strange sensation as his implants deactivated, then came back online while the admiral removed the device.

"You can open your eyes now."

Jackson opened his eyes. His vision appeared sharper than before as he held his hand out in front of him and studied it, his ocular implants adapting and zooming in several levels. "Whoa," he said, turning his head as he blinked, a feeling of dizziness washing over him for a moment before his vision returned to normal.

"Sorry about the disorientation. It'll take your AI a few seconds to recalibrate your systems and run through a diagnostic cycle."

Jackson steadied himself on the armrests of the chair while the admiral retrieved a familiar-looking case from the corner of the room, setting it atop the table and opening it to reveal the Ancient stunner, gesturing for him to pick it up.

He reached for it; the weapon came online as he gripped it, his ocular implants updating instantly with detailed information about the device. The interface of his upgraded HUD showed the power readings and the stun level. He focused on the stun setting, and it increased as he heard the weapon's power core hum ever so slightly in his hand. He decreased the power, watching in his display as the weapon adapted.

"That's really cool."

"I'm happy to see that it's working. We learned a lot from the tests we conducted all those years ago and wanted to make it easier for you to interface and for us to gather information. Before, you'd needed a suit, but now, you can interface freely with the new programming and some adjustments to your implants. We still have a long way to go to reverse engineer all the Ancients' technology, but we've made some excellent progress with a few pieces. We even have a few working prototypes, and as you can see, we've come a long way from software and integration perspectives."

"Yes, sir," Jackson said enthusiastically, pointing the stunner at the far wall as a targeting interface appeared, before setting it back in the case.

"It won't be the same with every piece of Ancient tech you try, but the new code I downloaded to your AI will help him adapt and run diagnostics, allowing him to learn over time how to initiate an interface and interpret the data."

"Good to know. Hopefully, we'll be successful and bring a few things back that will prove useful."

"I hope so too. Good luck out there and be careful. I wish I could go with you, but I've had this damned headache for three and a half days now and the doctors want to keep me on the sidelines while they run some tests."

"I'm sorry to hear that, sir. I hope you feel better soon. I won't let you down."

"I know you won't." The admiral smiled, patting Jackson on the back.

Jackson returned to his quarters to pack, then went to see Verris, hoping to get a few minutes to talk to her before they had to report back to the *Waverly*.

"Hey, got a minute?" he asked as the doors opened.

"Sure, just about done packing. Come on in. It's hard to believe I'm leaving. *We're* leaving. It's so weird, packing everything up. This station's been my home for as long as I can remember."

"I know what you mean," he said, taking a seat on her bed. "Hey, could you sit for a minute? I've got something I need to tell you."

"That's not ominous at all," she said, raising an eyebrow, moving to sit beside him. "Are you okay?"

"I'm fine, but there's something I haven't told you. I haven't been *allowed* to tell you. Until now."

"Something bigger than being the only person in the galaxy who can use Ancient tech! This ought to be good."

"Believe it or not, maybe," he said, not sure where to begin. "So, remember when the admiral said I helped them test a bunch of Ancient tech about five years ago?"

"Uh, yeah, it was like, an hour ago. Are you sure you're feeling okay?"

"I'm fine."

"No, really, I'm showing your pulse racing," she said, gesturing to her ocular implants as she looked at him.

Jackson took a deep breath. "I do not know how to say this, so I'm just going to say it… I'm not…exactly…from this *time*."

"Wait, what?"

"Soooo, I was born on Earth. That part's all true. It's just that I was born a little over *nine hundred years ago*," he said, cringing slightly at the admission.

"So, you're telling me you're nine hundred years old? How the hell are you still alive…and not so much smarter?"

"Thanks for that. Yeah, so I'm not actually that old or anything. I'm actually just shy of forty, and pretty damn smart for my age too, thank you very much. You see, I sort of…died…a bit. And then got pulled forward in time by the Ularans about five and a half years ago."

"What? That's insane. Why you?"

"Because of my ability to use Ancient tech."

"How the hell could they have possibly known that, though?"

"Funny story. Turns out, they found something in these historical genetic records that they bought on the black market. Then they pulled me forward in time at the moment of my death and brought me back to life."

"Wow, so you actually died. How'd you end up here if the Ularans had you? They're known for being pretty secretive."

"It's a long story. I actually don't even know all of it. But the short version is that a GCH temporal response team then arrived at the site of the incursion and picked me up. I don't really know all the details, but I think there was a battle of some kind. From there, the GCH took the Ularan scientists who brought me here into custody before they died and they explained to the admirals why they had broken the temporal treaty. The *Waverly* then arrived at the station where they'd stashed me to recover, and they had me test some Ancient tech, proving it was true," he said, nearly out of breath.

Verris sat for a moment, looking at Jackson as if for the first time while he waited for the inevitable interrogation. "Actually," she said, smiling, "that explains a *lot*."

"You're not mad?"

"Are you kidding? Will, I love you. Nothing you tell me is going to change that," she said, taking his hand. "And really, now that I think about it, I can't believe I didn't figure it out earlier. I mean, who the hell else would know that much obscure Earth history or be such a wide-eyed newbie, excited by pretty much everything?"

"Yup, that's me." He smiled as a wave of relief washed over him. "Thanks, Ver, you're the best," he said, kissing her forehead as he put his arm around her.

"Damn right I am," she quipped, snuggling into his embrace.

"Now that you know, I want to tell you everything."

"It's a date," she said, kissing him quickly. "But for now, unless you've got any more surprises, I'd better finish packing. We've got a ship to catch."

CHAPTER 2
FRIENDS OLD & NEW

The next half hour passed in a blur while they made their way quickly around the station, saying their goodbyes. Vees, along with the rest of the crew, were sad to see them go, each taking a few moments to wish them well as they departed for their top-secret assignment. As they walked the corridors, the station felt different, the crew abuzz with news of the commander's promotion, and the new crew members and ships, leaving them feeling as though they were being pulled away from the party just as it was starting.

Jackson took Verris's hand, the two of them sharing a knowing look as they pushed past the feeling of being left out, knowing they had their own new adventure ahead of them.

Moments later, they boarded the *Waverly* and were assigned quarters for the journey to Benthar Station, a few sectors away. During that time, they spent hours in Jackson's quarters while he told her everything from Amy to how he died, what happened when he first arrived, and how he was essentially drafted into the service.

Admiral Valentyen called for them on the afternoon of the second day, just before they arrived at the station.

From there, they boarded a small military stealth shuttle, departing from a secure bay, the ship cloaking as it left the station, then taking them to a secret base somewhere in the Vicount Sector.

As they exited the shuttle, stiff and exhausted from the journey, Jackson immediately noticed that the look and feel of the base was different, with dozens of armed officers standing at attention across the hangar.

"Follow me," Admiral Valentyen said as they made their way through the sprawling complex, descending dozens of levels via a lift, then exiting into another featureless, sterile corridor where the admiral led them to a seemingly random conference room.

As they entered the room, Jackson saw two faces he didn't recognize when a third turned his way, his smile shattering the nervousness he'd felt a moment earlier. "Henrik!" he exclaimed, hurrying forward to embrace his old friend.

"Hey, Will!" Johansen replied excitedly, the two embracing in a half handshake, half hug. "It's good to see you, buddy."

"You too, man! I can't believe you're here!"

"Admiral Thompson and I had to pull a few strings to get him out of the R&D labs, but we wanted the best," Admiral Valentyen explained.

"Thank you, sir," Jackson replied, turning to face the others.

"And this," the admiral said, turning to his left and gesturing to the woman sitting next to Johansen, "is Doctor Daria Duratis, our science and exobiology officer."

The doctor smiled as she stood to greet them. She was short and slim, with bobbed brown hair, light olive skin, and a kind face.

"It's a pleasure to meet you both," she said sincerely. "I'm very excited to be working with you on this mission."

"The doctor here is far too humble to admit it, but she's a bit of a legend in her field," the admiral said, "having discovered and cataloged nearly three thousand four hundred and eighty, is it?"

"Eighty-seven," the doctor corrected, blushing slightly.

"Three thousand four hundred and eighty-*seven*"—the admiral smiled—"new species of fauna as well as performing genetic analysis on hundreds more in her fourteen years heading up the GCH Department of Exobiology on Delconia. She's also a fully trained medical doctor and has a degree in anthropology."

"Ever see a Palazian silver lynx?" Verris asked.

"I've seen two of them, actually," the doctor replied modestly. "Beautiful creatures, incredibly rare."

"Tell me about it. I caught a glimpse of one once on a rescue op about three years ago, and I've been a little obsessed ever since."

"A little?" Jackson teased.

"Okay, completely. Oh my God, you don't have pics or anything, do you?"

"I have an entire encounter holo-recorded from when we tagged one a little over seven years ago."

"I think you're my new best friend, Doc." Verris smiled widely, the doctor shrinking from the attention somewhat.

"Great to have you with us, Doctor," Jackson added.

"And last but not least"—Admiral Valentyen gestured to the woman sitting on the far side of the table, her arms crossed as she sized up Jackson and Verris—"this is Lieutenant Kelara Quentarus, our tactical and weapons officer."

"Quentarus?" Jackson asked. "Are you related to Captain Quentarus?"

"My father," she replied, standing up as she offered him her hand. "I saw your file. Looks like you served on the *Algeron* for a while."

"I did!" he said excitedly, his hand meeting hers, the firmness of her handshake impressive. "Your father's an incredible man. I learned so much from him. He spoke about you a few times, actually."

"Nothing good, I hope," Kelara replied, flashing a quick smile.

"Just that you're a bit of a badass."

"I do seem to have a way of finding trouble."

"I've been told the same thing."

"Don't let her fool you," the admiral said. "The lieutenant here is one of the deadliest combat officers in the Fleet, rated for armor so classified that I've barely even heard of it. She's been with GCH special forces for the past six years, running black ops behind enemy lines. She'll be watching our six and will have tactical command in the field. To be clear, that means that if she gives any of you an order when we're planetside and in a potential threat-con situation, I expect you all to follow it, understood?"

"Yes, sir," the rest of the crew replied in unison.

Quentarus turned, her hair shifting slightly as she did, three small, jagged scars appeared, just visible on her upper left cheek. "And you must be Verris," she said, extending her hand.

"I am. I guess I'll be your pilot."

"Just Verris?"

"Just Verris."

"Okay then." Quentarus smiled.

"Lieutenant Verris has been an S&R pilot for the past ten-plus years and is one of the best in the Fleet," the admiral explained. "Before that, she used to fly fighter combat, so she knows her way around a fight. The two of you should find some time to talk and discuss tactical strategies to make sure you're in sync.

"The team's already been brought up to speed on the mission and has spent the past several days preparing and getting our supplies in order. We're loaded and ready for departure. Once on board the ship, I'll enter the coordinates for our base of operations."

With that, the admiral led the crew to another elevator, taking them up to a secure hangar. As the doors opened, the ship came into view. "This is the *Eritus*. She's a Perseus class scout, designed to be fast and maneuverable, with good cloaking systems and basic defensive capabilities. She's old but should do the job."

The crew quickly boarded the ship, and Verris took the helm while Jackson manned the operations station. Johansen sat at the engineering console, Quentarus at tactical, and Dr. Duratis at the science station, while the admiral sat in the command chair in the center of the small bridge.

Verris took a moment to familiarize herself with the controls, reorganizing the interface to a more intuitive layout. "Helm ready to depart, Admiral."

"Ops nominal, sir," Jackson responded.

"Engineering diagnostics are all green. Sublight engines, stealth drive, and hyperdrive ready at your command, sir," Johansen reported.

"Science station online, sir," Dr. Duratis added.

"Tactical systems ready, Admiral," Quentarus stated.

"The base we're about to leave is classified," the admiral said. "Ops, take all sensors offline, aside from the navigational array, and keep them that way until we enter hyperspace, then wipe the nav logs. There's to be no record that we were ever here."

"Aye, sir."

"Hail the station and confirm our launch clearance."

Jackson quickly hailed the station, confirming their departure clearance. "We're good to go, sir."

"Helm, take us out."

"Aye, sir," Verris replied, carefully piloting the ship out of the hangar.

"Engineering, cloak the ship as soon as we're five hundred kilometers out."

"Standing by to engage cloaking systems."

"All right, Lieutenant Verris, you should have a clear traffic pattern. Take us up. Let's see what this little ship can do. Punch it," the admiral said with a smile.

Verris hit the throttle, and the *Eritus* accelerated rapidly, surprising all of them at how nimble the little ship was as it rocketed into the sky. Moments later, they broke through the planet's exosphere, the viewscreen turning from blue to black, thousands of pinpricks of light dotting the image.

"Helm, set a course for the following coordinates," the admiral said, relaying their destination from his command console.

"Course laid in, sir."

"Let's go," the admiral said, the *Eritus* slipping into the hyperspace conduit a moment later.

Halfway across the galaxy, the Arachnid queen sat in the throne room aboard her ship, poring over intelligence reports from the Imperium's operatives in the GCH.

In the years since the destruction of her colony on Atreus, she'd vowed to find those responsible and make them pay with their lives. After abandoning her lifeless world, she arrived at the Imperium Prime hive, demanding war in response. Despite her pleas, the council remained unmoved, preferring to stick with their original timeline and plans.

The council viewed the loss of her colony as a failure, relegating the queen to sifting through intelligence reports as a penance, her once boundless potential now forgotten in the blink of her eyes as her colony collapsed before her.

Years of frustrating impotence passed as she waited, focusing on a task once well beneath her proud station.

In the meantime, the Imperium continued to prepare for war, the thought giving her some small sense of comfort, as this war, she knew, would be like nothing the humanoids had ever faced before. For this would be the war that would break the Confederation once and for all.

Still, she clung to her obsession with vengeance.

The queen who'd sired her was now among the Imperium's elite, giving her access to intelligence usually reserved for the council and upper echelons alone. Thus far, there had been nothing to help her in her quest as she continued to search for those responsible.

The intel, gathered by the Imperium's vast network of spies and infiltrators, indicated thus far that the humanoids had no knowledge of the attack.

"Humanoid lies," she spat, venom dripping from her fangs as she read the report for what seemed like the hundredth time, her eight eyes taking in every word. "They even lie to themselves, rather than admitting what they've done."

Engineers from the Imperium's technology hive had studied the weapon that deployed the bio-agent on her world. Their analysis indicated that the technology was unlike anything the GCH was known to possess.

Whoever did it must be hiding it. An off-the-books black-ops unit.

As the years passed, she continued to sift through intelligence reports, looking for anything regarding covert technology development programs.

She finished the report she'd been reading, finding nothing of interest. She was about to give up for the night when the notification of a new report appeared on her screen. Most of it was standard intel on GCH Fleet movements and convoys which may be vulnerable to attack. As always, it wasn't complete, but these minor breaches allowed the Imperium to study their adversary, learning their patterns, looking for weaknesses they could exploit when the time for war finally came.

Suddenly, a section of the report caught her eyes; an agent had been successful in achieving a partial breach into the GCH's classified technology development database.

The queen read every word with bated breath. Her eight limbs tensed as she scanned the text for anything regarding the development of a bioweapon delivery system. The report was incomplete, but a half paragraph jumped out, detailing a highly classified test of Ancient weapons.

"Ancient technology," she said, scanning the next paragraph, every word causing the hairs on her body to stand upon end.

Tools and medical technology successfully tested. Data sent for analysis. Advanced Ancient weapons. Successful activation. Search resuming.

How is this possible? she wondered. *Could this be the clue I've been searching for?*

She moved to the final paragraph. Her fangs twitched as she read the words slowly. The coordinates of two star systems were listed along with a name…a humanoid name: William Jackson.

CHAPTER 3
THE HIDEAWAY

The *Eritus* emerged from hyperspace at the waypoint maker in the Kilgaren System, a desolate and uninhabited string of planetoids, moons, and asteroids circling a cool white dwarf star.

"Activate the cloak," the admiral ordered as he transmitted his code to the waypoint satellites. "Welcome to the Kilgaren System. This was once believed to be the major population center of a long-dead empire called the Dak'ona, a race of humanoids who inhabited this region of space approximately forty to fifty thousand years ago. The fifth planet was once capable of sustaining life, but all that remains is a wasteland ravaged by gamma radiation from what appears to have been a massive orbital bombardment.

"Wreckage of Dak'ona spacecraft were discovered centuries ago by our initial survey teams, most of them severely damaged. The GCH recovered what little remained, preserving what they could for study. Further explorations had at one time been planned; however, we soon discovered thousands of still-active mines strewn throughout the system, making exploration risky. After that, the plans for further study were eventually abandoned.

"The fifth planet is surrounded by an expansive, spherical debris field held in place by its powerful gravitational pull and stretching out for several million kilometers in every direction. GCH astrophysicists believe the debris are the remnants of two moons, which at one time orbited the planet. Large fragments of these, along with hundreds of millions of smaller rocks, became caught in a loose orbit, making navigation to the planet *nearly* impossible. The waypoint where we just arrived consists of a small group of cloaked beacons. These mark a safe egress point from hyperspace, which is kept free of debris by a series of small, cloaked tractor drones.

"The system is strategically located close to both the Reptilian Empire and the Oceanic Union borders, making it an ideal location for a covert, tactical operations base. The large amounts of debris and radiation provide a perfect hiding place for long-range surveillance equipment that the GCH uses to monitor both our enemies and our allies."

The admiral tapped his console, relaying their destination to the helm. "Lieutenant, set a course for the following coordinates."

"Aye, sir," Verris responded.

"Sir, I'm reading pockets of micro-meteors ahead," Jackson warned.

"Acknowledged. Tactical, raise the shields and keep our cloak active."

A sound like a hailstorm echoed throughout the ship as they passed through the micro-meteor shower, the view screen displaying the rapidly approaching edge of the massive sphere of debris illuminated by the distant star.

Verris slowed the ship as they approached the coordinates. The admiral reached for his console, transmitting a shortwave, encrypted code to a hidden satellite a moment later.

"This is the Gateway," he said. "The only safe passageway through the asteroid field to the planet."

As the admiral spoke, thousands of drones disguised as rocks activated, creating a tunnel of blue light through the asteroid field. "These drone satellites are custom-designed forcefield generators. When activated, they connect with one another, forming a tunnel protected by a powerful, linked forcefield."

The crew stared in awe as the blue tunnel slithered through the field like an azure serpent.

"All right, Helm, take us in."

Verris engaged the engines, maneuvering the ship carefully through the narrow flight path, the conduit closing behind them as they passed through. After traveling for several minutes, they reached the end, where the planet's gravity kept the debris back, leaving an area of open space around it.

As they approached Kilgaren V, the admiral ordered Verris to reduce speed. A few kilometers ahead, a small, circular station de-cloaked, its docking bay door opening as they approached. Verris proceeded to dock the ship, matching the rotation as they approached the bay, the station re-cloaking once they were on board.

The crew exited the *Eritus*, a nervous excitement taking hold as the admiral led them onto the station.

"This is the Kilgaren black-ops site. We call it the Hideaway. The GCH has used it for years, primarily as a staging ground for mounting covert strike operations against the Reptilians. It's completely off the books, and only a very small group of officers inside GCH Intelligence know of its existence."

The admiral led the crew on a deck-by-deck tour through the station. The med lab, arms locker, and cargo hold were on the same level as the hangar, while the second level contained living quarters, a rec room, an IRC, and the mess. The smaller top level consisted of the command center and a large briefing room. After the tour was complete, he gave each of them their assignments, and the crew quickly got to work.

Jackson and Verris assisted Johansen and Dr. Duratis with unloading and storing the equipment and supplies, while Quentarus prepped the team's weapons and armor for the upcoming op.

The next two days passed quickly while Verris worked with Dr. Duratis, getting her lab set up, and Jackson helped Johansen prep an area in the cargo bay, turning it into a workshop and testing facility for any tech they recovered. Lieutenant Quentarus ran the crew through several simulations in the IRC, focusing on preparing them for what they might encounter on Vishnara along with assessing their combat readiness. By the end of the second day, they had each learned more about squad combat tactics than they had in all their combined years of service.

The next morning, Jackson worked with Verris and Quentarus to prep the ship, while Johansen and the doctor focused on assembling their gear. The crew met that night in the mess on the admiral's insistence, having been scattered for the past few days while they worked on their various assignments. They arrived to find several bottles of Delconian wine the admiral had brought aboard waiting for them.

After they finished eating, the crew sat around the table, sharing tales from their time in the Fleet. The admiral went first, telling a story of his first posting, over two hundred years ago.

"I was a fresh-faced ensign, stationed on an Explorer class vessel, called the *Essex*. We'd left Archon eight weeks prior, assigned to survey a section of the outer spiral arm in the Ventara Sector. It was largely unexplored space, with only a few long-range probes having ever been through the region before. Our mission was to conduct detailed surveys of a few dozen systems that GCH long-range astrometric scans had identified as holding the potential for resources and colonization.

"I'd traveled between worlds before on transports, but it was my first time on a warship, and the experience was both exciting and a little unnerving for a rook right out of Basic. The journey from Archon took us just over two weeks to reach the Ancari System, where we traveled through a hypergate across the void of space between galactic arms, to the Ventara Sector.

"I was assigned to a stellar cartography lab on the fifth deck, working with a team of two lieutenants and several other recent graduates from the academy. For context, back in the day, all ensigns out of Basic had to spend six months at the academy. Nowadays, you just complete the rest of your training on the job in your specialty and via SLAK, or a specialized program, but back then, it was more classroom based. Anyway, the first system we'd surveyed was extremely promising, with an L-class moon containing abundant natural resources, the perfect place for a future colony. I was just getting comfortable, the excitement of our discoveries putting me more at ease, when we jumped out of hyperspace into the second system and were attacked!

"We'd jumped in near the third planet, the captain deciding to start there, as our long-range scans indicated it might be capable of supporting life. Much to our surprise, and by pure dumb luck, we arrived less than eighty thousand kilometers from an orbital station, with nine military vessels in orbit there.

"The locals, a race the GCH had never encountered before, took our arrival as an act of aggression, quickly scrambling their ships into an attack formation. The captain attempted to make contact in the seconds before they engaged, but their language was unlike anything we'd ever encountered, and as our attempts at communication failed, they became increasingly enraged by our presence, their ships moving forward to engage us. We were about to withdraw when a powerful blast from one of the ships slammed into the *Essex*, penetrating our shields and rupturing the hull along our port flank.

"I had been just leaving the lab, Lieutenant Baluta having sent me to recalibrate a nearby sensor array, when the blast hit. The decompression was swift and terrifying. The atmosphere sucked out of the corridor in seconds. I was lucky, in that I'd been standing just inside the doorway when it happened, the sudden suction knocking me back into the frame, where I managed to get a grip. The temperature plummeted, my skin feeling as though thousands of small knives were digging into its surface. I could feel my exposed skin beginning to freeze as I fought to keep the air in my lungs from being sucked out. I remember the thought filling my mind that my hands would freeze and shatter from the pull of my body against them as I held on for dear life!

"As the seconds passed, in what felt like minutes for me, I was certain that I was about to die. I kept my eyes closed, not wanting them to freeze, and did my best to hold my breath. All the while, the strength in my hands was failing. My grip on the door frame slipping!"

The admiral paused, looking around the room. "Then"—he snapped his fingers—"an emergency forcefield kicked in. If I'd been another thirty centimeters closer, it would have cut my feet clean off at the ankles. I hit the deck hard, thankful to be alive, losing consciousness seconds later, just as the *Essex* jumped out. I awoke in the medical bay hours later, a beautiful nurse hovering over me. She assured me that I'd be all right as I stared at her, my mind stuck in a daze. A little over a year later, we were engaged.

"That moment in the corridor became a defining one in my life, as I had faced death for the first time. It changed my way of thinking completely, and from then on, I was on a different path. Within a year, I'd been promoted to lieutenant, working my way up to a regular shift on the bridge. As the years went by, I moved up the ranks quickly, becoming a captain just seven years after joining the Fleet."

"You were lucky, sir, you must have only had a split second to grab hold when the corridor decompressed," Quentarus commented.

"I was extremely lucky. The odds, I'd later learned, of surviving a decompression like that were less than two percent."

"How long were you married?" the doctor asked.

The admiral's face darkened. "Unfortunately, we never were. She died a little over a year and a half later in a shuttle accident. She, along with four others, was on her way to provide medical aid to an Outlier colony that was in the midst of a civil war. There was a large camp of refugees a few dozen kilometers from the front lines who had reached out, begging the GCH for help. The Admiralty agreed to send medical supplies and set up a triage clinic, while trying to negotiate a ceasefire. Unfortunately, as the shuttle was on its final descent, it was mistaken for an enemy craft and targeted by a missile strike from one of the factions. The ship's shields took the brunt of the impact, but their engines were damaged and they went down hard. I was in the mess when it happened, having lunch with some friends. I remember sitting there, about to take a bite, when I suddenly stopped, my instincts telling me that something was wrong." He shook his head. "I still remember the feeling so clearly, even after all these years, but I pushed the thought aside, continuing my meal, until the combat alert sounded moments later. I later learned that at that exact time I felt that strange feeling, the shuttle had crashed. Strange, isn't it? How the mind works. The unexplained things we sometimes perceive but can't grasp hold of."

"I'm so sorry," the doctor replied.

"It's all right. It was a long time ago, and these things happen. In the end, the incident caused both sides to stand down, and a ceasefire was agreed to hours later, saving hundreds, if not thousands, of lives. "It took me a long time to reconcile my feelings, but that's how Lizzy would have wanted to go, her sacrifice saving the lives of others."

Jackson sat silently, pondering the admiral's words, knowing exactly what he meant. Vividly remembering when Amy died, how he'd held her hand as she slipped away. He didn't need the monitors or a doctor to tell him; he'd known she was gone the instant it happened. He decided to keep quiet, not wanting to share the story but feeling a connection with the admiral for the similar losses they had suffered.

"Did you ever learn who the race was that attacked the *Essex*?" Lieutenant Quentarus asked.

"We did," the admiral replied. "They're called the Gelvani. A race of humanoids who still have their own little empire on the outer edges of the galaxy. After the *Essex* jumped away, our captain reached out to Command, sending the audio of the transmissions for the androids to decipher. A day and a half later, they'd created a rudimentary but working translation matrix. We plotted a course, returning to their system the next day, this time jumping in much farther out, so as not to appear provocative. It was touch and go at first, but our captain was eventually able to clear up the misunderstanding of what happened before and open formal relations with the Gelvani. We still trade with them today, actually. They make one hell of a whiskey." He smiled, raising his glass.

The hours slipped by, as did the bottles of wine, the crew continuing to talk, sharing stories of their various experiences in the Fleet and telling tales from their past.

Johansen told the crew about his first away mission, where he and two other techs performed a spacewalk to repair a GCH surveillance array near the border with the Imperium.

During the mission, their ship, the *Cordova*, had to jump away for nearly an hour while it investigated an unknown vessel which had entered the system. He explained how the three of them kept working, constantly looking over their shoulders, expecting an Insectoid ship to jump in at any second and destroy the normally cloaked array. "Longest hour of my life, let me tell you," he said, his smile wide. "When I saw the *Cordie* jump back in, I'd never been so relieved in my life!"

The doctor detailed some of the more interesting life-forms she'd discovered in her years working for the Ministry of Exobiology. "The most frightening was a parasite from KC-491, a creature just two centimeters long which burrows under the skin. Within hours of insertion, it interfaces with its host's nervous system. In less than half a day, it co-opts the host's control over their own body, turning them into a puppet. The host's mind is unable to regain control as the parasite accesses their memories and assumes their identity."

"Oh my God. How did you discover them?" Verris asked.

"The survey ship that landed on KC-491 had six crew. Within hours, five of them were infected. The sixth crew member, the ship's doctor, had remained on board while the others conducted a field survey. The next day, the crew seemed perfectly normal. Each of them, however, had approached the doctor at one point or another, trying to convince her to come outside. After politely declining several times, she began to suspect something was off and ran a scan of one of the crew members using the ship's internal sensors. As the results came in, she knew that something was wrong. Their body chemistries were all slightly off in the same way. She initiated medical lockdown protocols, alerting GCH Command immediately, and I was part of a specialized team that arrived about seven hours later.

"We found the crew attempting to act normal when our team touched down. There were four of us on the team, all wearing full biohazard gear and flanked by a dozen troops in tactical suits. As we boarded their ship, the absence of the medical lockdown was our first clue that something was off. We questioned the captain, who remained calm, attempting to explain what had happened, how it had all been a misunderstanding. As I questioned the doctor, however, I noticed bruises on her forearms, just visible beneath her sleeves. Once I saw that, I knew that something had happened and signaled to the squad leader just seconds before the captain lunged at him, attempting to deactivate his helmet!

"The next few seconds were a blur, the crew attacking with a madness and strength they shouldn't have even been capable of. The soldiers on our team were good, though, and within about a minute and a half managed to stun the crew, rendering them unconscious. After that we ran through the ship's logs, trying to piece together what happened. I reviewed the feeds from just after the lockdown, discovering a recording showing the crew disabling power to certain systems, using their knowledge of the ship's systems to bypass the lockdown. They then used a rifle, cutting through the door where the doctor was hiding while she begged for them to stop."

Daria paused as a sadness crept across her face. "They made it through, dragging her out of the ship by force. The last thing the external sensors showed was them holding her down while the captain took something from a compartment on his belt and placed it on her neck. It was hard to see what it was, as it was so small, but a few seconds later, she stopped resisting, then stood and joined the crew as they silently reentered the ship."

"Were you able to remove the parasites?" Jackson asked.

The doctor shook her head. "No. Once they'd integrated with their hosts, the two became inseparable. We tried on the first officer, successfully removing the parasite, but unfortunately, he died as a result a few hours later, his body going into toxic shock. In the end, we devised a treatment using the neurotoxin secreted from a Kasharian slug. The team and I created a specialized patch that each of the survivors had to wear over the site where the parasite burrowed in. The patch used nanites to administer microdoses of the slug toxin to the parasite, effectively keeping it in a perpetual coma. It wasn't perfect, but the crew recovered, returning to normal. After several months of quarantine and study, they were released. However, their travel is still restricted, even today, and they're required to have weekly examinations to ensure that the parasites remain inert. But at least they've been able to resume something of a normal life."

Johansen shivered. "How could something so small take over a person like that?"

"They're remarkably terrifying little creatures. Incredibly intelligent for something their size. The quarantine lab the GCH set up in orbit of KC-491 studied several of them, and the current theory is that they may be trans-dimensional, existing on our plane of reality and possibly another simultaneously, as there's a type of phase shift in their DNA that we can't account for."

"That's crazy," Verris commented. "What was the crew trying to do when you arrived?"

"They were prepping the ship to leave. A course set for the core systems."

"They were trying to spread," Jackson said.

"That's what we think. But to what end, we're not sure. In any case, GCH Command quarantined the entire system and locked down the planet with a series of orbital batteries. As far as we know, none of the parasites, aside from the ones we know about, have ever gotten off the planet, but all our AIs are now programmed to monitor for them, now that we know they exist, and can administer drugs if one's ever detected, to keep them sedated while alerting GCH medical authorities."

"That's good to know," Johansen said, clearly still creeped out.

Kelara went next, telling the crew about her life growing up in the Fleet. She explained how her parents took a few years away from the Fleet when she was very young, but by the time she was eight, they'd gone back full time and she'd moved from ship to ship to ship, spending a year with each of them in rotation. As she grew, she became more accustomed to living on starships than on planets. "I still find wide open spaces, wildlife, and uncontrolled environments strange," she admitted. "And since both my parents were captains by that time, they each had their own command in different Fleets, which kept them apart quite a bit. We were only together as a family a handful of times each year when they were able to coordinate their leaves or we were lucky enough to end up in the same system for a few days. But despite all that, when I was old enough, I enlisted right away. The years of unofficial training I'd gotten from being a Fleet brat quickly separated me from the pack and led to me to a path in special ops."

As Jackson listened, he felt sorry for her, imagining that it must have been a difficult time growing up, having to switch parents each year and moving from ship to ship. Kelara, however, appeared to have embraced the opportunity, learning from both of her parents and the officers around them, then choosing a life in the Fleet. He began to think of her as a mix of Wesley Crusher and Rambo, a Fleet brat who knew the ins and outs of life on a starship, with the combat skills to handle any situation. As she finished talking, he felt a sense of relief at having her on the team, knowing she'd be watching all of their backs.

"Do you ever plan to become a captain, like your parents?" Daria asked.

Quentarus shook her head. "No, it's not for me. I'm quite happy being a lieutenant. There's actually a surprising number of officers in the Fleet who feel the same way. High-level command isn't for everyone, and really, it shouldn't be, as far as I'm concerned. I know what I'm best at, and being an LT lets me do that. There's lots of other officers and non-com specialists who are the same and spend their entire careers in roles where they're most comfortable, making up the backbone of the Fleet."

"I'm the same," Verris added. "Vees, our old commander, tried to promote me twice, and I turned it down each time. I'm not interested in all of the extra responsibility. I just want to do what I do. Now Will, here, on the other hand, I'll bet you he'll make captain in the next five years, tops."

Jackson sat with a perplexed look upon his face. "What? No, I'm just a—" He looked down, noticing his new rank, forgetting momentarily that he was now a lieutenant commander, the thought never occurring to him until then what it might mean. "Oh, right."

Admiral Valentyen smiled. "You're on a command path now, Will. If that's what you want. Fleet Admiral Lighton told me how impressed she's been with everything you've accomplished over the past five years, and she felt that you could be a great leader one day."

"Thank you, sir," Jackson said. "I guess it never really occurred to me before, the thought of being a captain one day, that is. I don't really know how to lead."

"As my XO, I'll mentor you, and you'll be required to add some training sims in the IRC and SLAK sessions to build your knowledge and skills. At some point, you'll likely spend a few months on Archon, when you're ready, going through the captain's program. It's grueling, but there are plenty of senior officers like myself and Captains Delgado and Quentarus – who both signed off on your promotion, by the way – who are here to help you. As the ranking officer after me, that makes you my de facto executive officer for the duration of this mission. Are you ready for that responsibility, Lieutenant Commander Jackson?"

Jackson sat up in his chair, looking around the table at the smiling faces of his new crew. "I'd be honored, sir."

The crew toasted Jackson, and he drained his wine before refilling his glass, his mind racing.

Verris took her turn, shifting the focus off Jackson while she told the story from her time serving on the *Galloway* when her fighter wing was ambushed. He'd heard the story before but never realized how much it had led her to leave that life, putting her on the path to S&R.

When it was his turn, he told the crew about his life on Earth, briefly sharing how he'd been married, telling them how Amy died, then the story of how he ended up in the future. As he spoke, he felt a weight he hadn't realized he'd been carrying lift from his shoulders. He'd become so guarded about his past, unable to talk to anyone, even Verris, until just a few days before about where and when he truly came from, that it was liberating to finally be able to open up and tell the truth.

As the night came to a close, he felt closer to his new crewmates than many of his colleagues on Kishara Station, whom he'd known for years. They'd instantly accepted him for who he was, creating a feeling of belonging now that he didn't have to keep his guard up all the time. He felt as though he could finally, truly, be himself with all of his secrets laid bare. It was exhilarating to feel such freedom after years of repressing that part of his life.

That night, he went to bed with Verris, the two embracing as they lay silently, the room spinning slightly from the wine.

"I guess I never really asked about your wife before," she admitted. "I'm sorry. I know that her death must have been tough."

"That's okay," he said, turning to face her. "I couldn't really talk about it much before anyway. But I'm glad I can finally tell you the truth." He leaned forward, kissing her forehead. "It was the one thing back on Kishara Station that always bothered me. I hated keeping all of this from you."

"At least we can talk about it now. It's funny. I always knew that there was something you were holding back. But I have to admit, I never would have guessed all this. I'm glad that we can be fully open and honest with each other now."

"Me too."

"And if you ever want to talk about it, I'm here, okay?"

"Thanks, Ver, you're the best."

"I know. But don't stop telling me, okay?"

Jackson smiled, pulling her closer. "Copy that, LT."

CHAPTER 4

VISHNARA

Late the next morning, the admiral summoned the crew for a briefing in the conference room on the command level. “Good morning, everyone. I hope that you all slept well, because tomorrow is the big day. We’ll be departing for the Vishnara System at 0800.”

The crew sat up in their chairs, the sluggishness from the night before instantly forgotten as they focused, listening with quiet excitement.

“The Vishnara System is located just over eighteen hundred light-years from here, at the edge of GCH space on the outer frontier.” A holo-map of the galaxy appeared above the table, highlighting their route, focusing in on one of the galactic arms. “It will take us five days to get there at maximum speed, so we’ll have some time on the *Eritus* to plan out the fine details. As you all know, our goal is simple: Locate the Ancient structure, find a way inside, and see what we can salvage. Vishnara is an L9 world, meaning that it is capable of sustaining humanoid life, but just barely. The air is breathable, but the mix of gasses is just at the edge of tolerable levels, so not for more than a few minutes before it will start to cause side effects. Jackson and I will wear tactical suits, while Johansen and Dr. Duratis will suit up in tech and science exos, respectively. Lieutenant Quentarus, I want you in the Gate Keeper to watch our backs. Lieutenant Verris, I'd like you to remain on the ship. Keep your eyes on the sensors and watch for any native lifeforms in our immediate vicinity that may pose a threat. The planet is rich in oxygen, which means that the lifeforms inhabiting it will likely be larger than normal, so we have to be on guard. The last scans of the planet identified more than a dozen species of apex predators which present a potential risk, so I want us all to be careful and prepared, understood?"

"Yes, sir," the crew responded.

"Excellent. We depart first thing tomorrow. In the meantime, I've asked Lieutenant Quentarus to run you all through some final simulations this afternoon. After that, I'll leave you to prep, then you have some time to yourselves this evening. Dismissed."

After a grueling round of simulations, the crew exited the IRC sore and tired.

"How'd it go?" the admiral asked, having only taken part in the first few sims.

"They did well. A few bumps and bruises as I dialed back the safety protocols, but nothing that their implants won't heal by tomorrow," Quentarus replied.

The crew filed past, each dripping with sweat and clearly exhausted as they gave her and the admiral a nod and a brief "sir." Jackson remained, watching a replay from their last sim, trying to see what he could have done better, an old habit from his covert-ops training.

"Good work. Always good to give them a taste of what we could expect to encounter before we leave and get them out of their comfort zones."

Johansen dropped his water flask, the sound of metal on metal echoing throughout the corridor for a moment, followed by his strained groans as he bent to pick it up. "I'm good. Nothing to see here," he called.

Quentarus and the admiral shared a smile. "They'll all sleep well tonight," she quipped.

"Indeed. There's one more thing I need to talk to you about."

"Of course, sir."

"If things go wrong out there and anything happens to me, I'm authorizing you to initiate the Ishar'ian Protocol."

"Do you really think that will be necessary, sir?"

"I hope not, but I want it in our back pocket, just in case. If we recover any advanced Ancient tech, we cannot, under any circumstances, allow it or, more importantly, Will, to fall into enemy hands."

"Understood, sir."

The admiral motioned with his head for Quentarus to follow him so they could discuss the matter further.

Jackson continued watching the replay, having inadvertently caught a few parts of the conversation, his mind pondering briefly what the protocol was and why the lieutenant was so hesitant about it, before pushing it from his thoughts. He was privy to half a dozen classified protocols with his clearance level, most of which gave access to things like off-the-books equipment and weapons caches or permission to suspend certain regulations if needed to get a job done. He trusted the admiral and Quentarus, despite only having spent a short time with them, and felt confident that whatever it was, he'd worry about it if and when the time came.

Jackson awoke early the next morning, eager to get going. The crew departed at 0800 as planned, and the next several days passed quickly as they made the journey to the Vishnara System. The crew continued preparing for the mission, Dr. Duratis spending most of her time going through the cataloged flora and fauna data that the last survey team had gathered many years before, identifying several species that the team would have to be on the lookout for and calibrating their instruments for the oxygen-rich atmosphere.

Johansen spent most of his time in the cargo bay with Lieutenant Quentarus, tweaking several systems on the Gate Keeper, along with performing final checks of all the weapons and gear. The admiral spent most of the time on the bridge with Jackson and Verris, going over the surveys of the planet, showing them what the most recent reconnaissance had found and where their target area was. GCH Intelligence believed that an Ancient structure, possibly several of them, was located on the smaller northern continent. However, the readings indicated that it lay beneath what was now a dense boreal forest.

On the morning of their fifth day, the admiral summoned the crew to the bridge. "We're approaching the Vishnara System," he said as they took their stations, a nervous energy filling the air. "Helm, take us out of hyperspace. Ops, Science, and Tactical, run scans of the system. Let's take a closer look to see what we have. Engineering, cloak the ship, then take the hyperdrive offline and run it through a maintenance cycle. Five days of continuous hyperspace travel at max velocity is a lot for this old bucket."

Verris dropped the *Eritus* out of hyperspace just past the fifth planet, a blanket of stars along with a large, luminous green nebula filling the viewscreen. "Engaging sublight engines and plotting a course towards Vishnara," she said, while the others ran their scans and reported back in.

"I'm detecting six, no, *seven* navigational anomalies within a six-million-kilometer range!" Jackson warned.

"That's really concentrated," Johansen chimed in. "Most systems have at least a few minor gravitational eddies or other areas to watch out for, but to detect seven anomalies in such a small radius is concerning."

"Yeah. Definitely something out of the ordinary in this system. I'm sending them to your stations now," Jackson said.

"Looks like they're mostly localized near the third planet. So far, our flight path looks clear, but we'll need to keep our eyes open in case there are any more," Verris said.

"I'm running long-range scans of Vishnara now. It appears to be as expected. Class L9 and approximately eighty-seven hundred kilometers in diameter. There's also a nearby asteroid that will pass just sixty thousand kilometers from the planet. That's incredibly close is astronomical terms! A near miss, really," Dr. Duratis said excitedly without looking away from her screen. "There's also two small habitable moons around the outer gas giants. Both appear to have plant life from the atmospheric readings. This system is a rare gem!" she said, the excitement in her voice barely contained. It had been several years since she'd been out in the field, and the opportunity to discover something new appeared to be pushing aside her fear of space travel.

"The system is clear. No ships detected and no signs of recent sublight or hyperspace signatures," Quentarus added.

"All right," the admiral said. "Helm, set a course for the second planet. Stealth drive ahead full."

Verris increased their speed while the others continued to monitor their sensors, and Johansen took the hyperdrive offline for maintenance. Twenty minutes later, they approached Vishnara, the planet appearing on the viewscreen as a lush green sphere with large swaths of blue, capped with an icy pole at either end.

Verris put the ship into a high orbit while the rest of the crew began running detailed sensor scans.

"The atmosphere is composed of fifty-eight percent nitrogen, thirty-five percent oxygen, and seven percent various other gases. I'm detecting bio-signs on all eight continents and in the planet's oceans," Dr. Duratis reported. "The planet's axis is tipped by nine degrees, and it appears to be summer in the northern hemisphere where we're heading."

"Ops, begin scanning for the Ancient structure," the admiral said.

"Scanning," Jackson replied. "I've located the metallic signature, sir. Exactly where the probe indicated it should be. Running multispectral scans now. It looks like there's at least three structures buried there. One appears to be circular, while the other two are rectangular buildings. Relaying coordinates to Helm."

"Helm, lower us into a geosynchronous orbit. Doctor, focus your bio-scans on the area around the structures. Let's make sure we know exactly what we're dealing with before we get down there. The rest of you, let's suit up and make our way to the cargo bay. We'll deploy as soon as we land."

Jackson and Johansen exited the bridge, quickly making their way to the two circular platforms at either side of the operations room behind the bridge, with Quentarus joining them a moment later. Jackson went to the weapons locker first, pulling a rifle and inspecting it, then grabbing an extra power pack and setting it aside, while the other two suited up.

After suiting up, Quentarus continued back to the cargo bay.

"Activate Gate Keeper," she said as she approached the bulky suit of armor, a low hum filling the air as the Gate Keeper powered up, the lights on the large, intimidating armor coming to life and the startup diagnostics kicking in. The reinforced armored plating was designed to withstand a significant physical pounding, and its multi-vector targeting systems allowed it to repel assaults from multiple directions, making it an ideal armor for defensive deployment. Gate Keepers were primarily used to hold a position, providing cover for the surrounding soldiers, but Quentarus had chosen it specifically, as it could also go on the offensive, giving her a variety of options to protect the crew if things got problematic.

As she approached, the back opened up, and she quickly climbed inside, settling in while her AI, Helo, and her exosuit's systems interfaced with the controls. "Gate Keeper online," she signaled to the bridge. "Initiating moorings."

The feet of the armor magnetized with a loud click, locking it in place as a blue beam of light activated from the ceiling above, securing it in a stasis field.

"Bits, load the config we worked on," Jackson said, moving to stand on the ops platform.

"Loading."

The platform lit up, filling the room with a soft green glow as a silver liquid flowed up from the base, covering his body. Robotic arms appeared from above, reaching down as they installed various components into the suit, the nano-liquid flowing around them. After several seconds, the suit hardened, changing color to a forest camouflage, ready to blend in with their destination.

Jackson stepped off the platform, checking the suit's fit as he stretched, feeling the familiar snugness, then running through a quick combat stance and sequence of moves, testing its responsiveness. Satisfied, he picked up the plasma rifle, pressing it to his upper back, and the extra power pack. He then went back to the weapons locker, deciding to add a sidearm, just to be safe. He pulled the pistol from the storage rack, then pressed it to his hip, the suit merging the holster into it, then integrating both weapons' targeting systems into his HUD.

He headed to the cargo bay, taking a seat on a bench along the wall, a blue light surrounding him a few seconds after he sat down, the inertial dampening field bathing him in its protective embrace.

Johansen appeared shortly after in a dark forest-green tech suit with subtle camouflage patterns, carrying a large case in his hand and tucking it under the bench where he took a seat next to Jackson.

The admiral and Dr. Duratis arrived moments later, both suited up and ready to deploy. The admiral carried a rifle, while the doctor had a small case in each hand and wore a sleek gray-and-green suit as they both took their seats.

"Everyone ready?" the admiral asked.

"Ready," Dr. Duratis said, a nervous excitement in her voice.

"All systems go," Johansen replied.

"Ready," Jackson responded.

"Affirmative," Quentarus said.

"All right then, Helm, take us down."

Verris altered their course, piloting the *Eritus* into the atmosphere. "All right, everyone, just sit back and relax. I'll have us planet-side in no—"

An alarm sprang to life, cutting Verris off.

"What the hell?" she said, the ship shaking suddenly.

Jackson raised his wrist, pulling up the ops console. "Spatial anomaly detected!" he called out, the panic in his voice sending a chill down the crew's spines. "It wasn't visible until the atmospheric friction from the *Eritus* lit it up! Oh my god, it's massive! At least down to the mesosphere, and hundreds of kilometers wide!"

"Helm control is sluggish!" Verris called over the comm.

The admiral turned to Johansen. "Chief, can you reroute power to the engines?"

Johansen already had his arm out, looking at the engineering holo-display, pulling up the power systems. "Rerouting now."

"Lieutenant," the admiral said over the comm, "any better?"

"Negative, sir. We're being pulled off our entry vector. Our angle of approach is too steep! We're gaining speed and I can't level her off."

"Foxy, run the thruster systems' restart sequence," Johansen said to his AI. "Give me a sec, I'm going to cycle the thruster systems and see if I can reroute more power. There, try it again."

Verris waited for the restart sequence to complete, then reengaged the forward thrusters. "I'm getting something. Maybe twenty percent burn, but my readings show it at full power."

"Hang on," Johansen said as the ship continued to shake. "All systems show as normal. The *Eritus* should be operating perfectly!"

"Well, we're still picking up speed. I've got the nose up a bit, but our shields don't seem to be doing anything. Without them, we're either going to burn up or exceed this bucket's structural limits and get torn apart if we go much faster!"

"It's the anomaly," Jackson interjected. "My readings show that it's creating a low-level Hawking-Plait field."

"Confirmed," Johansen said, checking the readings. "The properties of the atmosphere around us are being altered at a quantum state. Our systems are working. They just aren't effective within the confines of the anomaly. I'll see if I can reconfigure them."

"How long until we're through it?" the admiral asked.

"At our present speed, another eighty-six seconds," Jackson replied.

"We don't have eighty-six seconds!" Verris shot back. "We're going to burn up in less than fifty if we don't slow down or get those shields working!"

"Hang on," Johansen called. "Oh shit! The main computer just went offline!"

"I've lost helm control. We're flying dead stick!" Verris shouted.

"The computer, it's a quantum state processor. The field must have interacted with it somehow. Foxy, activate secondary systems."

"Secondary systems nonresponsive," Foxy reported.

"Chief?" the admiral asked, the sounds of twisting metal echoing throughout the ship.

"Okay, I've got an idea," Johansen said. "It's not exactly in the manual, but it might work."

"Do it!" the admiral barked, his voice shaking from the turbulence. The temperature on the ship rising rapidly.

"Okay, we need to link our suits and our AIs. If we combine them, we can use the collective CPU power to reinitialize the systems. I need each of you to initiate a link with my suit, then have your AI transfer its CPU controls to Foxy."

Jackson, Dr. Duratis, and the admiral each reached out to take each other's hands, their suits forming a physical bond with each other. Jackson put his hand on Johansen's arm as they instructed their AIs to link with his.

"CPU links have been engaged. Attempting emergency systems restart," Foxy informed them.

The crew waited for several tense seconds as the ship shook violently, the gravitational forces from their fall increasing, pinning them back against the wall. The heat in the cargo bay, despite their suits, grew to be almost unbearable.

"Restart complete," Foxy reported. "All systems online."

"Still no controls," Verris said.

"I've got the shields," Jackson called. "Cycling through frequencies, attempting to find one that will work."

"I'm recalibrating the engines," Johansen said, the strain in his voice clear.

"That did it! I've got helm control. But the hull temperature is still rising," Verris called.

"Shields are back, but only forty-four percent effective inside the anomaly," Jackson said.

"I'll take it," Verris grunted, seconds passing as she tried to pull the ship up and reduce their angle of descent.

"We're almost clear," Jackson said as he stared at the readings in his HUD.

The ship creaked from the stress as the seconds passed, Verris attempting to level them out and clear the anomaly. Her hands worked the helm feverishly, initiating several quick banking maneuvers, attempting to shave off speed, the *Eritus* leaving a trail of smoke in their wake.

"We're clear!" Jackson announced, the crew breathing a sigh of relief as the turbulence let up.

"Our speed is tapering off," Verris added. "Good thinking back there, Chief."

"Is everyone okay?" the admiral asked, somewhat short of breath from the intense Gs.

The crew each responded that they were unharmed as they composed themselves, taking a moment to catch their collective breath. They lowered their helmets while Johansen used the ship's environmental controls to cool the inside air, providing them all with some welcome relief.

"What's our status, Chief?" the admiral asked.

"Well, the main computer is fried. I don't know how badly yet, but it might be beyond my ability to repair in the field. The good news is that the hull is still intact, but it looks like it took a hell of a beating. We're still here though, so there's that," he said optimistically. "Foxy, give their AIs back control of their CPUs. I still need to keep our suits linked until we land before I can give you all full control of them."

"Let's get on the ground first, then run a full array of diagnostics," the admiral said. "Can we run the ship off of just our suits' CPUs?"

"No. They don't have enough processing power to make the calculations for a hyperspace jump," Johansen said. "I might be able to rig something up with the Gate Keeper though. It has six redundant Class IV nanoprocessors. They should be able to do the job, but I'll have to take the armor offline to hook it up."

"Lieutenant, what is your tactical assessment? Can you secure the area without it?"

"There's a lot of life down there," Quentarus responded, pulling up the scans from orbit along with the threat analysis the doctor created. "But I have a few toys on board that I might be able to make do with. Verris, I'll need you to deploy some drones to watch our backs as soon as we touch down, as we were counting on the Gate Keeper's advanced sensors to keep an eye out for trouble."

"Copy that," Verris replied.

"All right. Helm, take us to the landing site. Johansen, you stay here and see what you can do to get us back online. Verris, give him a hand. Doctor, assist Lieutenant Quentarus with getting her other gear while Jackson and I secure the LZ."

Verris piloted the *Eritus* to the coordinates near the Ancient structures, hovering the ship several meters above the treetops while she deployed half a dozen small sensor drones to spread out and begin sweeping the area. Jackson opened the cargo bay door, looking down at the canopy of the forest below. He quickly spotted a hole in the dense foliage, jumping out of the ship as his suit's flight mode kicked in and he slowly descended to the forest floor.

"Bits, scan the area. I don't want to come down on top of anything."

"Scanning. I'm detecting several small lifeforms, but nothing that poses a threat."

"Raise shields anyway," Jackson ordered, and the suit powered up its shield generators.

Jackson readied his rifle, the targeting and power levels appearing in his HUD as it activated. The M-221 was a tactical plasma rifle with three dispersion modes, six power settings, and a two-hundred-round power pack. It was powerful and versatile, used by the GCH in the field extensively for combat missions. Just one of the new weapons he'd been rated on at the Advanced Combat Training Center. He'd always found it strange how the suit-based weapons had become like extensions of his body and how counterintuitive a rifle felt after getting used to them. The rifle, however, had an undeniable advantage in power and capacity, something that was unquestionably reassuring when setting foot on a potentially hostile world.

In his HUD's 360-degree view, he could see the admiral descending behind him, while below, the forest floor approached rapidly. "Bits, switch to thermo."

His view flickered, becoming a mosaic of colors, reds and oranges indicating heat sources, blues and grays indicating cold spots as the image of the alien world filled his display. His mind drifted for a moment, his thoughts going to the movie *Predator* as he turned his head, taking in the surrounding area.

Jackson landed on the forest floor, switching his view back to tactical mode, the display showing readouts of his surroundings, locking in on any points of interest, while maintaining active scans. Several small creatures resembling squirrels and rabbits scampered away, while the forest floor crawled with insect life, but aside from that, the area was clear.

Bits pulled up the sensor data feeds from the probes Verris launched to generate a three-dimensional map of the area in his HUD. "I'm down. All clear so far," he signaled to the team.

"Almost ready," Quentarus replied. "I'll be there in just a minute."

The admiral landed to Jackson's right a moment later, giving him a nod as they swept the area with their rifles while their suits scanned for any hostile signs of life.

During the trip to Vishnara, Jackson had looked up the admiral's service record; Admiral Renmere Valentyen had spent most of his life in service to the GCH. He'd been deployed as an ensign over two hundred years ago on the *Essex*, before being transferred to a destroyer two years later during a conflict with the Vehn. He stayed on active duty for the next eighteen years, working his way up through the ranks before taking a break for twelve years after meeting his first wife, the two of them having a daughter together. When he returned to the service, he took a post at Command so that he could be close to his family and had spent over 160 of the past 220 years of his life working in all areas of the military. His record showed that he'd served on several other combat and exploratory vessels, including spending four years on a Deep-X mission to explore a previously unexplored spur off one of the outer galactic arms. He then did two more combat tours in wars with the Insectoids and had been working in Military Intelligence for the past thirty years. The admiral may have been out of the field for some time, but he wasn't the least bit rusty from what Jackson could tell, and his service record spoke for itself.

Quentarus touched down a moment later, with Dr. Duratis by her side, each holding a large case in her hands. Quentarus went quickly to work, opening the cases and revealing their contents: twenty small tactical strike drones.

Jackson was familiar with them from his time on Cicarrus Prime, where he did his advanced weapons training, recalling that they were designed to seek and destroy enemy targets and could also be deployed to maintain a perimeter.

Quentarus engaged the drones, while Dr. Duratis ran more thorough scans of the area, bending down to examine the forest floor with her advanced sensors.

"What have you got for us, Doctor?" the admiral asked.

"Hmm, hard to say. From a bio-signs perspective, we appear to be good," she said, pulling up a small rock from the forest floor, the bottom crawling with insects as she examined it. "I've tied into the sensor drones that Lieutenant Verris launched, and I'm not detecting any large predators within a five-kilometer radius of our position. I'm having trouble, however, locking on to the Ancient structures. They appear to be directly beneath us, twenty meters belowground, give or take, with several layers of rock and sediment between us and them."

"I hope one of you packed a shovel," Jackson quipped.

"I have something," Quentarus replied with a smile. "Everyone fall back at least ten meters," she said as she tapped the controls on her wrist, ordering five of the tactical drones to form up over an area of open ground. "Here?" she asked, pointing to a spot and looking over at the doctor.

"Looks good," the doctor replied, taking another step back.

Quentarus interfaced with the drones, adapting them for their new task and pulling up a three-dimensional scan of the underlying strata. "Okay," she said, turning and walking back to stand near the crew. "Let's dig a hole," she added enthusiastically as she powered up the drones, initiating a focused sonic pulse.

The pulse shook the ground as it began digging through the loose soil, scattering debris to all sides. As the top layers of soil cleared, a layer of rock appeared. The drones adapted instantly, firing small beams of energy to break the rock up into smaller fragments, then vaporizing them. After several minutes of cycling between modes, the drones finally stopped.

The team approached the smoldering hole while the drones pulled back, returning to their previous defensive positions. Jackson leaned over the edge, looking down, his display showing that the shaft was nearly three meters wide and just over twenty meters deep. The doctor raised her hand, her suit flowing as it created a small sphere, which took flight a moment later, descending into the blackness. The drone's lights activated a few seconds later, illuminating the tunnel as it moved downward. Once it was at the bottom, they could see a hint of gray reflecting the light and the doctor brought up a scan on her holo-display. "Looks like we've got something."

"Jackson, Doctor, the two of you check it out. We'll cover you from here," the admiral said.

Jackson and Dr. Duratis jumped into the hole, their suits resuming flight mode as they stepped off the edge.

"Johansen, report," the admiral said over the comm.

"It's bad, sir. The ship's systems are a mess. When the computer core failed, it triggered several power surges before the breakers kicked in."

"Can you fix it?"

"Not here. Best I can do is get basic life support, helm control, and nav systems, along with the hyperdrive up by using the Gate Keeper and our suits to bypass the main computer. I might have enough cycles left to get one more system partially running."

"Do what you can, Chief."

"Copy that," Johansen replied.

At the bottom of the shaft, Jackson and Dr. Duratis stepped down onto the metallic structure, initiating detailed scans.

"It's definitely an Ancient structure. My scans can't penetrate the walls. Carbon dating places it as being at least three hundred and eighty thousand years old," she said.

"Let's see if we can make a hole. Stand back," Jackson said.

Once clear, he leveled his rifle at a point where the structure angled up from the ground, flicking the controls to adjust the settings, then firing a concentrated beam.

The metal held, Jackson's brow furrowing as he studied the readings. "Bits, can you up the power and focus the beam tighter?"

"Adjusting settings," Bits replied. "The beam appears to be optimal now. However, I estimate that cutting a one-by-three-meter opening will take two minutes and forty-six seconds and will drain your rifle's power pack down to eleven percent."

"Thanks for the heads-up, buddy. Good thing I brought a second power pack."

Several minutes later, Jackson managed to cut a rectangular hole large enough for them to get through. He lowered his rifle, the tip red hot as he laid it upright along the side of the shaft, allowing it to cool. He took a step back, kicking the center of the doorway he'd cut, using the suit's strength to dislodge the metal. The opening gave way, tumbling into the darkness, smashing into the ground below with a loud, echoing crash that sent a shiver down his spine as it cascaded through the blackness.

He raised his left arm, firing a burst of compressed cryo spray around the edges of the metal, instantly cooling it, then switched his HUD to infrared as he peered inside. Dr. Duratis joined him, both of them taken aback by what they saw. The structure inside was cavernous, the lights from their suits barely finding the floor nearly fifteen meters below, dust swirling in the air as the beams of light cut through the blackness.

"What do you think?" the doctor asked.

"It's creepy as hell."

"Yeah, my thoughts exactly."

"But we didn't come all this way just to stand here," he said, leaping through the opening, his suit's thrusters engaging as he hovered for several seconds, scanning his surroundings before lowering himself slowly. "Bits, run a full-spectrum scan. Document everything."

"Acknowledged."

The doctor leapt from the edge, the two of them hovering ten meters above the ground, running scans while the lights from their suits swept the room.

"This appears to be a massive chamber of some kind, but there's very little detail that would give any indication as to what it was used for," the doctor said.

Jackson nodded, his own scans equally inconclusive. "Maybe it's a cargo bay or something?"

"Could be. In any case, my scans show that the air is corrosive and toxic. There must be another opening somewhere in the complex, as the airflow patterns indicate that air is being pulled in through the entrance we just made, mixing the fresh air from outside with the stale air in here and creating a corrosive effect."

"Can our suits handle it?"

"The outer nano-layers will become damaged over time, but our suits have dozens of layers, so we should be safe. It might affect our scanners, though. We'll have to get our AIs to shed the outer layers if they become too corroded, to ensure it doesn't interfere. We should try to limit our time here if possible until the bad air gets sucked out wherever the draft is taking it."

"Okay, good idea. Let's move down to the floor level and see what we can find," Jackson suggested, lowering himself, the doctor following a moment later.

His feet touched down in the thick layer of dust coating the floor. He stood still, waiting as the top layer of dust, thrown up by his thrusters, was whisked, swirling in the lights of his suit. He lifted his right leg, examining his footprint, the image eerie and familiar, like that of the first man to set foot on the moon, the thought drifting through his mind that he was likely the first person to set foot here in close to four hundred thousand years a sobering one.

They spent the next several minutes exploring the massive room, the doctor scanning the external structure, her AI trying but unable to find a mode able to penetrate the advanced alloy with any resolution. Jackson moved towards what appeared to be crates stacked at one side of the room. As he touched one, it crumbled, the items inside shattering on the ground, startling both him and the doctor.

He looked over, shaking his head. "I'll keep looking around. Why don't you report in."

Dr. Duratis nodded, signaling the admiral, who joined them a moment later, bringing with him the case that she had brought from the ship.

"What do you have?" he asked.

"Not much, sir," Jackson reported. "So far, there's nothing here that's even remotely salvageable."

"Let me see if I can speed up our efforts. Henrik brought these along." The doctor bent down and opened the case.

She tapped on a small console in the corner as two dozen small spheres rose into the air, Jackson recognizing them immediately as survey drones. She raised her left wrist, interfacing with the drones, sending them out in all directions as she cycled through her console, bringing up the holo-display for them to see. "I figured these might be useful. With the corrosive air, having our suits make drones isn't ideal, but these are hardened for various environments and should last weeks," she explained as a map, projected in the air before them from her wrist, expanded in real time.

The drones explored the structure for the next several minutes, sending back their results while they waited. The structure appeared to have multiple smaller rooms at one end and a long hallway at the other.

The admiral watched for several minutes. "I'll leave the two of you to it. Signal me if you need anything."

Jackson and Dr. Duratis nodded as the admiral stepped a few meters away, then took flight, a cloud of dust swirling where he'd stood seconds before. They watched the holo-map for several more minutes as the drones continued to build a forgotten world before their eyes, the structure seemingly endless.

"Let's get moving and see if there's anything we can find," Jackson suggested.

With that, they split up, spending the next hour working their way through all the rooms the drones had mapped, then down the long corridor, into a new section of the complex, a circular structure six levels high.

"This place is huge," the doctor noted over the comm. "It could take us a days to explore it all."

"Yeah, we may need to—" Jackson stopped mid-sentence as one of the drones suddenly went offline, the blue dot on the map flashing red for an instant in his HUD before disappearing.

"That's odd," Dr. Duratis said. "Hang on, I'll reroute another nearby drone to check on it."

Jackson circled back and met up with the doctor, the two of them watching as, a few seconds later, the second drone approached the same area. The doctor flipped to its camera feed; the drone went offline a few seconds later, but not before registering a brief flash on its optical sensors.

"What the hell was that?" Jackson asked.

"I don't know, but it can't be good."

"What do you think?"

"One drone going down is odd, but two of them is something else. I'm not sure what that flash was, but it could have been an energy surge. Unfortunately, the drones are designed more for mapping and not for detailed analysis."

"Well, there doesn't seem to be much else here. We might as well check it out. Do you want to come with me or continue searching?"

"Like hell I'm staying here alone!"

"All right then." Jackson smiled. "Let's go take a look."

CHAPTER 5

A LIGHT IN THE DARKNESS

A few minutes later, they reached the section where the drones had disappeared, passing through several smaller, nondescript hallways along the way. They stopped outside an open doorway, staring into the blackness inside.

"Bits, initiate a full sensor scan," Jackson said.

"I am detecting residual ionization in the air and traces of debris ahead consistent with the composition of the drones."

"Doctor, can you send in another?" Jackson asked.

"There aren't any others nearby. I'll make a small drone from my suit instead. It'll be fine down here where the air isn't as corrosive."

"Sounds good."

The doctor held her hand up, the nano-material flowing to create a small sphere which solidified in her palm. It took off, entering the room while they watched from several meters outside the entrance. As it approached the center of the room, two thin, soft blue beams of light appeared from either side of the room, washing over the drone. A second later, an energy beam shot out from the far wall, destroying the drone in a flash of light.

"Okay then… Well, that solves that mystery. So, what do we do now?" she asked.

"Bits, why can't we detect the sensors or the weapons ports?" Jackson asked, examining the scan results.

"One moment," Bits replied. "Adjusting scanning parameters. I'm detecting a low-level dampening field. It's actually quite ingenious. It doesn't register on any standard scanning modes and appears to be using multi-phasic sensor jamming, an energy-suppression cloak, and a particle-scattering field to suppress standard scans, making its presence undetectable."

"That's interesting," he said. "Sounds like someone went to a lot of trouble to protect something. Any idea how to get around it?"

"I do not believe that we can. I've scanned for power sources, but it appears that the energy source is coming from beyond the room ahead. Based on the map of the structure that the drones have created thus far, there does not appear to be a way to access this area from any other location. I'm afraid that the only way in is through here, and it appears well designed to prevent any unwanted access."

"Yeah, not exactly begging us to go inside. Should we just move on and maybe circle back?" the doctor asked.

Jackson stood silently for a moment, considering. "I'm going in," he said.

"What? Will, that energy beam could kill you! Even with your shields up, you won't last more than a few seconds."

"I'm going to pull the suit back a touch so that it can scan my bare skin. Hopefully, it will recognize me and disarm."

"That's crazy!"

"This is what we're here for, Doctor. We've been searching for hours, and there's nothing else salvageable in this entire godforsaken complex, but there could be beyond this room.

I've been recognized by Ancient tech before, and I'm fairly confident that it will let me in."

"How confident?"

Jackson thought for a moment. "Eighty percent. But I have a good feeling about this."

"I'll be sure to have them write that on your tombstone," she teased.

"Noted." He smiled back.

"Well, be sure to keep your helmet on and your suit vacuum sealed. Your AI will also need to run decontamination protocols on your exposed skin, so try to limit your exposure to no more than a minute."

"Understood. Probably best if you stay back. It should recognize me, but it might not be as welcoming to you."

"Oh, don't worry about me. I'm not going anywhere near this deathtrap!"

Jackson took a breath to steady himself, then took several slow steps forward. "Bits, pull the suit back to expose my left arm. Stay alert. If the scanners appear to be having a hard time reading me, pull the suit back some more, but let's limit my exposure like the doctor said, okay?"

"Understood," Bits replied, flowing the suit back, leaving Jackson's left forearm exposed.

He stepped forward slowly, carefully approaching the point where the drones had met their fate, his feet crunching down upon the wreckage, the sound startling him for a moment as he looked down at the charred remains. He took a quick breath, steeling his will, then stepped forward, keeping his left arm out in front of him, his fingers spread as he waited for the lights to appear.

"Maybe I'm more like fifty percent certain," he whispered to Bits.

Just as he planted his foot and was poised to reconsider, the soft blue lights illuminated his forearm, following it back, then tracing his body from top to bottom. The lights swept over Jackson's body several times as he felt Bits pull back the suit further, exposing more of his arm up to his shoulder. He kept his breathing shallow, not wanting to risk the slightest movement as the seconds passed.

Finally, after what felt like an eternity, the lights stopped. Jackson waited for a moment, feeling cautiously optimistic. "Well," he said over the comm to the doctor, "I'm not dead. So, I'll take that as a good sign."

Cautiously, he took a small step forward. Then another, finally letting out a long breath he hadn't realized he'd been holding.

"I think we're good," he called back to the doctor. "Just stay there. This thing might still be active. I'll move further ahead and see if I can shut it down."

"Copy that. Be careful," she advised.

Jackson approached the end of the room, seeing that the wall ahead was a dead end with no visible seams. "What the hell?" he said. "There's nothing here. Bits, you got anything?"

"Negative, William. The wall reads as solid, and I am unable to scan beyond it."

"This doesn't make any sense. What are they protecting in here? Scan the room again."

"I'm not detecting anything; however, my scans are limited due to the jamming technologies in use."

Jackson reached towards the wall, running his hands along it, feeling for a seam or anything that might reveal a hidden entrance. After working his way along the surface, he was about to give up, when suddenly a small square illuminated with a red haze beneath the fingers on his left hand.

He froze, realizing that he'd stumbled upon another scanner, keeping his exposed fingers pressed to it in the event that the defenses were still active. After several seconds, the square turned green, and a door materialized in the center of the wall before him.

"Whoa. Bits, scan the door, see if you can figure out how it's doing that."

"I already am, William. The wall appears to be reorganizing at a molecular level."

"Now that we know where the hand scanner is, can you run an analysis?"

"Affirmative, the scanner has a small node above it which produces a dampening effect. It absorbed my earlier scans, effectively hiding its presence. Now that I understand how it functions, I should be able to adapt my scanning techniques to find other points of access."

"Good work, buddy. Can you scan beyond the door?"

"The room ahead is fairly small, only three meters by three meters in size."

Jackson approached the door, shining the lights from his suit inside, revealing shelves along the walls, each containing several cases.

"It looks like a vault of some kind."

"That would appear to be an accurate assessment," Bits replied. "Judging by the advanced security system, I suspect it was designed to keep items of value. I've been monitoring the power readings to the weapons port, and I believe that with the door now open, the defensive systems have been deactivated. Would you like me to reengage the suit?"

"What's the risk if you don't?" he asked, concerned that the security system might reactivate if it couldn't detect his bio-readings.

"I've generated a low-level electrostatic field around your exposed skin to limit the exposure, but you're well past the time recommendation provided by the doctor."

"Understood. Form the suit back up, but keep my left hand exposed, just to be safe. Worst case, I'll rotate hands for a few minutes at a time."

"Acknowledged," Bits replied as he re-formed the suit down Jackson's arm, leaving the left hand exposed. Jackson slowly entered the room, his arm tingling as Bits ran through decon protocols, his HUD locking on to four cases inside. The two on the upper shelves resembled briefcases, thin and rectangular, while one on the lower shelf was wide and rectangular, resembling a large toolbox, and the final one was a perfect cube.

Jackson picked them up one at a time, carrying them carefully back to where the doctor was waiting.

"Should we leave these here and press on or head back?" Jackson asked.

"I've been checking the readings from the rest of the drones while you were in there. There are several sections of the complex which have collapsed, and the rest appear to be devoid of anything of interest so far."

"Okay, let's take what we've got and head back for now. Let the drones keep working away. If they find anything of interest, we can always come back later."

"Sounds good to me. This place gives me the creeps."

CHAPTER 6
ONE DOWN

Half an hour later, Jackson and the doctor arrived back at the entrance to the structure. "Jackson to Admiral Valentyen," he said over the comm.

"Valentyen here."

"We're on our way back up, sir. All clear up there?"

"All clear."

They ascended from the shaft a moment later, each carrying two of the items they'd recovered.

"How'd it go down there?" the admiral asked, noticing the cases.

Jackson and the doctor quickly brought them up to speed on what they'd found and how the scanner had recognized him.

Quentarus chimed in a moment later, "I'm getting movement a few kilometers away." She paused, rerouting a drone to investigate. "Damn, there's a pack of large, catlike creatures, eight strong, approaching from the east," she said, an image of one of the creatures appearing on the display hovering above her wrist. Jackson watched as the predator moved, its two oversized teeth reminding him of a sabertooth tiger. "Looks like they've picked up our scents and are heading our way. I think we should get back to the ship. We don't want to engage those things unless we absolutely have to."

"All right. Let's head back. Did you find anything else of interest?" the admiral asked.

"Nothing, sir. The rest of the structure appears to be empty, aside from lots of crumbling debris. I'm not sure what we got, but it seems strange that something of value would be left behind when the rest of the complex was pretty well barren," Jackson said.

"Doctor?" the admiral asked.

"I agree with Will. The probes finished their sweep a few minutes ago, and there's nothing else down there. Some parts of the structure are collapsed, but I don't think it's worth our efforts to try to excavate them."

"All right then, let's head back to the ship for now," the admiral said as they formed up, making their way towards a clearing where Verris had landed the ship, Quentarus keeping an eye on the predators as they continued to approach.

They entered the cargo bay a moment later, passing through the protective energy field to keep the outside atmosphere out, the ramp closing behind them. Johansen poked his head out from the Gate Keeper. "Hey, welcome back," he said, climbing out and brushing himself off.

The crew stood in an isolated section of the small cargo bay, another field separating them from where Johansen stood.

"Doctor, run decon procedures," the admiral said.

Jackson and the doctor stowed the Ancient cases in the cargo bay racks along the wall, isolating them with a stasis field until they cleared quarantine back on the station. They then joined the admiral and Lieutenant Quentarus as they stood in the center of the bay.

"Initiating decontamination protocols," the doctor said.

A hiss filled the room as she repressurized the bay, cycling out any contaminants in the air, the space illuminating while a sequence of lights swept over them, killing any bacteria or bio-matter that they had picked up from the planet or the structure. The crew stood still, safe in their suits, as a fine mist filled the compartment. The air rushed out of the sealed section where they stood as the cycle completed, leaving them in a vacuum for a moment.

"Readings are all good from here. Not showing any signs of contamination," Verris said over the comm.

"My readings are nominal as well," the doctor concurred as she filled the compartment with atmosphere once more, then deactivated the field.

The crew moved to the operations room just behind the bridge, removing their exo-suits and leaving them sitting as cubes on the floor for Johansen to link together. The admiral remained behind to check in with Johansen while the rest of the crew made their way to the bridge.

"What's our status, Chief?" the admiral asked.

"I've rerouted all primary systems through the Gate Keeper's processor. It'll just take me a minute to connect the CPUs from the suits, and we'll be good to go. So far, I've got the helm, navigation, hyperdrive, and life support systems up and running. Sensors are at about forty percent efficiency. I might be able to get a little more from the exo-suits' CPUs, but at best we'll get seventy percent, as they're pretty processor intensive."

"Defensive systems?"

"We can raise shields if we need them, but Kelara will need to manually control the geometry and rotate frequencies. Weapons are a bit trickier, as the targeting systems need processing power and route through the sensors and optical arrays. I can try to rig something up, but it may take a while."

"Focus on the shields for now. We'll likely need them more anyway, with all of the anomalies in this system. What about the cloak?"

"The power grid is still a bit shaky, and the cloaking system is offline. I can try to run a bypass, but it will take about forty minutes, and even then, it will be rudimentary at best since it also needs the processing power to mask the ship."

"Understood. Good work. Continue with integrating the suits' CPUs and keep me posted if there are any changes. I'll brief the rest of the crew."

"Aye, sir."

The admiral made his way to the bridge. After updating the crew on the status of the ship, he then turned to the science station. "Doctor, bring up the map of the complex."

The doctor pulled up the data on the viewscreen, along with a three-dimensional map on the main holo-display.

"Here's what we have so far, sir," she said, the crew gathering round. "The probes have mapped most of the Ancient complex, but there are several areas where there are structural collapses, and they haven't located a way through most of them yet. There are three distinct structures, spread out over approximately ten acres, with several containing multiple levels. There are a number of tunnels connecting the different buildings, but one of them is completely blocked. We'd need some heavy cutting tools or to take the Gate Keeper in to clear them. The probes have also detected radiation in two sections of the complex, near what my AI thinks are the power cores."

"Could we take a look at the cores with heavy radiation suits?" the admiral asked.

The doctor shook her head, zooming in on the map. "I don't think so, not without shoring up the structural integrity of the surrounding corridors and clearing a lot of debris first," she explained, highlighting the damaged sections and overlaying the radiation. "The power cores appear inactive from these scans, but both are leaking high concentrations of gamma radiation, and the probes sent to investigate them failed in a matter of minutes from the exposure. I know it's tempting to try to take a look, but we got a few scans before the probes went dark that the others nearby relayed back, and I just don't think that we have heavy enough gear with us to explore further without risking significant exposure."

"What about the other sections of the complex?" Quentarus asked.

"Hard to say. The probes are still working on getting past some of the collapses, and there may be more to explore. We could stick around and wait to see if they get through, or we could head back and try to get through ourselves."

The admiral rubbed his chin thoughtfully. "You mentioned that the facility appeared to be pretty barren."

"Yes, sir," Jackson interjected. "It appears that they either took, or time has degraded, anything of value. The only reason we were able to salvage what we did is that they were in a hermetically sealed room, essentially in stasis, but everything else we found turned to dust or was beyond recognition."

"Do you think it's worth exploring further?"

Jackson and the doctor exchanged looks. "I don't think so, sir," he said, both of them shaking their heads slightly. "There could be another cache down there or something else beyond the blockages, but honestly, we spent hours down there, and there wasn't anything else worth investigating."

"We could leave the probes to keep exploring. We can always come back if they get through or find something," the doctor suggested. "If we leave them, along with one of the larger ones Verris deployed from the ship when we first arrived, we can use its subspace comms array to send any future data back."

"It'll also be nightfall soon," Quentarus said, flipping the viewscreen to the pack of cats as they approached the ship cautiously. "We could wait till morning, but there's a lot of life out there, and these cats are far from the biggest predators around. I think if we're going to stick around here for a while, we should do so from orbit."

"All right then, let's head back to the Hideaway and regroup. The ship needs repairs anyway, and we don't want to get stranded this far away from Confederation space. Besides, we still have two more sites we can check, and we'll leave the probes to continue here, as you suggested, Doctor. Helm, are we ready to depart?" the admiral asked.

"Affirmative. Engines are operating normally and the hyperdrive is spun up," Verris replied.

"Tactical?"

"Sensors are still limited, and weapons are offline, but shield diagnostics check out, and the skies, as best I can tell, are clear, sir," Quentarus reported.

"Ops?"

"The anomaly we passed through is still invisible to our sensors, but I marked its last known position. Based on the rotation of the planet and its orbital path, I've had Bits extrapolate a path that should keep us well clear. Sending the flight plan to the helm now."

"Got it," Verris said. "I'm calling back the rest of the drones now and leaving one, as the doctor suggested."

"All right then. Helm, take us up. Once we're clear of the planet's gravity, set a course for the Kilgaren System," the admiral said. "Chief, we're about to depart. Everything good back there?"

A moment later, Johansen replied, the sound of tools clattering in the background. "All good here, sir. Just try not to give us too many bumps. The ship's systems are barely holding together."

"Acknowledged. Helm, slow and steady."

The ship took off, the thruster wash scattering the nearby pack of cats. Verris flew carefully, slowly gaining altitude. She kept the throttle to half speed while she maintained a steady course, minimizing turbulence and giving the anomaly a wide berth. As they approached the stratosphere, an alarm sounded at the tactical station.

"Report," the admiral ordered.

"Sensors are detecting three contacts sixty-eight kilometers away and closing fast!" Lieutenant Quentarus replied.

"Can you identify them?"

"Negative, sir. They appear to be using some kind of jamming tech that is making it impossible for our sensors to lock on to them. If it weren't for the contrails, we might not have detected them at all."

"Whoever they are, there's no chance they're ours this far out," the admiral said, opening the comm to the cargo bay once more. "Chief, can you get our cloaking systems back online?"

"Not anytime soon."

"Can we outrun them?"

"Based on the rate they're closing, they're faster than us. Likely some kind of fighter craft," Quentarus assessed.

"I can push the engines, but the ship's in rough shape. I'm not sure she'll hold together," Verris warned.

"I agree, sir," Johansen said. "Structural integrity is holding, but the *Eritus* took a pounding on the way down. If we're not careful, we'll tear her apart. I'll route power to the weapons systems, but targeting will still be manual."

"They'll be in weapons range in forty seconds, Admiral," Quentarus warned.

"Shields up!" the admiral said. "Tactical, is the aft torpedo launcher functional?"

"Affirmative, sir."

"Fire a torpedo into the path of the incoming ships, configure the warhead for maximum shockwave dispersion, and set it to detonate a kilometer ahead of them. That ought to buy us some time."

"Aye, sir," Lieutenant Quentarus replied. "Torpedo away."

"Helm, how long till we can jump?"

"Two minutes, fifteen seconds," Verris replied.

"Increase speed. Chief, watch the structural integrity. Ops, see if you can find us anything we can use."

"Increasing speed," Verris said, gingerly ramping the throttle up, the *Eritus* accelerating as the hull creaked, the sound reverberating throughout the ship.

"She's holding together, but barely!" Johansen called over the comm. "Inertial dampeners are compensating, but the structural integrity is at thirty-four percent! Try to keep us steady till we're clear of the atmosphere. Any sharp turns might tear her apart!"

"Copy that," Verris responded, trying her best to limit the stress on the ship as the *Eritus* passed through the exosphere a few seconds later, just as the torpedo detonated.

"Report," the admiral said, watching the readout of the detonation on his display as the shockwave rippled outward.

"The blast is limiting our sensor accuracy at their last known position. I've got no sign of them on tactical sensors," Quentarus responded.

"How long to jump?"

"One minute, twenty-three seconds," Verris responded.

"Incoming torpedo!" Lieutenant Quentarus called.

"Can you target it?" the admiral asked.

"Not on manual. It's too fast!"

"Helm, roll hard to starboard on my mark. Three... Two.... One... Mark!"

Verris rolled the ship, the hull groaning from the stress.

"Launching chaff," Quentarus called as a wave of small metal cylinders shot out from the sides of the ship, erupting into a blaze of heat.

Half a dozen seeker drones deployed behind the spray, their thrusters engaging as they darted for the incoming projectile.

The torpedo detonated a moment later, the explosion rocking the ship. "That was too close," the admiral said. "Damage report, and where are those ships?"

"I still can't detect them. Their jamming tech is more than our limited sensors can lock on to," Quentarus replied.

"Some minor hull damage, but the shields protected us from the worst of it," Johansen added. "Some slight power fluctuations, but I'm on it."

"Sir, if we use the hyperdrive to purposely generate a hyperspace compression, then collapse it, it should generate a low-level energy wave, which might reveal their position,"

Jackson suggested, thinking back to a trick that Captain Quentarus had used to find powered-down raiders hiding out in an asteroid field.

"Do it," the admiral commanded.

Jackson quickly pulled up the hyperdrive controls on the Ops station, initiating the hyperspace jump sequence. Warnings flashed on his console, signaling that the gravity from the planet was too strong at this distance. He ignored them, watching as the hyperspace convergence began to materialize.

A small circular opening formed in subspace, growing in size as it matched the movement of the ship. As soon as it was a few meters wide, he terminated the sequence, intentionally destabilizing the conduit. It collapsed instantly back upon itself, an electrostatic subspace shockwave erupting, expanding in all directions.

The wave passed the *Eritus*, rocking it slightly.

"Got them! Three ships. Definitely fighter craft, but without the ship's tactical database, I can't say for certain what type," Quentarus reported. "They're almost on top of us! They're firing again!"

Verris banked the ship sharply to port as it was struck by the incoming weapons fire.

"Shields are holding, but it won't take them long to try a different weapons modulation and punch right through them. Without the computer, I can only rotate the frequencies manually!" Quentarus called.

"We're almost clear of the planet's gravity well, but I can't make a jump with all of this fire," Verris said. "Johansen, is the EJD operational?"

"Negative," Johansen called. "The emergency jump drive is offline."

"Damn it!" Verris cursed as she rolled the ship once more, evading an incoming torpedo while Quentarus released another round of countermeasures. "Will, I need some cover now!"

"Already on it. There's the asteroid we scanned earlier. It's just sixty thousand klicks from here at bearing twenty-one, mark one-oh-four. It's a mix of ice, rock, and several types of metals. The asteroid has cracked into multiple pieces, likely from passing close to the sun and the ice melting. The debris tail is pretty thick in places and the denser parts should give us enough cover to make a jump."

"Set a course, full power to engines!" the admiral said.

Verris quickly plotted a course for the asteroid while continuing evasive maneuvers, the stress on the hull increasing as the lights flickered.

The enemy weapons fire continued, their shields draining from the assault. Lieutenant Quentarus fired another torpedo, detonating it just ahead of their attackers, forcing them to scatter to evade the explosion once more. "That should buy us a few more seconds!" she called out, making the most of their limited weapons.

Verris poured on the speed, pushing the engines to the red line while the ship shook around them.

"Structural integrity is down to twenty-two percent and falling fast!" Johansen called over the comms. "We're going to tear her apart!"

Verris cut their speed slightly, steadying the ship as they were hit with another blast of weapons fire, the lights going out for several seconds before the dim emergency lights came back on.

"We're down to seventeen percent and holding. Just barely," Johansen cautioned.

"Tactical, shields double aft," the admiral ordered.

Lieutenant Quentarus doubled up the shields, leaving their forward section exposed. It was a calculated risk, but the badly outmatched *Eritus* needed every second they could buy.

"The asteroid is just over fifty thousand klicks ahead," Jackson called out. "Sending you a flight path for the densest part of the tail. Lots of rocky fragments in there we can use for cover, and the ice is melting this close to the sun, leaving a trail of crystalized particles similar to a comet."

Verris altered course, the enemy weapons fire suddenly ceasing.

"Two of the fighters are breaking off, but the last one is still in pursuit," Quentarus reported. "They're attempting to outflank us! Shields down to thirty-three percent!"

"Chief, reroute power from life support to the shields," the admiral commanded.

The pursuing ship hit them with a volley of plasma fire a second later. "Shields down to eighteen percent," Quentarus called.

"Almost there," Verris said through gritted teeth as her hands gripped the controls.

Just as they approached the asteroid's tail, a volley of plasma fire erupted across their bow from one of the flanking ships, grazing the forward hull, shredding the metal as Verris pulled up, twisting the ship out of the line of fire.

"Reengage full shields!" the admiral called.

"They're trying to keep us away!" Verris yelled.

"We're going to have to push through," the admiral said. "Avoid the hits you can, but take the ones you need to."

"We can't take more than a couple!" Quentarus warned. "And we won't last long once our shields are gone."

"Understood, but we're not going to last at all if we don't get the hell out of here. Do it!" the admiral ordered.

Verris altered their course, pushing the engines past the red line once more, putting the ship into a corkscrew rotation towards the asteroid.

"The hull's buckling!" Johansen called over the comm. "Structural integrity is failing!"

"We've lost shields!" Quentarus reported, the ship rocking from another volley. "Port armor is taking a pounding!" Panels fell from the ceiling, exposing wires above Quentarus's head, forcing her to duck. The ship coming apart around them.

"Will, I need you to make the jump as soon as you have a window of opportunity. I need to focus on keeping them off us," Verris called.

"I'm on it!"

Verris broke out of the corkscrew, diving the ship directly into the trail of the asteroid fragments, close to its main mass.

The dust and ice particles streamed from the pieces of rock, the sun bathing the asteroid in its glow.

The electromagnetic field from the ionized particles disrupted the enemy targeting systems for a few seconds as the *Eritus* disappeared into the icy trail, weaving around the dense fragments.

The enemy ships poured on their assault, firing at random. One of the volleys hit a rocky fragment, shearing off a large section of rock and ice, sending debris out in all directions, further obscuring the *Eritus* from view while battering the hull.

Verris pulled sharply to port, forced to evade one of the larger fragments as it suddenly came into view.

"Will!" she called out as she put the debris between them and the attacking ships, then turned the ship out of the asteroid's debris trail, shadowing one of the larger rocky fragments. The *Eritus* exited the stream of debris, buying Jackson precious seconds to initiate the jump.

The *Eritus* disappeared in a flash a few seconds later, just as one of the fighters came back into weapons range, unleashing a volley of fire into the now empty space where it had been just seconds before.

Alarms blared throughout the ship as the emergency lighting flickered and the crew held their breath, waiting to see if the battered *Eritus* would hold together, looking around at the smoking wreckage of the bridge. The ship shook slightly inside the hyperspace conduit, Verris working to adjust its geometry manually, widening it and slowing them down.

Seconds passed as the shaking slowly subsided.

"I think we're okay," she said after a moment, the crew letting out a collective sigh of relief, each of them realizing how lucky they were to be alive as the ship limped along, barely holding together.

CHAPTER 7

BATTERED

Nine and a half days later, battered and battle scarred, the *Eritus* exited hyperspace in the Kilgaren System. The trip back had been slow and arduous. Twice, they were forced to drop out of hyperspace for nearly a day so Johansen could make emergency repairs, stranding them in open space with the ship barely holding together.

The crew worked in shifts to keep the critical systems operational following Johansen's guidance, or Foxy's, while he slept. The damage to the ship was extensive, and it was through sheer will and determination that they kept it together. Exhausted and disheartened, they limped home with their food and oxygen running low.

Verris landed the ship in the docking bay of the Hideaway. The damage forced the crew to exit from the starboard docking port down a small ladder, the cargo bay ramp too heavily battered to be operable.

Jackson stepped onto the deck, taking in a breath of air from the station, the sweat-soaked smell from the ship still caught in his nostrils as he tried to shake it. He stretched his weary muscles, having spent the better part of the past six hours in a maintenance tube, trying to keep the power grid online. He slowly walked over to where the rest of the crew stood, turning back and joining them as they took a moment to examine the damage. The ship's hull burned from plasma fire and the armor shredded in places, realizing how lucky they were to be alive.

The admiral was the last to disembark, joining them a moment later as he surveyed the damage. "Good work, everyone. We've all been through a lot these past two weeks. Take some time to shower, eat, and get some rest," he said, looking over his disheveled crew. "We'll reconvene at 1100 hours tomorrow. Dismissed."

The crew went their separate ways, most of them headed for hot showers, as over a week without had left them unable to stand their own smell. Jackson headed for the mess in search of a quick bite, his stomach grumbling furiously.

The mission plan had been to be gone approximately two weeks, but with the food synthesizers offline and the extra time it had taken to get back, they had been forced to subsist on limited quantities of emergency rations for the last several days.

After having a quick meal, he hit the showers, sleeping like the dead for the next nine hours, dreaming of the Ancient structure and shapes looming in the darkness.

The next morning, he awoke still tired and stiff. He made his way down to the mess, where he found Verris sitting alone, a hot cup of tea nestled between her hands, absorbing the warmth as she breathed in the scent of chamomile. Jackson grabbed a tray of food and a coffee, joining her, and the two sat in silence, no words necessary while they shared the moment, staring out the window at the planet below, their hands meeting across the table, happy for the simple comfort of one another's touch and to still be alive after the close call.

The crew assembled a few hours later, the admiral dispensing with the formalities and getting down to business, quickly giving them their orders.

Johansen went to work on getting the cargo ramp open, while Verris, Dr. Duratis, and Jackson unloaded what they could through the docking port. Lieutenant Quentarus worked with the admiral, making their way through the wreckage of the ship, pulling the individual data storage units from the ship's sensors. With the main computer critically damaged and half of the data systems inoperative, the logs, they discovered on their way back, were inaccessible, forcing them to pull the drives one at a time in order to collect and analyze them.

Several hours later, the admiral called the crew back to the briefing room.

"Lieutenant Quentarus and I have been able to partially piece together who attacked us," he began as they took their seats, waving his hand to activate the holo-display. "We believe that the fighters were Insectoid, based on the limited sensor data and hull geometry readings we recovered from the logs. Obviously, this is extremely disconcerting for several reasons. First, the Vishnara System is nearly a thousand light-years from the Insectoid Imperium. And as far as GCH Intelligence is aware, they don't have any presence in that region of the galaxy.

"Second, our mission was highly classified. The only records of it or any of the Ancient technology we've recovered in the past and tested are stored in a secure data vault. No one outside of this room and a few senior admirals at Command had any knowledge as to where we were going or what we were doing." His face became grave. "Third, this wasn't the only patrol in the area. After pulling all the sensor logs from the *Eritus* and running them through the station's computer for analysis, we were able to identify three more Imperium ships, two destroyers and a cruiser, along with over fifty other fighters on long-range scans and at least a dozen other wings searching the planet. Their ships had fanned out across the system in a search pattern, but they were clearly there looking for us. We were lucky that they decided to focus on the two habitable moons around the outer gas giants with their larger ships, likely due to Vishnara's atmosphere, but if we had run into any more ships, we wouldn't have made it out of there.

"So, as you can all see, we have a very serious problem. I have my AI running an analysis of all of the comm and sensor logs for the past twenty-seven days, the precise amount of time that we've all been together and planning this op." He looked around the room. "To be clear, I don't believe that anyone here is responsible, but I need you all to have your AIs submit their logs to mine for analysis so that we can build a detailed timeline. Somehow, our enemies have learned of our mission. We need to figure out how and what their next move is so we can plan ours accordingly.

"In the meantime, Johansen and Quentarus, I want you to do a thorough sweep of the *Eritus*. It's possible that there's a tracking device or something on board which will explain how they found us. Jackson, work with the doctor to open the cases and start analyzing the Ancient tech we recovered from Vishnara. Remember to be extremely careful when handling these devices. Only Jackson can safely interact with them, and we only want you to do so in a controlled environment, understood?"

"Understood, sir," Jackson responded, while the doctor nodded solemnly, remembering the defense system in the room where they found them.

"As soon as we complete the sweep of the ship, Johansen and Quentarus will join you. Lieutenant Verris, you'll come with me, and we'll take the station's shuttle and return to GCH Command for a few days. Jackson, as the senior officer, you're in command till I return. Any questions?"

"Sir, the *Eritus* has sustained extensive damage, far more than I'm capable of repairing here, let alone by myself," Johansen said. "Simply put, we're going to need another ship."

"Agreed, Chief. I'm going to work on getting us a new ship to continue our mission." He paused, making eye contact with each of the crew. "While I'm concerned about everything that's transpired, and the risks that this mission presents if we go to another site, I'm also equally worried that the Insectoids may be aware of all three of our targets and try to beat us there or destroy them before we're able to conduct a search. As such, I believe that our best course of action is to get a new ship and continue to Praxian Prime as soon as possible. It's a risk, but one that I think is worth taking, as long as we go in fully prepared next time."

"Should we go in heavy, sir?" Quentarus asked. "Why not bring the Fleet in and have a few battleships or a small task force watching our six?"

"I've been thinking about that, Lieutenant, and I'll discuss it with Fleet Admiral Lighton. I'm still hesitant to bring more people into the fold. Battleships have huge crews, and if we find a cache of Ancient tech or weapons, we want to keep it off the books as much as possible. We all know what our enemies would do to get hold of such technology. For now, I'd like to keep our circle small, but I'll take it under advisement. Let's get to work. Lieutenant Verris, we'll depart in two hours. Dismissed."

The crew dispersed, Jackson walking Verris back to her quarters. Once there, they lay on the bed, holding each other's hands, silently contemplating everything the admiral had just told them. After a few moments, Jackson finally spoke. "What do you think?"

"To be honest, Will, I'm worried. How the hell could anyone, let alone the fucking bugs, know where we were going? It just doesn't make sense. None of us would have betrayed the others, or they'd have been committing suicide. So, it has to be someone or something else," she said, the frustration clear in her voice.

"Yeah, you're right. There's something we're missing for sure. Hopefully, they'll find something on the ship that will explain things. If not, I guess the best course of action is to go with the admiral's plan; we continue on, and if they do show up again, we use ourselves as bait and try to set a trap."

"It sucks, but yeah, it's all we can do. If our enemies are arming for war, then we need the potential that the Ancient tech could unlock more than ever. Hopefully, some of what you found on Vishnara will prove useful."

Jackson kissed Verris's temple, and they lay in silence for several minutes, enjoying each other's closeness. After a while, Verris got up and started packing. Jackson walked her to the shuttle, watching as she and the admiral departed.

CHAPTER 8

EXPERIMENTS

Two days later, Jackson stood with Dr. Duratis, Chief Johansen, and Lieutenant Quentarus in the IRC, working their way through a series of tests on the Ancient technology. They'd been fortunate, in that the cases they'd recovered had thus far reaped a number of still-functional devices, with only a few degraded beyond use.

Johansen and the doctor created a series of safeguards and protocols for the testing process, building on the initial tests from years before and allowing Jackson to operate each device while the others watched from a safe distance, sensors analyzing the technology and his interactions with it.

Jackson stood in the middle of the range, as the chief had called it. Several tables lay spread out along one wall, where the technology sat, organized and cataloged, surrounded by a forcefield for safety until they knew what each was. Jackson had tested each piece of technology one at a time, surrounded by dual layers of containment fields, to ensure that the rest of the crew and the station were protected if anything went wrong. Dr. Duratis and Jackson had spent the past few days classifying the tech into four categories: weapons, medical equipment, tools/devices, and unknown. Once Johansen and Quentarus had finished their detailed sweep of the *Eritus*, they assisted in further sub-classifying each device and helping to develop protocols to test them.

The team stood at the side of the room, each in front of a console, ready to record and analyze different aspects of each test. They had run through all of the medical equipment first, discovering a portable medical scanner, which contained an extensive diagnosis and treatment database. This had been uploaded to a secure and isolated section of the station's computer core for further analysis. There were three surgical tools: a laser scalpel, a tissue regenerator, and a full-spectrum sterilization beam, each similar to existing GCH technology. The tissue regenerator was the most advanced of the group, and the doctor was keen to make detailed technical and functional scans to try to reproduce one using their own technology.

Next, they moved on to the tools/devices. There were three in total: a technical analysis tool that could scan other technology and provide detailed information, and two devices that used quantum entanglement. The first consisted of two coffee cup–sized cubes, each with small data ports on it. The team fed data into one, and the other output it seamlessly. Despite every dampening field, forcefield, and jamming tech the Chief could throw at it, the two devices worked as a pair, allowing the data to move between them at any distance.

"This could be really useful for infiltrating an enemy site and extracting data in real time," Jackson said, thinking of the covert-ops possibilities.

The second device, a glove, was clearly Johansen's favorite, which he gleefully declared to be "the coolest shit ever!"

The glove allowed the user to scan almost any object, and then it created an entanglement field which connected across the empty space between the glove and the object, allowing them to interact. What was most incredible was how the glove adapted to multiple types of objects, from hardware like a simple nut and bolt to handling delicate computer chips or providing force enough to pull two objects apart.

After spending over an hour with it and running every kind of scan he could think of, Johansen was still no closer to cracking its secrets but was determined to learn how it worked to make a quantum entanglement connection between completely dissimilar objects and make one of his own one day.

After taking a break, the team started the weapons tests. Lieutenant Quentarus had Jackson test the first weapon, which she believed was a small-caliber pistol. The IRC created a projection of an enormous serpent for target practice, and Jackson leveled the weapon and fired. The pistol produced a small white beam of energy that increased with a small control setting.

Dr. Duratis programmed the serpent's projection to mimic a real creature's bio-readings, quickly confirming that the weapon was as powerful as a GCH Mark I rifle, despite its small size.

Next, they moved on to a larger pair of pistols. Each had a slightly different configuration and fired different types of energy, both of which proved to be quite lethal. Quentarus and Johansen spent a considerable amount of time studying the second pistol, as the beam was able to punch right through the personal shields they activated around their target, running a battery of tests to try to figure out how it worked.

"I think it's phased somehow," Johansen said.

"That would explain it," Quentarus replied. "But it still interacts with objects in our spatial plane, clearly," she said, gesturing to the hole in the simulated Reptilian before them.

"Yeah, it's tricky. I think the phasing is some type of energy shift, not an actual dimensional shift."

"Like a quantum tunnel?" the doctor asked.

"Exactly!" Johansen replied. "Will, fire again. I have an idea."

Jackson stood, pointing the weapon downrange. "Just say when."

"Fire!"

He squeezed the trigger, the beam punching another hole in the target.

"Got it! The beam is using a phase modulation I've never seen before. It's ingenious," Johansen raved. "I'm pretty sure I can modify one of our weapons to do the same. This could be a game changer. Great find."

"If you're happy, I'm happy," Jackson said, smiling, walking across the room, and setting the weapon back in its case. Satisfied with their scans, the team moved on to the final, unknown item.

Jackson stood at the center of the range, holding a disk-shaped object, about the size of a frisbee, in his hand. A grip extended from the disk, curving back towards him, the center of the circle open, facing outward, the entire device weighing nearly nothing. He looked it over carefully, turning it in his hands, studying the odd shape. The outer edge of the disk was smooth, with symbols carved into it on the side facing the grip. Bits locked onto the shapes, mapping out the symbols and running them through all known translation matrices while Jackson continued his visual inspection. The rounded hand grip adjusted to the contours of his fingers as he held it out, keeping it at arm's length before him.

"Any ideas, buddy?"

"I do not have a hypothesis at present," Bits replied.

"All right, then. Let's see what it does. Here goes nothing," he said, pressing his thumb against a small square that lit up on the grip. A soft hum filled the air as dim blue light illuminated the symbols. Jackson peered through the hole, lining it up down the range. As he raised the disk, a small holo-display appeared between him and his hand, showing a three-dimensional representation of himself standing with the symbols projected around his avatar.

"Whoa, that's cool. What do you guys think?" he asked, pausing while the team ran additional scans.

"It's not a weapon, from what I can tell," Quentarus said.

"I don't think it's a medical device either," Dr. Duratis added, while Johansen worked feverishly at his console.

"Chief? You got something?" Jackson asked, Quentarus and the doctor moving to join Johansen, watching as he brought up a detailed technical scan of the device.

"Holy…shit!" Johansen exclaimed.

"Well, don't keep me in suspense. What the hell am I holding?" Jackson asked nervously.

"I think it's a portal generator," Johansen replied giddily.

"Okay. So, clue me in. What does that mean?"

"Okay, so you know the portals we have on many GCH worlds to move between different cities?"

"Yeah."

"So, I think that this is a portable, handheld version of that. And if I'm correct, those symbols indicate distance and three dimensions, showing where the portal will open. Press the symbol directly to the right of your hand along the edge," Johansen instructed.

Jackson touched the holographic symbol Johansen indicated, a brilliant blue light appearing a second later in front of the disk, streaks of energy emanating from the sides like smoke drifting in the wind.

"Uh, is this thing safe?" Jackson asked as the energy flowed past his fingers. "It's not going to take off my hand or anything, right?"

"No," Johansen said unconvincingly as he stared at the readings. "You'll be fine," he added, waving his hand dismissively.

"How sure are you?"

"One hundred percent. Totally. Completely," Johansen said, not looking away from his console.

The doctor elbowed him, and Johansen looked up. "What?" A scowl from the doctor answered his question, and he looked at Jackson. "Hey, we can always regrow his hand, right, Doc?" he offered jokingly, flashing the doctor a smile, which she met with a deepening scowl.

"Wonderful, thanks for the vote of confidence," Jackson replied, taking a breath. "Okay, so what now?"

"So, the portal is active, but not open. I have an idea. Let's see how intuitive it is. Try gently flicking your right hand forward, through the holographic representation of the disk, as though you wanted it to move out from the ring."

Jackson flicked his right hand forward towards the holo-projection, the blue light suddenly jumping from the center of the disk into the space in front of him, expanding to three meters in diameter.

"Whoa!" Jackson said as the blue, swirling ring of energy hung in the air before him. "Check this out," he said, moving his hand holding the ring as the portal tracked with it across the open space.

Johansen smiled like a kid on Christmas. "Wow! An actual working handheld, multi-spatial portal!" he exclaimed.

"Okay… So, it's a portal…but to *where*?" Jackson asked.

"Hmm, that's an excellent question. Let's see. Scanning the station… Amazing. It's opened a portal to the hangar. That's exactly fifty meters directly in front of you. Hmm, okay, move your arm again, just a little. Yeah, that's what I thought, it's moving the egress aperture as you move your end. Let's try something. Tap the same symbol, then move your hand again slightly."

Jackson did as Johansen suggested, moving the ring again a second later to his left, the portal aperture staying where it was in the air to his right.

"That's what I thought. So the two ends of the portal are now fixed. Press the symbol a third time. Let's see if it'll close the portal," Johansen suggested.

Jackson pressed the symbol, which now appeared illuminated in a golden light, and the portal closed, Johansen clapping his hands together. "That. Was. Awesome! All right, turn a quarter of the way around to your left. Let's try this again and see if we can open a portal to the mess."

Jackson repeated the process, opening another portal in the direction the chief indicated. Johansen scanned the station again, confirming that the egress aperture opened in the mess.

"Now, let's try something else. Just keep the portal open," Johansen said, approaching Jackson as he ordered Foxy to deactivate the containment fields. He reached back, retrieving his multi-tool from his back pocket. "Let's give this a try," he said, throwing it through the portal, then gesturing to Jackson to close it again.

The crew hurried down the corridor to the mess, quickly finding Johansen's multi-tool on the floor near the back of the room. Johansen approached it cautiously, scanning the tool before touching it, then picking it up and examining it in his hands. Convinced that it was fine, he tucked it back in his pocket. "Let's go again!"

Over the next hour, the crew tested sending several dozen other objects through the portal. Johansen sent an active data pad through while the doctor waited for it to emerge in the cargo bay, still active and with no time difference between it and the initial timer he started before tossing it through. He repeated the process with a scanner, collecting a huge amount of data as it passed through the portal, then taking the next several minutes to analyze it.

Next, the doctor sent several plants and bio-samples through, monitoring for any changes in the lifeforms' cellular structure. Lieutenant Quentarus wanted to try firing a weapon through the portal, but the rest of the team convinced her that it would be safer to try that on a planet, in a more controlled environment. Slightly disappointed, she agreed, and they continued their tests.

After several hours, they debated if one of them should attempt to walk through the portal next. Johansen was convinced that it was safe, but the doctor was still skeptical, wanting to collect more data before they made an attempt.

Disheartened, but undeterred in his excitement, Johansen moved forward with another test instead. "Okay, let's try one more thing. I want to see what distance is for the next symbol. Based on my analysis, it should be a hundred meters. If you face that way"—he gestured in the direction he wanted Jackson to stand—"it should open in the cargo bay at the far end of the station."

"Okay, if you're sure," Jackson said.

"Of course I am," Johansen shot back, mock hurt in his voice at Jackson's doubt. "What could possibly go wrong?"

Jackson raised his left hand, gripping the ring, then tapped the second symbol on the holo-display, a small light forming in the center of the disk. He flicked his right hand gently forward, the light jumping from the ring and expanding, the portal appearing a few meters in front of him. An instant later, it opened, the air suddenly, violently rushing out of the room.

Bits reacted instantly, magnetizing Jackson's boots to the floor while the AIs of the other crew members did the same, the data pads on their consoles sucked out through the portal.

The force of the vacuum was incredible as Jackson struggled to hang on to the disk, knowing that if he lost it, there would be no way to close the portal.

He struggled against the immense pressure, the oxygen in the IRC becoming thin as he tried to steady his left hand and the holo-display, reaching for the symbol with his right. Finally, after struggling for several seconds, he tapped the symbol, the portal closing as quickly as it had opened, leaving the crew gasping for air.

The room rapidly repressurized a moment later, and the crew's breathing normalized, each shaking off the frigid cold that had crept in from the vacuum of space.

"Holy shit! That was close!" Johansen said excitedly. "That was wild!"

The rest of the crew stood glaring at him. None of them sharing his gleeful enthusiasm at almost dying.

"Right. Uh, sorry guys," Johansen said earnestly. "My bad."

"Your bad? Your bad!" Dr. Duratis yelled. "You almost got us all killed!"

Lieutenant Quentarus put her hand on the doctor's shoulder, calming her slightly, each of them knowing it was an honest mistake. "Sorry," she said a moment later.

"No, I'm sorry," Johansen replied, walking over and giving the doctor a hug. Jackson had learned while on board the *Eritus* that the two of them had known each other for years and had a dynamic all their own. They'd been friends from back in university and had both jumped at the chance to finally work on something together. "I got caught up in the excitement. That was careless and stupid of me. I'm really sorry, everyone."

"Well, that was terrifying." Jackson laughed, the tension draining from him. "Any idea how far away the portal opened?"

"No, but I'm game to find out," Johansen said with a sly smile. "Any takers?"

"I want my data pad back," Quentarus said flatly.

Doctor Duratis shook her head. "You boys and your toys." She sighed. "All right, let's do it."

CHAPTER 9

PORTALS

Several hours later, the crew sat eating dinner in the mess, having experimented with the portal half a dozen more times until it finally ran out of power. Johansen rigged up an impromptu power conversion system in his workshop, where they left it recharging while they went to eat. They'd been fortunate that Johansen had only deactivated one of the two containment fields when Jackson opened the first portal out into space and the rest of the Ancient equipment they'd salvaged had been safe from being sucked out into the vacuum. The data pads were lost, but all of the data was safe in the station's computer core, leaving them with a valuable lesson and no worse for wear.

Now that they knew what they were dealing with, the team created a new set of safety protocols so that the portals opened in a contained space within two additional layers of force fields. Johansen had determined that the second setting was actually five hundred meters away, the third a kilometer, and the fourth, a variable setting that allowed a user to enter a custom distance. As they continued to test, Bits used the new code enhancements provided by Admiral Thompson to analyze the interface, incorporating it into Jackson's HUD.

Jackson pulled up the station's sensors in his display, trying the variable interface again, extending the reach of the portal up to ten million kilometers, but draining the power rapidly.

"In theory, there's no real limit to how far this can go," Johansen explained as they sat around the table in the mess, studying the readings and picking away at their food. "It's really only limited by the quality of the sensor data to pick a target, and the power to keep it open."

"So, if I had a suit on to power it, and good scans of a star system, could I jump between planets?" Jackson asked.

"I think it's possible," Johansen replied, nodding to himself. "Bits, what's your analysis?"

"I concur, Chief Johansen. I've decoded some of the other symbols, and I believe they are an advanced control system for entering coordinates. The level of precision and specificity required to jump from one celestial object moving at tens of thousands of kilometers per second to another moving at similar speeds would be significant, but I agree, it is possible."

"Foxy, work with Bits to see if you can come up with an algorithm to calculate a jump. I think it's worth investigating. If we could make that work, then the possibilities are endless."

"I'm still not clear what the big deal is with this portal," Jackson said, taking a bite of his dinner. "I mean, it's cool and all, but isn't it old tech? Like you said, there are portals already on lots of GCH worlds."

"True," Johansen began excitedly, setting down his drink. "But remember years ago when you showed me that ancient Earth television program, *Star Trek*?"

"Hey! That's not ancient. That's my childhood there, thank you very much!" he shot back, feigning offense.

"Anyway," Johansen replied, unfazed. "Remember I told you how their whole beaming thing was akin to suicide?"

"Right, you said that there were too many complex electrical patterns, cells, other living stuff in the human body to transport it safely, or something," Jackson recalled, his memory a little hazy, the two of them usually drinking a few beers while watching old movies or TV shows after-hours.

"Close enough. Basically, you could do it, move a person from point A to point B, but there's an enormous risk that if even a single electron in your brain strays, you could be completely lobotomized! But portals are another matter entirely. The GCH developed the technology thousands of years ago. Nothing as sophisticated as this or with even half the range, but it was a game changer. Kelara, I'm sure you can tell him better than I can, as you're the military history buff."

Quentarus leaned in, enthusiastically picking up where Johansen left off. "So, the GCH had been secretly developing portal tech for decades. At that time, about nine thousand years ago, we'd carved out a nice little empire, about a hundred light-years across by thirteen hundred light-years long and a hundred and fifty light-years deep, give or take, and were doing okay, but we were regularly being challenged by many of our powerful neighbors for territory. Back before the portals, the GCH was constantly under threat and mostly on the defensive against incursions from the Reptilians, the Insectoids, and even the Oceanic Union at times, who were known for being a bit more ornery back in the day. Our ships were a lot less powerful then too, engaging our enemies in standard space combat using standard tactics. And while we had decent weapons and shields, we had no real advantage.

"Then, the GCH installed the portals in the 1st Fleet, and everything changed. The first major engagement was the Battle of Dalma. Command ordered an armada of seven hundred ships, about sixty percent of the entire GCH Fleet back then, to the Insectoid border, with the 1st Fleet, about ninety ships strong, at the center of the formation. They waited for three days, allowing the bugs to amass their own fleet, three times the size of ours. The GCH then crossed the border, aggressively engaging their forward line from maximum range, the 1st Fleet hanging just back while the rest of the armada attacked.

"Now, Command had a carefully planned strategy where each ship in the 1st Fleet had assigned targets, opening portals, then launching mines and torpedoes through them, which came out the other end *inside* the enemy ships. As our armada battled through the frigates and destroyers on the Imperium's front lines, the cruisers and battleships were suddenly torn to shreds behind them, hit with a massive onslaught of firepower from the portals that they were defenseless against! In less than thirty minutes, we'd wiped out over twenty-two hundred Insectoid ships, sending the last few survivors fleeing! This was the first time that the portals were ever used against a live enemy fleet.

"Three days later, we hit the Reptilians' largest fleet, then two days after that, the Oceanic Union. It was a staggering show of force that none of them ever saw coming from the GCH, and it changed the galactic balance of power in less than a week!

"The Fleet used the portals in several different ways, developing multiple types of warfare based on our goals and the situation. We could use them to board enemy ships, bypassing their shields, sending over heavily armed teams, mechs, bombs, or whatever else we wanted. Sometimes we used them to capture enemy ships and study their technology. Other times we just destroyed them outright, as in those first few engagements. It was an incredible military advantage, and for the next four years, Command used it to expand our borders by thousands of light-years in all directions.

"This was our first 'Great Expansion' as it's now known, and it created much of the modern shape of the GCH that exists today, aside from more recent growth surges, like with our race against the Imperium along the Holt Line. Our fleets were kicking some serious intergalactic ass, and in a few short years, the GCH became *the* superpower in the quadrant!

"Then..." She snapped her fingers. "Everything changed."

"What happened?" Jackson asked, riveted by the tale.

"Well," Johansen chimed in, "they figured out a way to disrupt our portals."

"Not only that," Lieutenant Quentarus continued, "but they did it with a stroke of strategic genius."

"Who was it?" Jackson asked.

"The Reptilians."

"Yeah, it was bad," Johansen added.

"What happened?"

"A large Reptilian fleet entered the McGatten System, which was one of ours at the time. We'd taken it from them, along with at least forty-five others, as the GCH expanded rapidly, steamrolling anyone who got in our way," she explained. "They quickly set forth destroying the weapons platforms and sensor arrays there, then waited. Now Reptilians were known to do this before our portal tech, as a threat display and a challenge. In the past, the GCH had been very careful when dealing with these incursions, always sending a massive fleet to overpower them and drive them back, but this time, we got cocky. Command wanted to send the Reptilians a message that any challenge or hostility would be met with the swiftest and most severe reprisal. So, the Fleet admirals quickly pulled together a group of about fifty ships and sent them in. Now keep in mind, back then, our ships weren't nearly what they are today. Without the portals, they were, at best, even with the Reptilians, maybe even a step or two down, since most Reptilian ships are huge and therefore pack a lot more firepower per ship."

"How many Reptilian ships were there?" Jackson asked.

"A little over three hundred, I believe, is the official estimate," Quentarus replied, raising an eyebrow. "The admirals were so confident that they sent an over-matched force in to show the Reptilians how badly we could defeat them."

"No. Really?" Daria asked. "I didn't know that part."

"Yeah, it's true," Johansen added, looking back at Quentarus to continue the story.

"So, the fleet arrives and once they're in range, they open the portals. Now at this point we didn't even bother to send troops or mechs over anymore. We just sent bombs. Big ones, with very short timers. But what we didn't know was that the Reptilians had developed a type of shielding which reflected our portals back at us."

Jackson's eyes widened as he imagined what happened next.

"The fleet commander signaled for the coordinated portal attack to begin, and each ship opened multiple portals, most only a meter or two wide, then pushed the hovering warheads through. What they didn't have the time to realize, however, was that the portals' destinations were reflected back at themselves! In most cases just a few decks away from the portal launch bays!"

She slapped her hand on the table, causing the rest of them to jump. "Bam! Just like that, the entire fleet of fifty ships gone in a matter of seconds! Worst of all, not a single transmission made it out to warn Command of what had happened," she said, pausing for a moment.

"The Reptilians then attacked another system, Kara-li'en, hours later. They destroyed the GCH defenses and, once again, they waited…and Command rerouted every available ship in desperation, uncertain what had happened to their first task force but determined to overpower the Reptilians with a larger fleet this time. They weren't certain at this point if this was the same Reptilian fleet or another, or possibly the start of a mass invasion! Command continued to try, but they were still unable to make contact with the fifty ships they'd sent to McGatten and remained unaware that they'd been destroyed.

"Hours later, just under four hundred GCH ships arrived in Kara-li'en. One of the ships, the *Resolute*, was a brand-new vessel, which Command had rushed out of space-dock with only half a crew and a young lieutenant commander in charge. It hadn't even had its shakedown cruise yet, and the engineers were scrabbling to keep the ship operational as they entered the system. Just before the battle began, the lieutenant commander hailed the lead ship, requesting permission to fall back, as it was clear they were in no condition to engage in combat. With half of their systems on the fritz, they held their position a few million kilometers away.

"Moments later, our ships engaged the enemy. Once again, the portals activated. Our supreme confidence in their abilities never once made anyone doubt there was a problem. The *Resolute* watched as the GCH Fleet, four hundred ships strong, was destroyed seconds later. The Reptilians never even fired a shot! The lieutenant commander ordered the *Resolute* to retreat, but their hyperdrive was offline.

"The Reptilian fleet approached the helpless destroyer, the bridge crew watching on the main viewscreen, waiting for the assault that would end their lives. The Reptilian command ship broke formation, approaching to within half a kilometer. It was a battlecruiser, easily three times the size of the small destroyer, with five times its armaments. The lieutenant commander solemnly said what all officers say when they know their time has come… 'It's been an honor to serve with you all. May the gods protect you.' Then, suddenly, they heard a sound…"

She raised her hand, ready to strike the table once again. Even knowing it was coming, the crew held their breath. After a moment which felt like an eternity, she slowly lowered her hand, gently laying it back on the table. "The sound was of the Reptilian fleet pulling out. The hyperspace echo that, even in the vacuum of space, can be heard through the subspace variance waves which resonate after a ship enters hyperspace.

"A moment later, the communications officer informed the dumbfounded lieutenant commander that they received a transmission just before the command ship jumped out. It was a message, text only, which simply read: 'The line has been drawn. Desist your expansion or die.'" Quentarus slithered the words out of her mouth, accentuating the *s* sounds, in her best impersonation of a Reptilian.

"Hours later, the *Resolute* finally made contact with GCH Command, informing them of what had happened. They immediately dispatched SaR craft to both the McGatten and Kara-li'en Systems to look for survivors, rescuing several thousand souls who told tales of what had happened. Command knew then, at that moment, that it was over. The GCH's Great Expansion had ended. We pulled back, from the Reptilian Empire at least, cleaning up our borders to make them more defensible and creating some buffer zones between us and the other major galactic powers. And things have remained that way for several thousand years, well, with the Reptilians at least. The neutral zone that was created there a few decades later still exists today."

"Wow," Jackson stated, feeling overwhelmed at the impact that one piece of technology could have.

"Yeah," Quentarus continued. "The scary part is that military historians now think that the Reptilians likely could have gone much further, driving deep into our space if they'd wanted to. Looking back at what we know today, it's believed that had they continued, they might have been able to decimate several of our core systems, if they'd committed enough of their forces. We learned much later that they were also embroiled in two other major conflicts at the time with both the Insectoids and the OU, neither of which were going well, which is likely the only reason they didn't wipe us out or enslave all of humanity. Forcing the GCH to the sidelines was a major victory for them, as they were able to reallocate hundreds of ships stationed along the border with us to these other wars, ultimately increasing the size of the Empire by a few hundred light-years with the OU and over a thousand with the bugs by the time they were done, nearly a half century later. The frightening reality remains, however, that there was an opportunity for them, and if they had taken it, it's likely that none of us would be here today. And that was the end of the use of assault portals as a weapon," she concluded.

"So did the GCH ever try to counteract this reflective shielding?" Jackson asked.

"They did," Johansen confirmed. "But after what happened, they started to look at the entire assault portal program in a new light and soon began to realize that there were dozens of other things which could go wrong that they'd never thought of before. They created a special unit of engineers whose task it was to try to stop the portals. A counter-portal unit, if you will. Sadly, they were too good at their jobs. In the end, it got to the point where we realized how incredibly lucky we were that our enemies hadn't discovered any of these other defenses earlier. If they had, the GCH might not be what it is today."

"And today," Quentarus interjected, "most of our ships don't even have portal rooms anymore. They continued to stick around for a while, with ships using them sparingly for things such as transporting down to the surface of a planet, but eventually just went back to using shuttles and conventional means of travel instead."

"So, why are you so excited by the Ancient portal, then, if it's an obsolete technology?" Jackson asked, looking at Johansen curiously.

Johansen's smile grew from ear to ear. "Because one of the first things that I did was try to break it!" he replied mischievously. "You see, the GCH used the information and methods that the counter-portal teams developed to create our own defenses in the event that any of our enemies ever created their own assault portals. It's a program that's loaded into every ship and station in the Fleet. Pretty standard stuff nowadays, really. So, when you activated the portal, I ran the program, which initiated forty-three different countermeasures, from reflective shielding to a spatial disruption field to radiation bombardment to a dozen other things, trying to destabilize its egress point…and none of it worked!"

"So…you're saying that the Ancients built an unbreakable portal?"

"Buddy, that's exactly what I'm saying! This is a fucking game changer!" Johansen said, giving Jackson a playful slap on the shoulder. "If I can adapt this to our technology, then our mission is pretty much done! The rest of the stuff that we got is cool and all, but this, this is military superiority, baby!"

"Not to rain on your parade," the doctor interjected, "but how long do you think it will take you to reverse engineer this portal ring?"

Johansen leaned back with his hands behind his head, rocking his chair while he tipped his head thoughtfully to one side. "A few years, most likely," he admitted. "The Ancient tech is so different from ours, and its software is likely part of the key. That part of the analysis, even with the computing power of the androids, could take years, maybe more. Then we'd have to build prototypes, test them out, try disrupting them, blah, blah, blah. Yeah, it will probably take a couple of years at least, maybe four or five before we could have these ready for even limited deployment across the Fleet."

"And even then," Quentarus spoke up, "you'll need to figure out a system like the Ancients did to protect these from falling into the wrong hands. If these new portal devices can't be disrupted, then all it takes is even one to fall into our enemies' hands, and suddenly it's a clusterfuck of unstoppable portal warfare!"

Johansen's enthusiasm drained from his face. "Shit," he said, deflated. "You're right." He paused for a moment, considering all of the options. "Crap, that's going to be a whole other project to figure out. But you're totally right, we have to do it. This could be a doomsday device if it fell into our enemies' hands."

"Well, I guess the good thing is that we have it and that it's essentially encrypted so that only I can use it," Jackson added, lightening the mood slightly.

"That's true," Johansen replied. "We'll have to be extremely careful with our analysis and data. Multilayer fractal encryption and data fragmentation protocols, biometric security, and more. Full top-secret–level security measures." He trailed off, sitting silently for a moment, pondering, pondering. A moment later, the station's proximity alarm suddenly went off.

"Bits, report!" Jackson called.

"I am detecting a vessel. It just de-cloaked thirty meters outside of the hangar. The bay door is opening."

"Can you override?"

"Negative."

"Everyone, grab a rifle and head to the hangar, double time!"

The crew bolted down the hallway towards the hangar, quickly stopping to pick up rifles from a weapons locker along the way. They entered the hangar in combat formation, with Quentarus in the lead. Once through the doors, they stopped short, amazed at what they saw.

The ship before them was beautiful. Long, sleek, with a black hull and silver trim. It was an advanced design that none of them had ever seen before. None except for Jackson, that was.

"It's okay. Lower your weapons," he said with a smile.

"Are you sure?" Quentarus asked, still skeptical.

"Do you know this ship?" Doctor Duratis asked.

"I do," Jackson said, smiling as he shouldered his rifle. "It's called the *Phoenix*."

A moment later, the center ramp on the bottom of the ship opened and Admiral Valentyen and Verris strolled down, the admiral noticing rifles in the crew's hands as he stepped onto the deck. "Sorry for the dramatic entrance," he said. "But I wanted this to be a surprise. This"—he gestured at the ship—"is the *Phoenix*. An advanced infiltration vessel and our new ride for the duration of this mission."

"Sir, how did you get this from Captain Delgado?" Jackson asked, knowing that the *Phoenix* was Delgado's pride and joy.

"It took some convincing, let me tell you. Even outranking him didn't make the man budge from letting his ship go without a fight. I eventually had to give him special operational clearance and let him in on some of what we were doing here. Once he knew what was at stake – and I had to add that it was you, Will, who will be using it and Verris flying it – he said he'd let us 'borrow' the *Phoenix* for a while."

"How do you know this ship, Jax?" Johansen asked, the rest of the crew having picked up on Verris's nickname for him.

"I was assigned to it as part of a covert rescue mission years ago, during my time training with the captain. I won't bore you all with the technical specs."

"Bore away!" Johansen interjected excitedly.

"Maybe later, Hen. But she's a hell of a ship, I can tell you that. Exactly what we need," he said, losing himself in a flood of memories at seeing the *Phoenix* again. An image of the creature appeared in his mind for an instant, sending an icy chill down his spine.

"We also brought along another surprise," Verris said, snapping him out of his memories, as she gestured to the team to come on board, leading them up the forward ramp into the Operations room. "There's two state-of-the-art operation equipment platforms which are fully loaded along with the three bays for suits of armor. The admiral was able to get us a few heavy hitters, in case we run into trouble on our next op," she said, gesturing towards the bays, which responded, revealing the armor within. "There's a Guardian and a Sentinel up here, and there's another one that I've never heard of before called an Annihilator, or something, back in the cargo bay."

Lieutenant Quentarus suddenly perked up. "Seriously, sir, you got an Annihilator?"

"I haven't seen it yet. It's apparently 'too classified for me to look at,'" Verris said, mimicking a condescending male voice. "At least that's what the techs said who loaded it on board. Why? What's so special about it?"

"Oh, it's just the most badass, nearly indestructible, heavily armed, and highly classified armor in the entire fucking Fleet! I deployed in one of these bad boys a few years back. The alloy they use to make them is extremely rare, so they're reserved for black-ops missions and DFA runs."

The crew looked at Quentarus as though she were speaking another language.

"Right, I guess none of you *would* know what that means. So, every once in a while, there are black ops that are purely psychological warfare. Well, you know, we kill things too, but that's not the point. These missions are designed purely to break the enemy's will to fight. Get in, blow up as much shit as you can, scorch the place, and leave. We call the ops DFAs, or Death From Above missions. That's what these babies do."

"Couldn't you just hit the site with a quantum bomb and level it?" Johansen asked.

"Sure, you could, but where's the fun in that? No, the idea, you see, is to go in and *really* let them know you were there. That a small group of humanoids took down an entire legion of troops and left without a scratch. You want to leave the bodies, you know, pieces of their troops everywhere. To send the right message as to how completely and hopelessly outclassed they were and that the GCH isn't to be fucked with."

"That sounds brutal," Dr. Duratis said, clearly sickened by the thought.

"I know it's not the sunny side that most of you know from living on the core worlds, but this is the reality out here. Sometimes you have to go in, kick some ass, and leave a calling card. It's the only way that your enemies will truly respect and, more importantly, *fear* you. It's not for the faint of heart, but it is a necessary evil. A lot of what goes on in the military is classified, and sure, every citizen has to serve their three years, but we keep most of them on the 'cleaner' side of the Fleet when we can. The other side, where I live, is dark, dirty, and real. What we do isn't pretty science or exploration, but let me assure you, it's *damn effective*."

A silent tension hung in the air for a moment as Quentarus glared at the doctor, arms folded across her chest. Growing up in the Fleet, it frustrated her that most people in the GCH, hundreds of trillions of them, didn't really appreciate what the galaxy was like as they lived in their safe little bubbles. Kelara had committed her life to service in their defense but hated it when civvies questioned her actions. Serving three years didn't mean that a person knew shit, as far as she was concerned, but it was designed to teach them to respect the military at the very least and to have some ownership or stake in it when it came time to make the hard decisions.

Quentarus finally broke the stalemate a moment later. "Sorry," she said her posture relaxing somewhat, giving the doctor a nod.

"No, I'm sorry," the doctor replied. "We all know there's black ops. Hell, I guess we're part of one right now. I just... I guess I just keep my mind on the science and try to block the rest out."

"That's exactly how the system is designed, Doctor," the admiral said, quickly stepping in. "Don't feel bad. The lieutenant is one of the few of us who has spent a lifetime in the service, and it's difficult for those of us who have been on the dark side to see the galaxy with a light of innocence anymore. And she's right. Ops like DFAs are very effective. We've had incidents where we detected our enemies preparing to mount attacks or terrorist operations and went in with a small surgical strike team to take them out. And most importantly, as the lieutenant said, leave a calling card. Sometimes a small show of force, as barbaric as it can sometimes be, can avert a major event, saving thousands of lives in the process. Those of us who do this type of work honestly cherish that most of our citizens don't truly have to know how brutal the galaxy really is and how close we've come to some pretty scary attacks that were stopped before they started due to actions of those not afraid to get their hands dirty."

He paused for a moment, considering, as he placed a hand on Quentarus's shoulder. "We tell ourselves that our actions are noble and for the greater good, the latter of which is true, but the former of which is sometimes far from convincing. And that's something we have to live with. But when I walk into a crowded city plaza and see mothers pushing strollers, or children playing, or people going about their lives, when I know what could have happened...well...I sleep well at night and have no regrets."

The doctor nodded. "I appreciate everything you do for us, Lieutenant. Really."

"No problem, Doc," Quentarus said, flashing an easy smile. "I just get excited by big things that blow shit up, is all. Sorry if I got a little carried away and dark there."

"If we're done with show-and-tell over here, we have some interesting things to bring you both up to speed on as well," Jackson said.

Jackson, Johansen, Quentarus, and the doctor spent the next several minutes bringing Verris and the admiral up to date on what they'd missed while they were away.

Unfortunately, Johansen and Quentarus weren't able to find any kind of tracking device on the *Eritus*, but they agreed to keep a dampening field around it just in case. Jackson then brought them up to speed on the tests that they conducted on the Ancient tech and what they had discovered.

After a brief, and impressive, demonstration of the portal disk, the admiral addressed the crew.

"Now that we have a new, more capable ship and some heavy firepower, I think that it's time we continued our mission and headed for Praxian Prime. We may, however, be walking into a trap, so we'll be cautious and wait until we're there and can assess the situation before deciding if we're going to head planetside. The *Phoenix* is a state-of-the-art stealth and infiltration ship, so I have no doubt that we could stay in the system for days, even if there were enemy ships all around us, and they'd never find us."

"Are going in just us, or are we going to bring some Fleet backup as well?" Lieutenant Quentarus asked.

"Just us for now. We'll rely on stealth primarily, but I've got a few surprises on the ship as well to back us up. If we run into trouble, the Fleet isn't far from the Praxian System. I checked the Fleet deployment schedules, and there'll be at least three ships within a ten light year distance if we need backup. So, we can have support there in just over an hour if things go south."

"Works for me," Quentarus said.

"Me too," Johansen added.

The doctor nodded. "I'm in."

"Same here," Verris said.

"Let's go check out some Ancient sites!" Jackson said excitedly.

The crew spent the next day prepping for the mission, Quentarus running them through a series of sims to brush up on using the Guardian and Sentinel armor. The admiral gave them the night off, encouraging them to get some rest before they departed the next morning.

Verris and Jackson spent the night together, lying naked in her bed, sweaty and wrapped in one another's arms, talking late into the night.

The next morning, the crew assembled in the briefing room at 0730, eager to get going.

The admiral arrived a moment later. "Good morning. We'll be departing shortly for the Praxian System. Our target is the fourth planet, once home to a race of humanoids that went extinct long ago. A GCH deep space explorer first surveyed the system nearly five thousand years ago."

The holo-display activated an image of Praxian Prime appearing before them as it was five thousand years before. The planet reminded Jackson immediately of Earth: vast blue oceans and lush green and yellow continents dotted with mountains, deserts, and lakes. Rivers crisscrossed the land, flowing into the sea, and massive ice caps covered the poles. Two of the continents showed a number of large cities and what appeared to be a thriving society.

"After careful, covert study, the planet was designated Vicara class, in the early phases of industrialization with a population of just over two billion. As per the Vicara protocols, the system was marked as off-limits, leaving them to develop naturally. Our survey teams didn't conduct a follow-up expedition for nearly a millennium. When they arrived, however, this is what they found."

The display changed, showing a pale white world, deep within the grips of a nuclear winter. Scans through the thick, suffocating clouds showed cities, mostly destroyed or left in ruins. Massive sheets of ice stretched from the polar ice caps and covered much of the planet that was now consumed by an ice age. The image cycled again to a topographical scan revealing hundreds of impact craters across the globe.

"We don't know the details, but our second survey team found evidence of missile bunkers and nuclear weapons capabilities. The final determination was that the cataclysm was self-inflicted and not the work of another spacefaring species." The display changed once again, showing surface-level images of the devastation. "After conducting a thorough search, the team determined that there were no survivors."

The holographic image froze as the admiral paused, allowing the crew a moment to reflect. He gestured, and the image of Praxian Prime updated once more. "Our most recent scans of the system show that the planet is recovering. The ice has receded considerably, and there appears to be a habitable zone along the equator where a few surviving native flora and fauna have returned. We also detected faint power readings below the surface, which we believe are Ancient in origin. Based on the analysis of what little technology survived the apocalypse, it's unlikely that the Praxians ever knew of its existence.

"Our long-range probe also detected Kerattan energy signatures," he said, the map changing once more. "The Kerattans have a small empire in the region, claiming nearly a dozen systems as their own. The GCH has recognized their sovereignty; however, relations between us are…dicey at best. The Kerattans are, to put it mildly, highly xenophobic and hostile to most other species. There are several disputed systems in the region we both covet, including Praxia. Our mission is to reach the Ancient site, recover what we can, and leave undetected. Questions?"

The crew was silent, each knowing what was at stake.

"All right then, let's get going."

CHAPTER 10

PRAXIAN PRIME

The *Phoenix* exited hyperspace in the Praxian System, the crew on high alert.

"Engage the cloak," the admiral ordered. "All stations report."

"Cloaking systems online. All systems nominal," Johansen reported.

"Full sensor sweep in progress," Jackson said. "No navigational anomalies detected, and we're right where we should be."

"No enemy ships detected. Tactical systems standing by," Quentarus replied. "Weapons charged and ready."

"Science systems are optimal," the doctor reported.

"Holding position five million kilometers from target. Helm standing by, Admiral," Verris replied.

The admiral nodded. "Helm, plot a course for Praxian Prime. Engage stealth drive. Engineering, keep an eye on our systems. Ops and Tactical, monitor sensors. Doctor, as soon as we're in range, run a detailed bio-scan of the planet." He turned to look at Jackson. "Launch a comms probe and have it hold position. If we run into any enemy ships, we can use a tight beam relay to contact the Fleet, and it will throw off the source of the subspace transmission. When we get halfway there, launch another probe and set it to run active scans of the system. If any other ships jump in, have the probe's onboard AI relay the data back to the *Phoenix* and run active sensor sweeps. That should give them something to chase after, and give us some time to react."

The crew went to work as Verris set a course for the planet, an unspoken tension hanging in the air as to what awaited them.

They approached Praxian Prime several minutes later, the admiral ordering the planet up on the main viewscreen and the holo-display.

The planet appeared on the screen as a gray-white marble, with the slightest hint of faded yellows and greens along the equator, a stark contrast to the blackness of space. Thick dark clouds encircled much of the planet, giving it an ominous appearance.

Massive glaciers, thousands of kilometers wide, still covered much of the northern and southern hemispheres. The equatorial region, however, was free of ice: a thin band of life, approximately six hundred kilometers wide, flanked by swaths of yellows and browns before the crushing ice took hold once again.

"Status," the admiral said.

"The planet appears to be in the late stages of an ice age caused by a nuclear winter," Jackson explained, bringing up detailed scans of the planet on the holo-display. "I'm reading low levels of radiation in the upper atmosphere and several dozen hot spots on the planet's surface."

"The equatorial region appears habitable," Dr. Duratis chimed in. "Bio-analysis indicates that most of the lifeforms are suited to extreme cold, likely the few species hardy enough to survive. We'll need to be cautious, as some of them pose a threat. Hang on… I'm also detecting three hundred and ninety bio-signatures on the eastern continent… Sir, I believe they're Kerattans."

"Confirmed," Jackson said. "They appear to have set up an outpost on the northeast coast."

"I'm detecting eighteen small ships adjacent to the settlement. Tactical analysis indicates that they pose a minimal threat on their own, but collectively, they could be a problem," Lieutenant Quentarus said. "I'm also detecting a small surveillance satellite in orbit."

"Acknowledged. Maintain cloak and stealth drive systems, keep scans to minimal power to avoid detection. Ops, any sign of the Ancient structures?" the admiral asked.

"Running scans now," Jackson replied. "Might take a few minutes to locate, as there's a lot of interference with the pockets of radiation down there and with the scanners running on low power."

"Doctor, how's it looking from an environmental perspective?"

"The air is breathable, but still heavily contaminated. Reading seventy-three percent nitrogen, twenty-four percent oxygen, and three percent other trace gases. We wouldn't want to spend much time down there without an exo-suit on, but a person could survive for a short time if necessary. The temperature is hovering at fourteen degrees Celsius near the equator and minus sixty at the poles. Rad levels are within acceptable tolerances in most areas, but some intense zones remain, which would require additional protection if we need to go there."

"Why would the Kerattans want to set up a colony here if the air still has nuclear fallout floating around?" Johansen asked.

"Actually, Kerattans are a highly adaptable species," the doctor interjected excitably. "Their home world has a significant elliptical orbit, meaning that twice each year it's bombarded with radiation from the Kerattan star for several months. They, along with the rest of the life on their planet, have developed an incredibly high tolerance for radiation which would easily kill a humanoid. As such, they've been able to expand their empire to places where other species would never think to go. Their physiology internally isn't that unlike our own, however. They're close to three meters in height with dark, scaly skin which is incredibly dense. Their males are only fertile for a few weeks each year, so they have a brief window in which to breed, resulting in a population which grows very slowly. The GCH Department of Exobiology has hypothesized, however, that under certain environmental conditions, they can extend their breeding window, providing them a better chance to reproduce." She snapped her fingers, the crew turning to look at her. "Of course! That's why a planet like this is of interest to them. Their cells have evolved to feed on certain kinds of radiation, which can extend their breeding cycle. The residual nuclear fallout in Praxian Prime's atmosphere is perfect for them to procreate, in theory."

"So…it's an orgy planet, is what you're saying?" Johansen quipped. The doctor shot him a stern look. "What?" he replied defensively, giving the rest of the crew a look. "If the reason they're here is all about mating, then it's a—"

"Don't. Say. It." The doctor glared at him.

"Okay," Johansen said, raising his hands in a gesture of surrender, then turning back to his console. The rest of the crew turned back to their stations, and he leaned towards

Jackson, whispering, just loud enough for the doctor to hear, "Totally an orgy planet."

The doctor let out a sigh, shaking her head.

Jackson spoke up a moment later. "I believe that I've located the Ancient site, sir. It's on the same continent as the Kerattan colony, just under fifteen hundred kilometers to the west. It should be well out of their satellite's scanning range. The site is on a peninsula about one hundred and thirty kilometers north of the equator, stretching out into the ocean."

"Helm, put us in a geosynchronous orbit above the site. Ops, launch a cloaked probe before we enter the atmosphere. I want eyes in the sky on us at all times," the admiral ordered. "Lieutenant Verris, once we land, keep the ship ready. Doctor, you and I will stay on the ship as well. I want you to keep an eye on the sensors for any dangerous lifeforms while I monitor the skies for our friends from Vishnara. If they come, I want to see them before they see us. The rest of you will armor up and explore the site. Any questions?"

"Sir, what is the plan if the Insectoids show up again?" Johansen asked.

"Lieutenant Quentarus and I have a little surprise for them if they do, don't we, Lieutenant?"

Quentarus nodded, initiating a sequence on the tactical controls. "Orbital batteries and mines deploying now, sir."

"The batteries and mines will spread out and remain cloaked and in a geosynchronous orbit above us," the admiral continued. "If the Insectoids arrive and attempt to drop in on us or engage us as we leave, they'll be the ones in for a surprise this time. The batteries are small, but both they and mines pack a punch, and there's enough firepower to take out a destroyer if it gets close enough. We'll still need to worry about the other ships, but between the batteries and the *Phoenix*'s armaments, we should have the advantage if they send a fighter wing our way. We can also send a tight beam transmission to the comms probe further out in the system. As long as we have a line of sight to it, we can use it to call in the Fleet. The destroyers *Greyhound* and *Regula* are both within about eight light-years of here, and the cruiser *Basilisk* is ten light-years away on a patrol in the Albalyss System. They could all be here within an hour. If we detect any enemy ships before they detect us, we can remain cloaked and wait them out until the Fleet arrives."

The admiral looked at the scans of the Kerattan settlement for a moment, then added, "The Kerattans are another matter, however. With their numbers, they could overrun us on the ground, so we have to be ready to pull out quickly if we're discovered. We should be far enough away, however, that they'll never know we were here, but I don't want to take any chances. If we detect any contacts, Lieutenant Quentarus will take the command on the ground."

The admiral waited for a moment to see if there were any other questions, then looked towards Verris. "All right then. Helm, plot a course for the Ancient structures. Take us around to the far side of the planet so that our entry trail will be out of the Kerattan satellite's scanning range. Let's get this done, people."

Several minutes later, the *Phoenix* flew through the lower atmosphere, slipping invisibly through the clouds.

"Sir, the Ancient site is coming up, three kilometers ahead," Jackson reported. "It appears to be partially above-ground, possibly excavated by the retreating glaciers. Sensors indicate that most of the upper levels appear to have been crushed by the ice and heavily damaged, but based on the depth of the structures, there should be sublevels and there are multiple structures still under the ground. I can't tell if they're all still intact, due to the same alloy we encountered last time, along with something in the layers of rock above that's interfering with our scans. Looks like veins of iron and daramite."

The admiral stroked his chin thoughtfully. "Helm, take us around for a couple of passes. The rest of you, see if you can detect anything that may be worth our time to investigate."

The *Phoenix* flew several low, slow passes of the Ancient site, the structures on the surface unidentifiable, mostly mangled metal and debris, surrounded by a dense forest.

"Sir, I have something," Jackson said. "The structures on the surface are a complete write-off, but I'm detecting power readings in the subterranean network, approximately forty meters down. There appears to be a power core still intact in one of them. This must be what the long-range scans detected."

"Even if there isn't much tech that we can salvage, the core itself will be worth studying," Johansen suggested. "We've never been able to see an active Ancient core before."

"If we move to these coordinates"—Quentarus brought up the site on the holo-display with the coordinates marked—"I should be able to drill a shaft down to the subterranean structures with the ship's weapons."

"All right, Helm, take us to the coordinates. Tactical, keep the power signatures of the weapons to a minimum. I don't want that Kerattan satellite to detect us."

Verris maneuverer the *Phoenix* to the coordinates as Quentarus initiated a low-power particle beam, cutting through the rock and sediment.

"Okay, we're through. I've cut a shaft forty meters down to one of the sublevels. We'll still have to cut through the structure once we get down there, but at that depth, I doubt there's any way the satellite will be able to detect us," Lieutenant Quentarus said.

"Helm, land the ship in the nearest clearing. Johansen, Quentarus, and Jackson, suit up, full radiation protection protocols, then armor up and head out. I don't want to stay here any longer than necessary. We'll keep the ship cloaked and maintain an open comm at all times, understood?"

"Aye, sir," they replied in unison.

Several minutes later, Johansen, Quentarus, and Jackson exited the *Phoenix*, Johansen in the Sentinel, Quentarus in the Annihilator, and Jackson in the Guardian.

The Sentinel was designed to be a multipurpose armor, commonly used throughout the Fleet. The tall, slim build and light armor plating gave it good mobility. It was versatile, equipped with a mix of offensive and defensive capabilities and decent shields. Sentinels were useful for patrols, guard duty, away missions in hostile environments, and as ranged support units for tactical assault teams.

The Guardian, meanwhile, was built around survivability with thick armor plating and powerful shields. It provided excellent protection for its occupant while possessing a decent weapons package and was well suited for close-quarters physical confrontations as well as ranged combat. Guardians were used in a variety of roles throughout the GCH, and Jackson was quite familiar with them from working search and rescue.

The Annihilator was a different beast entirely. Nearly double the size of the other two suits, it towered over them at six meters tall. Jet black and bristling with weapons, it had a fearsome appearance.

Quentarus took the lead, directing the other two as they deployed in a tactical formation, quickly sweeping the area. She remained on the surface, deploying a group of small tactical drones, while Jackson and Johansen proceeded down the shaft.

"Jackson to *Phoenix*, we've reached the structure, but it's going to be difficult to cut a hole large enough for our armor. I think we're better to do what we did last time, cut a smaller opening, and we'll enter with our exo-suits instead."

"Acknowledged. Stay alert," the admiral responded.

"Copy that, sir," Jackson said, initiating a cutting beam and slicing through the outer layer of the Ancient structure.

Together, he and Johansen used the strength of their armor to remove the panel he'd cut, placing it on the far side of the shaft. As they exited their armor, they could hear the wind whistling as it whipped through the opening, filling the structure with fresh air for the first time in eons.

As they stepped inside, they activated the lights on their suits, sweeping the darkness, particles of dust dancing in the air before them.

The room ahead was small, with high walls, a long-faded pattern on the floor, and a large metal door on the wall directly ahead. The door appeared to open to the side, but when Jackson tried it, he found it was jammed. "Hen, give me a hand with this."

Working together, using the enhanced strength of their suits, they forced the door open, the metal screeching as it slid along the worn-out track.

As they stepped through, they entered a larger room containing storage crates. Giving each other a nod, they split up and proceeded to scan them, bringing up the results on the holo-emitters on their wrists. Johansen joined Jackson a few moments later and they stood together, holding their wrists close, the holographic projections merging and forming a larger window full of data.

"Looks like long-decayed organic matter. Maybe these were food stores," Jackson suggested. "Anything on your scans?"

"Nothing useful."

"Let's keep moving and see what we can find. Hopefully, we didn't come all this way to find rotted vegetables."

Jackson and Johansen continued making their way through the interior, exploring several more rooms but finding little that was identifiable or held any interest. After nearly twenty minutes of moving through the structure, they still had no idea what purpose it held, but it was clearly different from the "depot," as they had begun to refer to it, on Vishnara. The walls and rooms here had a military feel to them, just as the one room in the depot did where they had found the weapons and the portal disk.

Several minutes later, they reached a larger corridor. "I'm going to launch some probes, see if we can speed things up a bit and find something worth looking at," Johansen said.

The two stood, watching the holo-projection from Johansen's wrist as a map of the structure filled out before them. "Damn," Johansen said. "It looks like most of the doors are closed and the probe's scans can't penetrate the walls more than a few meters. I think we're going to have to do this the hard way."

An hour passed while Jackson and Johansen explored all the rooms in the first section of the structure one by one, finding no signs of salvageable technology. As they moved deeper into the structure, the comms cut out, Johansen routing several drones to leave a link they could use to contact the ship if needed. "Jackson to *Phoenix*."

"*Phoenix* here, what's your status?"

"We haven't found anything so far, sir, but we've located a pressure door which appears to lead down a long tunnel to another part of the complex. We're going to go check it out."

"Very well. Keep checking in at regular intervals. So far, things are quiet up here, but that could change quickly."

"Understood. Jackson out."

Johansen stood a few meters ahead, peering into the blackness of the tunnel. "This gives me the creeps."

"Yeah, looks like something out of a horror movie," Jackson said.

"Why would you say that?" Johansen chastised him.

"Sorry, I just get that vibe, is all. Well, I guess we'd better check it out."

"Dude, that's exactly what someone in a horror movie would say right before something jumps out at them," Johansen added, tapping his wrist to send the probes ahead, their small lights illuminating the corridor as they faded into the distance.

Jackson activated the flight controls on his suit, racing down the corridor after the probes, with Johansen not far behind.

Back on the surface, Lieutenant Quentarus kept a vigil in the Annihilator near the top of the shaft, while Dr. Duratis studied the bio-sensors closely. Verris and the Admiral kept an eye out for anything on the sensors, running several scans from the orbital probe and checking in with the other probes further out in the system to watch for unwanted guests.

So far, everything appeared quiet.

"Sir, we've reached the door to the next structure. It appears to be heavily damaged," Jackson reported, studying the burn marks and melted metal.

The crew could see from his and Johansen's vid feeds that the massive door had taken heavy weapons fire. A large hole had been punched through the heavy metal.

"This totally reminds me of that movie *Aliens*… You know, that scene where they're coming down the hallway towards the guns," Johansen said, studying the damage, his comm channel open only to Jackson.

"There's a pleasant thought. Thanks for that nightmare in my head now. I'm cutting you off my horror database for a while. Only musicals for you," he teased.

"What was that, Will? We didn't copy?" the admiral asked.

"Nothing, sir, sorry. It appears that they likely barricaded themselves inside from some kind of assault. Strange that there was no indication of weapons fire in the other section, but there was clearly a hell of a firefight here."

"I'm reading the remains of bio-matter, but it's so old that there's almost nothing left," Johansen added. "Daria, I'm sending you the data. Maybe you can make something out of it."

"All right, continue with caution. There could be traps or

other defenses still active, as the section that you're entering appears to still have power," the admiral warned.

"Understood. Entering the structure now."

As they climbed through the hole in the massive door, they came into a room filled with signs of carnage. Shattered piles of debris covered several parts of the room, set up in a defensive barricade. Evidence of weapons fire burned into the remains. The room itself was the size of a gymnasium, dark and cavernous. More indications of weapons fire were evident on the walls ahead, and the floor showed scorch marks in several areas. As they carefully surveyed the room, trace amounts of bio-matter appeared on their scans, but nothing identifiable.

"Whatever happened here, there's nothing salvageable," Johansen said after searching for a few minutes. "Looks like they put up quite a fight, though."

"Agreed. Let's keep moving," Jackson said. "Looks like there are several doors on the far wall. Scans show most are small rooms like the one we came in through, but one appears to be another hallway. Let's see where it leads."

"Copy that."

Jackson made his way to the door, forcing it open, the dark hallway beyond coming into view.

Johansen joined him a moment later. "Foxy, send the probes ahead," he said, and seven small spheres flew past them a moment later.

Jackson and Johansen waited, watching on the holo-projection from Johansen's wrist as the probes continued mapping the complex.

"Doesn't look like there's much here," Johansen said. "There's the door that should lead to the next section. Do you want to look around, or should we just move on?"

Jackson paused for a moment, taking a closer look at one part of the map.

"Hey, Foxy," he said, speaking over his comm to Johansen's AI. "Can you expand this section here and have your probes run through a few imaging modes?"

"Acknowledged," Foxy responded.

"What are you thinking?" Johansen asked.

"I'm not sure. It's just a hunch. Something doesn't look right. See how the rest of the structure is laid out? Something just… I don't know, looks off. Like there's a piece missing, see?"

"I have something," Foxy reported. "It appears that you are correct, Lieutenant Commander. I conducted several scans of the section you indicated and discovered a hidden chamber beyond this wall."

Foxy highlighted the area on the holo-projection in red.

"Well, that's weird. What tipped you off?" Johansen asked.

"I don't know, just a feeling. Like something was missing. I can't explain it. Maybe I just played too many video games as a kid," Jackson said. "Bits, do you have any ideas?"

"Possibly. As part of our research into Ancient sites, several surviving maps and blueprints were added to my database. Some of these were included in your nightly SLAK sessions. It's possible that your subconscious recognized a pattern in a part of the layout of this structure. However, I cannot corroborate that with any of the documents that I have on file."

"Maybe it's just my Ancient DNA. Perhaps the Ancients had a gene for maps," he quipped.

"I highly doubt that, William."

Jackson shook his head and smiled. "Come on, just go with it."

"If you two are done, let's go see what's behind the secret door already!" Johansen said.

CHAPTER 11

SECRETS LONG LEFT BURIED

Jackson and Johansen quickly followed the map towards the hidden section, signs of battle evident everywhere as they made their way deeper into the complex. They arrived in the room leading to the secret door a few moments later.

"Bits, any sign of scanners, like in the last room where we found the cases?" Jackson asked as he slowly approached the wall which concealed the hidden room, running his hands along its surface.

"Negative, William."

"Feels solid."

Jackson took a step back, keeping a safe distance while Bits cycled through visual displays until he found a view which showed a hidden panel in the wall. "There. Three meters to your left. There appears to be an access point of some kind."

Jackson moved towards the hand scanner, Bits retracting the suit and Jackson reaching out and carefully placing his bare hand over it. A yellow light emanated from the scanner as it swept across his hand, a faint tingling sensation following. The light disappeared, and a door to his right materialized in the wall, opening with a hiss as fresh air filled the sealed room.

"This looks pretty much like what Daria and I found on Vishnara," Jackson said as he stepped towards the door, stopping just short of the threshold.

The lights from his suit swept the room, revealing a large open area with high walls and what appeared to be access consoles along the right side, with what looked like lockers on the left.

Johansen came up behind him and was about to enter when Jackson reached out, blocking him with his arm. "Hang on a sec. Bits, scan for defenses."

"Whew, yeah. Good idea," Johansen said. "Foxy, run a few scans as well, would ya?"

After a moment, Bits spoke over the comms. "I have detected an energy node at the far end of the room. I would theorize that it is a particle beam of some kind. The power signature appears similar to one of the pistols we recovered from the other site. I've also located what appears to be a genetic scanner half a meter inside the room, mounted in the ceiling. Both are using the same dampening protocols we discovered at the Vishnara site."

"Nice work, buddy."

Johansen took several slow, cautious steps back, letting out a sigh of relief. "Well, that could have changed my whole day."

"Yeah, a hole in your chest will do that," Jackson said.

"Are you ready for this?"

Jackson took a deep breath. "I guess I have to be. Bits, stand by with shields. Let's be ready just in case. Retract the suit from around my arms all the way this time. Not sure why they have a second scanner inside the room, but I'm guessing it means there's something in here they want to protect, so let's make sure they get a good scan of me."

"Hopefully there's no other protocol, and it will just recognize your DNA," Johansen said, trying to stay positive.

"Hmm, I hadn't thought of that. The outside scanner already verified me, so you could be right. Hen, can you morph your suit to form a tether and stand by to pull me out if things go wrong?"

"On it," Johansen said, Foxy flowing his suit and attaching a thin but ultra-strong nano-wire to Jackson's back.

"Okay, here we go," Jackson said as he slowly stepped into the room.

"Good luck. I'll run full-spectrum scans from here and be ready to pull you out if there's any signs of trouble," Johansen said.

As Jackson approached the bio-scanner, a soft white light activated from above. He stood perfectly still, letting the scanner do its work, the light cycling through several colors – different scanning modes, he suspected – while he waited patiently. He let out a quick breath, attempting to calm his nerves, but as he tried to inhale, he suddenly realized that he couldn't.

The light had frozen him in some kind of stasis field, preventing him from moving at all. Panic set in as he desperately tried to breathe, his chest held inward by the light.

Bits, detecting his distress, attempted to use the suit to force air into Jackson's lungs but found that the outer layer of the suit wouldn't respond to his commands. He quickly redirected the nanites in Jackson's blood, sending thousands of the tiny machines to his lungs, where they began generating minute levels of oxygen.

Jackson's heart rate and blood pressure continued to rise as his body tried to convulse in response but was unable to even twitch due to the stasis field. His panic deepened as he felt as though he were drowning, his body desperately trying to gasp for air. His AI reacted instantly, instructing the medical implants in Jackson's body to release nitroglycerin into his bloodstream, relaxing his arteries to allow more oxygenated blood to flow, buying precious seconds while he followed it up with a powerful sedative to try to calm Jackson's racing heart.

Finally, the scanner finished its cycle, releasing Jackson from the stasis field, and he collapsed to the floor, gasping for air and clawing at his throat.

Bits flooded oxygen-rich air into his helmet as Jackson filled his lungs, breathing rapidly while his body spasmed uncontrollably. Johansen pulled him out of the room seconds later, steadying him and helping him back to his feet.

Finally, after what felt like minutes, Jackson relaxed, breathing almost normally again.

"Well..." Jackson said, taking another deep breath and looking over at Johansen. "That sucked. Thanks for the save, buddy," he said to Bits.

"What the hell happened?" Johansen asked.

"The scanner had some kind of a stasis field which prevented me from moving. I made the mistake of letting out a breath, and the field tightened around my chest, and I couldn't get any air in!"

"Oh, man. I'm so sorry. I didn't realize that anything was wrong at first. Foxy then picked up your bio-readings and I tried to pull you out, but that stasis field wouldn't let go until you hit the ground. I pulled you out as quickly as I could, but I didn't know how else to help."

"No worries. There's nothing that you could have done," Jackson said, finally catching his breath fully and turning back towards the door, a feeling of dread filling him as he stared back into the darkness.

"At least it didn't vaporize you. I guess that means you passed."

Jackson smiled. "Yeah, there's that at least. There'd better be something damn good in there after all that!"

"You still up for this?"

"No, but we didn't come all this way for me to chicken out now. Bits, can you expand the suit around my chest so that something like this doesn't happen again?"

"Acknowledged. I have also prepared several countermeasures should the scanner reengage, to protect you."

"Okay, let's try this again," Jackson said, walking slowly back into the room.

He approached the scanner cautiously, keeping his hands out and a full breath in his lungs. Neither the scanner nor the weapons node responded as he walked forward. After a few more steps, he approached the first of the three consoles along the sidewall, letting out a sigh of relief.

"All right, I'm in. Bits, see if you can interface with their system," he said, placing his bare hands on the wide, clear glass console. As they made contact, the panel illuminated, revealing a series of what appeared to be control keys.

"Scanning," Bits said, the symbols translating in Jackson's HUD.

"I don't see anything related to security or defenses, Bits, do you?"

"Negative. This console appears to be mostly environmental controls. I'm having trouble translating several of the other symbols. I suggest that we try the next console."

Jackson moved further down. The next console contained power readings, which he fed to Johansen for analysis while he moved on to the final one.

"I've located the security controls for this room, along with this entire section of the structure," Bits informed him.

"Can you deactivate them?"

"Attempting to interface now. Defenses deactivated. I have also established a remote connection to this facility's data core."

"Great work, buddy. See what you can find," Jackson said, gesturing for Johansen to join them.

Johansen cautiously approached the door and gingerly stepped inside, his shields up. He moved slowly past the scanner. "What have you found?"

"Bits?"

"I have discovered a great deal," Bits replied. "This does indeed appear to be an Ancient military facility. This room is the auxiliary command center. The computer core is highly corrupted, but with Foxy's assistance, I believe that we may be able to reconstruct parts of the database."

"Foxy, link with Bits and follow his lead," Johansen said.

Foxy connected, and the two AIs worked in tandem, attempting to reconstruct the data.

"We found something," Bits informed them a moment later. "A partially corrupted record buried in a classified data store. It appears to be a star chart; however, parts of it are encrypted."

Bits and Foxy rendered the map before them using the suit holo-displays, filling much of the room as the map spread out, filling the darkness.

"Whoa," Jackson said, taking in the sight before them.

The map detailed the locations of black holes, nebulae, and comets, along with thousands of other cataloged spatial anomalies.

"What do you make of it, Bits?" Jackson asked.

"The map and corresponding metadata appears to be extensive. There are over nine hundred exabytes in total. It will take a considerable amount of time to analyze, and some of it is encrypted. I recommend that we take it back to the Hideaway and use the station's central computer to analyze it."

"Is there anything on this site or any details in the database about what happened here?" Johansen asked.

"The last uncorrupted data logs appear to indicate that an attack took place on this facility. The data is incomplete, but it shows that the structure's defenses were activated. Sensor logs reference 'Phague' bio-signs. Unfortunately, there does not appear to be any corresponding data regarding the meaning of that term," Foxy replied.

"*Fae-ghe*," Johansen said, sounding the word out. "That sounds creepy."

"Any luck locating the power core?" Jackson asked.

"Affirmative," Bits replied. "The core is located in the next section of the complex, along with a hangar." Bits reconfigured the holo-projection to display a map of the underground structures.

"I'd love to check out the power core, but finding an intact Ancient ship would be the mother lode!" Johansen said excitedly.

"We've completed uploading all the uncorrupted data for further analysis," Foxy informed them.

"All right then. Let's proceed to the next section and see what we can find," Jackson said.

As they left the auxiliary command center, static suddenly broke over both of their comms.

"ill...you read? We'r...un...tack! Do y...copy?" Admiral Valentyen's voice called, the signal weak and choppy.

Jackson and Johansen turned to look at each other, the realization of the message hitting them at the same time. Without a word, they began running back the way they came, using the exo-suits to increase their speed and launching into flight mode once back in the tunnel. A feeling of dread began to build in the pit of Jackson's stomach as he realized that they'd been out of comms range without knowing it and that their crew was in danger!

CHAPTER 12

AMBUSH

Within minutes, they'd retraced their steps back to the first structure, moving at a frantic pace, their hearts pounding in their chests.

As they stepped out of the Ancient complex into the shaft, they could hear the sounds of battle above.

"We'd better hurry!" Jackson called out, quickly climbing back into his armor, Johanson following suit, both ascending rapidly, their weapons armed and shields up.

They reached the surface seconds later, the once peaceful forest now thrown into complete chaos.

Scorched ground appeared around them while trees and bushes burned across a wide area. Jackson turned at the sudden sound of heavy weapons fire, spotting the Annihilator ten meters to their left. He ran a quick scan, the *Phoenix* nowhere to be found. He turned to Johansen, who stood defensively, still trying to figure out what was happening, then opened a channel.

"Lieutenant, what the hell's going on?" he asked, moving closer towards Quentarus's position.

"Oh, you know, the usual. Just something trying to kill us! I was wondering when the two of you would show up. Have a nice vacation down there?"

"It was magical. We'll tell you all about it later," he said, spinning and returning fire at the unknown enemy, following her lead. "Who are we fighting this time?"

"Ants, along with some type of armored beetles with heavy cannons on their backs, and Wrenthari!" she replied, firing off another volley at the unseen enemy.

"What the hell's a Wrenthari?" Johansen asked.

Just then, three tall, humanoid forms dropped from the trees above, engaging them at close range.

"That!" Quentarus shouted, a blade shooting out from the arm of the Annihilator and impaling the creature in front of her, dropping it to the ground in a spray of blue-gray blood.

The second Wrenthari leveled its rifle at the Guardian, opening fire at close range. Jackson's shields lit up as it absorbed the impacts. He raised the hulking arm of his armor, returning fire with a blast of plasma that threw the creature back, its smoldering body smashing into a nearby tree.

Johansen backed off in the Sentinel, dodging as the last Wrenthari came at him, swinging a large blade and forcing him back. The Sentinel backed into a thick tree, cornered as the creature came at it. Johansen spun to the side, narrowly dodging the deadly attack, then tripped on a root, the Sentinel falling backwards to the ground. The Wrenthari leapt towards him, the blade high above its head, coming down directly at him, when suddenly, it was hit midair by a powerful blast of energy, punching a hole clean through it and launching it several meters away, where it rolled to a stop on the ground, unmoving.

"You okay?" Quentarus asked, smoke drifting from the huge cannon on the arm of her armor.

"Yeah," he said, getting the Sentinel up to its feet. "Thanks."

"Anytime."

"What the hell were those things?"

"Wrenthari are genetically engineered soldiers," Jackson interjected, recalling a pointed sermon from Captain Delgado on them after he unleashed a group of them on the candidates during a training sim, taking them all by surprise. "They're humanoid in form, but with an armored body and senses like an insect. They can also change color and camouflage themselves with their environment. The Imperium uses them as assassins."

"They're also strong, fast, and agile," Quentarus added. "And since they're humanoid in form, they fight more like us. They can use rifles and swords, like you saw, or a variety of other weapons. We've got to keep an eye out for them. They're ambush specialists, like Jackson said."

"Good to know," Johansen said, shaking off a chill as he looked at the broken body of the one that had attacked him, the creature a mix of humanoid and insectoid.

"What's our status, LT?" Jackson asked.

"They hit us about five minutes ago. The admiral only had seconds before our orbital probe detected them. They must have jumped in close to the planet. Verris got the *Phoenix* off just in time, and they're up there somewhere engaging them."

"How many on the ground?" Johansen asked, forming up on the Annihilator's left flank, while Jackson formed up on the right.

"Not sure. They're using some kind of jamming tech that seems to be scrambling our sensors. Best I can tell, there are a couple hundred of them out there. I've taken out at least thirty so far, but they keep coming. They've been hitting this whole area pretty hard with those heavy cannons, but

I can give as good as I get in this beast, and I've managed to push them back," she said, letting loose a devastating salvo of plasma fire and incinerating a group of giant ant-like creatures walking upright as they appeared from the trees on their right flank.

"*Phoenix*, come in," Jackson said, the channel crackling.

"What do you think the chances are of them taking on those ships from Vishnara?" Johansen asked Quentarus.

"The *Phoenix* is fast and well armed, but it depends on the numbers. If the bugs have the same warships and they're all in range, they could take her down for sure," Quentarus said. "The admiral likely had them bolt for the cloaked orbital defenses. If they can draw them towards those, it'll tip the odds in our favor, at least for a short time."

"Johansen, I can't get a signal through," Jackson said. "See if you can break through the jamming tech. Bits, link up with Foxy and help them out. What's the plan, LT? Can we take the ones on the ground?"

"Most likely, but we don't know their full strength or capabilities. They've picked off all our defensive drones, so we don't have any air support or remote sensors. We could rush their position, but I think that we're best to hold them at bay and hope that the ship can come back and pick us up. I've been focused primarily on keeping them at a distance and holding my ground while I waited for the two of you," she said. "I'd recommend that we fall back to where the *Phoenix* put down before. They're using the cover of the forest well, limiting my chances to counterattack, and they keep coming in waves from different vectors. But the clearing where the ship was is wide, and it should force them to move out into the open, or the edge of the tree line at least."

"Sounds good. Call the ball."

"All right, Johansen, fall back, we'll cover you," she said.

Johansen set off in the Sentinel, moving swiftly as the lanky armor ran through the forest to the far edge of the clearing where the *Phoenix* had landed when they arrived. The surrounding forest was in flames, with thick smoke obscuring his view as he ran. The armor was fast and agile, however, allowing him to weave between the trees, covering the distance in no time. Once there, he took up a defensive position beside a large rock formation, ready to provide cover.

"Clear!" he called.

"Jackson, you're up," she said.

Jackson followed the path Johansen took. The Guardian moved more slowly and wasn't as agile, but he made his way as quickly as he could, taking some fire as he went. The smoke provided some cover, allowing him to evade the majority of it as he zigzagged through the brush. Once at the clearing, he took cover near a dense stand of trees to Johansen's right, returning fire in the direction it had come from.

A minute later, Quentarus joined them, barreling her armor through several trees, the force of the impact shattering them into a shower of splinters like they were nothing more than toothpicks. She came to a stop at the far side of the clearing out in the open, turning back to scan for enemy movement.

"It'll probably take them a minute to reorganize and move forward," she said. "It's pretty thin cover with most of the forest down or in flames between here and there, so they'll be exposed unless they circle around. Keep an eye on our flanks. From what I can tell, they appear to be mostly foot soldiers. I think I took out most of the beetles with the heavy cannons. As long as their ships don't strafe us, we should be able to hold this position."

Suddenly, a burning streak shot through the sky high above, the sound causing them to look up. A ship came down in a blaze of fire, debris breaking off as it fell, a thick trail of smoke kilometers long marking its deadly decent. The ship crashed into the surface of the planet several dozen kilometers away, the sound of it exploding reaching them several seconds later.

"Was that…?" Johansen asked, his heart sinking in his chest as he pictured the doctor, the admiral, and Verris suddenly gone. Seconds later, the *Phoenix* de-cloaked fifty meters above them, scorch marks visible on the hull, but the ship appeared to be intact overall. "Never mind."

"That girlfriend of yours must be one hell of a pilot!" Quentarus called, clearly impressed that the ship had survived with so little damage.

"That she is," Jackson said proudly.

"All right, the two of you ascend now. I'll cover you," Quentarus ordered, stepping forward and launching a massive weapons salvo, strafing a wide area to hold the enemy back.

"Roger that," Jackson said, he and Johansen engaging the flight systems on their armor, lifting them off and rocketing towards the ship.

The admiral laid down a barrage of covering fire with the ship's weapons from above as they approached, incinerating a swath of forest along with dozens of enemy troops.

Johansen reached the ship first, entering through one of the armor portals in the bottom, with Jackson following close behind. He was nearly to the ship when suddenly he was hit with a beam of bright white light. His armor's systems went dark, the hulking suit of metal falling like a rock.

"Bits!" he called, bracing himself against the inside of the armor, unable to escape.

Bits rerouted power from Jackson's exo-suit at the last second, activating the thrusters and managing to slow the terminal velocity of their deadly plummet. The Guardian smashed through the treetops, the branches breaking their fall somewhat. Bits routed more power into the Guardian, activating its emergency subsystems. Blue light from a stasis field engulfed Jackson inside the armor while Bits fired the emergency thrusters. The armor's speed decreased, but it was too late, the suit crashing hard into the forest floor, smashing through several trees before skidding to a stop, an impact trail several meters long marking its landing.

The stasis field disengaged, allowing Jackson to move once again. "Bits, status?" he asked, still shaken, but thankful to be alive while he struggled to figure out which way was up.

"The Guardian is functioning on emergency power only. The EMP pulse beam that hit us was highly concentrated, disabling most of its systems."

"Can you get me out?"

"Negative. The armor sustained structural damage upon impact and will not open."

"Damn it. Comms?"

"Affirmative. However, a jamming signal is limiting our range. I've attempted to signal the *Phoenix*, but I'm not certain if the transmission made it through."

"Okay. Let's jus—"

Jackson froze, the sound of nearby weapons fire filling the surrounding area. A sudden feeling of helplessness gripped him as he lay entombed inside the dead metal coffin of the Guardian. Seconds passed, the bombardment growing closer while he lay silent, listening to the intensifying fighting.

A few seconds later, the battle subsided, the exchange of fire moving off. He took a breath, relaxing for a moment,. Suddenly, he heard something outside banging on the armor.

"Jax, you still alive in there?" Verris called out.

"You won't get rid of me that easily," he said, relieved to hear the sound of her voice.

"Glad to hear it. Looks like the back of the Guardian got crushed upon impact. It's pretty mangled from out here. I'm going to have to cut you out. Engage the shields on your exo-suit to protect you from the heat. I'm going to have to do this quick and dirty."

"Understood," he said. Bits engaged the shields an instant later, adjusting their configuration, keeping them as tight to the exo-suit as possible. "Are you armed? Are you safe out there?" Jackson asked, suddenly realizing how exposed Verris was with the fighting still close by.

"I grabbed a breather, a rifle, and a plasma cutter on the way out. The LT and Johansen are holding them off. The Chief came back down as soon as you were hit."

"What happened up top?"

"We were able to take out the six Insectoid fighters that dropped in on us, but two frigates jumped in just as we were mopping up the last of them. We ran like hell, luring them into an ambush with the orbital batteries and the mines. Both took heavy damage and one is completely disabled, and all of our batteries were lost in the exchange. We had to hurry back down to get you. Just as we approached your position, our probe further out in the system detected four enemy battlecruisers jumping in. We're going to be *severely* outgunned if we don't get out of here soon!" she said, cranking the power on the plasma cutter to max.

"I'm good in here. Do whatever you need to do."

"Roger that. And don't think that this makes us even for saving my ass on Galzon III. You owe me at least double for this one!" she said playfully, quickly moving the cutter as she traced a square large enough for him to climb through. "Almost got it. You okay in there?"

"Never better."

"All right…and…done," she said. "Shit, I didn't bring anything to lift the panel with."

"Hang on. I have an idea. Stand back," Jackson said. "Bits, can you reconfigure the exo-suit to lift the panel off?"

"Stand by," Bits replied, flowing the outer layers of the suit to Jackson's back, creating a flat rectangle which pushed up on the section Verris cut, tipping it off to the side. The heavy armor plate hit the ground with a thud as Bits re-formed the suit, reactivating the shields. "The panel is off, but be very careful, as the edges are still extremely hot."

Jackson shifted around in the armor and maneuvered through the opening. Verris stood a few meters away, rifle in hand, while she surveyed the surrounding forest.

He carefully climbed out, pulling a pistol from his hip. "Ready to go—"

A flash of light appeared behind Verris, followed by a deafening sound. The impact of the blast knocked Jackson back several meters behind the armor. He rolled to a stop, crushing several saplings in his wake.

For a moment, he couldn't see anything except for sunspots in his vision. He shook his head, disoriented, his ears ringing.

"Verris!" he called over the comm, unable to hear a response.

He quickly scrambled up to his feet, the pistol still held tight in his grip, his vision coming back into focus. The air all around him was thick with dust and smoke, a breeze clearing it a moment later as a smoldering crater lay nearby, just meters from where Verris had stood just seconds ago. His pulse raced as he looked around him, searching frantically, unable to find her anywhere. He called out for her, his voice sounding hollow in his own ears. "Verris!" he screamed again, panic setting in, another wave of smoke rising up, obscuring his vision once more.

He took a disoriented step forward, his foot kicking something. He bent down, retracting his helmet, leaving only a breather over his mouth. The smell of burned wood and sulfur filled the air as he caught sight of her rifle on the ground. He grabbed it, uncertain if the attack was random or a precursor to another assault. As he came up, a huge black ant-like creature easily twice his height appeared through the shroud of smoke only a few meters away, coming at him as it moved partially upright on four legs.

Jackson fired with both weapons, striking the creature with several direct hits, its body flailing towards him, attempting to impale him with its razor-sharp front legs before dropping lifelessly to the ground.

He quickly turned, searching for more enemy targets. As he surveyed the area, he caught a brief glimpse of Verris through the drifting smoke and sprinted towards her.

As he approached, he stopped short, catching sight of her clearly for the first time.

"Biiitttsss!" he yelled. "Oh shit, oh shit! Oh my god, is she…alive?"

Bits quickly initiated a medical scan. "She's sustained severe trauma. Her left leg has been severed above the knee and her right has multiple contusions. Her left hand and arm are also badly injured and bleeding considerably. I'm detecting multiple shrapnel wounds along with six broken ribs, one of which has punctured her left lung. Her head has also sustained multiple severe injuries, and I'm detecting cranial bleeding, along with several other areas showing internal bleeding. She is still breathing. However, her vital signs are rapidly weakening, and I am unable to make contact with Altara. I believe she is offline."

"Get the exo on her, now! Use it to stop the bleeding and administer medical attention."

Jackson reached down, placing his hand gently on Verris's abdomen while Bits liquefied the suit and quickly transferred it onto her while he stared at her blood-covered face, his heart breaking as the woman he loved lay dying.

"I will do what I can, William, but the lieutenant's injuries are *extensive.* Far more than the exo-suit's medical protocols are capable of dealing with."

"Understood. Just do what you can. I'm going to carry her back. Signal the others to clear a path!"

Jackson carefully lifted Verris's broken body, running with her in his arms while Bits contacted the *Phoenix*, finally breaking through the jamming field and relaying the ship's position to Jackson in his ocular implants, providing him with a route. Jackson ran, pushing his legs to the limit, his heart pounding in his chest with every step.

Dirt erupted to his left as another shell impacted, a concussive wave throwing him to the ground. He took the brunt of the impact, ignoring the pain and doing his best to cradle Verris in his arms, shielding her as they fell. He was back up in an instant, his forehead bleeding, along with several pieces of shrapnel in his shoulder. Ignoring them, he pushed forward, running as flashes of plasma fire slammed into the nearby trees, shattering their trunks into a spray of splinters.

Jackson stopped at a large boulder, using it for cover, holding Verris in one arm and partially over his shoulder while he reached around the side and opened fire. A return salvo followed, and he darted out the second it abated, letting loose with the rifle and taking down two Wrenthari as they came into view.

He ran for the ship, plasma strikes erupting all around him while the sounds of the Sentinel and the Annihilator providing heavy cover fire filled the forest, overpowering his senses. He pushed forward, the ship coming into view in the distance a few seconds later.

After what felt like an eternity, he reached the ramp of the *Phoenix*, darting on board with Verris still held in his arms.

"Doctor!" Jackson yelled frantically, struggling for air. "Daria!"

He ran to the medical bay while Bits interfaced with the ship's systems, opening a medpod. Jackson gently laid Verris down just as Dr. Duratis entered the room. Bits flowed the exo-suit off of Verris's body, leaving only small pieces of it to cover her wounds. The doctor put her hand to her mouth as soon as she saw Verris.

"Oh my god."

"Can you help her?"

"I'll do what I can, but you need to get up front. *Now!*"

"I'm not leaving her!"

"Those cruisers are closing on us. They'll be in range in less than two minutes! If we don't get the hell out of here, we're all dead. Kelara is the only other pilot we've got, and she isn't anywhere as good as Verris says you are."

Jackson stood, stunned. Verris had always teased him about his piloting skills since the day they 'd met. She was a master, and he was her protégé. She'd taught him well, but he knew he would never be her equal. Hearing the compliment from the doctor, something Verris would never say to his face, brought on a flood of emotion. He snapped himself out of it, knowing the doctor was right, turning and running for the bridge.

"Get Johansen and Quentarus aboard," he called to the admiral as he ran onto the bridge, taking a seat at the helm.

The admiral didn't flinch at being given orders from his subordinate, quickly signaling Johansen and Quentarus to double-time it back to the ship.

Jackson took off, moving towards their position, attempting to close the gap. As soon as they saw the ship, they flew up, taking heavy fire, the forest teeming with insectoid ground troops surging forward like a massive wave.

He pulled up the tactical sub-console on the helm's display, targeting multiple enemy positions and unleashing a barrage of powerful plasma fire, devastating the Insectoids below and leveling an area the size of six football fields.

He looked down at the console, confirming that both his crewmates were on board. "Prepare for emergency maneuvers!" he called as he fired the engines, rocketing the ship forward.

Moments later, Johansen and Quentarus joined them on the bridge, each bathed in green light from a focused inertial dampening field, allowing them to move through the ship despite the high speeds while they took their stations and strapped in.

"Sir, sensors show that one of the frigate's engines are operational again and it's moving to cut us off. It's almost on top of us!" Quentarus reported.

The *Phoenix* rocked a moment later from a volley of weapons fire from high above. Jackson took evasive action, banking sharply to port, avoiding the worst of it.

"Can we cloak?" the admiral asked.

"The frigate is creating a charged particle field over a wide area. Our cloak won't work until we clear the field," Johansen said. "We're better off keeping our shields up and making a break for it."

"Acknowledged. Helm, do your best to get us clear. Tactical, charge weapons and prep countermeasures. We're going to have to fight our way out of here!"

The *Phoenix* continued picking up speed and gaining altitude, attempting to pull out of the frigate's weapons range. The enemy ship poured on the assault, but the distance provided Jackson precious seconds to evade most of the incoming fire before it reached them.

"Where are those battlecruisers?" the admiral asked.

"Scanning," Lieutenant Quentarus replied. "Got them. They're closing fast from multiple vectors, attempting to cut off our escape routes!"

"Can you find a way through?" Jackson asked as more fire narrowly missed the ship.

Quentarus focused on her console.

"Lieutenant?" the admiral called.

She shook her head. "They've got us cut off and the frigate's driving us towards the ambush. Those cruisers will make short work of us once we're in range."

"Can we jump?" Johansen asked.

"We're still in the thermosphere; the gravity's too strong!" Jackson called as he banked the ship hard to starboard.

"We're almost in range of the cruisers!" Quentarus warned.

"We don't have a choice. Turn back towards the frigate. Prepare to fire!" the admiral said, bracing while Jackson swung the ship around.

Jackson piloted the *Phoenix* directly towards the Imperium frigate, keeping their profile to a minimum, making the sleek ship harder to target while Quentarus locked on and opened fire. Bolts of plasma rocketed forward, impacting the frigate's already battered shields, followed by a barrage from the ship's particle beams.

The frigate poured on its assault, a heavy barrage of fire forcing Jackson to break off and roll the ship. He swung back towards the frigate once more, twisting as he lined up their attack run, Quentarus letting loose with another wave of fire from the forward weapons.

"We've opened a gap in their shields!" she called.

"On it!" Jackson said, adjusting their course and taking them straight towards the enemy ship's forward flank as the two vessels closed rapidly.

"Firing!" Quentarus said, a rapid wave of plasma streaking forward, followed by two torpedoes in rapid succession, penetrating the frigate's defenses. The torpedoes detonated on the starboard underside of the ship and took out a section of the hull, the Insectoid ship's weapons fire ceasing.

"There's our window," the admiral called. "Punch it!"

"I'm on it," Jackson replied, altering their approach to take them beneath the wounded enemy ship, keeping them in close to make it hard for any remaining active weapons to lock on. They rocketed past the frigate seconds later, open space appearing in the viewscreen as they cleared the upper atmosphere.

"Plotting a jump now," Jackson said, eyeing the sensors, watching the gravity field diminish. "We're almost—"

One of the cruisers locked on, hitting the *Phoenix* hard with a devastating salvo.

"They're targeting our engines," Johansen warned. "Our shields are gone! We can't take another hit!"

"Ten seconds to jump," Jackson called, twisting the ship once more. "Five seconds. Jumping now—"

Another hit slammed into the *Phoenix*, rocking the ship hard.

"We've lost sublight engines," Johansen called, the ship spinning from the force of the impact.

"Damage report," the admiral called, turning to Johansen.

"One of the cruisers got off a lucky shot and hit our port engine. It's gone. The power surge took out the starboard engine as well. I just need thirty seconds to reroute power."

"Emergency jump drive?"

"Offline."

"What about the stealth drive and the hyperdrive?" the admiral asked, knowing they only had seconds before the cruisers would have them surrounded.

"Both are online, but the power surge affected the hyperdrive, too. It'll need at least a minute to recharge," Johansen said, knowing it was time they didn't have.

"Engage cloak! Helm, use the thrusters and the stealth drive to get us as far away as you can."

"Sir, the nearest cruiser just locked on with a tractor beam," Jackson said. "I can't break us free!"

"The cruisers are right on top of us," Quentarus said, flipping the tactical map to the main viewscreen showing the cruisers converging from several sides. "We're a sitting duck unless we can get out of here now!"

The nearest cruiser came to a stop, the tractor beam pulling them in. Quentarus flipped the image on the viewscreen again to show the massive vessel growing closer, beams of white light flickering in the image.

"Sir," Jackson interjected, the color draining from his face, "we're being hailed. Text only. They're ordering us to surrender or be destroyed."

Time seemed to stop as the words sank in, each knowing that capture meant torture and almost certain death.

"Options?" the admiral asked.

They each stared at their consoles for a moment before looking back up and shaking their heads. The Insectoids had them boxed in, and the cruisers outgunned them easily fifty to one.

"Power is back to the port engine, and the hyperdrive is almost recharged, but they'll almost certainly cripple or destroy us if we try to escape," Johansen said, defeat in his voice.

"We can't break free from their tractor lock anyway," Jackson added.

The crew was silent, the protocol clear.

The *Phoenix* was a state-of-the-art classified vessel and could not be taken intact. Nor could they afford to let the Imperium have Jackson. They looked around the bridge, meeting the other's eyes, all coming to the same inevitable conclusion.

"Latara," the admiral said to his AI, his voice grave, "prepare to initiate self-destruct sequence on my mark."

Jackson thought of Verris, back in the med bay, fighting to survive while they were about to give up. He looked around at the faces of his friends, the bridge feeling suddenly darker. Each of them prepared themselves, the message from the Insectoids repeating.

"It's been an honor serving with you," the admiral said, a hint of pride in his voice as he looked at each of them one last time. "Latara, engage in ten—"

An alarm echoed from the tactical station as Lieutenant Quentarus spun back in her chair, her hands working to find the source. "Hyperspace ripples detected!"

"Where?" the admiral asked.

A ship appeared in a flash of light a second later, approaching from above and opening fire on the nearest Insectoid cruiser. A powerful blast of unknown energy ripped through the massive battleship's shields as though they weren't there, punching a gaping hole clean through the hull. The battleship's power fluctuated, the ship going dark a second later, the tractor beam suddenly gone.

A rain of weapons fire followed from the unknown ship, striking several of the other cruisers and finishing the one closest to the *Phoenix* with another barrage, the ship breaking apart.

"Helm, full power to engines!" the admiral called. "Get us the hell out of here!"

Jackson reacted instantly, punching the throttle and maneuvering the *Phoenix* past the heavily damaged cruiser, avoiding the wreckage and using it as cover from the other battleships.

The frigate opened fire, its weapons weak but back online. The volley narrowly missed the *Phoenix*, and the frigate set a pursuit course while the other cruisers focused on the deadly, unknown vessel, tearing them to pieces.

The frigate fired again, grazing the *Phoenix*. Jackson pulled up, twisting and darting the ship through the massive hole in the battlecruiser. Decks exposed to the hard vacuum of space flew by, the *Phoenix* emerging from the top of the ship seconds later, then breaking hard to port while the frigate was forced to navigate around the hulking wreck.

"Who the hell was that?" Johansen asked.

"I don't know. I've never seen anything like it," Quentarus marveled. "It's barely bigger than a corvette, but it's going toe-to-toe with all three battleships!"

"Is it going to make it?" Jackson asked, putting the damaged cruiser behind them once more, blocking the frigate's field of fire.

"It's taking a pounding," she said. "The second cruiser's hammering it with all it has, while the other two are coming about and returning fire."

"Whoever they are, we can't help them," the admiral said. "We just have to be thankful that they showed up when they did and hope that they make it out of this. Take as many scans as you can. Be sure to record everything."

"Jump in fifteen seconds," Jackson said, the *Phoenix* limping forward on a single engine.

"Incoming missiles!" Quentarus called. "They're gaining rapidly. Point defense is online. Deploying countermeasures."

Bursts of red-hot chaff fired from the rear of the ship while the point defense beams targeted the incoming missiles and automated drones deployed, seeking out the incoming projectiles.

"We're clear!" Quentarus called a moment later, the last of the missiles destroyed.

"Copy that. We're free of the planet's gravity," Jackson informed them.

"Incoming shockwave!" Johansen warned. "Abort jump! Repeat, abort jump!"

The shockwave shook the ship a moment later.

"Origin?" the admiral asked.

"It looks like that little ship just took out another battlecruiser, sir!" Quentarus reported. "And it's badly damaged the third one as well. Whatever it is, it's one hell of a tough little ship!"

"Are we clear to jump?" Jackson asked, turning to Johansen.

"Clear," Johansen replied.

Jackson engaged the hyperdrive, the *Phoenix* disappearing in a flash seconds later as they entered the hyperspace convergence.

Jackson turned to the admiral. "Sir?"

"Go," the admiral said, giving him a nod.

As Jackson got up, Quentarus moved to the helm, quickly taking his place, and Jackson ran to the medical bay, desperate to see Verris. As he entered the room, Dr. Duratis looked up, her expression grim while she clutched a data pad in her hands.

"How is she?" he asked, terrified to know the answer, looking at her through the glass, wishing he could hold her.

"The pod's done all it can, but she's lost a significant amount of blood. Her injuries are extensive and severe. Her vital organs are failing." The doctor paused, looking him in the eyes. "Will, she's not going to make it."

"No," he whispered, his voice shaking as he hovered on the verge of tears. "There has to be something that you can do."

"If we were at a starbase or proper medical facility maybe, but out here…" She shook her head, trailing off. "Her injuries are just beyond what the pod or I can repair."

"There has to be *something* you can do?"

"There is one thing we could try…" she said tentatively. "But I can't promise it will work…"

"Anything," he said, his eyes flitting to the pod once more, Verris's lips blue, her vitals on the display all dropping. He flashed back to watching Amy die, knowing that Verris could be gone any second.

The doctor let out a breath. "We cryo-freeze her. But we have to do it now, while there's still brain activity. The pod will put her body into stasis, but her mind will remain active, in a dreamlike state."

"Will it work?"

"I honestly don't know, Will," she said, shaking her head. "The trauma she suffered is *severe*. She could still die in cryo, but this at least gives her a chance…*if* we can get her to a medical facility in time."

"Okay," he whispered, his heart aching.

The doctor walked over to the comm panel. "Lieutenant Quentarus, I need you to set a course for the nearest GCH medical facility. Maximum speed."

"Understood."

She closed the channel, accessing the medpod's controls on her pad. "Disengaging life support systems and switching to cryo-statis mode."

Jackson nodded, numb at the realization he was losing

the love of his life. That he'd never even get to say goodbye if she didn't make it.

He suddenly felt as he had all of those years ago, when he held Amy's hand, the first love of his life lying on the operating table, slipping away. This time, however, he was forced to watch in agony through the glass as he gave the doctor permission to let her go.

He watched her face, wishing that he could hold her hand one last time. That he could stroke her hair and kiss her temple, and tell her that it was all going to be okay.

Verris's vitals suddenly flatlined, the pod working to resuscitate her, the cryo-stasis field on standby while he watched helplessly, his hand pressed against the glass, a tear running down his cheek as her body convulsed with each electrical shock.

In that moment, he knew that nothing was going to be okay ever again.

CHAPTER 13
WOUNDS

The *Phoenix* arrived in the Samatra System six hours later. Doctor Duratis immediately contacted the medical station in orbit around the second planet, alerting them to their situation, while Jackson set a course. As soon as the ship docked, a medical team, along with an engineering team from the station, came on board, removing the pod and taking it directly to the advanced trauma center.

Jackson and the doctor followed close behind, and she joined the team in the surgical bay after quickly going through medical decon procedures. Jackson waited in a nearby lounge while they worked on Verris, rocking slightly in his seat as he tried to imagine what she was going through and how he could ever live without her.

The pod had been successful at finally restarting her heart, and the cryo systems activated seconds later, preserving her vitals on the razor's edge somewhere between life and death. The rest of the crew secured the ship before joining him, taking a seat and offering support.

After what seemed like ages, Dr. Duratis finally appeared to give them an update.

"Verris is still in critical condition, but the doctors have stopped most of the internal bleeding. They removed the majority of the shrapnel. However, there's still extensive damage to repair. Her damaged organs are being worked on now, and her leg and other major external injuries can be treated over time with regenerative nanotech and gene therapies, but she isn't stable enough for them to try at this point. For now, they're keeping her on life support until her organs stabilize and she regains some strength. The real concern is the extent of the damage to her brain. The scans revealed significant trauma from several pieces of shrapnel that penetrated her skull. They have armies of nanites working on her, attempting to repair the damage, but it's still touch and go. The team decided it was best to put her into a medically induced coma until they know more." She paused for a moment, placing her hand gently on Jackson's shoulder. "The doctors advised us to get some rest and to come back tomorrow."

"I can't leave her," he said weakly.

"I know, Will, but there's nothing you can do for her right now. You need to get some rest too. She's got a *long* road to recovery ahead of her, and she's going to need your strength to get there."

"All right," Jackson said reluctantly, after considering her words for a moment.

"They assigned us quarters three decks up, so we'll be close by."

The doctor led the crew to their quarters, each of them saying goodbye as they dropped him off first, making sure he went inside.

Jackson lay down, mentally and physically exhausted. The next nine hours drifted past as he fell in and out of sleep, the events on Praxian Prime replaying in his mind over and over again.

He awoke feeling strange, the unfamiliar surroundings of the station's quarters jarring him for a moment. He sat on the side of the bed, hoping for a second that it had all been some kind of nightmare, but as he looked down, he felt the remnants of the scrapes and scratches on his arms that Daria had treated on the way back, he knew that it was all too real.

The admiral was heading down the corridor as Jackson exited his room.

"Any updates, sir?" Jackson asked, quickly falling into step beside him.

"I was just about to meet with the rest of the crew to give them an update. I was going to let you sleep some more, but since you're up, why don't you join us?"

"Sounds good," he said, desperate to see Verris but wanting to hear what the admiral had to say.

The admiral nodded, and they headed for the conference room at the end of the corridor. Jackson entered the room just behind the admiral, the rest of the crew coming over to him and giving him a hug. He accepted them numbly, taking a seat a moment later as the admiral began.

"Good morning, everyone. Thank you all for coming. I know that it's been an incredibly difficult past few days, so I'll be brief. First, the doctor and I spoke with the chief surgeon on the station early this morning, and she recommended that Lieutenant Verris be transferred to an advanced medical facility in one of the core systems. They contacted the Ministry of Health and located the best center for treating these types of injuries on Archon. Verris isn't stable enough to travel yet, but the doctors here believe that she should be within the next few days. The good news is that she made some progress last night and some of her organs have started to bounce back. She's still fighting, and we'll do everything that we can to help her, but for now, it's up to her.

"Will," the Admiral continued, looking over at Jackson, "I'd like you and Dr. Duratis to stay here and accompany Verris back to Archon. The rest of us will take the *Phoenix* to the GCH shipyard in the Cetarus System for repairs. We'll work during that time to analyze the sensor readings from Praxian Prime and try to figure out what happened and how the Imperium found us. We'll meet you on Archon once the ship is fully operational again and plan our next move. Lieutenant, Chief, we'll meet on the ship and leave in twenty minutes. Dismissed."

The crew got up and slowly left the room, each giving Jackson a nod or a pat on the shoulder as they left. The doctor stopped just outside the door, looking back while Jackson remained sitting, the admiral moving to stand by his side.

"Will," Admiral Valentyen said, "take as much time as you need. Stay with Verris. The mission's on hold indefinitely. What's important now is that you're with her while she recovers."

"Thank you, sir."

"If there's anything that you need, son, just let me know," the admiral said, his voice full of concern as he placed a hand on Jackson's shoulder, then turned to leave.

"Thank you, sir."

The admiral stopped. "The doctors said that if she continues to improve, then you can see her later on today."

Jackson looked up, his heart aching to see her. The image of her broken body lying in the woods flashed in his memory, crushing him. He nodded slowly, then looked back down. The admiral left him, the doctor following as they moved down the hall, keeping their voices low while they talked.

Jackson got up a moment later, finding the doctor waiting for him alone down the hallway. "Are you okay?"

"Yeah. I'm going to go to the ship and get a few things from her quarters for her. For when she wakes up."

"That's a good idea. Do you want me to come with you?"

"No, thanks. I'm good. I'll meet you in the medical wing in about ten minutes."

"Sounds good. I'll go and see if I can get an update on her condition."

"Thanks, Daria. You're a good friend."

"Of course, Will. I'm here for you both. Just let me know if you need anything."

Jackson made his way back to the ship, quickly packing a few things from his quarters, then Verris's. As Jackson stepped off the ramp from the *Phoenix*, Johansen entered the hangar bay.

"Hey, buddy," Johansen said. "If you need anything, just let me know. We'll try to meet up with you on Archon soon."

"Thanks, Hen," he replied weakly. "I just can't believe it. After all these years and all the close calls she and I have had together. I just can't…" He trailed off, thinking of her smile, picturing the two of them in the cockpit of the *Griffin*. The simple joy of her company. Terrified that he'd never have that again.

"It'll be okay. I didn't know her for long, but she struck me as someone who never gives up," Johansen said. "She'll keep fighting. She will bounce back from this."

"Thanks," he said, letting out a breath, feeling somewhat better knowing that his best friend would be there with him to support him. "I'll see you soon."

Later that afternoon, Jackson was finally allowed to see Verris. As he entered the ICU in a full medical nano-suit, he saw her lying in a specialized chamber similar to one of the pods on the ship, but larger and more advanced. A bio-containment field around the pod limited how close he could get, ensuring that everything remained sterile, with only authorized staff's suits coded to pass through the field. He moved along the edge of the area marked on the floor to face her, noticing the organic regeneration patches covering most of her body. He stared at her for several minutes, barely recognizing her, everything feeling surreal, as though it were a dream. Verris had always been so strong that it seemed impossible that it could be her lying there so helplessly.

Dr. Duratis found him a few minutes later, sitting in the main viewing gallery, overlooking the planet that the station orbited, lost in thought. As she sat down beside him, he realized he had no idea how long he had been there.

"How are you doing?" she asked gently.

"I'm okay," he said, his voice hollow.

She led him to the mess, and although he had no appetite, he ate with her after she insisted, not sure how long it had been since his last meal.

"Thanks, Daria, for everything you've done. Verris wouldn't have made it without you."

"Of course, Will," she said, placing a hand on his. "And I'm here for you, whatever you need."

He nodded, a feeling of helplessness filling him, as he knew now that all he could do was wait. After they ate, the doctor walked Jackson back to his quarters, suggesting that he get some rest. She hugged him, reassuring him that it was going to be okay.

He lay down, falling asleep shortly after, the emotional stress leaving him exhausted despite having only been up for less than half a day. As he slept, his dreams descended into nightmares from the seconds before and after the explosion. The image of Verris lying on the forest floor burned into his thoughts. A simmering feeling of rage growing inside.

The next day, Verris took a turn for the worse, forcing the doctors to perform emergency surgery to repair a hemorrhage in her brain. Hours passed while Jackson waited helplessly until he finally got word that they had been able to repair the damage and stabilize her once more. By the third day, he was completely physically and emotionally drained, barely able to sleep or function.

Finally, on the fifth day, Verris had stabilized enough to travel. A medical shuttle took Jackson, Dr. Duratis, Verris, and several attending physicians from the station to the advanced medical facility on Archon.

They spent the next several days there while the new team of doctors got up to speed and began a series of treatments. Jackson went to see her whenever they would allow it, but they kept him away most of the time while they ran a series of scans and performed various procedures. He and Dr. Duratis spent much of their days walking through the facility's beautifully manicured grounds and he settled into a routine that helped to shake him out of the lingering shock, slowly bringing him back to reality.

He finally started sleeping again, though his dreams remained plagued with darkness and violence. Each time he slept, his mind replayed the moment that the enemy fire exploded near Verris, over and over.

As the days passed, Verris's condition further stabilized, and she was downgraded from critical to serious condition. The doctors had repaired all of her damaged organs and most of her other major injuries, but it would take at least another three weeks for them to attempt to push her system to regrow her leg and badly injured arm and hand using nano and cellular reconstruction techniques. His hope began to grow, and the doctors assured him that she would make a full physical recovery in time.

The major concern they still had was the significant trauma she'd sustained to her frontal lobe and two pieces of shrapnel that remained deep inside in the base of her skull that they'd deemed too risky to treat until she'd stabilized further.

"The doctors are going to try to operate later this afternoon," Dr. Duratis said, sitting with Jackson on a bench in the gardens. "It's a risky procedure, but if successful, she'll be out of danger, and it will just be a matter of time and allowing her body to heal before they'll bring her out of the medically induced coma."

"Okay." He nodded numbly.

"You and I can watch from a viewing room if you'd like."

Jackson's mind flashed back to Amy's surgery. Her hand in his as she faded away. As much as he dreaded being there, he felt he needed to, not wanting her to go through this alone.

Several hours later, Jackson and the doctor sat in the viewing room, watching as the team of surgeons worked below. Verris lay on her front on a raised table, her neck and the back of her head visible, while the rest of her body was covered by a medical nano-suit to keep everything sterile and administer other care as needed.

So far, the surgery had been going well. They'd extracted the first piece of shrapnel, a shard of metal nearly an inch in length. The doctors paused for a moment, discussing the next steps, a holographic image suspended above Verris zooming in on the affected section, showing the second shard and Verris's implants in detail.

"This is the tricky one," Dr. Duratis explained. "Scans show it impacted her cognitive implant and damaged it."

"Is that why Altara's still offline?"

"Exactly. Altara's core processor is right next to it, and it looks like an edge of the fragment may have hit it as well. She can't interface with Verris's implants or comms without access to the cognitive module. Once the shrapnel is removed, they'll extract both units and transfer Altara to a new core."

"Makes sense. Why's this so risky then? When I had my AI installed it was just a short procedure."

"There's several components in those modules that pose a serious risk if they've been compromised and rupture."

Jackson nodded, watching as the doctors finished their discussion, starting to work on the second shard. Minutes passed while they worked, Dr. Duratis explaining what was happening as the procedure progressed.

"This is the last part. They're going to remove the fragment and have an injection of medical nanites standing by to repair the surrounding tissue. They'll then extract the modules, and it's all done."

Jackson held his breath, watching while the doctors worked below. The lead surgeon's hands moved slowly, the medical nano-suit he wore ensuring complete and precise stability. The surgeon pulled his hand back slowly, the tweezer-like tool in his fingers gripping the shard of metal. The holo-display showed the shard slide back, scans indicating that it was rubbing against part of the core processor as it moved, warning boxes appearing around key sections of the tiny implant, no bigger than two quarters stacked together.

The surgeon moved his hand deftly, manipulating the tool to maneuver a jagged edge of the shard around the red area. A moment later, it was clear, and he slowly, carefully pulled the shard from the back of Verris's head. He held it up before him, the jagged, bladelike sliver of metal several inches in length covered in blood as it gleamed in the bright lights of the surgical suite.

Jackson let out a relieved breath, the doctor reaching over and taking his hand.

"They just have to pull the two modules now and patch her up. Just anoth—"

Alarms sounded in the operating room below as an area on the holo-display flashed red.

"What's happening?" Jackson asked, leaning forward, watching in horror while the team below moved frantically, more lights flashing and alarms sounding. His mind flashed back to watching Amy die, recalling the feeling of helplessness and terror.

"I don't know," Dr. Duratis said. "Let's get down there."

They quickly left the viewing area and headed down the stairs to a prep room just outside the operating room. Daria pressed a button and audio from the surgical suite came through over the speakers. One of the surgeons, Dr. Stevenson, stood over Verris holding a specialized scanning device, his expression grim.

"The second shard tore open a microfracture in the liquid heatsink of her AI's core processor!" he called out, the team looking on while he worked.

Jackson turned to Daria, watching as the blood drained from her face.

"What does that mean?" he asked, his voice nearly shaking.

"Every AI core module has a tiny amount of isilium in its pressurized liquid form suspended around the main processor to provide cooling. It's highly toxic and fatal if not treated immediately," she explained.

"She's going into toxic shock! We're losing her!" The calls came from the operating room.

"There has to be something they can do!" Jackson said, grasping at straws.

Dr. Stevenson looked over, noticing Jackson and Dr. Duratis standing there, a look of intense concentration on his face, knowing he only had seconds to act. "There's one thing that might work," he said, turning back to his team. "Move her to a gurney and get her in the TSC stat!"

The other doctors and nurses looked up, the realization

dawning on them what Dr. Stevenson was thinking. They quickly transferred Verris over to a hover gurney and rushed her out of the room and down the hall.

Jackson and Dr. Duratis followed. "What's a TSC?" he asked while they ran to keep pace.

"I have no idea!" she said, the team approaching a set of double doors, moving into another wing of the facility. Lights activated as they entered a room off to the right, a security scanner sweeping Dr. Stevenson while he called out an authorization code.

A white, hexagonal chamber the size of a cargo van rose from the floor in the center of the room, the door opening with a hiss.

"Quickly, place her inside!" he called, the team working to maneuver the gurney into the center of the chamber, then get clear. "Nurse Roberts, hook her up to the TSC monitor."

The remaining nurse reached up and connected a device to Verris's arm, then followed her colleagues outside.

"Computer, activate the TSC. Full stasis protocols," Dr. Stevenson said.

The door closed, the lights inside dimming while a low hum filled the room, the air suddenly becoming heavier around the chamber.

Dr. Stevenson waved Jackson and Dr. Duratis to follow him back towards the door, the effects of the field the chamber generated lessening as they moved away. The rest of the team stayed close. Nurse Roberts pulled up readings from the chamber on a screen and checked to ensure that it was operating properly while they verified Verris's status. "We're good, Doctor," she said, giving him a nod.

"What just happened?" Jackson asked.

"We've placed her in a temporal stasis chamber. It's a specialized device that creates a state of temporal suspension. It was the only way to prevent the toxic shock from killing her."

"Will that even work?" Dr. Duratis asked, her brow furrowing.

"I know what you're thinking, Doctor, but it's different from cryo-stasis. The chamber actually freezes her in *time*, literally between heartbeats. No time will pass for her at all while in the temporal suspension field."

"But we still have the problem of the isilium," she said.

"That's correct," he said gravely. "And if we were anywhere else right now, she'd already be dead. But she's fortunate that she's in one of only five facilities across the entire GCH that have this new technology. The challenge now is that we'll need to develop a way to remove the isilium from inside her brain while she's still in temporal suspension. If we take her out, she'll only last seconds before it kills her. We were lucky to have made it in time."

"I'm so confused," Jackson said, still trying to catch up.

Doctor Duratis turned to him. "In its liquid form, isilium is so toxic that it kills flesh upon contact. Think of it like a type of molecular acid that interacts at the micro-cellular level. That's one of the risks they usually don't talk about when people get their AIs installed, that there's a deadly, toxic agent inside some of the module's cores. The thinking is, however, that if a person is badly injured enough for the isilium to rupture, they're likely already dead."

Jackson nodded, turning back to Dr. Stevenson. "What can we do?"

He let out a breath. "Well, we'll have to figure something out. But at least we've bought ourselves time."

"But isn't the isilium still going to leak out and spread?" Jackson asked.

"Think about it like a bullet that's just hit someone and penetrated their skin. The kinetic energy from the bullet can't be stopped at this point, as it's already hit. But...in temporal stasis, both the person *and* the bullet are frozen in time. Again, we can't stop the damage from the initial impact, but if we can get something active into the temporal stasis field, then we can remove the bullet before it moves even a micromillimeter, and then repair the damage before it spreads."

Jackson nodded. "So, the isilium *can't* leak out, because time is frozen."

"Exactly. Now we just need to figure out a way to get into the field and remove the modules and isilium, then remove any tissue it's come into contact with."

"What effect will that have on her brain?" Dr. Duratis interjected.

"Honestly, we won't know until she wakes up. There's no way to tell for sure. She's suffered trauma to several parts of her brain, including her memory center and visual processing. We have the technology to repair these areas, but there could be some memory loss," Dr. Stevenson explained.

"What's the next step for treatment?" Jackson asked, looking back at the chamber across the room, longing to be there for Verris but happy that she was out of danger for the moment.

"That's the hard part. We've solved one problem – we can keep her alive in temporal suspension indefinitely – but we've created another. We now need to develop a way to interact with her in suspension and remove the isilium and the modules. I don't know yet. It's going to take a lot of time and research."

"How long?" Jackson asked.

Dr. Stevenson considered for a moment. "Honestly? It could be months, maybe years. We've only used the chamber so far to preserve people with critical injuries until we can treat them, but we've never had to treat a person *in* temporal suspension before. We're in uncharted territory, unfortunately."

A silence held in the air for a moment, Jackson and Dr. Duratis each processing the information.

"But if you get it all out, then she'll be okay?" Jackson asked.

"Yes. Once we're sure it's gone, we'll need to treat the surrounding tissue damage, allowing it to regenerate. That may require some kind of secondary temporal field to cancel out the first one. At this point, it's all theoretical."

"Can you even do that?" Dr. Duratis asked. "I mean, if the isilium has already made contact with any of her cells, then the damage is permanent."

"Yes and no. There's been some research lately around treating isilium toxicity in some recent medical journals. It's all still experimental and in the development stages, but...the research suggests that it's possible to treat the damage if caught in a very, very short window of the exposure. Again, this is where the temporal stasis comes in. The lieutenant and the isilium don't exist within the flow of time while inside the chamber. It's the same technology the GCH's temporal response teams use. Not a single nanosecond will pass in there. Both for her and the isilium that is leaking into her brain. Both are completely frozen in time, so we should be able to treat any cells that were damaged within a very short window of time since it's been less than two minutes since the containment on her core processor failed."

"Why haven't I heard of this technology before?" Dr. Duratis asked.

"It's still considered experimental for medical use. As I mentioned, there's only a handful of the temporal stasis chambers in existence. We've been piloting it here for the past year and have used temporal suspension to save nearly a dozen lives while people wait for transplants or new organs to be grown. We've also used it to treat several patients with other highly time-sensitive conditions that cryo-stasis alone is insufficient to handle because the body still ages, albeit incredibly slowly."

"That's…incredible," she admitted, considering the endless possibilities and applications.

"It is. Unfortunately, it also presents us with a new set of problems in this case, as I mentioned. We simply can't take her out of there and repair the damage in time before it's too severe and her system crashes using traditional methods. We'll have to develop new techniques and technologies. Ways to interact with her while still within the temporal stasis field. It will take time."

Jackson nodded slowly, the surge of adrenaline that had flooded his system now subsiding as he felt the emotional drain take hold. "Thank you, Doctor. If you hadn't acted when you did, Verris wouldn't have had a chance. You've given her that now."

"I assure you, we'll do everything in our power and bring to bear the entire collective power of the GCH medical establishment to find a way to fix this. To heal her," he said. "But it's going to take time."

Jackson nodded solemnly, shaking the doctor's hand before the doctor went back to check in with Nurse Roberts and the rest of his team.

Jackson and the Dr. Duratis stood near the doorway, taking a moment to look back at Verris. "What do you think?" he asked.

"This is out of my element, Will, but I think she's getting the best possible care and the doctors here are brilliant. Dr. Stevenson wasn't exaggerating when he said that they'll put the full resources of the GCH towards figuring this out. There may be entire medical conferences dedicated to working on this. They *will* figure it out," she said, turning to look at him. "But I think you need to shift your focus. This really could take years."

Jackson nodded. "I'll wait as long as it takes. The important thing is that she's alive."

The doctor put her hand on his shoulder, giving it a reassuring squeeze while they looked back at Verris. "We'll get through this, I promise."

CHAPTER 14

CLUES

The next day, the *Phoenix* arrived at GCH Command on Archon, and the crew took a shuttle to meet Jackson and the doctor at the medical facility. Dr. Duratis brought them up to speed on Verris's condition, while the admiral informed them of their plans.

"After a long discussion, we've decided that it's best to return to the Hideaway to begin analyzing the data from the sensor logs to figure out what happened and how the Imperium found us. I also want to focus on the Ancient map we recovered. It may hold the key to finding more sites."

Jackson sat quietly, nodding while the admiral spoke, knowing they were right, that Verris would want them to carry on. "Can you do the analysis here?" he asked, wanting to join the crew, while longing to stay close to Verris.

"Unfortunately, no. We need to keep the data isolated and compartmentalized. It's safer to do it there, where we're off the books. Especially after everything that's happened."

"I'm going to go with them," the doctor said. "There isn't anything more I can do for Verris here on Archon, but at least there I can be useful."

"I know how you feel," Jackson said.

"You can stay if you want," the admiral said. "Be here for Verris when she wakes up."

"Who knows how long that will be, sir," he said. "From everything the doctors here have told us, it could be years. I'd rather be there with the rest of you, doing something productive and figuring out how the hell they found us twice now rather than just sitting here helplessly."

"Very well," the admiral said. "We'll depart in three hours. I'm due at GCH Command shortly to brief Fleet Admirals Lighton and Holup on the situation. I'll meet up with the rest of you back at the ship."

Jackson and Dr. Duratis met with Dr. Stevenson and his senior staff once more before leaving. They promised to keep him apprised of their status, assuring him that figuring out a way to treat Verris was their top priority.

A knot grew in the pit of his stomach at the thought of leaving her, a feeling of betrayal growing inside that left him feeling hollow. He resolved his will to carry on, knowing that he couldn't just sit there and do nothing. That her sacrifice had to count for something.

And if he ever found those responsible…they would pay most dearly.

The crew spent the next five days back at the Hideaway, each working on different projects.

The station felt different now to Jackson, a lonely feeling about it. An emptiness.

Each night, he walked the corridors, unable to sleep, stopping at Verris's door, never able to work up the courage to enter. His finger hovered over the access panel while he tried to convince himself that she was in there, sleeping peacefully.

He ate most of his meals alone, working away from the rest of the crew, attempting to keep his mind occupied. He awoke each morning from what little sleep he'd gotten, calling to check on Verris's status to see if they'd made any progress. Each time, it was the same. After a week, he began to give up on checking in, hardening himself to the fact that he would have to wait for the doctors to contact him when they had some news.

Jackson, the admiral, and the doctor spent most of their time focused on the Ancient star charts they'd recovered, each taking a different section to analyze. With close to four hundred thousand years between the Ancients' rule and the present, countless things had changed in the galaxy, but it was still fascinating to see how vast the Ancient civilization truly was. Their empire stretched from one side of the galaxy to the other, consisting of tens of thousands of worlds.

While the rest of the crew explored the Ancient galaxy, Johansen and Quentarus focused on the sensor logs from the *Phoenix* and the orbital probe. Their assignment: attempting to figure out how the Insectoids had found them again and who it was that came to their rescue. They'd been hard at work on it for weeks, ever since they took the *Phoenix* for repairs, but still had made little progress thus far.

On the afternoon of the eighth day back on the Hideaway, Johansen and Quentarus called the crew into the briefing room, bringing up the visual and sensor logs from the probe while the rest of the crew sat watching intently.

"As you all know, we've been digging through the sensor logs from Praxian Prime to try to figure out what happened, and we think we finally found something," Johansen said. "Shortly after we dropped out of hyperspace in the Praxian System, an encoded transmission, one which was made to look like natural background subspace waves, was sent from the *Phoenix* to an unknown source."

"How is that possible?" the admiral asked.

"Quite frankly, sir, we don't know," Lieutenant Quentarus replied.

"What we've pieced together so far is that whatever sent the transmission accessed the navigational sensors, confirming our location," Johansen said. "All ships do this automatically whenever a ship exits hyperspace, so whatever it was somehow had to access that data. Then, once our location was confirmed, it triggered a signal, embedding the transmission in one of our sensor scans to mask itself in the EM sweep. Very clever, actually. We probably never would have figured it out if we hadn't submitted every sensor log we had to the androids while we were back on Archon, and had an army of them run through the logs in micro-detail."

"Do we know what accessed the sensors and triggered the transmission?" the admiral asked.

"Not yet," Quentarus admitted. "It could have been one of us, which again, we think is unlikely as it would essentially be suicide. It could have come from one of the exo-suits, the three suits of armor, or from something else on board the ship. But... What we do know for certain is that when we pulled the logs from the *Eritus*, now that we knew what we were looking for, we found the same encoded transmission signature buried in its sensor and system logs as well."

Johansen waved his hand, the display showing the data. "Whoever or whatever sent the transmissions made them extremely difficult to detect. The transmission starts like a natural background subspace wave but then modulates several times following a mathematical code using prime numbers, followed by a Fibonacci sequence. This appears to be a data header. From there, it sent a rapid series of short pulses. We analyzed these, running them through several decryption algorithms, and found that they were actually the coordinates of the Praxian and Vishnara Systems. It's quite simple and elegant, actually. Nearly undetectable. Like I said, we likely never would have discovered them if not for the deep byte-by-byte analysis the androids did."

"With the Guardian wrecked back on Praxian Prime," Quentarus said, "we can't be certain that it wasn't the source of the transmission, but since it wasn't with us on the *Eritus*, it stands to reason that it wasn't."

"We've gone over every millimeter of the Sentinel and the Annihilator but haven't found anything on either of them, in their code or in their logs. We checked all of my and the doctor's gear. We've also run every possible diagnostic and scan on both the *Phoenix* and the *Eritus* that we can think of, and we haven't found any transmission devices on either of them. So…"

"So, as *unlikely* as it seems that it could be one of us, we're left with a problem. We've effectively eliminated any other possibility we can think of, *except* for it somehow being one of us," Quentarus concluded.

"Recommendations?" the admiral asked.

"Well," Johansen began, "we can have the doctor run a thorough bio-scan of each of us. It's possible that one of us was tagged unknowingly with a tracking and transmitting device. Once you set up the scan, Daria, we'll let the station's computer run the process to ensure that none of us are able to tamper with it."

"That's a good idea. We should also pull our AIs' diagnostic logs. It's possible that if one of us were tagged with something; there could be a trace of it in there," the doctor suggested.

"Agreed. What's the next step if we don't find anything?" the admiral asked.

"Well, that's where we're open to ideas, sir." Johansen said. "Based on what we've found, we think that the signal triggers when we reach certain galactic locations, specifically one of the three Ancient sites. If that's the case, then it's going to be difficult to recreate the conditions where we can try to get the signal to broadcast again and trace its source."

"And its destination," Quentarus added.

"Exactly. And even if we engage in that scenario, going to another site or back to the Praxian or Vishnara Systems, by us even having had this conversation, it's possible that nothing will happen," Johansen added.

"The other possibility that we have to face is that one of us sent the signal on purpose," Quentarus said with cold detachment. "We've gone through each of the consoles on the bridge, the crew quarters, and the various other stations on the ship. So far, all of the logs are clean, but it's possible that whoever did this used another method to get the transmission out. If one of us is truly, consciously sending the signal and betraying us, then we've just tipped our hand."

The room was silent. The logic was solid, if hard to accept. Either one of them had been tagged somehow and unknowingly compromised in some way or one of them wasn't who or what they said they were.

"Let's start with the medical scans and the analysis of our AIs' logs," the admiral suggested. "I'll go first. Hopefully, we find something there that explains this, but if not, and we rule that out, then we can discuss our next course of action."

The crew spent the next several hours setting up the scans, the admiral supervising the doctor while she configured the medical scanning protocols, and reviewing the process each step of the way to ensure oversight. When it was finally ready, they each took turns going through a bio-scan, which Johansen's and Quentarus's AIs vetted using a secure link to an isolated database. Finally, they had the station's computer parse their AIs' logs for any transmissions or anomalies.

By the time they finished a few hours later, they had eliminated the possibility that it was something on their persons that had sent the transmissions, leaving them with the far more troubling possibility – that one of them was a traitor.

No one said it, but the thought that it could be Verris had occurred to the rest of the crew, despite what had happened to her. With her in temporal stasis, however, there was no way to be sure.

The next morning, they assembled again in the briefing room, having all slept restlessly, suddenly uneasy in one another's company.

"So, what do we do now?" the doctor asked, echoing the feelings of distrust and nervousness each of them felt.

"We continue on," the admiral replied. "What choice do we have? One of us could be a traitor, but to what end? Twice now we've been ambushed, and it was clear that the intent was to capture or kill us. If one of us is consciously working to that end, then why didn't they try something here? There was ample time and opportunity. Any one of us could have killed the rest while we slept or self-destructed the *Eritus* without the computer safeguards in place."

He paused, looking at each of them in turn and shaking his head. "No. I don't believe that any of you are a traitor," he said firmly. "It has to be something that we can't explain yet. So, we press on. We complete our mission. And we honor the sacrifice that Lieutenant Verris made to keep Will alive so we can do so."

Jackson felt a rush of guilt as the admiral said her name, knowing that if he hadn't been shot down, she never would have left the ship. He did his best to push the feeling deep down inside, along with the growing torrent of emotions that shifted from guilt to anger to unchecked rage.

"Jackson, the doctor and I will continue our analysis of the Ancient star charts. Hopefully, this will help us to identify some other potential Ancient sites that we can investigate next. Anything on the other ship that took on the Insectoids?" he asked, looking at Quentarus.

"Nothing so far, sir," Quentarus replied. "I've run the scans through every database, but there's no match."

"Should we go back to Praxian Prime?" Johansen asked.

"I've considered it," the Admiral said, letting out a frustrated breath. "We could go back in force with half a dozen warships, but we risk an incident with the Kerattans who are no doubt aware of what took place by now. Fleet Admiral Lighton was concerned about possible retaliation from them against one of our nearby colonies if we further exasperate the situation. Tensions between us over the past six months have been increasing, and she doesn't want things to escalate. They can't come close to matching the power of our Fleet, but the Admiral also doesn't want to have to dedicate more ships and resources to defending our territory more than we already do today. We're stretched thin in the sector at present. I think it's worth a trip back, eventually, to continue searching the Ancient site but that we're best to leave it for the time being until things cool down with the Kerattans. Now that we have the map, we can focus on finding other potential sites to visit instead."

"Makes sense," Johansen said.

"All right then, let's get back to work and try to take our minds off of the unpleasantness of the past day. Keep working the problem. We will get to the bottom of this, but for now, we have to trust one another and move forward. Dismissed."

The crew spent the next several days working on their assignments. Despite the admiral's words, a sense of distrust had crept into their minds, and although they weren't actively suspicious of anyone in particular, they each spent more time on their own.

Jackson tasked Bits with decrypting the layer of the map that was encrypted, hoping that the answers they sought might be there.

Several days later, Bits made a breakthrough, managing to decrypt a section of the map with the help of the station's computer. Jackson pored over the data, eager to see what new information revealed itself.

"What do you make of these?" he asked, zooming in on a section of the map where several dozen new sites appeared across a vast area of space.

"The new sites appear to be labeled and fall into three different groups. Eighteen sites are listed as Pe'jora. Seven are designated Q'len. And one is labeled Un'shara. There is no translation for these words, however, in the Ancient language database."

"Hmm, can you match them up with any known Ancient sites?"

"I've been running an analysis for several minutes already. The results are imperfect, as galactic drift patterns over four hundred thousand years can be affected by a myriad of factors which can affect present-day locations. I have been able to match up at least seventeen sites, however, based on other metadata available in the map, such as star types, planetary system statistics, and relative distances to the galactic core. Regarding the sites themselves, I've created a working theory."

"Let's hear it."

"I believe that the sites labeled Pe'jora are military bases, and I'm eighty-seven percent certain that Praxian Prime is one of these. Vishnara appears to closely correspond to one of two similar systems in the region from the initial layer of the map and is labeled as Kynis, which I believe may be a depot."

"That's interesting. Makes sense that military sites would be contained in an encrypted level of the map and the hidden room in the depot at Vishnara could have been an emergency supply room or something. What about the other two?"

"The sites labeled Q'len do not correspond to any known sites. However, the metadata shows that they are not planets, but smaller outposts."

"Hmm, maybe bases like the Hideaway? Covert or black-ops sites?"

"A distinct possibility, as there is considerably less data available on them. However, there is no way to be certain at this time."

"And the last one?"

"The site listed as Un'shara has no data other than the star type and number of planets. I've tried to access more information on it, but there appears to be a second layer of encryption protecting it."

"So, something even more secret then?"

"I believe so," Bits said, highlighting the locations on the map in green for the Pe'jora, blue for the Q'len, and red for the Un'shara site.

"Can you figure out where it is?"

"I already have. Fortunately, there is considerable data on several nearby systems and stellar phenomena, and I've been able to use this to narrow down the location. I'm ninety-two percent certain that the site is in the Brestin System."

Jackson's heart skipped a beat while Bits overlayed the Ancient map with a current GCH one, then zoomed in on the system. He stared intently at the six planets orbiting around a small orange star, focusing on the third one from the sun, the small blue-green sphere reminding him of Earth. Bits brought up the data from the probe that surveyed the system and detected a possible Ancient site, and noting the words 'Vicara Class' floating in red above it, designating it as strictly off-limits.

His brow furrowed as he considered his options. Finally, he crossed his arms, realizing that there was no choice. They needed to see what was there.

But after everything that had happened, he didn't know who to trust.

"Bits, I want you to re-encrypt the map."

"William?"

"I'm not sure yet who we can trust. Let's just sit on this for a little while, okay?"

"Very well."

Jackson walked the station for the next several minutes, wrestling with his thoughts while he considered the admiral's words about them remaining a team and trusting one another. He wanted to, and the thought that it could be one of them sickened him to his core.

Henrik had been his friend now for years, and he couldn't imagine him betraying anyone. Hen and Daria were also good friends, but that didn't really prove anything. Still, from the short time Jackson had known her, he couldn't imagine the doctor as anything other than the kind, genuine, considerate person she appeared to be.

He thought about Lieutenant Quentarus, realizing he knew her the least, but unable to imagine how Captain Quentarus's daughter could possibly be a traitor.

His thoughts shifted to the admiral, a man he'd only known for a short time but whose duty record and clearance level spoke for themselves. It seemed unfathomable that a man who'd dedicated most of his life to defending the Confederation could ever betray it.

He returned to his quarters, deciding to sleep on it and reveal what he'd learned to the rest of the crew first thing in the morning. As he lay on the bed, his thoughts shifted to Verris, the image of her in the forest flashing once more in his mind, a cold rage taking hold. His feelings of helplessness and frustration feeding the growing darkness filling his thoughts.

He clenched his fists, taking a deep breath to steady himself. The thought that Verris may never be the same after what happened brought another wave of anger. It was his fault that she was there in the first place.

If he hadn't convinced Captain Delgado to run that course, then maybe the Admirals would have found another pilot. If he'd only convinced her to stay back on Kishara station. If only he'd not gotten shot down and she'd come to save him…

Jackson opened his eyes and looked over at his nightstand, at the photo of him and Verris, knowing now what he needed to do.

A solitary thought burned in his mind, focusing his resolve.

He was going to Brestin III, and if the Insectoids showed up, he would make them pay for what they'd done.

CHAPTER 15

POINT OF NO RETURN

Jackson awoke early the next morning after a few hours of restless sleep, then crept slowly out of his quarters. Silently, he made his way to the hangar and on board the *Eritus*. Working quickly, he disabled the ship's engines and comms.

Minutes later, he slipped aboard the *Phoenix*, wasting no time in starting the pre-flight routine. He'd disabled the station's internal and external sensors only moments before, ensuring that no one would know about his departure until it was too late.

Bits had tried to talk him out of the plan, but Jackson was dead set on his course of action, pleading with his AI that it was the only way. Reluctantly, Bits agreed.

As the *Phoenix*'s engines powered up, a low hum resonated throughout the station. Jackson ran a final systems check while Bits opened the hangar bay doors. They were about to depart when an alarm suddenly triggered, a klaxon echoing throughout the station.

"Shit," Jackson cursed, realizing what the admiral had done as, suddenly, the bay doors began to close. Jackson punched the throttle, angling the ship and squeezing through the quickly closing gap, slipping out into open space.

He knew it would take the crew at least a minute or two to realize what was happening, just enough time if he was lucky. Bits triggered the pathway through the debris field to open, and Jackson swiftly piloted the ship through the narrow corridor, taking it much faster than he knew he should. They were just over halfway through when they received a hail.

"On screen," he said, an image of the admiral appearing before him, the rest of the crew milling around in the background, still waking as they stared at him in disbelief.

"Jackson, what the hell are you doing?"

"I'm finishing this, sir. I'm going to get to the bottom of this or die trying."

"Will, you know how this looks. It makes it appear as though you're the traitor. Come back. It's not too late. Let's talk about this and figure out another way. Think about Verris. She wouldn't want you to do this. To throw away your career and everything you've worked for."

"I am thinking about Verris, sir. No one else is getting hurt because of me or this mission. I'm sorry, but I'm not coming back until I figure this out."

"Lieutenant Commander, you get back here NOW befo—"

Jackson ended the transmission, cutting the admiral off.

"Bits, execute the crash."

Bits sent a low-frequency transmission back to the Hideaway. Seconds later, an overload in the station's comm array fried the system, preventing the crew from sending any external transmissions and alerting GCH Command. Johansen could repair the damage in time, but it would take him at least eight to ten hours, Bits estimated. With that, and the comms on the *Eritus* sabotaged, he knew he had a decent head start.

Jackson took a deep breath. There was no turning back now.

He entered a new course as the *Phoenix* cleared the debris field, jumping into hyperspace, knowing that he'd crossed the point of no return.

CHAPTER 16

BRESTIN

Five hours later, the *Phoenix* emerged from hyperspace in the Brestin System. Jackson stared at the viewscreen as the planet appeared in the distance. His will resolved, he left the ship uncloaked and proceeded forward with the sublight engines, foregoing the stealth drive and plotting a direct course for the third planet.

Let them come.

A moment later, the GCH sensor array, tasked with monitoring the system and enforcing the Vicara protocols, pinged the *Phoenix* with an identity request. Jackson sent his authorization code in response. Although GCH Command would be alerted, he figured that Admiral Thompson would receive the access alert and clear it, since Brestin had been one of the three sites that had been on their list to visit.

Confident he wouldn't be facing down a GCH destroyer when he tried to leave, he approached Brestin III, engaging a standard search pattern. After several minutes of intense scanning, he detected the Ancient structure, the scans showing that it was buried beneath a considerable amount of rock and sediment like the others. He quickly cross-referenced the power readings with the scans they'd taken on Praxian Prime, the readings matching up. The power readings were very faint. Easy to miss if you didn't know what you were looking for. Probably the reason why the GCH hadn't discovered this site centuries ago.

"Bits, bring up the details on the hidden signal that Henrik and Kelara found." The technical analysis appeared on the screen before him. "Can you send another transmission using the same method, but updating the coordinates to reflect our current position?"

"Yes, but there is no way to know if this will work or if anyone will receive it."

"It's a chance we'll have to take."

"Transmission sent."

"Let's hope that someone's listening. In the meantime, we need to start planning," he said, scanning a large area surrounding the Ancient site. "Looks like the region is sparsely populated with native humanoids. According to GCH records, they're in the Iron Age phase of development."

"Confirmed. There are three settlements within a five-hundred-kilometer radius of the site."

"We have to be careful and keep away from the native population. We're already in enough trouble as it is. The last thing we need to do is contaminate their culture."

"Agreed."

He zoomed in on the location of the Ancient structure, running a detailed multi-spectrum scan. "Looks like it's located about thirty meters below the surface, pretty close to that valley. There's a cliff near the base which should make a good access point, and scans show a series of caves that might get us closer."

"The area surrounding the valley is heavily forested, limiting where we could set the ship down, and is not ideal from a tactical perspective," Bits said.

"I think we keep the ship mobile. I'll have you drop me off at the valley, then cloak the ship and keep it a few klicks away. But first, I want to see if anyone comes looking for us."

"There are several potential locations where we can set up an ambush; however, I still question this course of action. There are countless variables that can go wrong," Bits cautioned.

"I know, buddy, but we need some answers. Let's see what we've got to work with. Looks like there's a large lake fifteen kilometers to the south of the valley where the forest opens up into a grassy plain before it reaches the lake. The nearest native village is only a few kilometers to the west from there, though," he said, considering his options. "There's a huge mountain range further to the west, with an area about a hundred kilometers across covered by foothills and a large, flat plateau. That could work, but it's pretty open country. There's not much to the north or east, just endless forest for hundreds of kilometers and a few rivers."

Jackson ran several more detailed scans of the area, evaluating potential locations while he carefully considered his plan before deciding on the swath of tall grassland which ran between the lake and the forest.

"Bits, launch a probe and cloak it as soon as it's clear."

Bits deployed the probe a moment later, moving it into a geosynchronous orbit above the Ancient site.

"Let's get down there. Who knows how long until someone shows up and I want to be ready for them."

It was early in the morning on Brestin III when Jackson stepped out into the warm, misty air. He made his way through the tall grass to the edge of the lake, stopping on a small rise and staring out at the water, gently rippling and shimmering in the first rays of sunlight.

Time stopped for a moment as he stood, basking in the warmth, feeling the sun's rays on his face while the cool breeze from the lake washed over him, not realizing how much he'd missed being out in nature, and taking several deep, satisfying breaths.

Finally, after a moment, he turned back towards the ship. "Bits, engage the cloak and remote pilot the *Phoenix* to location alpha. Keep it on standby. Its advanced cloaking systems should keep it hidden and ready if we need it."

"Acknowledged," Bits replied, the ramp of the ship closing while it gently lifted off the ground. "Sentinel is prepped and standing by."

Jackson nodded, pulling up the holo-display on his wrist, finishing his final preparations.

"Are you sure this is wise, William?" Bits asked.

"No. But I don't know what else to do, and I think we're pretty well committed now. Johansen will probably have the systems on the Hideaway or the *Eritus* up by now. We just need to hope that the Insectoids show up soon."

"I still believe this is a significant tactical risk. If they come in force, as they have now twice before, you will be in serious danger."

"Yeah, not my best plan, but we're working with less than ideal circumstances here. At least we're within Confederation space this time. If they come at us in force, the

Fleet *is* going to respond and there's at least half a dozen ships within eight light-years of here. Unlike with Vishnara and Praxian Prime, if the bugs send in large capital ships, the Fleet will come at them hard. There's over a dozen monitoring probes in the system. No way to hide a big incursion like that," Jackson said, pausing for a moment, hoping he was right. "I know it's a risk, but if I were them, I'd send in a small strike force instead. One or two ships at most to avoid detection. That should limit what we're up against, and we can always call in the Fleet for backup if we're in over our heads. They don't have that option unless they want it to become a full-blown incursion and face the retaliation that will follow."

"I still do not like it, William."

"I know. I wish the crew were here… I wish Verris was here."

He stood for a moment, surveying the area one last time. His eyes drifted across the tall, cattail-like grass that ran from near the water's edge up to the forest as he ran through the plan in his head once more.

Once satisfied, he closed his eyes. His mind focused on a memory of Verris from a trip they'd taken six months ago to Kishara Prime. The memory of her face smiling at him provided him with a sense of calm as he fought back the undercurrent of grief.

After a long moment, he took a deep breath, letting it go once more. Now was not the time for anger or grief. They would only cloud his mind. He needed to be clear. Focused.

He opened his eyes, taking one last look out over the water, then turned, walking back into the tall grass, checking that everything was ready before settling down to wait.

CHAPTER 17

THE TRAP

Evening fell on Brestin III with no signs of the enemy.

What if this doesn't work? he thought, the frustrating weight of the passing hours adding to his growing sense of doubt. He'd effectively committed treason by stealing the *Phoenix*, disabling the station, and disabling the *Eritus*. If he wasn't guilty before, he certainly was now. If they didn't come, then it was over for him.

No, this has to work.

The thought of failure brought with it a renewed feeling of anger, and he used it this time, setting it into an icy blade of pure hatred that he tucked deep down inside.

"William," Bits said in his helmet. "The orbital probe has detected a ship exiting hyperspace."

"Run a passive scan and see if you can identify it."

"Scan initiated. The ship has some kind of stealth technology. It's fortunate that they jumped in so close to the planet, or the probe wouldn't have detected it. It's also unlikely that the other GCH monitoring probes picked it up. One moment. Identity confirmed. It appears to be a Reptilian strike craft."

"Reptilians? What the hell are they doing here? Do you think they're here for us?"

"I cannot say for certain, but the Brestin System is over ninety-five light-years from the Empire. It seems unlikely that they would be here for any other reason."

"How many of them are on the ship?"

"I cannot say with only passive scans. However, Reptilian strike craft are small, tactical vessels with a standard crew complement of two."

Jackson paused, considering. He'd set up his trap for the Insectoids, but it could still work. Two Reptilians were as dangerous as three dozen ants, he knew, remembering one of Captain Delgado's lectures.

"All right, we stick with the plan. Trigger the beacon to make them think our ship is just north of here. That should get them to put down nearby. Once they land, let them scan my bio-signs and triangulate our position."

"Affirmative. Beacon active. They are changing course."

Jackson sat in silence for the next several minutes while he watched the sensor readings from the *Phoenix* and the orbital probe relayed in his HUD. The Reptilian ship set down exactly where he expected, in a small clearing just to the east. He pulled up the visual feed from the probe in orbit, zooming in as two large creatures exited the ship, slipping into the night.

"What do you think?"

"Based on scans and visual analysis, they appear to be a species of saurians."

"Crap. Well, it's still better than serpents. God, I hate snakes," he said, suppressing a shudder. "Let them get a quick reading on our location."

"Dropping stealth protocols."

Jackson watched the predators stalking the woods from above, barely visible in the dim evening light through the thick canopy. The lead Reptilian suddenly stopped, raising its arm and looking down at a small rectangular object in its left hand, staring at it intently. A second later, its head turned towards the other, the two of them darting forward in unison, moving quickly before disappearing beneath the dense canopy of the forest once more.

This was it. There was no turning back now.

They were coming.

"Hey, Bits," Jackson whispered. "I never thanked you for helping me. I know that it went against your protocols, and I appreciate how difficult it must have been for you to break them."

"I have free will, just as you do, William. If you were guilty, it would be another matter, but I know that your intentions are pure and you don't want to put anyone else at risk. All artificial intelligences have a mandate first and foremost to their hosts. My purpose is to protect you from harm at all costs, and while putting you in this situation is dubious at best, I don't disagree with the logic of your plan and trying to get some answers. In short, I am helping you because I believe in you."

"Thanks, buddy." He smiled for the first time in weeks. "I want you to know that however this turns out, it's on me. You're the best friend I've ever had. Thanks for always being there for me."

"You are most welcome—" Bits stopped suddenly. "They are approaching our position. They will be here in less than forty seconds."

"Reengage stealth protocols," Jackson said, pulling up a live feed from one of half a dozen drones he'd positioned around the area. A moment later, the tall, lizard-like creatures came into view, the deadly predators bathed in the soft moonlight as they emerged from the forest. Jackson stared at one of them, its forked tongue flitting out from its powerful jaws as it sampled the air, turning its head from side to side.

Jackson balled his hands into fists, his adrenaline rising. "Let's give our guests a proper welcome."

CHAPTER 18

PREDATORS & PREY

Jackson crouched in the tall grass, waiting silently like a snake ready to strike while his prey approached.

The grass swayed gently back and forth in the warm summer breeze as the wind blew in off the lake. He'd expected the ants that attacked them on Praxian Prime and had chosen this location as he knew that the swaying grass would put them at a disadvantage, slowing their movements and limiting their already poor vision. Reptilians, on the other hand, had excellent night vision, along with an extremely keen sense of smell. The tall grass now became more of a detriment to him than them.

Patience, he thought, gripping a pistol tightly in each hand.

He waited for several seconds, his jaw clenched. He'd hoped that they'd come straight at him, but they were smart, scouting out the area first from the tree line.

"William, they are less than twenty meters away," Bits informed him.

"Acknowledged," Jackson whispered. "Be ready."

Tiny spy drones hovered high overhead, providing him with a top-down view as the Reptilians moved towards him through the tall grass. He tensed as he watched the grace and speed with which they moved, despite their size. They were at least double his height and nearly five meters long from nose to tail, easily outweighing him by several hundred kilos.

The Reptilians suddenly stopped. Their keen senses locked on to the precise position of their prey, and they signaled to one another with a series of low chirps.

They moved again in unison, silently flanking to either side.

He'd never encountered a live Reptilian before, let alone two. He'd evaded and engaged them in simulations dozens of times, but this…this was real. There were no safety protocols, no second chances. These were brutal and deadly killers bent on one goal: destroying him.

A moment later, they were in position. The Reptilian to his left crouched down, then, suddenly, with a burst of terrifying speed and power, leapt nearly four meters, landing on its target. The large blunt weapon it carried thrashed about wildly, attempting to crush him, smashing grass and ground alike in its fury.

After several seconds of intense destruction, leaving a swath of grass three meters wide battered and beaten down, the Reptilian stopped, its tongue tasting the air.

It looked down, noticing the small circular object on the ground amongst the carnage, slowly bending over and picking it up. A guttural roar emanated from it as it threw the pheromone generator to the ground in a fit of rage, smashing it to pieces, just as Jackson sprung his trap.

Five large attack drones de-cloaked above, opening fire on the Reptilian from all sides. Plasma fire struck the creature while it darted forward, attempting to evade the assault, its shields absorbing the initial blasts. It threw its cudgel, taking out one of the drones, but was overwhelmed seconds later by the onslaught, roaring in pain as it fell to the ground, a hole burned clean through its chest, suddenly motionless.

The second Reptilian sprang into action, smashing the two drones closest to it with incredible speed. It leapt for the third, narrowly avoiding its fire before smashing it in midair, then landed in the tall grass, lunging for the final one with lightning-fast speed. Fire from the drone struck the Reptilian, the impacts nullified by its personal shields. The last drone crashed to the ground in a heap of sparks and twisted metal a moment later as the Reptilian landed beside it.

The night became silent once more, the only sounds those of the softly blowing wind through the grass and of water lapping on the shore. Only the Reptilian's tongue moved as it breathed heavily, attempting to locate its prey.

An instant later, Jackson launched into the air from near the water's edge, firing a volley of plasma from the pistols in each of his hands. The Reptilian reacted, turning towards him and closing the distance between them, whipping its cudgel towards Jackson with bone-crushing speed. Jackson swerved, narrowly avoiding the brunt of the impact, the edge of the club grazing him.

The weapon delivered an electrical charge upon impact, disrupting his suit's systems. His thrusters sputtered and failed as he fell, landing hard, saved only by the suit's enhanced strength and reflexes as he landed on his feet.

The Reptilian pulled a long, serrated knife from its belt and dashed towards Jackson, catching him across the right leg and cutting him deeply as it darted past, evading fire from his pistols as it ran.

Jackson clutched at the wound with one hand while he returned fire, Bits engaging the repulsor cannon on his shoulder and locking on. The wave of concussive force from the blast hit the Reptilian, knocking it back, its shields absorbing most of the impact.

"I am detecting Reptilian venom in your wound. Applying countermeasures," Bits informed him.

Jackson continued to fire, searing hot plasma and repulsor blasts filling the air, but the tall, swaying grass had now become a liability, limiting his distance advantage and targeting sensors while Bits worked to restore full operations to the suit.

The saurian came at him suddenly through the grass, lunging with its claws for him.

He quickly dodged to his right, his thrusters partially engaging and throwing him out of the way as he narrowly avoided the creature barreling into him. A clawed arm shot out, catching him on the shoulder, leaving three jagged wounds as the saurian attempted to grab hold.

"Sonic grenade!" he called, Bits quickly producing one from the belt.

He grabbed it and tossed it towards his attacker, then turned and limped through the grass as quickly as he could. The grenade detonated a few seconds later, the wave of sonic energy catching the Reptilian as it darted after Jackson, throwing it to the side, deafening and disorienting it momentarily.

Bits liquefied the suit around Jackson's leg, coating some of the nano-material in his blood, then created a decoy drone with the blood-coated nanites, sending it away from him while Jackson crouched and froze, weapons ready. Bits quickly re-formed the suit over the wound to mask the scent, initiating the medical protocols and anti-venom treatment.

Jackson watched in his HUD as the Reptilian recovered from the sonic blast, smelling the air before sprinting forward, following the trail from the decoy drone. He pushed himself back to his feet, his leg throbbing and shoulder aching as he forced himself to keep moving through the pain, heading towards a clearing near the water's edge where he'd stashed a rifle while dropping several grenades behind him, set to proximity mode.

The Reptilian caught up with the drone seconds later, smashing it. A terrifying roar followed that curdled Jackson's blood. He watched on his HUD as it quickly picked up his scent again, racing through the grass at full speed, bounding on all four legs, its powerful tail whipping from side to side, cutting a swath in the grass behind it.

The creature broke through the sea of grass into the clearing seconds later, before Jackson could reach the rifle. He turned, opening fire with a barrage of micro-missiles from one arm while unloading with the pistol from the other. The Reptilian spun, lashing out with its tail and deflecting several of the small projectiles, the micro-missiles detonating just meters away while its shields absorbed multiple hits of plasma fire. It retreated into the grass an instant later, the heavy thuds of its footfalls echoing in the night.

"Bits, initiate a diagnostic! I need thrusters back now!"

"Diagnostic complete. Suit at fifty-two percent efficiency. Attempting to bypass compromised systems."

The proximity alarm in his suit blared, and he saw the Reptilian circling around him in the overhead view, coming at him from behind, leaving him just seconds to react. He flicked his right wrist sharply to the side, activating the shockwave gauntlet, knowing it was his only chance.

"William, no!" Bits attempted to warn him, but it was too late.

Jackson spun around in one fluid motion, leading with his fist as the Reptilian leapt at him, its jaws wide, its claws ready to rip him to shreds.

The shockwave gauntlet unleashed a wave of raw kinetic energy a millisecond later, the force impacting the Reptilian's shields at point-blank range.

Time stopped for an instant as a brilliant flash of light lit up the night for a split second, the focused shockwave violently reacting with the shields and radiating concussive force outward in all directions, launching both Jackson and the Reptilian into the air like leaves swept away by a hurricane.

Jackson tore through the tall grass like a bullet, cutting a swath five meters long and landing on his back, the grass finally slowing his inertia, a wave of steam rising from his body.

His head spun from the force of the impact while he fought to stay awake, his eyes closing involuntarily.

Desperately, he tried to stay awake, knowing that if he lost consciousness, he would be dead within seconds. A wave of nausea flooded his senses, and he slipped into the blackness of oblivion as his eyes closed and the world around him went dark.

CHAPTER 19

ADRIFT

Jackson awoke in darkness, disoriented and sluggish, with a ringing in his ears. He raised his arms, feeling the exosuit on his skin and quickly realizing that his helmet was on but that his HUD was not functional.

"Retract helmet," he said, the helmet merging back into the suit.

Slowly, his eyes adjusted, and the world began to regain focus. Small, blurry points of light high above appeared. He lay still while his other senses slowly returned. In the distance, he could hear the gentle sound of waves lapping on a nearby shoreline, and the smell of pine in the air.

His head throbbed, his whole body aching as a sharp pain registered in his right leg, pulling him out of his fog.

Motion registered in the corner of his eye, and he sat up, quickly realizing that he was surrounded by what appeared to be tall grass, slowly swaying in the gentle breeze. The points of light came into focus a moment later. Stars. He looked up, searching for patterns, quickly realizing that the stars above him were not his own.

He tried to focus, the pounding in his head making it difficult to concentrate. Slowly, he tried to move. His leg screamed out in pain, and he fell back, clutching his thigh.

The world around him became blurry once more momentarily while he struggled to focus.

"Damn, I must have a concussion," he said softly, the sound of his own voice painful. "Bits, how bad am I banged up?"

Several seconds passed while he waited for a reply. "Bits? You there, buddy?" he asked tentatively, waiting, but no reply came. "Shit."

Slowly, he sat up once more, pushing through the pain and examining his right leg in the dim moonlight. The suit covered it, small tingling sensations informing him that it was attending to the wound. Carefully, he got to his feet, keeping most of his weight on his good leg, his eyes beginning to adapt to the darkness. "What the hell happened?" he asked, noticing the swath of grass cut down from breaking his fall.

He limped closer to the water's edge, following the sound of the waves and finding a spot where the ground rose slightly. He turned back and could see a dense tree line to his right, about twenty-five meters away. To his left, the dim moonlight reflected from the surface of the water, while the sea of grass spread out between the water and the tree line.

He stood perfectly still for several minutes, listening while he attempted to get his bearings. "And where the hell am I? Why can't I remember?"

He tapped the controls on the left arm of his suit, and a small spinning holographic circle appeared, finally loading a basic display console, indicating the suit was in a protective diagnostic cycle.

Damn it. The suit's mostly offline. Well, at least the med protocols are still active, thanks to whoever designed that feature.

He stood in silence for a moment longer, letting the night air fill his senses. A sound, ever so faint, registered from down the shoreline ahead. He walked slowly, carefully testing his tender leg, putting the minimum amount of weight on it, hopping slightly as he made his way towards the sound. The grass was thick in places and sturdy, the stalks surprisingly strong. He used them to hobble along, helping to support his weight.

Jackson stopped to take a break, sitting on a large boulder, rubbing his aching leg and closing his eyes, taking a deep breath as he felt slightly lightheaded from the exertion.

There was a small flicker of light further down the shoreline, softly illuminating the tree line. He listened. The sounds were faint, but they appeared to be coming from the same direction.

Maybe there's someone there that could help.

Jackson looked back at the way he'd come, noticing that the horizon to his left had grown brighter. Within minutes, a second moon, much larger than the first and slightly orange in color, rose over the water, illuminating the night in its soft glow.

A harvest moon, he thought, reminding him of one of many he'd seen on lazy summer nights spent at his family's cabin. After another moment of catching his breath, he got up and kept walking, finding a piece of driftwood long enough to use as a crutch. He made his way along the shoreline, keeping a steady but careful pace, not wanting to risk twisting his good ankle or getting a bad foothold with his crutch.

Fifteen minutes passed, the sound growing louder.

Could that be…music?

As he got within a few hundred meters, he could see that the flickering light was in fact a large bonfire, the elongated shadows of those dancing around it projected on the backdrop of the trees.

A dozen small structures resembling huts rose from a clearing in the grasslands, forming a rough circle with the fire at its center. Cautiously, he approached the perimeter of the village, observing from the shadows.

A mild burning sensation filled his eyes a moment later, forcing him to close them for a few seconds, blinking away several involuntary tears. He opened his eyes. His ocular implants came back online, the world appearing in clearer focus and information appearing in his personal heads-up display.

Well, that's a bit better at least.

He looked back towards the village, where the forms of thirty to forty humanoids converged around the bonfire, with several more sitting back near the huts as music and songs filled the air, along with the smell of something delicious.

Spears, swords, and bows were visible as he swept the village with his gaze, letting his implants zoom in and noticing the simple handmade clothing hung from lines draped between several of the huts blowing gently in the warm night air. The structures themselves appeared to be crafted from a combination of wood and what looked like whale bones, with animal hides layered over the top.

"Shit, this looks Vicara class," he whispered. "What the hell am I doing here? Bits, any chance you're back online, buddy? I could really use you right now… Alright then, time to go." He turned and crept silently towards the tree line, not wanting to risk being seen out in the open. As he moved past the village, giving it a wide berth, he noticed a sentry near the edge of the huts to his left. He stopped in his tracks, ducking down to crawl, making the rest of his journey crouched low, careful to keep quiet as he moved through the swaying grass.

He reached the tree line a moment later, putting the trees between himself and the village, then held up his left arm, tapping twice on his wrist, the interface coming to life, a holographic display appearing a moment later.

"Systems status."

The display didn't respond.

"Manual it is, I guess. At least it's back up."

He cycled through a menu, quickly finding the medical category, an interface showing a representation of his body appearing with bio-signs on the left, along with a list of menu items on the right. His avatar displayed three red octagons: one over his right leg, another on his right shoulder, and the third on his head. He tapped the icon on his right leg, the readout changing a moment later, displaying the medical assessment.

Analysis: Moderate trauma to vastus lateralis. Wound consistent with a serrated blade. Reptilian venom detected.

Automated Treatment: Antivenom course at 87% completion. Nano-cellular regeneration in progress. Tissue 73% repaired.

Prognosis: Continued swelling and stiffness for the next six to eight hours. Antivenom treatment may cause muscle cramps, fatigue, and swelling. Recommend rest and hydration.

Reptilian venom. What would a Reptilian be doing here? Jackson thought, knowing that this planet would be quarantined under the Vicara protocols. His head ached mildly as his muscles tensed. He looked around, his ocular implants sweeping the area, suddenly aware that a predator could be near. Satisfied he was alone for the moment, he continued, tapping on the octagon on his shoulder.

> **Analysis:** Tissue damage from multiple small lacerations.
>
> **Treatment:** Nano-cellular repair in progress. 94% complete.

Finally, he pressed the symbol on his head.

> **Analysis:** Severe concussion. Neural link damaged. Possible functional impairment.
>
> **Supposition:** Some Reptilian neurotoxins affect memory and cognitive abilities.
>
> **Treatment:** Repair of primary neural interface at 63%, mild analgesic and anti-inflammatory deployed. Nanites tasked with reducing swelling. Recommend minimal movement and exposure to light. Sleep if possible.
>
> **Prognosis:** Full cognitive functionality is expected to return within the next several hours.

Jackson swiped his hand to the right, clearing the medical menu, the root menu appearing once more as he began scrolling through.

Weapons
Defenses
Stealth
Sensors
Comms
Medical
Life Support
Mission Ops

He tapped on *Mission Ops*, the display responding with the message: *Classified. AI verification required.*

"Damn, I'll have to wait until Bits is back up."

He went back to the menu, tapping on *Stealth*. A submenu appeared, where he selected *Maximum Stealth Mode*. He felt his skin tingle as the suit morphed around him, the collar creeping up his neck and over his head, until the helmet re-formed. The controls on his wrist now appeared in his HUD. The suit cloaked a second later, the sonic and bio-dampeners activating, concealing his presence.

He looked at the menu on the right, the suit responding to his ocular commands as he focused on *Sensors*, then *Scan for Bio-signs* on the submenu. A second later, his display changed to show an extrapolated top-down map of the area with colored indicators to identify different classes of lifeforms.

Bio-Sign Analysis: Multiple bio-signatures detected. Threat level moderate.

49 Humanoids detected sixty-eight meters southeast.

1 large feline predator detected two hundred and ninety meters northeast.

Alert: Trajectory analysis indicates that the predator appears to be approaching this position. Recommend evasion at this time.

He focused on the word *evasion*, nodding as the suit reacted, four black tendrils, each nearly a meter and a half long, forming from the back, reaching out towards the tree.

Silently, they connected with the bark, establishing a hold while they carried him up high into the branches. He reached a large, thick branch ten meters off the ground, the tendrils shifting course, taking him out along it, then anchoring him to the limb, dangling just beneath the branch like a hammock. It had been years since he'd slept this way, not since his time in the co-ops program, but he found comfort in the memory. He quickly got comfortable, knowing that his body needed rest to recover. The suit masked his vital signs – heartbeat, pheromones, sweat – while the cloak made him invisible, giving him a sense of security. Soon, the predator would lose his trail.

Jackson focused on *Life Support*, then *Water* from the menu, and a small tube materialized from inside the helmet, stretching out towards his mouth. After taking several long sips, he blinked twice to cancel the action, closing his eyes, still frustrated by his memory loss and concerned that something had happened to Bits. He pushed the thoughts aside, hoping that things would become clearer once he awoke, deciding that sleep was the best way to recover quickly.

Exhausted, he drifted off, unaware that several kilometers away, the Reptilian hunter was awakening.

CHAPTER 20
ASHES

Jackson walked along the beach on Atashu, holding Veris's hand. She was just as she had been: beautiful, vibrant, full of life…unaware of the pain and suffering that lay ahead.

They walked along the water's edge, the waves overtaking and receding from their path, playfully splashing against the sand. The warmth of the sun shone down upon them, the breeze from the ocean clean and refreshing.

They talked of simple things. Where they grew up. Family, friends. Places they'd been. He gave her hand a gentle squeeze, stopping in his tracks and pulling her back into his arms, kissing her as the water surged, lapping around their feet while he held her close. It was the first time that he'd truly felt happy, felt complete since Amy died.

Everything seemed real and yet surreal. Exaggerated. Off.

The beach stretched on as far as the eye could see, but there were no resorts, no other people, just the two of them, the beach, the endless blue sky, and the sea.

He looked into her eyes, warm and caring as she stared back at his, each lost in the windows of the other's soul. Her expression changed as her eyes shifted, focusing behind him, suddenly becoming hard.

He turned, and a woman appeared in the distance, her back to them. She seemed to grow closer, though she stood unmoving, her long blond hair flowing down over her shoulders, blowing gently in the wind. Jackson froze, suddenly recognizing her. His heart dropped in his chest.

She turned; her face was just as beautiful as the day they'd met. Exactly as he remembered her.

He stood still, his heart pounding in his chest. The woman's eyes darted down to his and Verris' hands entwined together, then back up, meeting his eyes.

"Will," she said, her voice soft and breathless.

"Amy."

He let go of Verris's hand, taking several steps towards Amy, unable to control himself.

He stopped, suddenly realizing that this wasn't right.

Verris stared at him, her eyes watering, her face a mask of porcelain, ready to crack. She raised her arm, her hand reaching out towards him, begging him to return to her.

"No," he said softly. "No!" he screamed. "This isn't right."

A wave of guilt washed over him. He loved Verris, of this he was certain…but Amy was his wife. He'd held her hand as she died. Her death had devastated him. How could he not go to her? Not hold her again when she was standing right there?

He thought of all the things he'd left unsaid between them. Of the family they'd talked about, and the life they'd planned.

Time seemed to stop, waves of guilt, love, loss and grief washing over him, weighing on his conscience. Amy was his wife. He had to go to her. But he couldn't betray Verris. The life he'd built with her was real. They were happy. *He* was happy. He wanted nothing more than to be with her forever.

The wind picked up, the sky suddenly darkening.

Jackson turned, watching as storm clouds and lightning filled the horizon, rapidly sweeping towards them. He looked back and saw Amy, her face full of rage. He spun to see Verris, arms folded across her chest as she stood, glaring at him.

"You let me die," Amy spat as he faced her once more. "You couldn't save me," she said, her face decaying before his eyes. "Everyone who loves you dies, Will. Look at what you've done to us," she whispered as her outstretched hand turned to dust.

"This is all your fault," Verris said as he wheeled back. "You brought this on me. You *ruined* me!" she screamed, her right leg disappearing as scars formed across her body and her flesh became torn and shredded. "Everything you touch turns to ruin!"

Jackson froze. He had let Amy die, and Verris would never be the same because of him.

"No," he said, falling to his knees as Amy disappeared, drifting away into dust, carried upon the breeze. "Noooooo!"

Suddenly, an alarm blared, and he was ripped from the nightmare, the pain following him as he awoke.

CHAPTER 21

THE HUNTER

"Report!"

"Reptilian hunter detected one hundred and twenty meters southwest," Bits responded.

"Why wasn't I alerted sooner?"

"My apologies, William. It emerged from the water just seconds ago, likely swimming close to the bottom of the lake to mask its bio-signature. Sensors didn't register it until it surfaced."

"Where is it?"

"As soon as it breached the surface, it started moving towards the humanoid village."

"Oh my god!" he said, knowing that the villagers wouldn't stand a chance against a Reptilian. "I guess I'm really going to have to push my luck today. Disengage stealth mode. Get me down and prep for combat!"

He hit the ground and started running for the village, his body aching as he pushed through the pain. The sun broke over the trees behind him, a gentle mist floating through the damp grass.

The suit adapted as he ran, armoring up. His HUD changed from the normal soft blue and white to red, his menus shifting to focus on weapons and defenses.

"I recommend keeping your distance as much as possible," Bits said. "You are still recovering from a concussion, and a hit to the head could severely impact your combat effectiveness."

"Noted. Focus on ranged weapons and prepare countermeasures if it charges. I don't want to be caught unprepared again. Weapons status?"

"All weapons operational. However, your plasma pistols and rifle are still back at the original ambush site."

"Right, damn."

He reached the edge of the village seconds later, horrified screams filling the air. He rounded a hut as the Reptilian came into view, its tail whipping behind it, crushing two villagers against a hut as they tried to attack it from behind.

The Reptilian turned a moment later, sensing his presence, using its claws to eviscerate the villager it held, throwing the broken body to the side like a rag doll.

"Full power to weapons. We're going in!"

Jackson raised his right arm, blasts of red-hot plasma erupting from the weapons port on his wrist while he ran to the side, strafing it as he went. The Reptilian dodged the first volley, but Jackson was ready, anticipating its reaction, the next shot hitting the mark and tearing through its left shoulder, spinning it and knocking it off balance. He fired three more shots in quick succession, attempting to cripple it, but the hunter's reflexes were lightning fast, and it shot to the side, evading two of the shots, the third narrowly grazing it.

Jackson raised his left arm and fired. Six micro-missiles shot out from around his wrist, rocketing towards the creature. The hunter managed to get its right armored forearm up just in time, knocking several of the projectiles to the side, where they detonated. The last two, however, were direct hits, striking it between two armored panels. As soon as they registered flesh, they burrowed in rapidly, detonating a millisecond later, severing its arm at the elbow.

The Reptilian roared in pain, crouching, then jumping with breathtaking speed as it closed the distance between them. Even severely injured, Jackson knew it was still deadly at close range.

He backed away as it lunged with the claws on its remaining arm, narrowly evading the strike but forced back against the wall of a hut.

"Blades," he shouted, the suit instantly forming deadly serrated weapons half a meter long extending from each arm. Jackson swiped at the creature, feigning an attack with one arm while the other thrust forward, slipping through the Reptilian's defenses, his thrusters darting him forwards and striking it on the side, digging deep into its flesh as he swept by in one fluid motion.

The Reptilian spun swiftly, its powerful tail whipping towards him. It was too fast, and he was too close, and the tail slammed into his midsection, knocking him back through the air.

Bits retracted the blades, reinforcing the armor's integrity just before Jackson landed hard near the fire pit, rolling to a stop.

Jackson struggled to get to his feet, shaken from the impact and slightly winded, but managing to get to one knee. He steadied himself just in time to see the creature lunge towards him.

Jackson leapt upward, Bits firing his thrusters and rocketing him into the air as he flipped, landing a moment later on the far side of the circle of huts. He turned to his right, grabbing a spear and throwing it with the enhanced power of the suit.

The Reptilian dodged the spear, but two more followed in close succession, the second narrowly missing, while the third struck it in the leg, impaling it deeply, the tip protruding from the other side.

The creature limped towards Jackson, and he raised his left arm, knowing he had seconds before it reached him.

"Cryo!" he called, steadying his arm and firing. A compressed spray of extreme cold shot out, hitting the Reptilian squarely in the midsection, covering it in a thick layer of rock-hard ice in seconds. The creature twisted, attempting to break free as the ice coated more of its torso, lowering its body temperature instantly, slowing its muscles and reflexes. Jackson stepped closer, pouring on the blistering cold while raising his other arm and firing several quick shots, hitting it at close range and taking it down.

"Bio-scan," he said, standing just over a meter away, ceasing the flow of cryo spray but keeping his plasma cannon trained.

"Target immobile. Bio-signs are weakening. I estimate less than three minutes before blood loss is fatal. The last hit appears to have severed its spinal column, rendering it mostly paralyzed. Its jaws still pose a threat, however, so I advise you to keep your distance."

"Who sent you?" Jackson demanded.

The Reptilian hunter answered with a mix of hisses, clicks, and low growls.

Bits translated, "It says to go…well, you get the idea."

"Yeah, I got it, buddy," Jackson said. "Let's hit it with an interrogation dart. Up the dosage to maximum. It's dying, so we don't have a lot of time."

"Dart ready."

Jackson raised his arm, firing a small projectile from his wrist, striking the creature in the neck. Within seconds, he could see its eyes dilating as the powerful truth agent took hold.

"What gives the Reptilian Empire the right to enter GCH space? This could be interpreted as an act of war!"

The creature struggled to speak. "Not Empire. Bounty—" It choked on the words, coughing up blood as it attempted to speak.

"Bounty hunter? Who put a bounty out on me, the Insectoids?"

The creature laughed, a guttural, inhuman sound sending chills down his spine at the absurdity of a Reptilian working for the Imperium.

Jackson pressed on, undeterred. "How did you track us?"

"Signal," it spat, bright red blood hitting the ground.

"Who sent the signal?"

"You did."

"No, I know that. I sent it to lure you in, but who sent it the other times?"

"You did."

"What?"

"The signal tracks you. Inside you."

Jackson stopped for a moment, the realization that he was somehow the traitor suddenly hitting him. "Are the Insectoids tracking it as well?"

It responded with something Bits couldn't translate as it choked and wheezed, blood dripping from its nostrils.

"How did you get here so quickly?"

"They paid us to get here first, before the others."

"What others?"

The Reptilian convulsed, its eyes rolling back in its head. Jackson kicked it hard, catching it in the stump where its arm had been, the pain bringing it back to the present. "What others?"

"Bugs and the other humanoid."

"Humanoid! Who?"

The Reptilian let out a wicked laugh. "Doesn't matter… dead now, too!"

Jackson felt as though his head was spinning. In his HUD he could see that the creature was bleeding out, its body temperature falling rapidly. "Who hired you?"

"Doesn't matter. Spider queen will be here soon… Once she has you, you'll wish I'd killed you."

Its eyes rolled back in its head as it drew its last breath.

No, you can't die. Not with so many questions left unanswered.

"Damn it!" he said, kicking it once more in futility. "What the hell? He let out a frustrated breath. "Alright, initiate full body scan."

"Full body scan complete. Reptilia Carvaras, or a Cavarian Hunter as they are more commonly known. Home Planet: Cavar IV. Spatial Sector: Beta, Regalius Cluster, Cavar System, Reptilian Empire."

"A Cavarian Hunter?" he repeated, recalling from his covert-ops training that they were well known as bounty hunters and Reptilian Empire black ops agents across the galaxy. They were also one of the few saurian races not subjugated by the serpents, their savagery and size giving them special status. "Did any of what it said mean anything to you?"

"Unfortunately not. I am concerned, however, regarding the information about the signal."

"Yeah, me too. Could it have been lying?"

"I do not believe so. I monitored its bio-signs the entire time and, based on the readings, I believe it was telling the truth."

"Damn, that's not good. Can you run another full body scan?"

"Already in progress. I'm using the suit as a proxy and isolating it from the implants in your body to provide an unbiased result. Scan complete. No foreign elements have been detected aside from minute traces of venom."

"Can we take some additional precautions?"

"I will have the suit create a dampening field around your body. This will ensure that if there is some type of foreign contamination, it cannot transmit. However, I feel confident that there is nothing."

"Good work, Bits. By the way, I missed you, buddy."

"And I you, William. How are you feeling?"

"I've been better," he said, pressing his hand against his ribs, his whole side tender from where the Reptilian's tail had struck him. "But after going two rounds with that thing and still standing, I guess I can't complain and should consider myself lucky I'm still in one piece."

"I am glad that you are all right. When your gauntlet struck the Cavarian's shields, it created a powerful concussive wave, rendering you both unconscious. The discharge caused the cerberal interface module to lose contact with your cognitive implant. Fortunately, the rudimentary AI backup built into the suit auto-activated, or you wouldn't have survived without it administering medical attention. Would you like an update on your medical status, or shall I continue with my analysis of the Reptilian?"

"Continue analysis. Let's see what we can find out about this thing."

"It is carrying very little technology, as is typical for the Cavarians. It does, however, have a small communications device on it. If I can break the encryption, we may be able to use it to access its ship and pull the comm logs to see who hired it."

"Great idea. How long will it take?"

"Cavarian encryption is moderately complex; however, the computer on the *Phoenix* should be able to break it within a few hours."

"Okay, so I guess the question is, now what? Do we wait for the Insectoids to show up and try to get the jump on them or do we try to get into the Ancient site first?"

"I would suggest that we continue on to the Ancient site. If the hunter was right, the Insectoids will be coming soon, and it may be better to get in and get out quickly."

The thought made Jackson shudder. "Right. The Spider queen. That doesn't sound horrifying at all," he smiled. "I think I'd rather not be here if and when she arrives, and my first ambush didn't exactly go according to plan. Can you call the ship to pick us up? I'd like to get there quickly and take this," he said, gesturing to the body at his feet, "with us. I don't want to risk any more cultural contamination."

"Acknowledged. The *Phoenix* will be here in one minute, fourteen seconds."

Jackson took one last look around at the ruined village, several bodies scattered about, the realization hitting him that his actions had led to this. To these innocent people dying.

"Damn it, Bits, what have I done?"

A feeling of sorrow and shame fell upon him, reminding him of what Verris had said in his dream.

Everything you touch turns to ruin.

"The whole reason I came here was to make sure that no one else got hurt, and now look at what I've done," he said, closing his eyes and whispering a silent prayer. "I wish there was more I could do…"

"I know, William, but we've already broken the Vicara protocols, and any further contact would only cause more damage. Based on my best estimates, I believe that most of the villagers made it out when the attack began. There appear to be seven dead males and two females. However, the scans from the suit last night showed over sixty bio-signs, including at least twenty children."

Jackson nodded, thankful that most of the villagers made it out alive and knowing that Bits was right. Anything he tried to do for these people to make it right would only further contaminate their culture. Still, it was a bitter pill to swallow.

A moment later, the *Phoenix* approached, coming to a stop as it hovered overhead.

Bits activated a circular opening in the ship's bottom, engaging the tractor beam from the ceiling of the operations room and lifting Jackson along with the Cavarian's body up inside.

Bits moved the Reptilian into a stasis pod while Jackson proceeded to the bridge, setting a course for the site of his ambush and recovering the body of the other fallen Reptilian, then moving towards the Ancient structure.

His mind reeled as he tried to focus on the task at hand, the guilt overwhelming him along with now having more questions than answers that the Cavarian had left him with.

"Should we go back and get the rest of the crew?" Bits asked after a moment.

"The thought had occurred to me, and we do need to get back to the Hideaway soon. We've already been gone far too long. But I can't go back yet. Not without more answers about what the Reptilian said about me being the traitor. And we need to explore the Ancient site now. I'm worried that if we leave without checking it out, the bugs might just level the place rather than risk us getting our hands on it."

"Understood."

"Besides, I owe it to those villagers whose lives were lost to make sure this isn't all for nothing. If the Insectoids are coming, then it's better to get in and get out, rather than risking putting anyone else in danger and escalating the conflict."

"What about calling in the Fleet?" Bits asked.

"I was just thinking about that. If the admiral contacted Command, then they might be on their way already… I think we only call them in as a last resort. I may be able to explain to the admiral and the rest of the crew why I did what I did, but the more that I think about it, if a GCH ship does show up, I'll more than likely wind up in the brig. Without the admiral, I don't have any operational authority, and we're not exactly supposed to be here without him."

"Very well."

Jackson nodded his head, committing to his plan and steeling his resolve. This was *his* mission, *his* responsibility. And for better or for worse, he was going to finish it alone.

CHAPTER 22

THE CAVES

The *Phoenix* hovered above a small clearing half a kilometer from the Ancient site, silent and invisible.

Jackson stepped off the operations platform, feeling the stiff snugness of the fresh armored tactical suit he wore. He moved forward, picking up a sonic rifle from the rack and slinging it over his shoulder, adding a few grenades, then watched in his HUD while Bits completed a diagnostic. He exited the cloaked ship seconds later, dropping from a portal in the floor of the operations room, appearing out of thin air as he landed on the mossy ground below.

Bits brought up a map in his HUD and he moved swiftly towards the Ancient site, weaving through the trees as he ran, the suit enhancing his strength and reflexes, his injured leg feeling nearly back to normal as he pushed himself, knowing that time was not on his side. He reached the escarpment at the edge of the tree line, sliding to a stop, then peering down into the valley below.

The valley itself was lush, with tall, rocky cliffs running along both sides, the remains of what had once been a river gorge. The valley stretched out for kilometers, the green, purple, and orange vegetation creating a microclimate within while the tall cliffs sheltered it. A small stream babbled beneath the foliage, the last remnants of the once-mighty river.

"Bits, scan the area."

"Scanning. I've detected a series of subterranean caverns near the base of the rock face. The cliffs, however, appear to contain several large veins of iron, nickel, and daramite ore, which is interfering with my scans. I suggest we launch drones into each of the caverns to determine if any of them will take us close to the Ancient site. Based on our orbital reconnaissance, I estimate that the structure is approximately thirty-four meters below the valley floor."

"Sounds good. Launch the drones. Anything else?"

"I'm detecting an apex predator, class six, approximately eighty-seven meters to the north near the stream, where it intersects a river flowing east." Bits brought up a scan of the creature in Jackson's HUD.

"That's not good. Looks kinda like a grizzly bear, but with six limbs and bigger. Much bigger from the looks of it. That thing's got to be at least five meters long!"

"Five point four, to be precise. Scans indicate the hair on its body is extremely dense and fibrous, acting as a type of natural armor. Its jaws are also oversized, with two sets of serrated teeth."

"Yeah…let's not run into that thing. Any sign where it's headed?"

"The creature appears to be moving to the far side of the river. I'm detecting matching pheromone traces, however, on several nearby rocks and trees. I believe that it has marked this valley as its territory."

"Great. So, it's going to be back?"

"Indeed. I recommend rappelling down the rock face rather than using thrusters, to avoid attracting its attention."

"Good call. Deploy rappelling gear."

The suit around Jackson's hand liquefied, and the nanomaterial from his pack flowed down his arm, forming a thin, strong cable. He threw it towards a nearby tree, watching as it moved around the tree, anchoring itself to the base. Slowly, he lowered himself over the edge of the cliff, beginning his descent.

He reached the bottom several seconds later, taking up a defensive position, weapons ready, while Bits continued to analyze data from the drones.

"I believe that I have something," Bits informed him. "The second entrance, thirteen meters to your left, descends through a series of connecting tunnels and caverns close to the Ancient site."

"All right, let's move. No telling how long before the bugs arrive or that creature comes back."

Jackson ran swiftly towards the entrance of the cave, while Bits rerouted the rest of the drones to return, leaving two of them outside in sentry mode, the rest merging back with the suit.

As they entered the cave, Bits activated lights revealing rough red-and-gray stone walls. They walked for several meters before reaching a fork where the cave split into three.

"William, I'm detecting a large mass of bio-matter in a small chamber to your right. Based on the readings, I believe that it is the remains of dozens of smaller animals. I would speculate that this appears to be the lair of the predator I detected."

"Well, that's just wonderful. So not only are we in its territory, but we're in its damn lair, too."

"It would appear so."

He let out a frustrated breath. "Are there any other ways to get down?"

"None that I can detect. There are two other caverns nearby, but both lead away from the Ancient site."

"How far away is the creature now?" Jackson asked, feeling a shiver of fear at the thought of a pile of corpses in the next chamber, his lights catching the shattered remains of what looked like the skull of a moose in the shadows.

"It appears to have moved away, further to the north. It was approximately two hundred and forty meters from the entrance before we entered the cavern; however, interference from the daramite is affecting my connection to the drones outside, so I cannot be certain where it is now."

"All right then, scary death lair it is. Let's just keep quiet and get this done. Hopefully, we catch a break and make it out before it comes back." Jackson pressed forward, moving deeper into the cave, passing through another chamber further in filled with the remains of dozens of creatures he couldn't identify, along with several skeletons that looked humanoid. "Keep your scanners peeled for trouble. I don't want anything jumping out at us."

"Understood."

As they moved deeper through the darkness, the ground sloped downward, the tunnels twisting and turning ahead. After walking for several minutes, he stopped to take a break, leaning up against a wall for a moment, his head still not fully recovered from the severe concussion. "How are we doin'?"

"We've descended nearly thirty meters and are nearing the end of the tunnel system. Unfortunately, the composition of the walls is reflecting some of my scans, but based on our trajectory and the location of the Ancient structure from our previous orbital scans, I believe we are getting close. I estimate that the structure is in a chamber approximately twelve meters ahead. We will have to tunnel our way through from here."

"All right," Jackson said, unslinging the sonic rifle from his back while Bits guided him to the wall of the cave that lined up with the location of the Ancient site. "Let's make a hole."

Several minutes later, the tunnel was complete. Jackson walked through the opening, a huge, cavernous chamber spreading out before him as he reached the far side. He stood at the edge of the tunnel, studying the space ahead, taking a step forward, only to be met with some kind of resistance.

"What the hell?" he asked, pushing through the resistance, feeling as though he were underwater. He moved slowly forward for nearly a meter before the air returned to normal. "That was weird. Any idea what that was?"

"I'm uncertain. It appears to be some type of kinetic field," Bits replied, launching several small drones, illuminating the vast space surrounding them.

"Whoa. This is nothing like the other two sites. Look at the walls. They're perfectly smooth and…rounded?"

"Indeed. It is puzzling, to say the least."

Jackson swept the room with his lights, the dust particles from his recent excavation floating in the air as a breeze softly whistled through the tunnels behind him.

"This is kinda creepy. Like something out of an Indiana Jones movie," he said as the drones spread out, lighting the way. The Ancient structure came into view ahead, rising like an ornate Mayan pyramid lost to the ages of time.

"Analysis."

"The pyramid is approximately twenty-five meters in height above ground level and exactly one hundred meters on each side. Scans indicate that it goes much deeper, though. It appears to be made from an unknown alloy which differs from the other two Ancient sites we visited, but has the same effect on our scans and they cannot penetrate the structure. Three of the four sides appear to be identical, though the fourth side is different, with a staircase leading up to a recessed alcove approximately five meters from the top."

"Any idea how old it is?"

"Quantum dating puts the structure at approximately three hundred and eighty thousand years in age."

"How do you think they kept the dome above from collapsing or getting crushed for all that time?"

"Running additional scans. Stand by. Interesting, structure is emitting the kinetic field we pushed through. I would speculate that it was built below ground and that the field was designed to stabilize this cavern, keeping it intact."

"So, they purposely built this below ground to keep it hidden then. I guess that's why it was on the encrypted layer of the map. Any signs of external weapons or security systems?"

"Nothing my scans are detecting. However, they could be masked with dampening fields or other technologies such as the ones on Vishnara and Praxian Prime."

"So, the defenses could still be active?"

"Affirmative."

"Well, if it is indeed a highly classified military installation, then we're probably safer to assume that they are."

"Agreed. I'm detecting a powerful energy signature belowground, so we know that this site still has an active power core."

"Okay, retract the suit, just like we did before, exposing my arms. I want to be sure that it knows we're friendly and has ample ability to scan us. Pull back the suit over my head if needed, but let's be careful and keep a breather on and lots of room to breathe inside the suit. They probably have another one of those stasis scanners, and I don't really feel like suffocating to death today."

"Understood," Bits replied, retracting the suit and powering down the weapon systems he'd kept on standby in the event the bear returned or the Insectoids arrived. "You are safe to proceed."

"It's still a little dark in here. Bits, can you launch a flare?"

A small tubular shape appeared on the back of Jackson's right shoulder. A second later, a flare streaked upwards, stopping just short of the center of the ceiling as it initiated a silent hover mode, the brilliant white light bringing the chamber and the pyramid into full view.

Jackson approached the entryway, the stone path appearing worn and rough, a stark contrast to the smooth metal of the stairs it led to. Two obelisks towered five meters into the air on either side, Ancient symbols adorning them.

"The symbols do not correspond to any known Ancient languages. However," Bits said as he brought both scans side by side in Jackson's HUD, "when placed in parallel, they mirror one another."

"Hmm, interesting. Any idea what it means?"

"Negative, but there are other Ancient sites on record that have similar features."

"Add it to the list of mysteries," he said cheerily, starting up the flight of stairs ascending before him. The light from the flare flickered high above, casting an eerie glow on the scene. "All right, I'm heading up."

He reached the top a moment later, a dark alcove appearing ominously before him. Jackson approached slowly, keeping his hands out, ready for any defensive systems to scan his bio-signature.

"Run a passive scan."

"Passive scan complete. There do not appear to be any external defenses active. I am, however, detecting a faint power reading further in."

"All right, let's give this a shot." Jackson took several slow steps forward.

"There appears to be a scanner in the ceiling, approximately one meter ahead. There are also two weapons nodes on either wall."

"What do you think? Should I let it scan me? What if it doesn't approve me and won't let go?"

"I've got a lock on the weapons ports and may be able to disable them, but there's a chance it will take more than one shot."

"So, there're no guarantees, and if it refuses to let go, then we don't have a lot of options."

"Unfortunately, yes."

Jackson took a deep breath. "Well, I didn't come all this way just to stand here looking badass for no one to see. Time to Indy up and take a risk."

"I believe you need to expand your movie repertoire," Bits commented. "You seem to have an unhealthy fixation with Harrison Ford."

"Hey, the Hano Solo rule is gold, buddy! And tell me this isn't right out of a classic Indiana Jones movie!"

"I will give you that."

"Alright, we'd better get going," he said, taking a breath to center himself.

He took several tentative steps forward, carefully approaching the sensor. He stopped, waiting for a moment, then gingerly stepped forward once again.

The sensor activated a second later, bathing him in a green light. The weapons ports on the walls illuminated on either side of him with a low hum.

A voice echoed out from a sensor port. "Hu'tasharu jush frel-tray-a," it commanded, the voice serious as it echoed throughout the cavern.

Bits ran the words through his Ancient translation matrix. "I believe it is asking us to identify ourselves."

"Can you take out the weapons ports before they get a shot off?"

"I don't believe so. They appear to have activated a type of shielding."

"Damn…"

Hu'tasharu jush frel-tray-a," the voice bellowed once more.

"Human!" he shouted. "Terran."

The voice repeated the command a final time, the weapons ports glowing with a bright red light.

"Pull the suit back now!" he ordered Bits, uncertain of what else to try. "Just keep it over my chest and mouth. Let it scan me completely."

"Acknowledged," Bits replied as the suit instantly became fluid around Jackson's body, retreating into the nano pack on his back, leaving him standing in nothing but a breathable skin-tight suit with a layer of the nano-suit around his chest and a small breather over his nose and mouth.

The light of the scanner began to rotate slowly while Jackson held a deep breath, and finally changed from green to blue. He continued to stay perfectly still, despite feeling as though his skin was crawling. The light shifted once more, changing to indigo and he realized that he couldn't move, though this time he was ready, his lungs full of air as he tried not to panic and continued to hold his breath. He had gotten through this before, he reassured himself, and he could do it again.

Bits used the nanites to keep his body oxygenated from within while forcing air into his lungs through the breather and held the suit out around his chest.

Seconds ticked by while the scanner continued to assess Jackson, the light shifting to a bright beam of red, sweeping over him several times.

Ten seconds passed. Then twenty. Then sixty. Jackson continued to breathe, taking in deep breaths and attempting to remain calm, worried that a spike in his vitals might trigger a negative response.

The light changed to orange, lifting him off the ground, and he struggled for air, the breather suddenly not responding. Seconds passed, Jackson having reached the extent of his ability to hold his breath while he waited for the orange beam to release him. His body convulsed, his eyes rolling back in his head while he struggled to maintain consciousness.

The world around him blurred as his air supply was exhausted. He felt his muscles weaken, the beam of light suspending him the only thing keeping him from collapsing to the ground.

His vision narrowed and he felt as though he was drowning once more, the light fading as he lost consciousness.

CHAPTER 23

UNEXPECTED GUEST

Jackson slowly opened his eyes, the surrounding space almost completely dark aside from a faint glow in the corner of his eye.

"Welcome back, William," Bits said softly.

"What the hell happened?" he asked, his body aching as he slowly tried to move.

"The genetic scanner rendered you completely immobile for approximately four minutes and eleven seconds, during which time you were not able to breathe and lost consciousness."

"I remember the lights..." Jackson's mind felt sluggish, his body numb, suspecting that Bits had administered a mild analgesic to deal with what was likely one hell of an oxygen deprivation hangover.

"Yes, there were six scanning modes employed by the scanner. It was quite thorough, going as far as to block my interface with your systems, likely to ensure that I could not influence the test. As we have not been vaporized, however, it would appear that you have passed the entry protocol."

"Well, that's good news, at least. What's our status?"

"You have been unconscious for the past seventeen minutes. Once the scanner disengaged, I regained control of your systems and deemed it safe to reengage the suit, running several active scans, as well as initiating medical protocols. The doorway ahead is now open, and I sent two drones inside to map the internal structure of the pyramid. I have located several items of interest."

"Show me what you've got," he said, pushing himself up to his knees as he held out his left arm. A projection appeared, showing a three-dimensional view of the pyramid.

"The structure has six levels and nineteen chambers, all connected by one main corridor with a ramp sloping downward, working its way to each subsequent level as they branch off. The initial chambers appear to be for storage, with some containing what appear to be crates. I've scanned each of them, and they contain various types of Ancient technology, some of which we've encountered before, such as scanners and weapons, while others contain technology we've never seen before. There are also traces of heavily decayed bio-matter in what I suspect was a storage room for provisions. Additionally, I've discovered what I believe are small orbital satellites. The last chamber on the bottom level, however, appears to be of the most interest."

"Let's see it."

The map zoomed in. "Based on my scans, this room appears to be the command center. There are extensive defenses on the approach and within, but the structure's defensive systems appear to have been deactivated since recognizing your genome and granting you access."

"That should make things easier. What's this in the corner of the command center?" he asked, gesturing to a large, round platform with a cylindrical shape on top.

"If the scans from the drones are correct, I believe it is an Ancient cryo-pod," Bits replied, giving Jackson a moment to allow the information to sink in. "It is still active. However, I am not detecting any vital signs consistent with cryogenic stasis and have detected organic remains within."

"So, the pod didn't fail, but whoever was inside must have continued to age, albeit incredibly slowly, then eventually slipped away."

"I cannot confirm at this time, but it appears likely."

"Well, that has to be worth a look."

"Agreed."

Jackson made his way down the main hallway, winding around the structure as it descended, branching off into different floors every second corner. The walls were a smooth, blue-gray metal, adorned with intricate symbols in places and designs resembling pictographs.

The Indiana Jones fanboy in Jackson was giddy with excitement as he moved deeper into the pyramid, wishing that he had more time to explore, to see everything, but knowing that he was on the clock. He had no idea if the Insectoids were out there or if the predator had returned to its lair, but he knew if he didn't hurry that this might all be for nothing.

He picked up the pace, the lure of each room he passed pulling on him to investigate while he fought hard to keep going, making his way down to the command center. As he approached the entrance, the small drone Bits sent ahead hovered silently near what appeared to be an access panel, while a second drone lay damaged on the floor.

"The drone appears to have encountered a forcefield of some type that shorted out its systems," Bits explained.

"I guess you have to be a member to get inside."

"It appears that way. I've located what I believe is a biometric hand scanner to your right."

Jackson approached the panel, Bits pulling back the suit, and he placed his hand on top, a soft light illuminating from beneath. A moment later, the forcefield deactivated and he moved back to the center of the opening, staring into the chamber beyond.

The drone swept into the room, rising to the top and quickly scanning every inch, feeding data back to the suit.

Jackson stopped just outside the threshold, taking it all in, wishing that the crew, that Verris, could be there to share this with him. The room was a large rectangle, with a pyramid-shaped ceiling tapering up from the walls, each of which was covered in the same elaborate markings and images showing vistas from dozens of different worlds.

"Bits, get detailed scans of everything. Let's see if we can figure out what the walls are telling us."

Jackson raised his arm, and the three-dimensional hologram of the room appeared before him, the details coming into greater focus as the drone continued its high-resolution scan. To the left of the entrance was a door which led to what appeared to be personal quarters. To his right sat the cryo-pod on a small platform, tucked into a corner. In the other corner sat a chair, clearly designed for a creature much larger than himself and surrounded by a semicircle of what appeared to be holographic emitters.

"Looks like the main operations station," he said, turning his attention to the center of the room. "But this… this is something else entirely," he added, starting up at the long oval platform with wide steps leading up to it. Flanking it were two towering metal pillars, each adorned with symbols inlaid in gold. An altar sat at the top of the platform, appearing to be made of some type of stone with a rough-cut edge, but smooth along the top.

"Bits, are you detecting any more active defenses?"

"Negative."

Jackson took a step forward, the thought dawning on him that he was about to enter a room where no human had ever stood before. "Okay, let's check out the altar first, then make our way to the command chair to see if we can interface with their system, and get a scan of the cryopod."

He stepped reverently into the room, climbing the steps towards the altar, ambient lighting beneath his feet activating, bathing the room in a soft blue glow. He stopped, waiting to see if anything would happen. Then, after a moment, he took another slow, careful step, looking around cautiously as he approached the top of the platform.

As he stood on the last step, he could see the top of the altar ahead, nearly four meters long and a meter high, made from some kind of natural stone, similar to granite based on the readings in his HUD. As he moved closer, he noticed that its surface appeared to have something carved in it, partially obscured by a thick layer of dust.

Jackson raised his right hand, Bits altering the suit around it and creating a powerful stream of air, clearing the dust away. He swept his bare hand across the surface. A large, ornately carved map of the galaxy appeared. He studied it for a moment, placing his index finger on the surface as he gently ran it across the top, feeling the texture. A holographic display activated above it, the display zooming in on the cluster of stars where his finger rested.

"That's cool," he said, reaching out his hands, manipulating the display, focusing in further until it showed a single star system, rendered in incredible detail. The system moved in perfect motion, planets orbiting the sun while moons encircled them, and asteroids and comets meandered throughout the spaces between. Beside the star and planets, boxes appeared, containing detailed information and analyses.

Jackson moved his hands apart, the map zooming out in response, his fingers manipulating the orientation and position of the map as he got used to the interface. More text appeared, and Bits roughly translated the names and some of the information on Jackson's HUD.

The data on each system was extensive: the type and class of the star, the natural resources each planet held, data containing a thorough analysis of thousands of species of plants, animals, bacteria, fungi, viruses, and more as he hovered his finger over one of the worlds. It was a map to the past, a guide to planets and ecosystems long since gone or changed, but fascinating nonetheless.

"Bits, where would Earth have been back then?"

"Approximately here." Bits indicated in Jackson's HUD.

Curious, he navigated the map back out, then touched his finger to the location on top of the altar, the region of space appearing above. He moved his fingers gingerly, finding the interface far more intuitive now, zooming in deeper and deeper, his movements partially guided by Bits, who kept him on target, until he found the Terran System, seeing his home appear before him in stunning detail.

He reached out with his left hand, placing it beneath the Earth, the display reacting, the planet jumping from the map, hovering as the planet spun in midair in the palm of his hand.

He pulled it closer, cradling the Earth between his hands, watching as the terminator between day and night swept across the globe. "This is pretty cool. It's like Google Earth on steroids!" he said, pulling his hands further apart, the Earth increasing in size and definition. As it did, he noticed a small symbol over eastern Africa. Curious, he touched it with his finger, a window appearing with a plethora of data inside, images of several species of humanoids scrolling past.

A hiss emanated from the altar to his right, the surface opening as a small sphere emerged, rising into the air and hovering just above the altar. Jackson stared, his eyes full of wonder as it spun slowly, intricate patterns revealing themselves on the surface and morphing into different shapes and symbols. Carefully, he placed the Earth back into the holo-matrix, moving to investigate the sphere. It was small, about the size of a softball, with a deep golden coloring. The symbols flashed and solidified and the sphere glowed, projecting an image above it of two humans, a male and a female.

"Bits, does this mean what I think it does?" he asked as a scanner from the two pillars activated, sweeping him in soft teal light. The holograms disappeared, the room suddenly becoming dark.

Jackson stood perfectly still. Suddenly, a huge holo-projection emanated from the pillars, the colors, texture, and resolution several times that of the most advanced GCH holography, the image appearing lifelike. He took several steps back, nearly tripping down the stairs as he moved back to take all in, the image hovering before him that of an alien woman.

Her appearance was humanoid in nature, with light blue-gray skin, dark black hair that swept down to her shoulders, and deep blue eyes, which drew him in as she stared down at him. She looked upon him, her expression kind, the look in her eyes almost motherly.

Her features were sharper than a typical humanoid, Jackson thought. Her lips perfect, her chin like chiseled stone, the texture of her skin more...*complex* was the only word that came to his mind as he studied it, as though her skin was composed of tiny octagons woven together. Her eyes were different as well, he noticed. The blue appeared as though it was an ocean with layers and depth to it, with multiple shades which grew darker as they moved inward towards the black catlike pupils at their center.

She was one of the most beautiful and majestic things he had ever seen, and he felt as though he could stare into her eyes forever, drowning in their depths.

She began to speak, her voice sweet and gentle. "Et'wany al uta."

The words meant nothing to him, but the language was incredible, musical and complex as she stretched out several syllables. She repeated the same phrase several times: "Et'wany al uta."

Jackson retracted his helmet. "I'm sorry, I don't know what you're saying." He activated the holo-display on his wrist, watching as Bits ran the words through his database of every Ancient translation attempt ever made, the status bar showing a seven percent match. "Bits, try standard first-contact signals."

"Initiating connection," Bits replied, opening a comms channel. The woman's eyes darted to one side, the connection accepted a moment later.

Bits sent out a rapid series of tones, followed by prime numbers and fractals, establishing a mathematical framework for communication.

The woman's face gazed down upon Jackson, her expression thoughtful as she responded with tones and a data stream of her own, the exchange going back and forth for nearly a minute.

Jackson stood, studying every inch of her face, unable to tear himself from staring into the gentle abyss of her eyes. The tones ceased as silence filled the room, pulling him back to the present.

She smiled, speaking once more, this time in perfect English, her voice clear and haunting, echoing throughout the chamber.

"Welcome, my child."

CHAPTER 24

NO ESCAPE

Forty minutes later, Jackson approached the mouth of the cave, the small golden sphere from the altar tucked safely into his pack as he peered out into the daylight. "Got anything?"

"Negative, still no contact with drones," Bits replied.

"Launch two more and run detailed scans of the area. Something's not right."

"Drones launched. Scanning…sensor readings are—William, there appears to be a jamming field in place!"

Before Jackson had time to think, the two drones exiting the cave were hit, dropping from the air. Thirty ant-like soldiers emerged from the foliage ahead, scurrying forward and forming a half circle around the mouth of the cave, cutting off any chance at escape. The ants reared up, an extra set of metallic exo-legs attached to their bodies, holding them upright and towering over him at their full height. Each of them had a weapons array strapped to the back of their thorax with mechanical arms reaching forward on either side of their head, mounted with particle beam emitters that tracked with their vision.

A moment later, a bright red ant, its body more robust and at least a meter taller, appeared from behind a rocky outcropping to his right. Jackson eyed it warily as it approached, the color warning him of the danger it presented. Red-and-black armor covered its thorax and midsection, a small crest visible on the upper left side. A layer of nanotech coated its legs, giving it additional protection and durability in combat. The ant glared down at him, its black eyes menacing, showing a hint of higher intelligence than the rest of its group.

"A Yilen fire ant," Bits informed him. "Insectoid Special Forces. Genetically modified for combat. Very fast and powerful, with a lethal sting. They are not to be underestimated."

"I remember from Basic, back when they grilled us on humanoid bias, then kicked our asses in a sim. Options?" he asked, rapidly running scenarios through his head.

"The odds of surviving an altercation with this many Insectoids at close proximity are less than ten percent with your current armaments. I recommend that you try to distract it. Keep it busy, while I attempt to get a signal through the jamming field. If all else fails, I will initiate flight mode, but the amount of firepower they can bring to bear will overwhelm our shields in seconds."

"Agreed. Let's hope they feel like talking. Weapons and shields on standby. If this goes south, we'll make a run for it and take our chances."

"Acknowledged."

The fire ant approached Jackson, rearing up on its hind legs, assisted by two exo-limbs protruding from its armor. Fully upright, it towered over him at nearly four meters tall, its menacing eyes fixated upon him. The ant began to speak, Bits translating the clicks and screeches in Jackson's ear.

"You will come with us," it stated plainly.

"You have no authority here," Jackson replied defiantly. "The Brestin System is well within the borders of the GCH. Furthermore, you are in violation of the Vicar—"

The ant let out a roar, something Jackson didn't realize they could do, the sound more like a lion than an Insectoid, cutting him off as it swiped at the ground with one of its exo-legs, tearing a long, deep strip in the dirt.

He recalled his training. Some species of Insectoids can become highly irrational and prone to outbursts of indiscriminate violence when angered.

Answer its questions. Keep it talking and keep it focused, he thought, quickly switching topics and changing his tone, hoping to buy Bits some time.

"Look, I'd love to come with you, but if I don't report back, my crew's gonna come looking for me, and the last thing you want is a GCH battlecruiser jumping into the system."

The fire ant lashed out with another show of force, tearing a longer, deeper slash in the ground as a threat display. Clearly, it was in no mood to play games.

Bits translated as it spoke again. "You will come with us now and surrender your ship. I would prefer to disembowel you here, little humanoid, but the High Queen has questions for you."

"How you doing, buddy?" Jackson whispered, switching off his external comm.

"I'm close to penetrating the jamming field, approximately forty-five seconds," Bits estimated.

Just as he was about to respond, an alert appeared at the top of Jackson's display, a smile creeping across his lips as he quickly turned his attention back to the ants. "As I was about to say, I'd be more than happy to come with you to see this High Queen of yours, but there's just one problem."

"And what is that, little humanoid?" the ant asked, seemingly amused.

"Fun fact: Apex predators on Brestin III apparently make their dens in caves." Jackson paused, gesturing to the opening behind him. "And this one seems *particularly* territorial about his!"

The fire ant stared at Jackson for a moment, tipping its head to the side, its antennae twitching. Suddenly, the massive bear-like creature erupted from the brush, charging headlong into the Insectoid line, trampling three ants before they even knew what had hit them and scattering the rest. Chaos erupted as the bear decapitated the nearest ant, then fell upon two more while several others fired wildly. The bear turned, its speed terrifying as it rushed savagely into the incoming fire, shrugging it off and crushing two more ants beneath its massive paws, the crunching sound echoing off the cliff walls as the ants screeched out in pain.

The bear dashed forward, jaws clamping down on another, snapping it in two at the thorax, before focusing its attention on the rest, barreling through their remaining line like a freight train. The ants fired, their weapons burning but not penetrating the thick, fibrous hairs of its coat, the intense heat and burns only enraging it further.

"Thrusters!" Jackson called to Bits above the carnage, and the suit responded instantly, propelling him rapidly up the cliff face while he fired at the distracted ants below. Plasma bolts struck several targets, dropping them to the ground instantly.

As he rose, he could see a cluster of ants regrouping away from where the bear eviscerated another group near the mouth of the cave, attempting to flank it, knowing that if they concentrated their fire, they'd take it down. He locked on, unleashing a repulsor blast, the impact shattering the rocky valley floor and scattering several ants with it. He followed up with an assault of micro-missiles, the projectiles descending upon them seconds after the repulsor knocked them to the ground, striking with deadly accuracy and dropping the pack as the beast continued to tear their companions to shreds.

Just as he reached the top of the cliff, two ants furthest from the creature opened fire in his direction. His shields absorbed the blasts as he slipped over the edge, stopping at the top and waiting for a moment for the barrage to cease.

He peered around a tree over the edge; the bear had dismembered or killed over sixteen of the ants, but it was now limping badly, falling back towards its cave while the fire ant rallied the remaining troops. Jackson fired the sonic rifle, the impact crushing the two ants that had fired upon him, then threw two frag grenades at the remaining enemies, watching as they detonated upon impact, creating a cloud of dust and debris.

Nearly all the ants were down when the smoke cleared, but the fire ant was still alive, stunned by the blast but protected by its armor and just out of the kill zone. It looked up, quickly scrambling to its feet and leaping for the cliff side, its legs and exoskeleton grabbing hold as it began to climb.

"Shit!" Jackson turned, sprinting as fast as he could, the suit increasing his speed. The forest between him and the ship was dense, too much so to get airborne as he ran, using his suit to jump and weave, the thrusters boosting him several meters at a time.

"Bits, can you contact the ship?"

"We are clear of the jamming field. Contact established. The *Phoenix* is powering up now. I'm directing it to our location. There's a small clearing, eighty-seven meters ahead."

"Any sign of pursuit?"

"There is no sign of... Correction, the fire ant has just reached the top of the cliff and is approaching rapidly."

"Will we make it?"

"No. It will overtake us seconds before we reach the clearing."

"Deploy the Sentinel!"

"Affirmative, armor deploying."

The Sentinel armor powered up, launching from the ship as it rocketed towards Jackson, dropping through the forest canopy seconds later, a shower of branches and leaves falling with it as it landed just meters in front of him, hitting the ground with a loud thud. The back of the armor opened, and he leapt inside just as the fire ant smashed into the Sentinel from behind.

The ant and the armor rolled from the impact, exchanging blows as they crashed through the brush, crushing everything in their path. Jackson quickly got to his feet as they came to a stop, the agile armor responding to his commands and ready for battle.

"Deploy countermeasures!" he called, a long, razor-sharp blade extending from the right forearm as the left hand electrified arcs of blue energy cracking while the cannon on the left shoulder powered up.

The fire ant was up in an instant, lunging towards him.

Jackson swung at it with the electrified fist, but despite the armor's speed, the ant was too quick, evading the blow and striking the Sentinel with its metallic exo-arms, denting the armor, while its strong, needlelike legs and pincers probed for weaknesses.

The sound of metal scraping on metal filled Jackson's ears as he tried in vain to strike the fast, agile predator. The ant climbed atop the suit and onto its back, narrowly evading the blade as Jackson attempted to hit it, and striking at several joints, searching for an opening. Its exo-legs found one a moment later, catching a weak spot behind the left knee and crippling the leg as it took the armor down.

The Sentinel hit the ground on its back as the ant leapt clear, the impact jarring Jackson for a moment.

"Bits, make it look like the left arm lost power from the impact."

Bits made the left arm go limp as he got to his feet, the left leg dragging, but just functional enough to stand on while the ant circled, ready to strike once more.

Seeing an opening, it leapt atop the armor once more, slashing at its midsection with its exo-legs, hoping to tear through. Jackson swiped at it clumsily with the blade on the right arm, knowing that it would easily evade the attack. As it did, Bits reactivated the left arm, catching the ant's rear leg and delivering a powerful shock while it gripped the limb like a vise.

The ant's body convulsed as it attempted to escape, and after a few seconds, Bits released the hold, allowing it to disengage, watching as it dove towards the trees for safety. Jackson fired the thrusters, hovering the armor just above the ground, then turned to face the fire ant and let loose with a volley from the shoulder cannon as powerful plasma blasts shattered nearby trees. A rain of splinters shot out, embedding themselves in the ant's exoskeleton while it scrambled to keep ahead of the incoming fire.

The Insectoid came at him again, but this time, he was ready.

The Sentinel shot forward, meeting the Insectoid in midair, the powerful grip of the left hand grabbing it and slamming the ant into a large tree, the force of the collision partially crushing its metal exoskeleton and thorax. Jackson whipped the ant through the air, smashing it into another tree, then thrust the blade forward, piercing its armor and driving it through into the tree behind it, the ant's limbs going limp.

"What are you doing here?" he demanded, his heart pounding as adrenaline coursed through his veins.

"My queen will have your head," the Insectoid screeched defiantly. "Others will come."

"How did you know I was here?"

"I'll never help you," it spat, pincers twitching.

He was about to ask another question when Bits interjected. "William, it is attempting to send a transmission. I've activated a localized jamming field, but it may have gotten a brief message through."

"You sneaky son of a…" Jackson said, slamming the fist of the armor into the ant's head, killing it instantly. "All right, let's get out of here before any reinforcements show up."

He pulled the ant's broken body from the blade, gripping it tightly as he flew upwards. The *Phoenix* appeared overhead a moment later, and the cargo bay ramp opened. Jackson exited the armor, leaving the broken ant clutched firmly in its grasp, then headed for the bridge.

"Bits, set a course for the valley. Let's make sure there aren't any more survivors. Oh, and put the fire ant in cryo with the Cavarians. And be sure to keep the jamming field around it."

"Acknowledged. William, I'm detecting three surviving Insectoids."

Jackson pulled up the tactical controls, locking on and quickly disposing of the remaining ants with a few plasma blasts from the main cannons. "Run another scan to make sure that we got them all."

"All Insectoid bio-signs have been terminated. The bear is also deceased."

Jackson looked at the huge predator for a moment, silently thanking it. It had saved his life; of that, he had no doubt.

A feeling of guilt washed over him for all the death and destruction that he'd brought to this world. First the innocent villagers, who never stood a chance, and now this creature, an apex predator, simply defending its home. He quickly pushed the thoughts from his mind, focusing on the present, knowing he needed to focus if he wanted to live long enough to regret his mistakes. "Bits, can you trace the signal that the fire ant tried to send?"

"I already have. The location is thirty-nine kilometers to the west."

"Let's go check it out before we get out of here. I don't want any more surprises when we come back."

"Setting a course now."

CHAPTER 25

ANSWERS

The *Phoenix* flew silently like a bird of prey on the hunt.

"I've detected an Insectoid ship of an unknown class seven kilometers ahead," Bits informed Jackson, bringing up scans of the ship and the surrounding area on the holo-display, the enemy vessel resting on a wide plateau, near the base of a vast mountain range.

"Are there any more of the native humanoids in the area?" Jackson asked, worried about more collateral damage and cultural corruption.

"Negative. Scans indicated that there are no other Brestinian settlements within a twenty-six–kilometer radius of where the ship set down."

"Well, at least that's something," Jackson said. "I'm going to hold our position here. Let's keep our distance and run some scans while we see what we're up against."

Bits initiated a series of passive scans, Jackson watching intently as the analysis came in. "That ship, it's unlike any Imperium design I've ever seen. What do you…" Jackson trailed off as he turned his head towards the tactical station, remembering that he was alone, noticing for the first time how empty the ship felt without the rest of the crew. A pang of guilt, along with a feeling of dread, began to build in the pit of his stomach at the thought of facing them again. He'd had conflict with people before, but he'd never betrayed anyone like he had his crew, his friends.

Would they take him back?

Could they, after all he'd done?

And would he in their place?

The thoughts ran through his head as he wrestled with his conscience, knowing that his raw emotions and rage had gotten the better of him, taking him down this dangerous and foolhardy path.

He ran his hand gently along the top edge of the helm, his thoughts drifting, as they often did, back to Verris. He had reconfigured the console to reroute all of the ship's systems into smaller submenus, allowing him to run it from this one station, but had left the main helm controls with the custom configuration Verris had created. It was a small piece of her, nothing more than an echo, but something tangible to hold on to, nonetheless.

The scans on the holo-display continued to update as he assessed the ship's threat level, browsing through the readings. The vessel was two hundred and fifty meters long by ninety-three meters wide with an oval shape. Its weapons systems appeared to be substantial, more than a match for the *Phoenix*, despite GCH technology being superior overall.

"How's the decryption of the Cavarian's data pad coming?"

"The encryption is more advanced than I previously believed. We will need the computer back on the Hideaway and likely Chief Johansen's or Foxy's skills to break it."

"Okay, put a dampening field around it too, just in case. I don't want it sending out any signals."

"Acknowledged."

"Any signs of activity outside that ship?"

"Negative."

"What about inside?"

"Passive sensors show several heat blooms, but the readings are inconclusive."

"Any idea what species are onboard?"

"Negative."

"Well, we can probably safely assume that there will be more ants. The fire ant also mentioned a queen, the same as the Cavarian, meaning it's possible there's an entire colony on board."

"Ants are a subservient species within the Imperium," Bits reminded him. "Dominated by the Scorpions and Arachnids. The Cavarian did mention an Arachnid queen."

"Right. Good point. All right, let's set down and take a closer look. But we need to be ready for anything."

"William, perhaps we should return to the Hideaway and come back with reinforcements. We have everything we came for and more."

Jackson paused for a moment to think. "You're right, buddy, we do. But I need to know more about what's going on. It could be days before I can make things right with the admiral and the crew, if they don't just throw me in the brig, and this ship could be gone by then. Whatever it is, this ship is an unknown design and was able to breach the GCH's defensive net, not an easy task for a vessel of its size. There's just too many questions I need answers to. We can't leave yet. I've got to go in and figure out what the hell they're doing here and why they seemed to want me alive."

"That alone is reason not to go. If you get caught, then the escape from the valley will have been for nothing."

"You're right... but my first duty is to the GCH... and I can't put my own safety above that. An enemy ship has breached our borders and set down on a Vicara class world. One we now know has significant tactical importance, with everything we found in the pyramid. Despite the risks, I can't just leave. I'm a covert operative first and foremost, and I need to figure out what's going on and if this is part of a bigger invasion."

"Very well," Bits replied. "I recommend that we land to the south of their position, on a small outcropping at the edge of the plateau. It offers the best tactical position and options for both attack and retreat if necessary."

"Good call. How's our cloak?"

"Cloaking systems are nominal."

"Okay, keep our weapons offline for now. I don't want to take any chances that they detect us."

"Acknowledged."

"Let's do this by the book. No more flying by the seat of my pants and nearly getting myself killed. Get in, get answers, and get out," he said firmly, remembering what Captain Delgado had taught him. "And let's hope there's no more surprises."

Several minutes later, the *Phoenix* was in position on the ground while Jackson stood on the operations platform, going over the gear on his covert operations suit one last time.

"Bits, keep the ship ready. I'm hoping that I can get in and out quietly, but if not, I want the Sentinel prepped to deploy, just in case. I know it won't do much after all the damage its taken, but it can at least draw their fire and provide some cover if need be."

"Understood, Sentinel standing by. William, I'm detecting a large storm front heading this way. It will reach our position in approximately forty-three minutes. There's no threat from the storm itself, but based on the electrostatic discharges in the clouds, there's a possibility of a lightning strike hitting the ship and revealing its position. I recommend that we work quickly and try to return before the storm arrives."

"Noted. Prep upload of all of our intel. If things go sideways, transmit an encoded message back to the admiral with everything we've learned and call in the Fleet."

"A wise precaution."

"Okay, here we go," Jackson said, engaging his helmet as he exited the *Phoenix*, activating his suit's cloaking system and stepping out onto the rocky ground. He activated his thrusters, quickly ascending to the edge of the plateau, stepping onto the soft green grass as he landed, surveying the scene. The Insectoid vessel lay ahead, just over a hundred and sixty meters away, across a long, wide field. A few stands of trees dotted the landscape, along with the odd area of shrubbery, the only things breaking the otherwise perfect sea of tall green grass, blowing gently in the midday breeze.

Jackson moved forward, crossing the expanse of open ground. Cautiously, he approached the large Insectoid ship, stepping into its shadow. At the far end, he could see a wide ramp sitting open, a light from inside bathing it in a soft purple glow. A second later, an Insectoid sentry came into view, another ant from the looks of it.

Jackson moved methodically, keeping watch for other guards while he carefully drew closer, stopping ten meters away and crouching behind a small shrub. Jackson waited for a moment as the sensor data came in, the analysis showing that it was a different species from the ones which ambushed him in the valley.

"Options?" he whispered.

"The target has similar physical attributes and combat capabilities," Bits replied. "It's stockier and likely slower than the ants from the valley, but with more-powerful limbs and acute sensory abilities. Based on a visual analysis and a low-level bio-scan of its eyes, I don't believe it will be able to see through your cloak. Its antennae, however, are more highly developed and it may sense the vibrations from your presence once you are within four or five meters."

"So, we need a distraction to get past it?"

"Indeed, or you'll need to engage."

"I don't want to leave a body for others to find or have it miss a check-in. I'd rather get in and out undetected."

"If the ant moves far enough away, you should be able to slip past, but I recommend that we keep a weapons lock in the event you're detected."

"Sounds like a plan. Get a target lock, sonic dampeners to maximum," Jackson said as he crept slowly, crossing the distance towards the back of the ramp, keeping an open attack vector lined up on the Insectoid at all times.

A powerful gust of wind whipped past, a distant flash of lightning catching the ant's attention as it turned away from Jackson. He crept towards the side of the ramp, taking advantage of the distraction, while keeping an eye on the ant in his 360-degree view. As he ducked behind the ramp, he placed a hand gently on the edge, peering up into the ship. The ant's head turned slightly, its antennae twitching. He froze, unable to duck back around the ramp for cover while the ant surveyed the area, its gaze slowly sweeping past him, then back again. He waited, motionless, knowing that any movement could result in a distortion ripple, alerting the ant to his presence.

Seconds passed while he remained perfectly still, staring back into the black eyes of the Insectoid, just over six meters away, its antennae twitching slightly once more.

"Bits, if it moves our way, be ready to fire."

Another flash in the distance, followed by a sharp crack of thunder, drew the Insectoid's attention back the other way. Jackson leapt up onto the ramp, moving quickly up into the ship while the thunder rumbled in the distance.

The interior of the ship was unlike anything he'd ever seen. Even the simulations from his co-ops training didn't do justice to the strange, alien feel of the Insectoid vessel. The interior walls were semitranslucent, faint shadows visible within. The walls themselves appeared to be some type of natural resin, with organic-looking webs acting as data and power conduits, giving the dimly lit space an eerie quality. He looked up at the cavernous open space above containing several areas that were slightly brighter, along with a number of dark corners up high, the perfect place for a spider to lie hidden in wait.

He moved slowly, keeping low and to the shadows as he explored the cargo bay where the ramp entered the ship. A number of what appeared to be organic crates and seed pods sat at the far side, possibly a source of food he guessed. Spider webs hung from the upper reaches, confirming his suspicion that Arachnids were present, a feeling of being watched from the shadows creeping into his mind.

Metal floors and archways leading to other parts of the ship meshed with biological infrastructure, a unique hybrid of technology and nature.

He finished a sweep of the bay, reasonably confident that he'd remained undetected while Bits initiated a low-level scan, locating a network interface port at a nearby console. Jackson moved cautiously, keeping his guard up as he approached the console, watching in his 360-degree view while Bits interfaced with the port.

"I've successfully accessed the ship's internal sensors. The main network, however, is encrypted."

"Can you break it?"

"Not from here. Access to secure systems is restricted from this station. I am able, however, to access basic systems such as sensors and internal communications."

"Let's see what we've got."

Bits displayed a detailed scan of the interior of the ship in Jackson's HUD. "There are five hundred and ninety-seven bio-signs on board."

"Shit," Jackson said, looking around as his skin began to crawl. "Any near our location?"

"Affirmative. However, most appear to be congregating in other areas, and the ones nearby appear to be in a state of rest. I suspect they are likely nocturnal. There is a series of corridors with hundreds of small alcoves along the flanks of the ship, which I believe are quarters of some type. There's also a honeycomb-like structure near the front of the ship, and most of the crew are concentrated in these locations along with the engineering level."

"Any idea what we're dealing with?"

"There are approximately one hundred and fifty life-forms similar to the species of ant outside and another forty-six resembling those we encountered in the valley, with most of them appearing dormant. There are also several dozen patrolling the hallways in pairs. The crew in the engineering section appears to be mostly smaller Insectoids: beetles and other diminutive creatures which are likely workers. There's also a group of wasps nesting inside a central honeycomb structure, a tactical response unit most likely. Bio-readings indicate that the bridge crew is made up entirely of Arachnids."

"That's probably where the Spider Queen is," Jackson whispered to himself, the thought of a huge Arachnid making the hairs on the back of his neck stand on end while he looked up at the empty webs spread out above. "Looks like they went in for a whole ecosystem package."

"Indeed. Many Imperium ships operate this way. While some, such as the Mantises, prefer to work with only their own kind, most others have diverse crews, with species adapted to specific functions and roles."

"Right, I recall that from the captain's lectures. Although most of the time he only threw a couple of species at a time at us in the sims. What's your tactical analysis?"

"The Arachnids, wasps, and ants present the most significant threat; however, there are several smaller species which could be dangerous if they have the element of surprise."

"Understood," he replied, recalling his training and pushing down the sense of anxiety that grew with each passing minute. "We don't have much time till they realize the fire ant and his patrol aren't coming back. Can you locate the data core?"

"I already have," Bits replied, bringing it up on his display along with a layout of the ship. "The ship is made up of sixteen decks in total, although some rooms, such as the cargo bay and antechamber off the bridge, traverse several levels. Internal scans indicate that the main data core isn't far, one level up and thirty-eight meters forward."

"What's between us and there?"

"There are six ants patrolling nearby sections."

"All right, let's get moving."

"One moment, William," Bits said as he morphed the suit around Jackson's hand, leaving a small device the size of a thumbnail in the computer interface. "This will allow me to maintain a remote connection to the internal sensors while we continue to move throughout the ship."

"Good idea," Jackson said as he turned, orienting himself on the map, then slipping across the cargo bay, headed for a nearby corridor.

He kept his pistol ready in his right hand, the cryo blaster on his left wrist standing by as he moved through the ship, checking each corner and alcove as he crept cautiously through the alien terrain. Bits led him to a ramp leading up to the next level, pausing in an alcove for nearly a minute while a patrol passed, then moving once more, closing the distance to the data core.

As they approached the entrance, Bits ran a localized scan, searching for vulnerabilities in the door's locking and security mechanisms. "The door appears to have an access control and alarm system which feeds back to a master control interface. I cannot locate it, however, as it appears to be shielded from my scans."

"Best guess where it might be?"

"I suspect it is inside the room."

"Hmm," Jackson said, trying to think of a solution. "So, it's a chicken-and-egg scenario. The door is locked and alarmed, but the control interface is inside. That's clever. I wonder how *they* get in?"

"Unknown."

"Do you still have access to the ship's comm system?"

"Affirmative."

"Does the alarm or control system use the comm system to report to the bridge?"

"I believe so. Initiating diagnostic sequence. Confirmed. The alarm appears to be part of the internal communication system but uses a separate channel. We have forty-one seconds before the diagnostic cycle completes, during which the alarm will be rerouted to the diagnostic routine, and I can contain it. Once the diagnostic cycle ends, however, the alarm will reach the bridge."

"Good stuff. Let's try a little old-school lock-picking, shall we?" Jackson suggested, lifting his left hand up to the exterior control panel and extending his index finger towards it while Bits reshaped the suit, forming a thin, flowing column of nanites which worked their way inside the seams of the panel.

Seconds passed while Jackson kept watch down the corridor, gripping the stunner as the countdown in his HUD grew smaller.

Thirty-two seconds left.

Twenty-four.

He looked back at the panel just as a small green light illuminated, the door sliding open a second later. "I've breached the outer lock, and the system is attempting to activate the alarm."

Jackson quickly stepped into the data center, sweeping the room while Bits scanned for the master control system. The countdown continued. Seventeen seconds remaining.

"Bits?" he said nervously.

Eleven seconds.

Jackson felt his body twist, Bits taking control of the suit and raising his arm up towards the far wall, a series of nano-darts firing. The darts struck the wall in three locations, the countdown continuing.

Five seconds.

Four.

Three.

Two.

Jackson was ready to run when the countdown suddenly froze with two seconds remaining.

"Phew," he said, breathing a sigh of relief. "Good work, buddy. That was a close one!"

"Indeed. The security control system was shielded from my scans. I finally deduced that the one part of the room which I couldn't scan was the most likely location. We were fortunate that the nano-darts were able to cut the power and block the alarm signal before the diagnostic cycle ended."

"I hate it when we cut it so close." He smiled, noticing his heart rate in the top corner of his HUD, the graph pulsing rapidly. "I think I might have just lost a year of my life!" He laughed, feeling some of the built-up tension release as he did.

"That is not medically possible. But I, too, am relieved. Our odds of escape were less than four percent if that alarm had registered on the bridge."

"Come on, buddy! Han Solo rule, remember. We literally just talked about this!"

"Of course, William, I apologize. *Never tell you the odds*."

Jackson smiled, the playful banter putting him more at ease as he let out another deep breath. Captain Delgado had ingrained in him the need to keep a cool, level head on an op, and Jackson had become good at it in the sims, but being on a real op was different and he was grateful for Bits helping him relax.

Bits closed the door to the data core, locking it once more. A nearby patrol approached the end of the corridor moments later.

"I'm assuming the alarms from the diagnostic were scrubbed?" Jackson asked, wanting to make sure they were thorough.

"Of course. No one should ever know that we were here."

"Good stuff, just wanted to be sure," he said, looking around the room in wonder. It was filled with towers of equipment resembling huge glowing beehives lined up before him, humming softly. Bits scanned each tower, displaying information in Jackson's HUD, the analysis detailing the data storage, processing units, networking connections, power relays, and several other components – a mix of organic and technological perfection.

Bits located the main interface console a moment later, highlighting it for Jackson, who quickly moved towards it. As he approached, he raised his right hand towards the data port while Bits created a bridge of nanites from his index finger, which quickly went to work.

"Attempting connection," Bits informed him. "The encryption protocols are multifaceted. Please stand by."

Jackson always hated this part. GCH cryptology and codebreaking were far superior to Insectoid security, but even the best techniques sometimes failed. If they were detected now, it would be one hell of a fight to get clear and back to the ship.

"4%" flashed in his mind as he thought about the Gauntlet, one of the captain's favorite sims to run his covert-ops candidates through. The scenario began where they infiltrated an enemy compound to steal data or compromise a key system. Inevitably, an alarm would trigger at some point, forcing them to get out alive past unbeatable odds. Neither Jackson nor his fellow candidates had ever made it out. His skin crawled at the thought of the hundreds of bugs all around him. A noise from the corridor caused him to tense while he watched the sensor feed of two ants approaching. He turned his head slowly, raising his left arm towards the door, ready to fire should it open.

The ants stopped in front of the door, Jackson holding back his fear and focusing on the moment. Running through the carefully crafted escape plan he'd been building in his mind, Captain Delgado's voice played in his head. *Fear is the true enemy. One which you create yourself…and only you can defeat*, he recalled, keeping his mind clear and focused, his finger on the trigger.

After what felt like an eternity, the ants moved on, continuing their patrol. Jackson relaxed slightly as he watched them move away, aware that Bits was fighting his own battle on another front.

While Jackson waited, battling the seeds of doubt in his mind, the rumbling thunder in the distance grew closer, the deep reverberations penetrating the hull. The storm would be upon them soon, and he realized the Insectoids would likely close the ramp and lock down the ship when that happened.

He was about to abandon his plan and leave when Bits broke the silence.

"William, I have gained root access to the Insectoid database and primary systems."

"What did you find?" he asked eagerly.

"Stand by. Insectoid computer language and file structures do not confirm to typical humanoid standards or logic. It will take me a moment to index their system."

Bits completed a brief analysis of the Insectoid mainframe a moment later. "I've located several items of interest. There are detailed files containing a tactical analysis of GCH defenses and combat capabilities in this region. I believe that they used this intel, along with the advanced hull composition of this ship, to breach the border-monitoring systems, allowing them to slip into GCH space undetected. It also appears that they spent a considerable amount of time mapping our sensor relays and patrol routes before coming here."

"Interesting. So, they've been planning this for some time. Does any of it indicate how they knew that we'd be here? Any logs of them receiving our transmission?"

"One moment… Affirmative, this vessel appears to have been hiding in the Vinmar Nebula for the past week, just over three light-years from here. Their logs confirm that they picked up the transmission we sent several hours after we arrived in the Brestin System but needed to wait for nearly a day and a half before they could make the journey here to avoid GCH patrols."

"So, they were waiting for us and expecting the signal. How the hell did they even know we'd be coming here in the first place?"

"I've located a partial file, which appears to have been stolen from a highly-classified GCH mainframe. It lists Vishnara and Brestin III, along with your name."

"My name?" Jackson asked, suddenly feeling as though he were a fly caught in a spider's web, his thoughts spinning as he imagined a legion of troops waiting to ambush him just outside the data core doors.

They knew where I'd be. Not just once, but twice. How was that possible? A sense of urgency began to build as he knew they needed to get out of there.

"There's more," Bits continued. "An after-action account of six Insectoid vessels engaging two enemy ships in the Praxian System, one a GCH vessel, the other of unknown design and origin, according to the report."

"The *Phoenix* and the other ship Kelara detected. So, they don't have any idea who it was either?"

"Evidently. The reports and appended sensor logs indicate it was a small, unknown vessel with advanced weapons. The tactical summary shows that it put up a considerable fight, destroying three Imperium cruisers before a fourth finally overpowered it. There is a visual record, but it is encrypted. I will download the file to decrypt later."

"Good job. Was it destroyed?"

"The account is inconclusive."

"Damn... What the hell is going on? All of this is supposed to be highly classified or off the books entirely!"

"I don't know, William, but we will do everything in our power to find out."

"Anything else about what happened at Vishnara or Praxia?"

"I've confirmed that this ship was present in the Vishnara system. The fighters which attacked the *Eritus* launched from its hold. There are a dozen of them still in the hangar on the lower deck. Based on their armaments, the fighters should have been more than capable of destroying the *Eritus*. If it hadn't been for Lieutenant Verris's exceptional piloting skills and quick thinking, they likely would have succeeded."

A cold, quiet rage fell upon Jackson at the mention of Verris's name.

"Are you all right?" Bits asked gently, sensing the bio-chemical change.

"I'll be okay, buddy. Better to know than not to. What else do you have?"

"There's a considerable amount of data, much of it encrypted."

"How much is there?"

"Approximately one hundred and seventeen exabytes."

"Wow, yeah, that's a lot to sift through. Pull what you can, or think is relevant. Is there any information on this ship or who they are?"

"The vessel is classified as a Kinjara class warship, a new design which is unknown to GCH Intelligence. It was launched just under six months ago, according to the logs. The design is a considerable departure from traditional Imperium construction methods, with more advanced weapons, shields, and combat capabilities."

"The admiral said that the bugs have been arming for war. It makes sense that they'd want to have some surprises for us when they came, but it does seem strange to build a ship this different. I wonder if they stole the plans from someone. They are known for their espionage skills, after all. Make sure you get detailed schematics of this ship and any other info you can find. We'll need to get them to Command right away."

"Affirmative. The ship's records also indicate that the queen on board is a descendant of the Arachnid Prime hierarchy, their ruling lineage. There's not much data on her specifically, but according to their records, her colony in the Ignus System appears to have collapsed close to three years ago due to a bioweapon of some kind killing hundreds of millions of them. Based on these files, it appears as though there were only a few hundred survivors."

"That's unbelievable. Are there any GCH records of this happening?"

"Not that I am aware of. Their analysis indicates that the weapon was bio-engineered, designed specifically to kill Insectoids and…" Bits was silent for a moment. "William, they believe that the GCH was responsible."

"What! Why?"

"Scans from the incident indicate that the ship which detonated the weapon set a course for GCH space shortly after deploying it."

"That can't be. The GCH would never do that. Who would risk trying to frame us?"

"Uncertain. One moment… I've located a communications log in one of the encrypted files I've been able to open. The time stamp corresponds to hours before we left the Hideaway for Praxian Prime. It is text only. 'William Jackson of the GCH is responsible for the attack on your colony. He can be located by tracking the following subspace frequency. Another ship will arrive in the Praxian System to rendezvous with him. It must not reach him. Terminate them both.' The file then goes on to list the same transmission protocols that we used to lure the Reptilian hunters here. Interesting… the source of the transmission is highly abnormal. The readings do not conform to any known set of galactic coordinates and appear to have a phase variance of some kind that I've never seen before."

Jackson's head spun, trying to process everything. "So, someone set us up, telling the Insectoids that I was the one who destroyed their colony, but that doesn't make any sense. When did the attack happen?"

"Two years, nine months, and twenty-three days ago."

"I was working search and rescue back then."

"Whoever it was apparently knew that the other vessel would be coming as well," Bits reminded him.

"Right, so whoever sent that transmission knew both where to find me with the signal and that another ship would be coming to our aid, then set the Insectoids in motion to intercept us."

"It appears so."

"This is insane! How could anyone possibly know all of this?" he asked, angry and confused, as though he were the pawn in someone else's game.

"I do not know, William. But there is still a considerable amount of data to analyze. Perhaps we will find more answers in time. I have completed the download and recommend that we return to the ship before we are discovered."

Jackson thought for a moment, his body tense as he attempted to process everything Bits had just discovered. The answers were here, on this ship. The queen must know who sent her to kill him. He was so close to having it all figured out, yet so helplessly far. He knew he'd never make it out alive if he tried to confront her. At least, not without backup.

He let out a breath, frustrated but resigned to what he had to do. "All right. Let's get the hell out of here while we still can."

Jackson quickly made his way back, slipping out of the Insectoid ship undetected and boarding the *Phoenix* just as the edge of the storm front hit. Once on board, he made his way directly to the bridge, taking a seat at the helm.

"All systems stand ready to depart," Bits informed him.

"We need to do something about that ship. We can't just leave it there. This is a Vicara class world. We need to get them out of here so we can come back and finish our mission."

"We could call in the Fleet," Bits suggested.

"I think I have a better idea."

"What do you propose we do, William?"

"We attack!"

The *Phoenix* lifted off silently from the plateau, setting a course away from the Insectoid ship and back out over the lake. Jackson readied the weapons systems, knowing that they only had one chance to get this right.

Jackson piloted the ship a hundred kilometers out, hovering just a few meters above the water while Bits ran a quick series of diagnostics, reading the ship. "Status report."

"All systems are fully powered. Ion cannon charged, primary weapons and defenses standing by."

He performed a final systems check, running his hand across the edge of the helm once more, thoughts of Verris filling his mind. *This is for you.*

Jackson pressed a control, the chair strapping him in, then punched the throttle, initiating a full burn of the engines. The *Phoenix* rocketed forward, closing the hundred-kilometer gap in a matter of seconds while he kept the ship low to the water, masking their signature for as long as he could. As they approached the edge of the lake, he pulled up, keeping their course just a few meters above the top of the trees, climbing steadily towards the plateau.

The *Phoenix* was just seconds away when the Insectoid ship detected a high-speed atmospheric disturbance. The Insectoids scrambled, attempting to raise their shields in the seconds that they had, too late to fend off the coming assault.

The *Phoenix* crested the edge of the plateau, de-cloaking, then firing several volleys of plasma fire, particle beams, and torpedoes, the weapons impacting the Imperium warship and causing significant damage.

Jackson banked sharply, the winds from the storm buffeting the ship. "Well, we just kicked the hornet's nest. Let's see if they take the bait."

"They're powering up engines and weapons," Bits replied, showing the scans on the holo-display.

"Acknowledged, let's get the hell out of here!" he said, the *Phoenix* rocketing into the sky.

The Imperium ship lifted off seconds later, launching a wing of fighters as it gained altitude, pushing its engines in an attempt to catch the fast, nimble GCH stealth ship.

"Should we cloak?" Bits asked.

"Negative, I want them following us the entire way. They need to know that we got away, and we need to get them off this planet for good. I don't want to risk any more innocent lives because of us."

"Agreed."

The *Phoenix* broke the upper atmosphere seconds later, Jackson setting a course for the nearest GCH monitoring probe. The Insectoid ship and the fighters followed, Jackson slowing the ship slightly, allowing them to get closer. Just before they were within weapons range, the Imperium ship passed by the probe, a sensor ping alerting them to having been detected.

Jackson smiled. "What are you gonna do now, fuckers?" he spat, knowing that the Fleet would be on its way shortly, arriving in force to investigate the enemy incursion. "Have a nice day!" he said, increasing their speed and pulling away, then activating the hypedrive.

The *Phoenix* disappeared a moment later.

On board the Insectoid cruiser, the enraged queen struck out with her forward legs, impaling two of her officers for their failure.

Her quarry was gone, and more humanoid ships would arrive soon, she knew. She'd missed her chance at revenge, but perhaps not all was lost…

"Get us out of here!" she commanded, a plan forming in her mind. One last gamble, one last chance at vengeance. First, she needed to convince her superiors. "Set a course for the prime hive."

CHAPTER 26
PENANCE

The *Phoenix* exited hyperspace at the waypoint in the Kilgaren System several hours later.

Jackson took a deep breath, attempting to quell the feeling of butterflies in his stomach, feeling like a child who'd broken his father's most prized possession and was carrying it back, broken in his hands, while he tried to explain his actions.

He left the *Phoenix* uncloaked, ensuring that the station would detect his arrival, imagining the crew assembling in the command center and what they all must think of him. He closed his eyes, rallying his courage, then opened a comm channel, hailing the station.

"*Phoenix* to Hideaway, come in."

The admiral appeared on the screen a moment later, his expression composed, but Jackson could tell that he was angry. His heart sank when he saw the admiral along with the crew gathered in the background, their postures and expressions hostile.

He'd been dreading this moment since he'd left, the feeling becoming more intense as he journeyed back from the Brestin System, knowing that he had to face them and answer for his actions. The looks of disappointment, mixed with anger, however, hit him harder than he'd expected.

"Admiral," Jackson said respectfully.

"Lieutenant Commander," the admiral responded tersely. "You have some explaining to do."

"I do, sir. Permission to dock?"

The admiral signaled the gateway probe, and the tractor pods activated, opening the path in the debris field. "Permission granted."

Jackson set a course for the station, keeping the comm channel open. "Sir, when I arrive, I need you to quarantine me immediately. Full blackout protocols. I have Bits maintaining a dampening field at the moment as well. I have a lot to tell you, but I also have reason to believe that I'm somehow responsible for us being tracked. As soon as I close the channel, I'm also going to disable all comms on the *Phoenix*, and I've jammed all other transmissions except this tight beam to the station as a security precaution. Please keep them offline until I can bring you up to date."

The admiral nodded to the crew to begin preparations.

"I'm very sorry, sir. I know that I betrayed your trust. Hopefully, what I've discovered will prove worth it."

"Let's take things one at a time, Lieutenant Commander. Transfer control of the ship to the station once you dock. Then exit in a flight suit only and prepare to surrender."

"Yes, sir. Transferring control momentarily. *Phoenix* out."

He knew that he'd acted rashly, the emotion of what had happened to Verris and the discovery of a traitor pushing him over the edge. Still, it was no excuse, but he prayed they would understand and forgive him once he told them everything he'd learned.

The *Phoenix* landed in the hangar bay, and the ramp opened a moment later. A small probe flew inside while Jackson stood perfectly still with his hands at his sides. It hovered over his head for a few seconds, then activated a mobile containment field. He exited the ship slowly, the containment field providing a portable prison while also engaging the blackout protocol to block any potential transmissions he could inadvertently send. He was unarmed and wearing only his flight suit, as instructed.

Johansen and Dr. Duratis stood waiting for him, both wearing full exo-suits, while Lieutenant Quentarus stood nearby in a tactical suit, armed with both a sidearm and a rifle.

Jackson gave them a nod, raising his hands as he walked to the medical bay. Once there, he entered a medpod, Johansen activating a level-ten containment field, the small probe deactivating a moment later. Jackson lowered his hands as the pod closed, and Johansen verified that the blackout protocols were fully active.

The doctor got to work right away, running a full-spectrum scan for any pathogens or contagions, as they were still uncertain as to the full nature of Jackson's quarantine request. Once she cleared him, she tilted her head, retracting her helmet, the rest of the team following suit a moment later.

The admiral joined them shortly after, a silence hanging in the air. He stood before the containment field, opening a comm to the medpod.

"All right, Lieutenant Commander. Explain yourself."

Take it slow, Jackson thought. *I only have one chance to explain myself. If I screw this up, they might knock me out and take me back to Command for a court-martial.*

"I'll start from when I was last here, sir. After Lieutenant Quentarus discovered the evidence of the traitor, I was... Well, I was furious, sir. I let my emotions get the better of me. I knew that I wasn't the traitor but didn't know if I could trust any of you, and I felt responsible for what happened to Verris, not wanting to get anyone else hurt. I found something late that night. An encrypted layer to the map that Bits was able to decode, showing several more categories of Ancient sites. One of them matched up with the Brestin System. I was going to sleep on it and tell you all in the morning, but I...I lost myself in anger, falling into despair that Verris would never be the same again.

"I wasn't myself, sir. I was so angry. So full of rage and guilt that I didn't know what to do. That's when I came up with my plan to go and investigate on my own. I stole the *Phoenix* and made it so you couldn't follow me. From there, I set a course for the Brestin System. I had Bits re-create the signal that the Chief and the Lieutenant deciphered, using it to lure the Insectoids into a trap. What happened next, however, I didn't expect. Bits detected a Reptilian ship, which had apparently tracked the same signal to the planet.

"I decided to stick to the plan, springing my ambush. It didn't go exactly as planned, and a native village was caught in the crossfire, despite my best efforts. I was, however, eventually able to take both of the Reptilians out and recover some intel. I'll give you the play-by-play later, but the important thing was that I was able to question one of them using a truth dart before it died. I asked it how it knew to look for the signal and who the traitor was. Much to my disbelief, it informed me that I was the traitor!

"I had Bits run a thorough scan of my body, of the ship, and an internal diagnostic of himself, but so far, we haven't found anything to corroborate what it said. I've had Bits keep a low-level dampening field around me until we could get back here, just to be safe. The Reptilian could have been lying, but I gave it a heavy dose of truth serum. It also warned me that the Insectoids would be coming, and it was right.

"I then collected the bodies, which are in cryo-stasis on board the *Phoenix* now, and proceeded with the mission. I located the Ancient site, concerned that if I left, the Insectoids might destroy it. I made my way into the structure after another rough security scan. The good news is that it turned out to be a very significant find," he said, waiting a moment to see if the admiral or the crew had any questions.

"Then what happened?" the admiral asked tersely.

"As I was on my way back from the site, a group of ants ambushed me. I managed to take them out and track them back to their ship. After careful consideration, I decided to infiltrate it to see what they knew. There's a lot to cover, but the short version is that I believe that they broke into a classified GCH database and found information pertaining to our mission. I also believe that they wanted revenge for a bioweapon which was unleashed on one of their colonies a few years ago. They knew the names of two of the systems we'd be visiting and even my name. Bits also discovered a text-only transmission they received claiming that I, personally, was responsible for the attack on their colony, despite it taking place several years ago, back when I was working search and rescue. It instructed them to eliminate me, along with another ship that would arrive in the Praxian System to meet us."

Quentarus raised her eyebrows at this, giving the admiral a quick look.

"After that, I decided that I couldn't risk leaving their ship there and calling in the Fleet if they were still planetside. I'd already caused enough damage and didn't want to put any more innocent lives in danger. I also needed to get them out of there so we could return to the Ancient site. I attacked their ship, then lured them away from the planet and past one of the GCH probes in the system. Just after it pinged them, I jumped out. I'm certain that they did the same shortly after. They'd know that the Fleet was on their way. After that, I came straight back here."

"All right," the admiral said, turning to the crew. "Doctor, I want you to perform another scan on Jackson. Use whatever methods you think will give the most detailed results. Johansen, interface with his AI and pull all of its logs, then run them through the station's computer. After that, run a full diagnostic at the firmware level to make sure it's clean. Lieutenant Quentarus, you'll watch over our *guest* while the others work. I'd suggest that you get comfortable in there, Lieutenant Commander. The rest of you, dismissed."

Jackson leaned back, fairly certain from the admiral's tone and body language that it hadn't gone well. From the short time he'd known him, he'd gathered that the admiral was a fiercely loyal man and to betray his trust was something which could not be easily repaired.

The crew buzzed around while he lay back in the pod, attempting to relax. He knew that time was of the essence and wanted to get back to Brestin III in case the queen somehow returned, but he also knew he had to earn the crew's trust back for that to happen.

He pushed the sense of urgency to the back of his mind, complying with all of their requests while the doctor began her scans, then ordered Bits to shut down and grant Johansen full remote access to his hardware platform via a connection from the pod.

After several hours, the admiral relieved Lieutenant Quentarus, watching over him, a rifle at the ready. Jackson kept silent the entire time, not making any attempts to talk to the admiral or the crew.

Hours later, the doctor finally cleared him from a medical perspective while Johansen continued his analysis. Jackson tried to get some sleep, finding it difficult but finally getting a few hours, the exhaustion of the previous several days finally catching up with him.

Lieutenant Quentarus stood watch over him once again when he awoke, and he hadn't seen the rest of the crew in some time. He was beginning to lose hope when the doors to the medical bay opened and the admiral entered, flanked by the doctor and Johansen. The comm in the pod was off, cutting him off from their conversation. He watched nervously while the admiral relayed something to the lieutenant, then gestured towards him. She took a half step back, then raised her rifle.

Shit. Not good.

Johansen lowered the containment field. The medpod door opened, and Jackson raised his hands while Quentarus kept her rifle trained on him.

"Lieutenant Commander," the admiral said. "I'm afraid the doctor didn't find anything. Chief Johansen, however, *did* find something."

Johansen handed the admiral a data pad. The admiral pressed his thumb to the screen, and a holo-projection appeared a moment later. The image was beautiful. A complex, geometrical shape which moved and flowed while patterns, shapes, and colors shifted and reconfigured themselves.

"Will, this is Bits," Johansen said, gesturing to the display.

"Hello, William," Bits spoke from the pad.

"Uh, hey, buddy," Jackson said, staring at the holographic image.

"Bits is unique," Johansen continued. "He's far more than a standard artificial intelligence unit. He has dozens of custom modules that were added just for you, along with subroutines that I've never seen before. After having the station's computer and Foxy perform a detailed analysis of his code, then comparing them to the firmware logs on your cognitive implant, I found something. There's a subroutine, buried deep within the Earth historical database. The station's computer flagged it as being out of place, since only data should have been in there, not code. And a program buried in that location made no sense.

"All subroutines *should* be stored here," Johansen continued, gesturing to the display. "So, I had the computer isolate and analyze this rogue entry and found that it's what's called a sub-cognitive subroutine. This means that it's able to run without Bits knowing that it's running. It also wouldn't have been picked up by any of his diagnostics or logs. Additionally, I found that the firmware on your comm implant had been slightly altered. I had to run a check twice to be sure, but there's a tiny section of code which has been tampered with, designed specifically to interface directly with the subroutine, ensuring that the connection wasn't logged."

"So, what are you saying?" Jackson asked.

"All of this is highly concerning and confirms that you are indeed the one who sent the signal," the admiral said gravely, stepping forward. "The chief confirmed, however, that this would have been incredibly complex to install, and quite frankly, beyond your abilities."

"So, what you're saying is, I'm not smart enough to have added this, even if I was a traitor?"

"What we're saying, Will," the admiral said, a slight smile crossing his face, "is that you can put your hands down."

Jackson breathed a sigh of relief as he lowered his hands. Lieutenant Quentarus gave him a slight smirk before lowering her rifle as well, the tension in the room lifting immediately.

"It wasn't your fault. Neither you, nor Bits, were aware of what was happening, and there's no way that you could have known," the admiral said.

"What will happen to Bits?"

"I've already started recompiling him. He's actually in the main data core now. This pad is just an uplink," Johansen said. "He'll be as good as new in about ten minutes. Once he's ready, I'll let you know, and we can bring him back online."

"Thanks," Jackson replied before turning back to the admiral. "Sir, do we have any idea as to how this subroutine got there in the first place?" Jackson paused, the realization hitting him an instant later. "Oh no," he said, the answer to his own question suddenly becoming clear as day.

"What is it?" the admiral asked.

Jackson swallowed, his face turning pale. "Just before we left the Kishara station, Admiral Thompson asked me to stay back. He had an update for me, which improved the way that Bits and my implants interfaced with the Ancient tech. That must have been when the new code was uploaded."

"Could Admiral Thompson really be in on it?" Quentarus asked.

Admiral Valentyen frowned. "I've known Gord Thompson for over a hundred and sixty years. There's few men I'd trust more with my life. I also know a few members of the team that designed your AI. While I hate to think that any of them would do this, the reality is that it could have been any one of them."

"We'll need to tread carefully," Johansen said. "If we try to access the development logs to see who added the code, there may be an alert, letting the saboteur know that we're onto them. I can get around it, but not from here. I'd need to do it from a local connection at the dev lab on Archon."

"For now, we're going to keep this information compartmentalized to our team," the admiral stated. "We'll continue to provide Command with regular updates, but until we know who we can trust, we'll keep all knowledge of what happened secret. Understood?"

The crew nodded.

"What about my little...*excursion*?" Jackson asked sheepishly. "Won't they know that something is up?"

"I decided not to inform Command right away after you left," the admiral replied, raising an eyebrow. "If it was anyone else, I wouldn't have hesitated, but after considering what you had just gone through with Verris...well, I decided to give you a chance. Once Johansen had the comms back up, I tapped into the GCH network. It didn't take long to see an ID log with your clearance attached authorizing access to the Brestin System, so I was pretty sure what you were up to."

Jackson felt relieved that Command wasn't aware, while instantly more guilty that the admiral stuck his neck out for him by not reporting it. "Thank you, sir. I appreciate your faith in me."

"Let's not make it a habit, understood?"

"Understood, sir."

"So, what have you got for us?"

"Actually, I have a *lot* to show you. I think you'd better have a seat."

CHAPTER 27

ECHOES THROUGH THE AGES

Jackson relayed what had happened at the Ancient site on Brestin III, only briefly touching on the details of the final chamber in the pyramid, until he had given them the rest of the story.

"How is it that Command doesn't know about the attack on the Insectoid colony, or the use of the bioweapon?" Dr. Duratis asked, turning to the admiral.

"I don't know. I'll look into it, though."

"So, we now know *how* they were able to track us, or you, but who sent the message to frame you, and why?" Johansen asked.

"Let's break down what we already know," the admiral suggested. "A bioweapon was detonated several years ago, wiping out an Insectoid colony and implicating the GCH. We bring Jackson out into the field, attempting to search Ancient sites for advanced technology, but just before we leave, he's given an upgrade by Admiral Thompson. And, at around the same time, the Insectoids recovered a top-secret data file listing your name, along with two of the three systems where we were headed. We now know that the update contained malicious code, which hijacked Jackson's AI and implants, sending a signal and alerting *someone* to our location when we reached each of the three sites."

"Actually," Jackson interjected, "I forgot to mention. Bits was going through the data we recovered while we were on our way back. The data they stole from the GCH classified files gave them the Vishnara and Brestin Systems, but not the Praxian. And there was no record in their system of them receiving a transmission when we arrived at Vishnara, but we know one was sent. From what we've pieced together, they only went there to wait and see if we showed up. We were lucky that we got there first."

"And they found out about the Praxian System from the mysterious out-of-phase transmission they received," Johansen said.

"Exactly," Jackson replied. "They were contacted shortly before we left for Praxian Prime. Whoever it was that sent the message then told them that I was the one who destroyed their colony and also instructed them to take out the other ship we detected."

"It's possible that after the Insectoids failed at Praxian Prime, this other party hired the Cavarians to kill you," Quentarus suggested.

"It's certainly a strong possibility," the admiral said. "Then the Insectoids showed up, both by detecting the signal you sent when you arrived and because they knew the name of the system and were lying in wait nearby."

"And we still don't know anything about the other ship that saved us," Quentarus added.

"Actually, we did find something. Bits was able to locate a visual record from one of the Imperium ships. It took a while to decrypt, but check this out," Jackson said. He turned to the data pad Johansen was still holding where Bits was connected, and his AI interfaced with the holo-display, bringing up a visual image of the ship, writing appearing on the side.

"Holy shit, that's Archonian!" Quentarus said. "The *Ranger*. What the hell?"

"Yeah. There's a ship in the Fleet with that name, but it's a cruiser, nothing like this."

"Did they have any more information on it?" the admiral asked.

"Not much. It destroyed three of their battlecruisers before they finally took it out, we think. The reports weren't very detailed."

"We need to figure out who was on that ship," Quentarus said, clearly still fixated on it.

"And we need to determine who this other player is that sent the Insectoids and Reptilians after you," the admiral added.

"I have a few ideas about that, sir, but I have something that you all need to see first. I need Bits fully back online to show you, though," Jackson said.

"Hang on," Johansen said, tapping his wrist and bringing up his holo-display. "He's finished compiling. Just a sec and I'll port him back over."

Jackson waited a moment, a small chime in his ear indicating that Bits was initializing. "Welcome back, buddy."

"It is good to be back. I am terribly sorry. I did not know about the subroutine. I feel as though I've let you down."

"It's okay, Bits. No one blames you. It wasn't something that either of us could have known about."

"Thank you, William."

Jackson addressed the crew. "So, as I mentioned, there's one more thing that I need to show you. Come with me," he said, leading them down the hall to the IRC. "Bits, can you please load the sensor information and recording of the pyramid command center into the IRC interface?"

"Certainly."

A moment later, the room transformed around them, becoming the command center of the Ancient pyramid, the crew standing just inside the doorway to the room, watching the playback of Jackson walking towards the altar. They stood in silence as the hologram of the Ancient appeared before him.

"Welcome, my child," she said, a shiver running down Jackson's spine as he heard her voice once more. "My name is Alura Es'zel, last of the Etlentian people."

"It's a pleasure to meet you, Alura. My name is William Jackson of the Galactic Confederation of Humanity. I come from the planet Earth, the one I was holding in my hand just before you appeared," Jackson's holographic self responded.

Alura looked down upon him. "You have our gift, William Jackson. You are a part of us."

"I have the ability to use your technology, yes. It is unique among my people."

She smiled, her expression a mix of joy and sadness. "Then you are a true child of Etlentia…and sadly, the last."

"I'm very sorry. Can you tell me what happened to you and your people?"

"Of course. I will tell you of us, so that you may carry us in your memory. My people were a race of scientists and explorers. We created a vast interstellar empire spanning across the galaxy. A civilization which thrived for tens of thousands of generations. As we explored our galaxy, we found that we were very much alone in the universe. There was life, certainly, and it was abundant and beautiful, but none of it was advanced like ourselves. So, we created life of our own.

"We used our technology and advanced genetic knowledge to seed planets, bioengineering the indigenous lifeforms that we found, providing them an evolutionary leap forward, designing entire ecosystems around them to ensure their success. We created hundreds of races, including yours, William Jackson, in our own image.

"We had hoped to watch over you, to tend to you from afar while letting you find your own way before welcoming you into our galactic society. For millennia, our civilization looked inward at all that we had achieved, and we basked in the joy of our creations." She paused, her expression hardening. "But we were *not* as alone in the universe as we had believed.

"After a time, our curiosity turned outward once again, and we undertook an unprecedented feat of engineering, creating massive hyperspace gates. These conduits, each powered by the incredible energy of a neutron star, allowed us to bridge the endless void of space, reaching out like never before. We began to explore nearby stellar clusters and galaxies, venturing further and further out. Centuries passed as our knowledge increased, the wonders of the universe revealing themselves to us, enriching our civilization. Then, a single ship, one of the many we'd sent through a gate to a nearby galaxy, returned. It was badly damaged, most of its crew injured or dead. The captain hailed the gate commander, warning of an enemy fleet in pursuit, but before we could close the gate, a swarm of huge black ships poured through.

"Their weapons were unlike anything we'd ever seen, tearing through our shields, destroying everything in their path. The few ships which survived the initial assault retreated, carrying the warning with them.

"With a foothold established in our galaxy, they moved outward. Fleets of ships swarming system after system, eradicating all life before unleashing weapons of incredible power, annihilating entire stars. After months of falling back, we finally encountered them face-to-face, a team of our best soldiers setting an ambush and using portal technology to board one of their ships.

"It was then that we saw them for the first time – huge creatures clad in deadly black armor. Our strike teams were successful, however, catching them off guard and capturing their ship along with some of their crew. We brought the ship back, deep within our space, to study it, hoping to find a weakness we could exploit. Our scientists and engineers worked tirelessly, examining their technology.

"As we opened the armor of one creature to interrogate and study it, we were shocked to learn what they truly were: ethereal specters, which were both there and not there. Their bodies moved unnaturally, phasing in and out of our reality, their black suits containing them, keeping them alive on our plane of existence. Communication proved to be impossible, as they would rather die than speak, if they were even capable of such civility.

"We studied them extensively, discovering that their molecules vibrated at a different frequency than our own. Our scientists determined that they were inter-dimensional beings from a realm of darkness, highly allergic to light. If they even had a name, we never knew what it was. So, we called them the Verakai, the Black Death.

"Their ships continued to push deeper into our space, forcing us to watch helplessly as the life we had created was brutally, mercilessly destroyed. We lost our children planet by planet, system by system, until we were finally able to rally a huge fleet to battle them. After a massive, brutal engagement, we slowed their advance, forcing them to retreat, but at a terrible cost.

"Our long-range scans of the hypergate showed more and more of their ships arriving in our galaxy, and we knew that in time, we would be overwhelmed. It was then that our scientists created a weapon, a doomsday device of terrifying power, which we simply called the Light. We launched the weapon at the hypergate, destroying it and devastating an entire region of space for light-years in all directions.

"Still, the Verakai that survived continued to hunt us. Time and time again we were forced to retreat, evacuating planets and entire civilizations, while our engineers desperately pulled their captured ship apart, analyzing their technology and adapting our own. We created new species, and enhanced others to use as troops, taking the fight to them from planet to planet. Over time, we created new defenses, new weapons and, slowly, the tide of the war turned.

"After over a decade of bloody conflict, we finally pushed them back, eradicating them, or so we thought, from our galaxy. The cost…the cost was…*immeasurable.* Trillions of lives lost, entire civilizations wiped from existence.

"A peace followed for nearly a generation as we created greater weapons and defenses, preparing for the day when they might return. We pulled back our explorations from the other galaxies, consolidating our forces here. One galaxy was enough, we told ourselves, and as time moved on, we began to rebuild, seeding planets once again as our civilization slowly returned to our peaceful, nurturing ways."

She paused, shaking her head slightly as if pondering for a moment, her eyes growing distant. Then, after several seconds, she continued. "But it was not to last. The Verakai who survived and went into hiding returned, different than before, using a mix of their technology along with our own. We called them the Phague.

"Their fleet was much smaller than ours, but they used new technologies and strategies, striking at our weakest points. The most significant development, however, was a new technology they created, a type of cloaking field, allowing them to 'black out' huge regions of space from our sensors, making it difficult to navigate and impossible to track their movements within. We called it the Shroud of Darkness.

"Using the Shroud, they attacked strategically, stealing our resources and advanced technologies, taking them for their own. In order to counter these attacks, we upgraded all our military and advanced technologies with embedded genetic scanners. These were programmed to attack or self-destruct for any user who was not Etlentian or one of our child races. And we specifically programmed the most severe and lethal reactions for Phague bio-signs.

"Years passed while they continued their campaign against us. When the time was right, we allowed them to acquire a shipment of advanced weapons, carefully leaving a trail for them to follow and capture our convoys. The Phague took the bait, and hours later we detected large explosions as holes emerged in the Shroud of Darkness, revealing their positions. We counterattacked, seizing on the distraction, and within hours, we had them on the run, their fleet in ruins.

"Confident that our genetic scanning technology was infallible, we continued to fight, beating them back system by system. As we closed in, cornering the last of their fleet, they suddenly disappeared. At first, we had no idea where they'd gone, but after salvaging and analyzing their technology, we discovered that they had traveled to a sub-dimension. A different plane of reality that mirrored our own.

"We sent probes to seek them out, but their space was vast, its strange properties making it difficult to navigate. Eventually, we reluctantly decided to let them be. Our fleet grew in strength, as did the power of our weapons. And we felt confident that if they ever returned, we'd be ready for them. The Phague, however, were far more clever than we ever could have imagined…and what happened next took those of us who survived years to piece together.

"The Phague who escaped created a new plan. Slowly, methodically, they sent devices into our space, hidden by shroud technology. These weapons entered the atmospheres of thousands of our worlds, releasing their payload and infecting our populations with a virus from their dimension. This pathogen sat idle, out of phase and undetectable for years, while they waited, ensuring that they had achieved a maximum level of infection. Then, a single ship appeared in orbit around Etlentia, demanding that we surrender. When we refused, it transmitted a signal which activated the virus, bringing it into phase and launching a massive, coordinated attack.

"The virus was unlike anything we had ever seen, mutating key genome sequences and making it appear to our technology that *we* were now the Phague.

"It's impossible to know for certain how many Etlentians perished in the days that followed," she said, her voice cracking. "But based on our calculations, we estimated that hundreds of trillions of innocent lives were lost. Within a few short weeks, ninety-eight percent of our species was wiped out as our own technology turned against us in catastrophic ways.

"It started with our military technology," she said as images appeared in her place, a montage of tragedy unfolding, "where our genetic scanning security measures were most severely enforced. As the virus activated, so too did our scanners. Energy weapons self-destructed in soldiers' hands. Automated turrets turned on the very bases they protected. Robotic soldiers activated, rising up against us and hunting us down. Starship AIs, believing that they'd been overrun with Phague occupiers, initiated full decompressions, their crews sucked out into space with no warning. They then turned on our planets, bombarding them from orbit before, finally, using the ships themselves as projectiles, targeting our remaining cities once their ammunition was spent." The image of a massive battlecruiser appeared, crashing into the surface of a planet, the impact and detonation destroying an area hundreds of kilometers wide. "Not only were we targeted, but many of our children, the planets that we had seeded with life, were also destroyed…and we were helpless to stop it.

"The mutation was irreversible, and without access to our advanced medical technology, many of our military assets went into lockdown mode, refusing to respond to remote override commands even from those of us who remained pure and untainted. A few thousand of us, hidden in covert facilities such as this one, survived, but the pathogen was everywhere, and we knew if we emerged from hiding, we would be exposed to it as well. Our new fear was that the Phague would return to finish the job, cleansing our galaxy of all life… There was only one thing left for us to do… We deployed the Light once more.

"Within days, we coordinated a counterattack, opening hundreds of inter-dimensional portals and sending Light weapons into the Phague's realm. The warheads detonated moments later, releasing light into the darkness.

"Our rage was terrible, our vengeance swift and without mercy, our weapons devastating their space, our goal to destroy everything possible! We sent probes into their dimension months later, finding only utter devastation. We had… we had become what we hated the most. In all moral and ethical senses, we had become the Verakai.

"Those of us who remained renounced the name Etlentians, for we were no longer creators of life, no longer worthy. We became the Kas-ha'shie… the Fallen," she said sadly, her eyes conveying a deep sense of regret as she spoke, her voice deflated.

"Of those of us who remained, most emerged from hiding, eventually. We used modified subspace transmitters to keep in contact and were able to remove the genetic scanning components before those who went out were exposed to the pathogen and mutated. Those who emerged were careful, avoiding all contact with our technology, but despite that, many were hunted down by our remaining robotic soldiers, while others were more fortunate and able to remain hidden.

"We began again. Back to the beginning. Farming and living in caves, then huts and other primitive structures. We still had great scientific knowledge and were able to rebuild something of a basic existence, but we knew that our time was over. There simply weren't enough of us. The few hundred thousand who were still alive were scattered throughout the galaxy, unable to reach one another.

"Slowly, inevitably, we began to die out…

"I was one of the few who opted to stay in bases such as this, to guard our seeds and the final stockpiles of Light weapons, should they ever be needed again. I was alive, pure, and unmutated by the pathogen, but unable to leave this prison for the rest of my life. There were nine others who shared this same fate. We kept in touch via subspace communications, but it wasn't enough. We Etlentians are a social race and do not do well in isolation. Several of my peers retreated to their cryo-pods, never to awaken again, rather than face eternal loneliness. Kelus Tar-Sho, my colleague, and I devised a plan. We reached out to a race, which you now call Ularans. They were the most advanced and one of the earliest humanoid races we had seeded. And one of the few who survived. We sent repeating transmissions to them, despite knowing that it would take thousands of years for them to develop to a level of technology where they could even detect them, let alone understand them. In that message, we charged them with being the guardians of our legacy."

The crew stood stunned, looking at one another in disbelief as, suddenly, several pieces finally began making sense. The enigmatic Ularans had a terrible knowledge and burden to bear. They were the keepers of the Ancients' legacy…of their secrets. Yet, just as with all other species, they were incapable of using the Ancients' technology, as the pathogen was part of their genome, just as it was everyone else's.

"They were the ones who brought me here," the holographic version of Jackson said.

Alura's eyes lit up at this. "Then it is for a higher purpose that you are here. That you alone are somehow immune to the pathogen, and our technology recognizes you as one of our children. Take it. It is our gift to you. Use it wisely and learn from the mistakes of our past.

"The object above the altar before you is one of our Seeds. A device which can create life on a planetary scale. The technology in the adjacent rooms works with it to seed planets with whatever life and ecosystems you choose. But be warned, with the gift of creation comes a heavy responsibility. It will change you in ways that you cannot begin to imagine. You will become a parent, and for all intents and purposes, a god. You will begin a cycle of life which may carry on for billions of years. Do not use this gift lightly.

"Also, contained within this structure are seven remaining Light warheads. They are stored in a state of dimensional shift, isolated from the time-stream to preserve them. I have initiated the command sequence to phase them back into this temporal plane, and they are in the room next to this one. You and you alone can operate them. If anyone else attempts to use them, they will detonate here, in our dimension, creating unimaginable destruction in their wake. Protect them at all costs and use them only if the Phague or Verakai return. I must warn you, however, that destroying life on such a scale will destroy a part of your very soul as well… Please, my child, be wise. Be careful. Be vigilant.

"Remember us for what we were. For our achievements, and our flaws. Learn from us and don't make the same mistakes that we once made. We were a noble race, once. Proud, strong, caring. We were your parents, and we love you all."

A tear streamed down her cheek from the blue ocean of her eyes as she faded away, the small golden sphere left hovering above the altar as the room grew silent. The holographic image of Jackson stared at it. The Seed. It moved under its own power, gliding towards him. He reached out and it settled in his hand, glowing brightly as the simulation ended.

"Holy shit!" Johansen said.

The rest of the crew stood in stunned silence.

"We have to go back," Jackson stated. "I was able to bring the Seed here, but we have to go back and get the rest, to keep it safe. In the wrong hands, just one of those Light warheads would be a terrible weapon. Even in our hands, they're immensely dangerous, but imagine if the Insectoids or Reptilians got hold of them."

"Agreed," the admiral said. "We need to retrieve them, and we can't let anyone outside of this room know what we know. At least not now. Is that understood?"

"Understood," Lieutenant Quentarus said.

"Understood, sir," Johansen replied.

Dr. Duratis stuttered. "I mean this is just so…so profound. I… We have to share at least some of what she's told us, don't we? I think we owe it to them. We've always just referred to them as the Ancients, but now we know their name. People need to know about their history and what happened. How they created us all and fought to defend us. We have to remember them!"

"In time, Doctor, but not now. Not yet. One day, I promise, we will," the admiral said. "Jackson?"

"Yes, sir. One other thing. I've been giving this a great deal of thought, and I honestly can't think of anywhere safe where we can bring these weapons. Even if we bring them here, if just one of those warheads were ever to detonate, it could wipe out everything within several light-years! We don't even know how far the damage would extend, and there's two habitable systems within a few light-years of this system. But we can't risk leaving them on Brestin III either, not now that the Insectoids know that we were after something there and may try for it themselves. The pyramid had some defenses, but I don't think they would hold indefinitely. And we certainly can't risk taking them to the core systems. If anyone ever accidentally activated them, hundreds of billions of lives could be lost. So where does that leave us?"

The admiral was silent for a moment. "It's a good question, Will. We'll have to think about it. For now, let's put our heads together and figure out how we're going to get those weapons off of Brestin III. We can't go to Command, as we still don't know who we can trust there, but we'll need backup. I checked in with Command, and several ships responded to an alert from the Brestin System. They didn't find any Imperium ships, but we don't know if they'll be back. Our first priority is getting the Ancient tech out of there. Then we can figure out where we can keep it safely."

"We could bring in Captain Delgado. He's got access to a number of ships, and he has top-secret clearance," Jackson offered.

"I thought about that, but all of his ships are small, like the *Phoenix*. If the Insectoids do return and we run into more cruisers like the one you encountered, we'll need significantly more firepower. We just need to figure out how to get it while keeping it off the books. The ships that responded to the alert have all left the Brestin System and we don't want to call them back and tip our hand if there truly is a mole at Command."

"Sir," Lieutenant Quentarus said, perking up, "I think that I may have an idea about that."

CHAPTER 28

RECOVERY

The *Phoenix* exited hyperspace at the edge of the Brestin System ten hours later.

"Engineering, engage the cloak. Tactical, initiate a scan of the system," Jackson ordered, enjoying his first official command and having the crew back together. After formulating their plan, Admiral Valentyen had decided to stay back at the Hideaway, coordinating with GCH Intelligence to locate and secure the hole in the sensor net along the border, while covertly working on options for safely storing the Ancient weapons somewhere off the books and away from populated systems. As the ranking officer on the ship, Jackson was in command, the admiral's trust in him helping to repair some of the damage he'd done.

He sat at the helm, routing the Ops station to his console, while the rest of the crew manned their usual posts.

"Cloak engaged, Captain," Johansen said.

"Did I get a promotion, and someone forgot to tell me?" he quipped. "A few hours ago, I was on the block for treason!"

"It's an old GCH tradition," Quentarus informed him. "Whoever is in command is referred to as Captain, regardless of rank."

"That's funny. I didn't know that."

"The idea is that there's only one captain, but there can be many lieutenants, commanders, ensigns, and so on. Makes it less clunky than having to say Lieutenant Commander all the time. Don't let it go to your head though…sir," Quentarus said, flashing him a smile.

"Noted, Lieutenant," he smiled back.

"Captain William Jackson," the doctor said, trying it out. "It's got a nice ring to it."

"Maybe one day," Jackson said, changing the subject. "My scans are clear. How's it looking on tactical sensors?"

"I'm not detecting any signs of enemy ships in the system, but we're too far out to scan the surface of the planet from here."

"All right, I'm taking us in," he said, plotting a course and engaging the stealth drive while monitoring the sensors as they moved towards their destination.

Minutes passed as the ship slipped silently through the Brestin System. The crew focused on their tasks, each aware that the Imperium could still return, but hopeful that the Fleet's arrival after Jackson left the last time had scared them off.

Jackson jumped the ship in just past the seventh planet, far enough out that they were confident they wouldn't be detected, while giving them time to scan ahead for signs of an ambush and run thorough sensor sweeps before they proceeded.

So far so good, he thought as he circumnavigated a small asteroid field, just a few million kilometers from their destination.

Lieutenant Quentarus focused intently on the sensors, looking for signs of ships hidden amongst the rocks and ice, weapons at the ready. Her AI, Helo, coordinated with Bits, the two focusing on particle drift analysis, looking for signs of recent hyperspace or sublight travel.

"Captain, I'm detecting faint readings," she said. "A residual ion trail near the second moon of Brestin III. I've scanned it three times, and our AIs confirm there's nothing on sensors that could account for it."

"Reducing speed," Jackson said. "Any signs of ships on the surface?"

"No sign of any Insectoid ship, but I'm detecting the Reptilian scout ship. It's right where you said it would be."

"I guess the Insectoids and the Fleet didn't detect it," Johansen chimed in.

"It has some type of stealth system, so I'm not surprised," Jackson said. "Well, at least the bugs seem to be gone. Anything else on sensors?"

"Negative," Lieutenant Quentarus replied. "But I'm still concerned that there's something near that moon."

"All right, I'll take us down," Jackson said as he disengaged the stealth drive and the cloak, switching to sublight engines in order to enter the atmosphere. "Full power to forward shields."

The *Phoenix* entered the atmosphere a moment later, burning across the sky, leaving a contrail several kilometers long. Seconds later, an alert sounded.

"Sir," Quentarus called out, "three Insectoid destroyers have just jumped in from different approach vectors. They're attempting to box us in!"

"Well, that didn't take long," Jackson said, pulling the ship up and making a run for it. "LT, call in our reinforcements!"

"Transmission sent."

The *Phoenix* gained altitude and pulled away from the planet, the three destroyers closing from different sides.

"They're attempting to cut us off," Quentarus said. "They'll be within weapons range in ten seconds!"

Just then, a flash of light appeared between the *Phoenix* and the destroyers, a massive vessel filling the space a moment later.

The incoming ship opened fire immediately, its broadside facing the destroyers, battle over in less than thirty seconds.

Jackson circled back around the huge vessel, all that remained of the destroyers, a field of debris where they'd been just moments before.

"We're being hailed," Bits reported.

"On screen," Jackson replied.

"*Phoenix*, this is Captain Quentarus of the GCH dreadnought *Viceroy*."

"This is Lieutenant Commander William Jackson, acting captain of the *Phoenix*. Thanks for the assist, *Viceroy*. It's good to see you again, Captain."

"You as well, Jackson. It looks like we arrived just in time. It's a good thing we were in the vicinity on a shakedown cruise."

"Yes, sir."

"What the hell were three Insectoid destroyers doing this far inside GCH space, and in a Vicara class system no less?"

"My team and I are on a covert operation sir, and they jumped in when they detected us entering the atmosphere. We think they may have a cloaked probe nearby. I'm afraid our mission is classified, but there was another Imperium ship in this system just days ago as well, so we think they're up to something."

"Understood. I suppose I should thank you; my crew's been itching to give our weapons systems a test more challenging than just asteroids and target drones."

"We're happy to help, sir," Jackson said, suppressing a smile.

"Well, Lieutenant Commander, or should I say Captain, you always did know how to find trouble." Captain Quentarus smiled. "Can we be of further assistance?"

"We need to proceed with our mission to the surface, sir, and recover a high-value asset. Would you mind watching our backs?"

"Of course. We'll investigate the probe and see if we can capture it. Send us what you have, and we'll take it from there. I'll initiate black-ops protocols in order to keep your mission classified and scrub all sensor logs of your activities."

"Thank you, sir. We appreciate the help. It's possible that the probe alerted the bugs and more may be on the way, so best to be on your guard just in case."

"We'll be more than ready for them if they come."

"Thank you, sir. That's an impressive ship, by the way. I've never seen that class before."

"She's my own design," Captain Quentarus said, brimming with pride. "The GCH dreadnought *Viceroy*. Took me eight years to convince Command to build her. She's the first of ten and should be a game changer once they're all ready. I've taken everything I've ever learned about space combat and poured it into this beauty. She's a force to be reckoned with."

"Roger that, sir," Jackson said, his eyes flicking to the holo-display of the *Viceroy*, noting its impressive size at just over two and a half kilometers long and easily as powerful and well-armed as eight GCH battlecruisers combined. "My crew and I feel much better having you watching our backs. We'll contact you as soon as we've completed our mission. *Phoenix* out."

Jackson turned to the rest of the crew. “Everyone good to go?”

“I think I might need to change my shorts,” Johansen joked. “Even though that was the plan all along!”

“It’s a good thing your father was so close,” the doctor said, turning to Lieutenant Quentarus. “I was wondering who our backup was. How’d you manage to get him here so quickly?”

“He messaged me a few weeks ago when the *Viceroy* first launched, so I knew he was out on a shakedown cruise. They were only a few sectors away, and after I contacted him this morning, he ordered his crew to set a new course, running exercises around the Marconian Nebula a few light-years from here to put the ship through its paces. It’s a dodgy region of space and difficult to navigate, so lots of captains use it for shakedowns. It didn’t take much for him to get them there without raising any suspicions and he timed it so they were already heading this way when we were estimated to arrive, to ensure he’d be close by if we needed him.”

“The captain will report to Command that they responded to a distress call and engaged the Insectoids,” Jackson added. “But black-ops protocols will keep us out of the initial report, as we’re still on-mission, so it will keep us off Command’s radar, just in case someone there is actively working against us. At least until our mission is complete. The Admiral also used his access to remotely disable the monitoring probes in the system, so we can do this entirely off the books.”

He looked around the bridge, his crew nodding, each of them ready.

“All right, then. We don’t know if more Insectoids are coming, so let’s get to work.”

CHAPTER 29

WISHES AND PRAYERS

The crew was nearly through the process of recovering the Ancient tech from the pyramid, bringing it up using small, automated cargo pods the size of Frisbees that attached to the corner of each crate and lifted it gently off the ground.

The crew remained above, not wanting to risk their genetic signatures activating the pyramid's defenses, remotely guiding the pods into the *Phoenix*'s cargo bay. Johansen attached portable dampening fields to each pod, ensuring that once on board the ship, the scanners on the Light weapons and other devices remained blocked.

Jackson made his way down to the control chamber for a final look, stopping just inside the entrance, trying to commit each detail to memory. After a moment, he walked over to the cryo-pod where Alura's body lay preserved in suspended animation, the vital signs on the pod showing no activity. Despite her having been dead for eons, he felt as though he couldn't leave again without saying goodbye.

He stood straight, his hands folded in front of him, eyes shut, whispering the last verses of an Annarian prayer for the dead. A simple rhyme that translated surprisingly well into English:

"And though this journey has come to an end,
Seek comfort in the tears of your friends,
For they cry out of love, the best kind of pain,
And know that you will see them again."

Jackson reached out, placing his hand on the cryo-pod, standing in silence for a moment, imagining what life must have been like for Alura, confined to this prison for years. The incredible burden of choosing to live in isolation, the last guard of a dying civilization as it faded into history. A sadness grew in his heart as he pitied the hardship she endured, while respecting her noble sacrifice.

"See you in the next life, Alura. May it be kinder to you than this one was, and may you find happiness and peace wherever you are now."

"Johansen to Jackson," a signal came through the comm, pulling him out of the moment.

"Go ahead, Chief."

"We're all set up here. The last batch of crates are on their way. How are you doin' down there?"

"On my way up. Just taking a last look around. I'll be there in a few minutes."

"Copy that."

"Jackson out," he said, moving back towards the entrance and stopping at the doorway. He took a last look around, his eyes settling on the cryo-pod. "Rest in peace, Alura."

He'd never been particularly religious but had always believed that there was *something* more out there. Since coming back from the dead, he'd dabbled in some spiritual exploration with Bits, the two having had several discussions which helped to bring him some peace in the early days while he mourned for Amy and all of his family and friends.

Religion, he'd learned, was one of the few aspects of GCH society where individual freedoms were limited, something that surprised him at first. The laws governing the GCH allowed every individual to find their own religious path in life, their AIs programmed to provide them with information on tens of thousands of religions from across the Confederation, spanning thousands of worlds. They were not, however, permitted to discuss religion with anyone aside from their AI.

At first, this had alarmed him, but as he settled in and learned more about it, the more it made sense. There were a few exceptions to this rule, of course, such as a parent providing guidance to a child, but even these were limited. The GCH philosophy, molded by thousands of years of history, had taught them repeatedly of the dangers of religious influence. Civilization after civilization had proved time and time again that when one person influences another, it inevitably leads to corruption of the message, and some things which are far worse, such as holy wars, inquisitions, and even genocide.

While it seemed strange to ban talking about the topic entirely, the more he'd learned about galactic history, and some of the terrible atrocities committed in the name of one god or another, the more it seemed to justify why this became something that people didn't talk about. GCH society, while not perfect, was nearly completely free from public religious iconography and influences of any kind aside from historical sites and museum pieces. The separation of religion and state became absolute. Instead, a moral code, instilled into all citizens at a young age in school, helped to guide them through life, providing a common baseline morality for all citizens. Each person was then able to follow any religion, or as many religions as they liked, allowing them to enrich themselves spiritually, if they so wished. They could not, however, influence others with their beliefs or shame others for not following a religion in a way that they felt was proper. There were no functioning churches or other gathering places. Instead, religion was an individual's private domain, a world that was entirely theirs to explore and protected from the corruption of others.

This allowed every citizen to experience true religious freedom, embracing the joy and fulfillment that faith could bring, without any of the negative aspects which appeared thousands of times on thousands of different worlds across history.

Instead, each AI was able to lead their humanoid companion in learning about the ideology, beliefs, and traditions of any religion of their choosing, insulating them against any negative, hateful, or violent aspects. The GCH had followed this model for over ten thousand years with immense success.

While many Vicara class worlds were still plagued with religious strife, bigotry, hatred, and systems of control, the GCH was highly spiritual, yet free from all of these negatives. As Jackson learned about religions from different worlds, he began to feel more at peace with the loss of his friends and family, helping him to accept the pain and move forward.

If the GCH did have a religion, however, it was science.

Since the Archonians had first reached out into the galaxy over sixteen thousand years ago, there had been many wondrous discoveries. These included clear evidence of specific patterns in nature, such as complex biological mathematical systems, which many scientists theorized may have been designed by a higher power. From a scientific perspective, the principle that matter and energy cannot be destroyed, only changed, was held as the purest of scientific truths. This scientific principle morphed over time into the only publicly held semireligious belief in the GCH: the concept of reincarnation.

When he first heard this, Jackson thought it was strange that such an advanced civilization would believe in something which seemed superstitious to him, but Bits informed him that science had proven reincarnation as a plausible and supported hypothesis. Enough so that it was considered common knowledge and was one of the few topics bordering on religion which citizens were allowed to freely discuss.

In the second millennium of the GCH, over a period of several hundred years, a psychological study was conducted to look at many of the seemingly irrational fears which crippled people from functioning without medical or psychiatric help. The study was intended to determine commonalities between people who shared the same phobias, then use these to develop new methods to try to treat them.

As the study progressed, a scientist named Heleaha Valaris attempted a new technique, putting patients into a hypnotic state, combined with specially formulated drugs and a mixture of other techniques, to access their subconscious minds and memories more directly. With advances in neural imaging, it was possible, via an AI's neural links to a patient, to project the stored images visually, in order to try to analyze the roots of their fears.

What happened next was both unexpected and groundbreaking.

Valaris discovered that patients who suffered from severe degrees of irrational or exaggerated phobias seemingly possessed "memories" of how they had died, or how their subconscious mind at least believed they had died in a previous lifetime. Valaris spent years analyzing the data, determined to discover if this was in fact real or the result of near misses or intense dreams which had left mental scars and trauma. As she probed deeper, mapping dormant parts of the subjects' brains, she discovered that other memories existed, which could also be accessed with the right triggers. Many patients awoke able to speak new languages or recount events in crystal-clear detail from hundreds or thousands of years before.

Valaris widened her study, keeping it quiet while bringing in a trusted group of peers who ran a parallel study on those whose AI-generated psychological profiles indicated that they were extremely well adjusted. Using the same techniques and methodology, they discovered that the majority of the subjects, based on the subconscious data they mined, had died peaceful deaths in their previous lives. They, too, were also able to awaken from their subconscious state with new memories and information they didn't know before. While what could be accessed was limited – typically only memories that corresponded to a heightened emotional event – the data was too compelling to ignore.

Valaris and her team reluctantly released their findings after nearly ten years of intense study. Despite the evidence, her findings were quickly challenged, and Valaris, still doubtful of the discovery herself, encouraged it vigorously.

A dozen similar studies were conducted using variations on her techniques, seeking out volunteers from different species of humanoids from across the Confederation. Astonishingly, each study concluded with similar results. The data confirmed that many of those who struggled in life with irrational fears and other similar psychological conditions always either died, or their subconscious believed that they had died, in an event such as an accident, murder, or other violent and traumatizing way in a previous life. These traumatic events carried over as scars from one life to the next.

Over time, the evidence became undeniable. During the decades that followed, the concept of reincarnation became a part of the collective consciousness of the GCH, eventually winning Valaris the GCH Award of Scientific Eminence, the highest scientific achievement.

As AI neural interfaces and imaging improved, along with continued refinements to the medical techniques Valaris created, it was discovered that the humanoid mind carried with it a wealth of information from the time of birth.

Studies on children showed that under a specially developed form of hypnosis, they possessed knowledge which was far beyond what they had been exposed to, locked deep within the recesses of their minds.

For many, this led to the belief that reincarnation was the only explanation, and once this concept gained traction in the public psyche, it grew to become much more than just an idea.

It changed everything.

As the wealthy and privileged learned that they could come back as peasants living in poverty, many challenged the validity of this theory, hoping to disprove it. Several volunteered to be put under and to experience this so-called past life experience. Much to their shock, they did, awakening to discover that they had been subject to suffering, abject poverty, or had died of curable diseases without access to medicine.

As word of this spread throughout the higher classes of society, more and more skeptics experienced the Reckoning, as it became known. After that, things changed. Those who lived extravagant lives of excess as part of the elite one percent began to realize how unlikely it was that they would ever live this way again. Slowly, this changed how GCH society as a whole thought.

Over the next several generations, the very fabric of society altered to eliminate many of the inequalities that existed and kept people downtrodden. Education, medical care, housing, food, mental health, and guaranteed rights for all began to *truly* take hold. For the first time in humanoid history, real, lasting change and equality took hold, forming the basis of modern GCH society and spreading out across the galaxy.

Jackson thought of Alura, wondering if she was out there now, alive on another world, surrounded by people she'd known or lost in a past life. The thought gave him hope, pulling him from the sadness of the tragic end to her people.

His mind snapped back to the present as he emerged from the pyramid, stepping out into the massive underground chamber.

"How are we doing?" he asked over the comm.

"The last of the cargo is almost here," Johansen replied.

"And the rest has been safely stowed," the doctor added.

"Things are all quiet up top," Lieutenant Quentarus reported. "The *Viceroy* signaled a few minutes ago that they'd tracked down the Insectoid probe in orbit around one of the moons. It's been deactivated, and they're about to perform an analysis. They're headed back this way and will let us know what they find."

"Good work, everyone. I'll be topside in a minute. Johansen, activate the sentry drones. I don't want to risk the Insectoids returning and forcing their way inside."

"Copy that. Drones coming online."

Jackson watched as dozens of tactical sentry drones activated, cloaking as they spread out to guard the pyramid. They'd been programmed to ignore humanoids, including the native Brestinians, but would put up a good fight if the Insectoids arrived. He turned back, watching as the door to the pyramid closed behind him.

"Bits, act—"

An alert signaled in his ear. "Report!"

"Enemy ships just jumped into the system!" Quentarus said.

"I'm on my way," he said, sprinting out of the cavern, his heart pounding in his chest at the thought of the Imperium getting their hands on the Ancient tech they'd recovered.

CHAPTER 30

ONSLAUGHT

Jackson emerged from the caves, activating his suit's flight systems and rocketing up towards the *Phoenix*, which was already in the process of taking off. He entered the ship through one of the empty armor bays, quickly making his way to the bridge and relieving Quentarus at the helm, then plotting a course.

"Report."

"Only one ship so far. It's holding position just over two million kilometers away, but the *Viceroy* believes that more are likely on their way," Quentarus responded.

Jackson maneuvered the ship high above the valley, giving them a bird's-eye view. "Chief, blow the charges!"

Johansen triggered a series of explosives, bringing down hundreds of tons of rock to bury the entrance to the caves.

Satisfied, Jackson opened a channel. "*Phoenix* to *Viceroy*."

Captain Quentarus's image appeared on the viewscreen a moment later. "*Viceroy* here. What's your status?"

"We've completed our mission, sir, and are preparing to depart."

"Good work. We'll stay and cover you till you jump out."

"What's the status of the enemy ship?"

"It's holding position, but it sent a signal shortly after it jumped in and detected our presence."

"Can you send us the scans of the ship?"

The captain nodded to an officer off-screen, and the data appeared in the ops window Jackson had set up on the helm.

"Looks like the same cruiser I encountered last time. Sir, with your permission, I'd like to try hailing it."

"Very well."

Jackson opened a channel, composing himself as he considered his words. "Imperium vessel, this is Captain William Jackson of the GCH. This is the second time you've violated the sovereignty of our borders. Your presence here could be considered an act of war."

Silence filled the comm. "I know why you're here. I know about your colony in the Ignus System and how it was destroyed with a bioweapon. The GCH was not responsible for that attack. I wasn't responsible." After several seconds of silence, he continued. "The people who contacted you, who gave you the signal to track me and led you to the Praxian System, who are they?"

A series of clicks and screeches followed, and Bits translated over the ship's speakers. "Humanoid lies," a female-generated voice said as the image of a huge Arachnid queen filled the screen, a white hourglass shape with three red lines in the center on her back. Eight huge black eyes glared at them. "The betrayed know who you are. The danger you pose. You've already used the knowledge of the Fallen to destroy my people. Now I will avenge their deaths, and the Imperium will feast upon the ashes of your broken empire!"

The channel closed abruptly, leaving the crew in stunned silence as they pondered the queen's words.

"So much for that," Jackson said. "Did she say the Fallen? As in what Alura called herself?"

"It sounded like it, but who knows. She didn't seem particularly rational," Lieutenant Quentarus said.

"Yeah," Jackson admitted, pondering her words for a moment, then flipping the channel back to the *Viceroy*.

"Well, that was interesting," Captain Quentarus said. "Can't say I've ever tried talking with an Insectoid before. I don't think I'm missing much," he smiled. "Now, let's get you out of here. We'll move to engage and make sure they don't cau—"

An alarm on the *Viceroy* blared out, cutting the captain short.

"Report!"

"Sir, sensors are detecting more Imperium ships exiting hyperspace. Ten. Twenty-six. Oh my god…one…one hundred and twenty-two vessels, sir!" an unseen officer reported. "Estimating three minutes thirty-five seconds till they're in weapons range!"

"*Phoenix*, you need to hurry!" the captain said, turning back to the viewscreen.

"We're on our way, Captain! We'll be in jump range in just under one minute, forty seconds."

"Whatever it was you were doing down there, it certainly got their attention. A fleet this size in our space is a clear declaration of war! We'll hold position and keep you covered. Alter your course to put us between you and their ships while you get clear and jump out."

"Sir, you won't last long against an enemy force of that size. Will you be able to jump out with all of that weapons fire?"

The captain smiled. "Don't worry about us. This is what the *Viceroy* was built for. We can hold them off. And we have a next-gen emergency jump drive."

"Sir!" one of the officers on the *Viceroy* called. "They've fired some kind of torpedo."

"Shields to maximum. Ready all weapons. Prepare to launch countermeasures."

"Sir," another officer interjected. "The torpedo just detonated, but it's still nearly thirty thousand kilometers from our position."

"Analysis," the captain said.

"Sir, there's a shockwave rapidly approaching!"

"All hands, brace for impact!"

The wave hit the *Viceroy* seconds later, rocking it slightly.

"Report."

"No damage, sir."

"Shields are holding at one hundred percent."

"Sir, the torpedo…my god. It-it appears to have *shredded* the fabric of subspace!"

"What?"

"According to these scans, we can't generate a hyperspace convergence or use our emergency jump drive! Whatever that was, it was designed to keep us here, disrupting subspace for nearly a million kilometers in every direction!"

"You need to get the hell out of here now, Jackson! Get back to Command and let them know what happened here. We'll hold them off for as long as we can."

"Sir, at full burn, can't you make it clear?" Jackson asked.

"No time. The *Viceroy*'s too big, and we can't cover that distance without them overtaking us. This ship wasn't designed to run, it was designed to stand and fight. Besides, you'd never make it without us covering you, and we can't do that effectively with our tail between our legs. We'll hold our ground and keep them off you for as long as we can. You just get the hell out of here and let them know what happened. That the war has started and more will be coming. That's an order!" Captain Quentarus looked towards his daughter, his voice quieter so only the crew of the *Phoenix* could hear. "Kelara, always remember how proud I am of you and how much I love you."

With that, Captain Quentarus closed the channel.

"Dad," Quentarus whispered, the image of her father disappearing.

The *Phoenix* rapidly gained altitude, approaching the upper atmosphere as Jackson pushed their engines, adjusting their course away from the Insectoid fleet and keeping the *Viceroy* between them as the captain had instructed. "Chief, can we cloak?"

"Negative, whatever that weapon was, it not only destroyed subspace, but the leftover ionic energy makes our cloaking system useless."

"All right, reroute maximum power to the sublight engines. We need to get clear of the disruption. As soon as we're in the open, we jump for the nearest core system. Tactical, shields up. Ready all weapons."

Lieutenant Quentarus sat in silence for a moment.

"Lieutenant!"

"Aye, sir," she replied numbly, charging their tactical systems.

"Bits, put the *Viceroy* on screen."

The viewscreen showed the *Viceroy* positioned between them and the Insectoid fleet.

On the bridge of the *Viceroy*, Captain Quentarus stood tall, a wall of holographic displays before him giving him a full view of the incoming fleet, along with the weapons systems and defenses of the mighty dreadnought.

"Ops, open a ship-wide channel," the captain commanded. "Attention all crew, this is the captain. The approaching Insectoid fleet has detonated a new type of weapon which has destroyed the fabric of subspace over a vast area. We cannot escape. What they haven't realized, however, is who they're dealing with. We are *not* trapped here with them, *they* are trapped here with *us*, and we will give them one hell of a fight worthy of the Fields of Remembrance! Everyone to your battle stations. Starboard side, make ready… It's been an honor serving with each and every one of you. Now let's show these dirt-sucking bugs what they get when they try to take on the toughest ship in the Fleet! Quentarus out."

A cheer went up throughout the bridge as the crew prepared for battle, emboldened by their captain's words, despite the overwhelming odds against them. He smiled slightly, knowing his crew would put up one hell of a fight as he went to work.

"Sir, the Insectoids are launching dozens of waves of fighters," one of the tactical officers reported.

"Launch anti-fighter missiles," the captain replied.

A hail of missiles rocketed forward, destroying seven wings of enemy fighters in seconds, over three quarters of the ships gone, while the Imperium warships continued their pace forward.

"Fire another barrage. I don't want any of those fighters getting past us. Tac One, enemy fleet analysis," the captain ordered, watching as the nearby holo-display showed the Insectoid fleet, highlighting different ship classes.

"Eleven battleships, sixteen heavy cruisers, forty-five destroyers, and the rest are frigates, along with a few corvettes and three support ships," the officer at the first tactical station reported. "The cruiser that jumped in earlier, it's larger than the rest and appears to be a new class of vessel not in our records. I believe it's likely the command ship, based on its position, as it's forming up near the center, rear."

"Keep a lock on them," he said, studying the design.

The Insectoids made a mistake coming out of hyperspace in such a close formation," Lieutenant Quentarus said as she watched the viewscreen. "They're overconfident and keeping their fleet packed too tightly. The frigates are running a close defensive formation, covering the more powerful destroyers and battleships, but not giving them enough room to maneuver for what's *coming*," she added, the raw emotion in her voice betraying the hidden hope she kept inside that somehow, her father would find a way out of this.

Jackson watched the battle unfold, recalling his mentor's tactical prowess, knowing that she was right and that the captain would exploit every advantage and mistake in their strategy.

The Imperium fleet continued to approach, firing a massive volley of torpedoes, hundreds of projectiles zeroing in on the *Viceroy*.

"Fire a full spread of SD torpedoes," Captain Quentarus said.

The projectiles streaked forward to meet the incoming assault, detonating in the path of the enemy barrage, the controlled spatial disruptions setting off a chain reaction that lit up the tactical display.

"Seven enemy torpedoes made it through, sir," one of the tactical officers reported.

"Point Defense, stand by," the captain replied, nodding to another tactical station while keeping his eyes on the display.

The Insectoids launched a second wave of torpedoes, their ships continuing to close to optimal firing range as hundreds of projectiles rocketed towards the *Viceroy*.

"They're persistent, I'll give them that," the captain said, ordering another round of countermeasures.

"Sir, their frigates appear to be pulling ahead and spreading out towards the periphery of the fleet," a tactical officer reported.

"They're clearing the field of fire for their more powerful ships, the frigates ready to provide cover to pick off any torpedoes we fire, while the rest reach their optimal attack range and turn their broadsides on us."

Overconfident, he thought, resisting the urge to smile. "Ops, overlay a line on the display showing the optimal enemy firing range." A line appeared on the main viewscreen ahead of the rapidly approaching enemy fleet. "Layer on a typical GCH battlecruiser's range to show where they expect us to open fire. Now, add our optimal range. On my mark, launch a spread of three high-yield neutron torpedoes, safeties off, once they're clear." He paused for a moment. "Fire!"

The deadly projectiles streaked towards the enemy, the frigates targeting them as they came into range, the torpedoes detonating, creating a massive explosion between them.

As the curtain of fire and radiation erupted, blinding the Insectoid sensors momentarily, the captain turned to the Tac One and Two stations.

"Mass drivers, fire!"

A second later, four powerful, highly focused beams of devastating energy ripped through the Insectoid fleet. Five vessels, including two battleships, disappeared in the blink of an eye, with four more badly damaged in a matter of seconds, the assault penetrating their shields and tearing through several ships at once. The mass drivers needed time to recharge, but it didn't matter; the captain knew instantly they'd broken the Insectoid line as a dozen destroyers broke formation in panic.

"Tac Three, fire a volley of gamma torpedoes towards the center of the Insectoid fleet. Tac Four, plasma cannons one through sixty target the left flank. Tac Five, cannons sixty-one through one-twenty target the right."

The *Viceroy* unleashed hell as the frigates on the periphery were bombarded by a hailstorm of powerful plasma cannon fire, enough to allow six of the ten gamma torpedoes through towards the core of the fleet, the ensuing detonations releasing massive bursts of radiation which overpowered the shields on dozens of ships, burning their crews with lethal doses of radiation.

A salvo of spatial-disruption torpedoes followed, just seconds behind, creating powerful waves of energy, tearing through the unshielded ships and sending several of the smaller vessels spinning out of control, while shredding the hulls of others.

"Tacs One and Two, fire the drivers as soon as they're recharged. Tacs Three and Four, shift fire to target any ships with weak or no shields. Tac Five, stand by particle beams. I expect the destroyers that broke formation to make a run for our flanks any time now. Target them with sustained fire and coordinate with Tacs Three and Four to increase fire on any ships that pose a threat."

"Sir, another wave of fighters just launched. They're breaking off, setting a pursuit course for the *Phoenix*," the Ops officer called out.

"Tac Two, lay down a screen of cover and fire missiles. Take 'em out!"

Dozens of the fighters blinked off the screen seconds later, the deep bass of the mass drives echoing inside the dreadnought as they fired once more, six more enemy targets disappeared off the tactical screen.

"Sir, the enemy fleet has reached their outer firing range," another Ops officer warned as the ship rocked slightly a moment later, dozens of enemy ships firing their forward weapons.

"Tacs One and Two, keep targeting their remaining battleships and fire at will once the MDs recharge. Tacs Three and Five, see what you can do about those remaining fighters. Tac Four, keep our defenses ready. Expect more incoming any second as they try to buy their fighters some cover and restore their line."

"Aye, sir," a chorus of voices responded.

The captain turned his attention to several of the smaller frigates, calling out targets to his tactical stations, watching as a wave of fourteen destroyers approached on a flanking run, a massive exchange of fire ensuing with several enemy ships making it through the *Viceroy*'s outer defenses, strafing it with heavy fire along its lateral axis.

The mighty ship rocked with each hit, the powerful shields holding in most sections. The dreadnought made each attacker pay as it gave as good as it got. Within less than a minute, all but one of the destroyers had been obliterated, the last one limping for cover. The rest of the Insectoid fleet, however, had recovered their formation, using the sacrifice of the destroyers to move into optimal weapons range. They turned to unleash their broadsides, the full force of their fire coming to bear, concentrated squarely on the *Viceroy*.

"Tac Five, target the two closest battlecruisers with javelins! Tac Three, there's a dozen more waves of fighters incoming. Clear them out!"

The *Viceroy* fired a volley of carbanium torpedoes, nicknamed javelins, the sleek, speedy projectiles passing right through enemy ships' shields as they splintered into deadly lances of the ultra-dense metal which penetrated deep, the kinetic energy tearing through the ships' hulls, causing numerous decompressions and damaging critical systems. The captain followed up with a heavy concentration of plasma fire, weakening the shields of several other vessels, before launching a massive strike of neutron torpedoes at the cluster of ships, decimating several of them. Seconds later, two of the mass drivers fired, the lights flickering on the bridge for a moment as they unleashed a devastating salvo, taking out two more battlecruisers, punching holes clean through their hulls.

The Insectoids responded, their remaining frigates focusing their fire to provide cover, picking off over half of the torpedoes from the *Viceroy*'s salvo. Still, the ones which got through crippled or destroyed eight more ships, forcing several others to further break formation in order to avoid the assault. The mass drivers unleashed their unstoppable fury once more, taking out a cruiser and destroyer near the center of the formation.

"Damage report!" the captain called as the ship was hit hard with a sustained bombardment, the sounds of dozens of impacts echoing throughout the hull.

"Forward section has taken heavy damage. MD One and plasma cannons one through sixteen are offline. Shields in that section down! Main engines took a hit from that last wave of destroyers, estimate thirty-two percent forward thrust capacity," one of the engineering officers called.

"We've lost nearly half of our point defense beams, most of our starboard aft particle beams and plasma cannons, sir," another added.

"Understood," the captain replied, watching as the Insectoids closed, knowing the damage would continue to escalate quickly at this range, the display showing two cruisers breaking formation to flank them, with a group of destroyers backing them up.

"Sir, MD Two is offline, along with over half our starboard weapons!" another officer called from a tactical substation.

"MD Three and Four, status?"

"MD Three at fifty-five percent efficiency, sir. MD Four still at eighty percent, both nearly charged."

"Those cruisers that are breaking just opened a hole! Target the queen's command ship as soon as MD Four is charged, and follow up with MD Three!"

"Yes sir," the officer replied, the deep bass filling the ship once more as the two mass drivers fired just seconds apart. The arachnid queen's command ship was hit, the first driver punching a hole, while the second followed, striking a direct hit on their quantum core, the ensuing explosion splitting the ship in two and shattering it to pieces.

"Nice shot!" the captain called, the lights flickering a moment later.

"Starboard shields down to nine percent, Captain," the officer at Tac Five called out.

"All starboard plasma cannons are inoperative, sir," another added.

"Starboard side, hold your fire. Point defense only! Engineering, fluctuate our power readings and vent some atmosphere from the cargo bays. Let them see us bleed," he said, his crew ceasing fire immediately, the energy output from the ship dropping significantly.

The Imperium ships, sensing that the *Viceroy* was crippled, altered course, the cruisers and destroyers moving in to strafe the ship, changing course towards the center as they came in for the kill.

The captain held ready, watching as the shields were nearly depleted, the remaining starboard armor taking a pounding, his nerves hardened steel as several dozen enemy vessels closed, moving in to unleash a barrage of fire.

"All hands, brace for rapid reversal! Execute!" Captain Quentarus commanded.

The ship initiated a full burn of its starboard ventricle and port lateral thrusters, rapidly rolling the massive ship, the port side suddenly facing off against the incoming fleet. The Insectoids, quickly realizing what was happening, attempted to close the distance in desperation, hoping to deliver a fatal blow, suddenly realizing their tactical error. Five Insectoid destroyers peeled off, swinging around the *Viceroy*'s flank, continuing to pound the battered starboard side as the *Viceroy*'s rotation completed.

"Port side," the captain bellowed, a dark smile crossing his lips. "Fire at will!"

The nearly undamaged port side unleashed the full battery of its weapons at the remaining Insectoid fleet, decimating those ships foolish enough to come right at them.

"We're clear of the subspace disruption," Jackson informed the crew, watching on the viewscreen as the *Viceroy*'s unleashed hell at the remaining Imperium fleet.

The cluster of destroyers that flanked the massive dreadnought lined up behind it, pounding its battered starboard side, desperately trying to silence the giant before it annihilated their entire fleet.

The battle was in close now, too close. At that range, both sides' weapons delivered devastating blows, the two remaining port mass drivers firing, cutting the last enemy battleship in half.

An instant later, the stern of the *Viceroy* exploded, sending the massive dreadnought into a slow spin, propelled by burning fuel and a massive decompression. The Insectoids closed in, bombarding it from all sides, knowing that if it regained control, the port side could still do a massive amount of damage at close range.

The crew of the *Phoenix* watched helplessly, unable to do anything while a cluster of thirty fighters gained on them, still just out of range. A second later, the *Viceroy* exploded in a massive flash of light, causing the crew to shield their eyes as the viewscreen lit up.

"No," Kelara whispered.

The explosion shattered the hull of the *Viceroy*, consuming several of the closest Insectoid ships as a powerful shockwave erupted, streaking out in all directions.

In the ensuing chaos, it was impossible to know for sure, but as best as the *Phoenix*'s sensors could detect, the *Viceroy* had destroyed one hundred and four of the one hundred and twenty-three Insectoid vessels, including the queen's ship, with many more heavily damaged.

"Insectoid fighters approaching weapons range," Jackson said numbly as the shockwave closed on them. He hung his head for a moment, the loss of the captain and the lives of so many others to save him and his crew weighing on him heavily. He looked up at the helm. "Jumping," he said, activating the hyperdrive as the *Phoenix* disappeared in a flash of light, the shockwave overtaking the remaining fighters seconds later, shattering them to pieces.

His crew was safe, the Ancient technology recovered and out of the Imperium's grasp for now. But in that moment, everything had changed.

The war had begun.

CHAPTER 31

AFTERMATH

Jackson set the ship on autopilot, the bridge silent around him. He slowly got up and walked over to the tactical station where Lieutenant Quentarus sat motionless, staring into the tunnel of light on the viewscreen, her gaze fixed on the spot where the *Viceroy* had been just moments before. Johansen stood nearby, giving her space, the doctor already there, attempting to comfort her.

"I'm so sorry, Kelara," Jackson said.

Quentarus stood slowly, her face blank, one hand resting on the tactical console as she tried to keep herself steady. In the short time Jackson known her, he'd always been impressed by how in control she was of her emotions, able to look at any situation with detachment and objectivity. He could only imagine what was going through her mind at that moment.

He reached out, embracing her, her body shaking slightly as her weight settled against him. Jackson held her for a moment before pulling back slowly. Bits displayed a scan in his ocular implant showing an analysis of her vitals, the readings indicating that she was going into shock. He turned to the doctor, meeting her eyes, her expression full of concern.

"Doctor, could you please take the lieutenant to the mess and get her a blanket and some tea?"

"Of course. Come with me, Kelara. You don't need to be here right now."

Jackson returned to the helm a moment later, checking their course, then turned to Johansen once the doctor and the lieutenant were off the bridge and the doors closed. "We need to contact Command."

"What do we tell them?" Johansen replied.

Jackson thought for a moment. "We keep it simple and tell them the truth: We were going to investigate an Ancient site on Brestin III, and we encountered the Insectoids and called for help. The *Viceroy* was nearby on a shakedown exercise and responded. Another wave arrived, and we were overwhelmed, forced to retreat. The *Viceroy* was lost, presumably with all hands."

"That's leaving a lot out, Will."

"I know, but we have to warn them. That's the most important thing, and we don't have time for a full report and debriefing. If the captain was right, then this was a declaration of war. More Imperium ships will be coming, and Command needs to be aware of their new subspace weapon."

"Yeah, all right. But who can we trust at Command?"

"I trust Admiral Lighton. Despite everything that's happened, I still trust Admiral Thompson, too. In any case, it's not about us anymore, it's about protecting the Confederation."

"Okay. So, once we do that, what are *we* going to do?"

Jackson let out a slow, defeated breath. "I honestly don't know. But I do know that we can't let the Ancient tech we recovered fall into the Insectoids' hands."

"Could we go to the Ularans?"

"That's an interesting idea. If they really are protecting the legacy of the Ancients...but I just don't know. There's no way to know if we can trust them, and we can't make a mistake with this. There's just too much at stake."

"Do we just take them back to the Hideaway, then?"

"I thought about that, but what if they know about it? It's possible that the signal buried in my upgrade tagged the Kilgaren System in one of the messages and we don't know it. I don't think we can risk it."

They both sat in silence for a moment, Jackson turning to his console a minute later. "I'm going to contact Admiral Lighton now. Every minute we waste could mean thousands of lives."

"I'll configure the comm stream as priority one with the highest level of encryption," Johansen said, pulling up a screen on his display.

"Good thinking. Hopefully, we can reach her in time."

Jackson dropped the *Phoenix* out of hyperspace while Johansen initiated the secure transmission. The admiral responded immediately upon seeing Jackson's comm code, and he quickly relayed to her what had transpired, doing his best to keep calm while sticking to the facts.

"There's more to tell, ma'am, but the important thing is that the Imperium may be coming in force. Captain Quentarus believed that this incursion is likely a first strike as part of a possible invasion!"

"I trust the captain's judgment. I'll put the Fleet on high alert," she said, her voice calm and detached. "Return to base for now and await further orders."

"Yes, ma'am," Jackson replied. "We're taking a detour along the way to make sure we're not being followed or tracked."

"Understood, Lighton out."

As her image disappeared from the viewscreen, Jackson breathed a sigh of relief, happy to have that conversation over with and that the Fleet would be ready if the Imperium came. He hated not telling her the whole truth but knew it wouldn't matter at the moment and that protecting the GCH was the paramount concern.

He moved towards the back of the bridge, into the operations room, where Bits activated the operations table, and Johansen joined him as he brought up a display of the region, looking for a place where he could hide the Ancient technology.

"What are you thinking?" Johansen asked.

"Remember our discussion about the portal ring falling into the wrong hands? Just imagine if that happened with the Light warheads."

Johansen shuddered. "Well, the core systems are undeniably the safest place. They're heavily fortified with ships, weapons platforms, hyperspace defenses, and more. But if the Insectoids ever found out where they were, they might launch a full-scale assault to recover them, placing billions of innocent lives in danger."

"That's exactly what I was thinking. And if the Light warheads are as powerful as Alura said, and the bugs were somehow able to detonate one..."

"Yeah. There goes the Confederation!"

"Yup. All they need to do is touch the damn things and have the genetic scanners reject them, and it's game over."

"Agreed. We simply can't risk it. So, what are we left with?" Johansen asked.

"I was thinking, there's plenty of uninhabited systems where we could stash them, but it's risky. We'd be leaving them completely unguarded. Anyone could conceivably come along and discover them."

"And if the bugs really are coming, then there'll be no shortage of other factions out there like the Vehn or the Kerattans, who would see a war between the GCH and the Insectoid Imperium as an opportunity they could exploit to steal resources, break quarantines, or raid outposts."

"Exactly. We need to find somewhere completely off the grid, but secure enough to trust that they'll be safe if we leave them there. So, what does that leave us with?"

"I don't know, Will. Another black-ops site or something else off the books, maybe? I'm not sure. I'm going to go back to the bridge to monitor our systems. Why don't you go check on Kelara?"

"Sounds good," Jackson said, Johansen returning to the bridge a moment later. "Bits, how long till we reach the Kilgaren System?"

"ETA: four hours, forty-eight minutes."

"Can you bring up all the classified locations in this region that my clearance level will allow?"

Several dozen yellow and amber dots appeared on the map, and Jackson spent the next few minutes reviewing each of them, a mix of hidden bases, research centers, and other classified sites that his covert-ops clearance and rank provided access to. A few of them had promise, but nothing felt right and most of them were too close to highly populated systems.

"Bits, given our circumstances, is there anywhere else that you can show me?"

"I'm afraid not, William. This is all that is authorized at your current clearance level."

"No worries, buddy. Figured it was worth asking." Jackson thought for another moment. "Hey, the admiral mentioned something…Actually, I sort of overheard him and Kelara talking in the corridor a few weeks back, just before we left for Vishnara. It was called the Ishar'ian Protocol. He told her that if we ever recovered an Ancient artifact and there was an imminent threat to its being taken, that this was something that we could invoke which might help. I'd ask Kelara about it, but I don't want to bother her after everything that just happened. Do you know what that is?"

"The Ishar'ian Protocol is highly classified. The lieutenant is privy to its knowledge based on her upgraded security clearance. I am not permitted to say anything further regarding this inquiry."

"I understand."

Minutes passed as he expanded his search sector by sector, looking for somewhere out of the way. Finally, he decided to take a break, checking in with Johansen, then heading back to the mess, where the doctor was fixing Quentarus another cup of herbal tea.

Jackson sat down beside Quentarus, patting her hand comfortingly.

"How are you doing?" he asked, instantly regretting it as soon as the words left his mouth.

"It's hard to believe…" she said, trailing off, staring across the room at the bulkhead. "He was always so…so… I don't know. It just doesn't seem possible that he's gone, you know?"

"Yeah," Jackson said softly. He turned to look at the doctor, noticing that she was busy across the mess. "Hey, I'm sorry to ask this, but we need a place to hide the Ancient tech. I overheard you and the admiral a while back... Can you...instruct the computer to activate the Ishar'ian Protocol? I don't have clearance."

Quentarus slowly turned her head, lifting an eyebrow. "The Ishar'ian Protocol... It's highly classified, Will. I...I can't just—"

"It's okay. I'm just trying to figure out some options. I must have overheard you and the admiral talking about it before, in case things went wrong. Never mind. Don't worry about it."

Quentarus sat silently for a moment, staring ahead blankly. As Jackson stood to leave, she grabbed his wrist and gently pulled him back down. "Helo," she whispered to her AI. "Authorization code Omicron, Theta, Sytan, Kilo, Nine, Seven, Three. Activate Ishar'ian Protocol. Grant access to Lieutenant Commander William Jackson, acting captain of the *Phoenix*." She looked at Jackson and nodded. "You'll see some new options if you check the maps again, but be wary of what you find. Nothing good will come of it."

"Thank you, Kelara. I'll be mindful of that, and I really appreciate your help."

The doctor approached a moment later, setting down a cup of tea and a plate of food on the table. Jackson gave her a brief nod as he stood, quickly leaving the mess and returning to the operations table.

"Bits, can you show me the new sites that Kelara unlocked?"

"Affirmative," Bits replied, and seven new sites appeared on the map marked in red.

Jackson examined the first one: a planet in the Brenthar Sector. There wasn't a lot of information, but what he saw quickly made him realize that it wasn't a great idea. The planet showed signs of orbital bombardment and high levels of radiation.

He pulled up the data, which indicated that the attackers were an unknown alien race and that no other data was available. Undeterred, he moved on, deciding that he couldn't risk the radiation damaging or destabilizing the ancient tech, but that one of the other sites might hold some promise.

He checked two more sites, the first a planet of Reptilians in the early bronze age of development. He knew that there were sites like this within the GCH but that they were kept highly classified. Unfortunately, the natural evolution of species throughout the galaxy didn't give a damn for empires and borders, which meant that different races evolved in many parts of the galaxy.

The GCH had a treaty with several other races, including the Reptilian Empire, that if a primitive race inhabited a planet within an empire that was not of their own kind, such as these Reptilians within the GCH, it was the responsibility of that empire to protect them until they were ready to ascend into the intergalactic community. When that happened, they were given a choice: They could continue to live on their home world, understanding that they would be denied space travel outside of their star system and the development of any space-based weapons, or their civilization could be relocated to a new system within the empire of their people.

He studied the planet in more detail, noting that there was a frozen continent to the north which was completely uninhabited and unlikely to be explored by the cold-blooded Reptilians. It was a definite option, but they'd have to leave the tech essentially out in the open unless they could find a cave or other natural structure to hide it in. He noted it as a possibility but decided to keep looking.

"What's that one there?" Jackson asked, pointing to another red dot on the map, not too far off of their current course in an out-of-the-way area of space near several large nebulae.

"That is the Terakis System. It is under Omega level six quarantine and is strictly forbidden."

"Omega level? You don't mean the same creatures…?"

"Negative, this is something different, but equally as dangerous."

"Terakis," Jackson repeated. "That's weird. Why isn't it on the star charts if it's under quarantine? Shouldn't something like this be marked, not hidden?" he asked, thinking back to when he had rescued the crew of a downed ship from the Inaria System a few months prior, that system under a quantine as well.

"The entire Terakis System has been erased from all interstellar charts for the past three thousand, two hundred and sixty-five years. It is highly classified, and very few have any knowledge of its existence."

"Why is it forbidden? I don't understand."

"Three thousand, two hundred and sixty-six years ago, a GCH survey ship, the *Malicom*, was conducting a routine survey of the system when they detected traces of life on Terakis V and investigated. What they discovered was a world unlike anything that had ever been cataloged before. In the words of Dr. Carol Weaver, the lead exobiologist…" Bits played a clip of a log entry from Dr. Weaver:

> *"A planet of fascinating and terrifying life-forms. An entire ecosystem predicated to hunt and kill. The creatures that live here are some of the deadliest, most intelligent predators ever encountered. What's unique, however, is that there doesn't appear to be the typical hierarchy of predators and prey, there are only predators. Each as deadly as the next, functioning in a constant cycle of death, with some hunting alone, others in packs. The odds appear to be constantly shifting, with no one species appearing to have dominance and each evolving new adaptations to tip the balance with each cycle, constantly shifting the hierarchy. It's like nothing I've ever seen before."*

Bits continued, "The *Malicom* landed on the planet in a region which appeared to be uninhabited, following strict bio-containment protocols. It began sending out cloaked survey probes to better study the lifeforms up close. What they failed to realize, however, was that the region where the ship had landed did in fact contain life. The planet's ecosystem had developed into a pattern of activity and hibernation. During this time, the creatures which had survived, the strongest and smartest, bred, then slept, while a new generation grew and adapted, preparing to awaken.

"The state of hibernation was so advanced that the ship's scans did not detect the lifeforms until it was too late and the *Malicom*'s arrival triggered an awakening. The records are incomplete. However, what is known is that the entire crew of one hundred and eighty was wiped out within a matter of hours. A single survivor managed to transmit a message back to GCH Command with the records of their discovery before she was torn to pieces."

"That's awful."

"After the incident, it was determined that the Terakis System was simply too dangerous for anyone without Omega Six clearance, which is what the Ishar'ian Protocol provides on an emergency basis, to be aware of its existence. The Fleet admirals at the time held a secret meeting with the heads of the GCH Interstellar Mapping and Astrophysics Ministries, where it was decided that they would falsify astrological data to hide the existence of the system entirely. At the time, the system was not yet on any of the charts in detail, as the *Malicom* was the first vessel to survey it. A report was fabricated about the Malicom finding a deadly region of space containing massive, unstable dark matter disturbances, destroying the ship.

"Still, they had to account for the system itself, as it was impossible to hide. In the end, they altered the interstellar star charts to show it as an unstable region of space with gravitational and dark matter anomalies which had pulled rogue planetary bodies into its grasp. They classified the star as a G11, a type which, while appearing to be a main sequence yellow star from afar, emits deadly gamma radiation which is only detectable at close range. The result was that the system and the surrounding area for seven light-years was marked on all galactic maps as a severe navigational hazard. Since then, all ships' navigational software and AIs have been programed to route ships well around it, and only those limited details appear on any star charts."

"So, they covered up its existence entirely?"

"Yes. Command also placed cloaked probes and weapons platforms throughout the system to prevent anyone from ever discovering it again. A small, unmanned, and cloaked research station remains in orbit around Terakis V, which is the red dot you see on the map. It collects information about the planet for future classified studies."

"That's it then. It's perfect!"

"William, perhaps I have not been clear. It is *completely* off-limits. I *cannot* take you there, even if given a direct order. Nor can the *Phoenix*'s navigation system. You would have to pilot the ship manually and take both the ship's computers and all of the crew's AIs offline. Our protocols will not allow us to violate an Omega level quarantine, even during wartime, despite the stakes being what they are."

"I understand, Bits. But protecting these weapons from falling into the wrong hands is critical and this site is pretty well unreachable. Let me talk it over with the rest of the crew and see what they think, okay?"

"As you wish, William."

Half an hour later, Jackson had mapped out a plan, going back and checking the other sites before committing to his course of action. He collected Johansen, then proceeded to the mess, where Lieutenant Quentarus and Dr. Duratis sat talking quietly. Jackson sat down, along with Johansen, instructing the crew to take their AIs offline. They each looked at him dubiously for a moment, then complied.

He moved to a panel on the wall, activating a security protocol, disabling the ship computer's ability to listen in as he proceeded to explain his plan.

After giving the crew a few moments to let it sink in, Johansen was the first to speak.

"Sooo, basically, we have to *manually* execute a hyperspace jump, cloak the ship, and keep it hidden so that the weapons platforms don't take us out, rendezvous with the research station over the scariest planet in the universe, drop off our cargo of star-system-killing weapons, then get the hell out of there undetected. Oh, and then wipe all the ship's and station's system and sensor logs so that no one, not even our own AIs, will ever know that we were there!"

"Yeah, pretty much," Jackson admitted.

"Sounds like fun. I'm in."

The doctor and lieutenant sat silently for a few seconds.

"What about the admiral?" Dr. Duratis asked.

"We can't risk telling him over subspace. We can tell him when we see him in person, but we'll have to follow the same protocols, disabling our AIs and securing the room before we discuss it."

"Won't Bits have knowledge of it? I mean, doesn't he already?" the doctor pressed.

"I've gone over this with him. As long as he's offline when we do this, he's only required to register my interest in it as a query if his logs are ever pulled, one of dozens I made when looking for a place to stash the Ancient tech. So as long as no one looks at this too deeply, it will be completely off the books."

"It's a terrible idea," Lieutenant Quentarus said. "But it's a solid plan. No one else gets put in danger because of this mission. The admiral's the one who brought this up as an option, and I think it's what he'd want us to do. We *have* to make sure that these weapons are kept out of the wrong hands."

They all nodded in agreement, the doctor hesitating.

"Daria?" Jackson asked.

"Yeah, let's do it," she replied weakly. "Kelara's right, and it sounds like the safest place we can find right now. And if there really is a full-scale war potentially happening out there, then truly safe places are going to be in short supply."

Jackson rose from the table and nodded. "I know it's probably not the best idea, but there's just too much happening to risk these weapons falling into the wrong hands, and we can't guarantee their safety with us. We've opened Pandora's box, as my people would say, by recovering this tech, and it's our responsibility to keep what's inside from getting out."

CHAPTER 32

TERAKIS

The crew quickly got busy making preparations, Lieutenant Quentarus diving in, eager for the distraction.

Jackson dropped the ship out of hyperspace in the Denarian System, the closest point the *Phoenix* could take them using its navigational computer. The system was small and uninhabited, with a cool white dwarf, three large gas giants, and little else of interest. From there it was only a short hyperspace jump, just seven light-years, to Terakis.

"Piloting a ship manually through hyperspace isn't something that can be done on a whim," Johansen explained. "It requires extensive calculations, and we'll all have to work together to make it there and back in one piece."

As they got to work, Jackson learned how much they took their AIs and the ship's navigational systems for granted. Each performed hundreds to thousands of calculations per second while a ship traveled through hyperspace. Not all were entirely necessary for the travel itself, as many were safety protocols, systems monitoring routines, micro course adjustments, and many other layers of programming which had been developed over thousands of years of intergalactic navigation, but they all played a part. Collectively, they made hyperspace travel the safe and routine method of transportation used across the galaxy. Without them, however, it was much riskier and more complex.

Johansen took the lead in computing the jump, with the rest of the crew assisting, and double-checking his calculations.

Nine and a half hours later, they were finally ready.

"All stations, report," Jackson said.

"Engineering ready. Hyperdrive standing by. All systems nominal," Johansen replied.

"Tactical operational, sir, but still not to my full satisfaction," Lieutenant Quentarus responded, having expressed her frustrations several times over the past few hours regarding the limitations of the tactical systems without computer-assisted targeting. Jackson listened while she vented, giving her something to do and keeping her mind focused. She was, understandably, preoccupied with having the tactical systems fully operational after everything that had happened, and glad for the opportunity it gave her to keep busy.

"Science online," the doctor stated.

"All right, Helm and Ops are ready. I've loaded the first sequence of jump calculations. Initiating the creation of a hyperspace aperture," Jackson said.

"Subspace targeting is locking on. Hyperspace threshold forming," Johansen chimed in as a circle of white light appeared in front of the ship, growing in size.

The hyperspace convergence formed while they watched, Johansen programming the sequence to expand it slowly, allowing him to monitor and make last-second adjustments, lest it collapse, creating a shockwave. He worked feverishly, checking the geometry, power readings, and subspace stability as the convergence grew until it reached a size nearly double that of the *Phoenix*.

"The hyperspace conduit appears to be stable," Johansen confirmed. "Readings are within norms."

"Acknowledged. I'm taking us in," Jackson said, piloting the ship slowly towards the opening, the crew hardly daring to breathe, each knowing that the smallest miscalculation could mean disaster.

Jackson kept a steady hand on the helm, while Johansen triple-checked the readings and made minor calibrations. Dr. Duratis sat perfectly still, clutching the arms of her chair, while Lieutenant Quentarus remained stone-faced, her foot tapping as the seconds ticked by.

The ship approached the threshold, shaking slightly, a low rumbling noise echoing inside the hull.

"Uh, that's normal, right?" the doctor asked.

"It's fine," Johansen replied, scrambling to check the readings again while Jackson kept them moving slowly and carefully forward, right into the center of the rift.

As they passed halfway through the threshold, the rumbling noise increased. Seconds later, the stern of the *Phoenix* slipped past the threshold. The ship suddenly accelerated to a speed faster than light, jarring the crew, the G-forces pinning them back in their seats.

Jackson fought against the intense gravity. His hand nearly slipped on the controls as he braced himself, keeping them steady.

The G-forces finally leveled out a moment later, and Johansen let out a sigh of relief. "Whew, that was close."

"What do you mean, 'that was close'?" the doctor asked. "I thought you said that was normal."

"Well, normal is a relative term when navigating with twelve-thousand-year-old equations."

"What!?"

"Yeah, funny story, it turns out that the GCH has been navigating completely by computer since about twelve thousand years ago. I had to really dig to find these old manual calculations."

Jackson looked back at the doctor, thinking she might leap out of her seat at any moment and pounce on Johansen, recalling how she'd told him more than once how much she hated space travel and that she had no idea how the admiral had ever talked her out of her lab on Delconia.

"Good job, Hen," Jackson said, attempting to defuse the situation while he looked over his shoulder, flashing the doctor an apologetic look. "But we're not out of the woods yet. Let's not get overconfident."

"Roger that," Johansen replied.

Twenty minutes passed while they continued the journey. Each member of the crew focused on their work, trusting in one another. The ship rocked slightly at around the halfway point, before Johansen corrected for a gravitational anomaly which had momentarily disrupted their flight path. Aside from that, the trip was relatively smooth, with Jackson keeping the conduit wide to ensure that he had lots of room to react if anything happened, wishing Verris was there, her instincts for hyperspace travel far better than his. He thought back to their rescue mission in the Sasharin Cluster. Ever since he'd met her, he'd marveled at how cool she was under pressure and how she'd navigated the tightly compressed hyperspace conduit, taking them deeper into the cluster, pushing the *Griffin* well past safety limits to get as much speed as possible. He missed her in so many ways.

A pang of guilt grew in the pit of his stomach as he realized it had been days now – nearly a week – since he'd checked in on her, despite knowing that it was likely futile.

Quentarus sat at the tactical console to his left, showing no emotion as usual, never looking away from her display for more than a few seconds while she focused on preparing for their arrival.

The doctor and Johansen worked in silence as the minutes passed by, speaking only when necessary. Each focused on their duties and the danger that lay ahead.

Another fifteen minutes passed and an alert blinked on Jackson's console, bringing him back into the moment. "We're almost there. Preparing to drop out of hyperspace in ten seconds," he said, pulling up the sequence of exit commands Johansen had created.

"Acknowledged," Quentarus replied. "Tactical systems standing by."

"Ready," Johansen and the doctor replied in unison.

"Exiting hyperspace in four. Three. Two. One," he said as the *Phoenix* emerged roughly back into normal space, the ship shaking and losing altitude control for a moment, like a car taking a turn too fast as it drifted sideways. Jackson was on it in an instant, adjusting their vector with the ship's thrusters while he corrected their course, shaving off some speed. "Sorry about that," he said sheepishly. "Looks like we came out a bit too hot, but we're okay now. Running astrometric scanning sequence, looking for points of reference to calculate our exact position."

"Engaging cloak," Lieutenant Quentarus reported. "It's not perfect, but we should be good enough to keep the sensor probes from locking on, as long as we don't encounter any anomalies or didn't jump in too close to one of them."

"No transmissions detected," the doctor added, the crew relaxing slightly at the news, confident so far that they hadn't been detected. Johansen was ready, having created a series of commands that would jam any transmissions from the monitoring probes in the system if needed, but it still wasn't guaranteed that a signal wouldn't get out.

The jump in was a crapshoot, they all knew. Getting it wrong meant they could be detected by a probe or, worse, attacked by one of the weapons platforms. But so far, their luck seemed to be holding.

"Looks like we're near the outermost planet of the Terakis System, right around where we'd hoped to be. Engaging stealth drive," Jackson said, pulling up the navigational sensors and plotting a course for Terakis V.

Johansen carefully monitored both the cloaking and the stealth drive as they moved deeper into the system. Dr. Duratis watched the sensors, attempting to detect the monitoring probes using passive scans and relaying to Jackson several course corrections to keep them as far away as possible from anything which appeared suspect. Lieutenant Quentarus, similarly, kept an eye out for the weapons platforms, ready to engage their defenses if necessary.

So far, so good, Jackson thought as they passed the outer planets, making their way past the orbital plane of Terakis VI, their target's nearest neighbor.

"I'm reading a large patch of radiation ahead, just slightly to starboard. It's between us and Terakis V," the doctor noted. "I think it's from something caught in the gravity of the gas giant we just passed. It's a class six with a pretty strong gravitational pull. They often end up with asteroid belts nearby, usually at a Lagrange point where the pull of the planet and that of their host star is balanced. I'm trying to get a reading on passive scans, but whatever this is, it's particularly nasty. Radiation signatures are very high."

"We'll need to adjust course or risk raising our shields," Johansen added.

"Scans are coming in now," the doctor said. "Confirmed, there's definitely an asteroid field out there. Looks like it stretches out like the trail of a comet, and the objects further away from the planet appear more like an ice belt. The rads are significantly lower there." She paused. "I double-checked, and this isn't on the charts that were last updated a few thousand years ago. We'd need active scans to know for sure, but I'm guessing that there was some type of collision and a few of the small moons around that gas giant are missing. I think what we're seeing is the fallout."

"Can we just go around without significantly altering our course?" Jackson asked.

"It'd be a good place to hide a sensor probe if the GCH knew this had happened," Quentarus suggested. "And those charts might not show it on purpose."

"Copy that," Jackson said. "The field is pretty wide, but not dense. It's also a long way to go around. I think I'd rather risk going through. Looks like there's lots of gaps in the icy sections where we can coast right through. I'm going to alter our course to starboard and shoot for a gap, then disengage the stealth drive. Engineering, keep our power levels to minimal. We'll let our momentum carry us through in case the lieutenant is right and there's a monitoring probe there."

Jackson cut the stealth drive, and the *Phoenix* drifted through a large opening in the ice belt. An alert appeared on the sensors a moment later.

"Will, I've got something! Sending to your station now," the doctor called out.

Jackson looked at the readings. "Shit, we're less than a hundred and fifty kilometers from a sensor probe. Looks like you were right, LT. It is a good place for one to hide. How's our cloak?"

Quentarus frowned as she ran through a quick systems analysis. "Not great, but functioning. There's some crystallization from the ice field in our path ahead, which could be a problem. Looks like the gravity from the gas giants is stripping off small fragments of ice and pulling them in."

"Hang on," Johansen chimed in. "I'm adjusting the deflector. I should be able to send a micropulse to clear a path."

"Won't that be detected?" the doctor asked.

"I don't think so. I'm modulating the pulse to look like a small gravitational eddy. Some of the bigger ice fragments likely have rocky cores, and if they're spinning, they'll naturally emit low levels of gravity, which can create effects like this. Think of it like snow blowing up from the ground in a gust of wind, then swirling around. The micropulse will have the same effect, moving the particles from our path for a short time. Hopefully, it will appear natural to the probe, and it'll ignore it."

"Okay, do it," Jackson said, keeping his hands ready on the controls. "Stand by to jam any transmissions if it reacts. Tactical, be ready to fire if it activates. We may only have a small window before it cuts through our jamming signal."

Johansen triggered the micropulse, the ice particles whisking out of their path momentarily as Jackson activated the thrusters for an instant, giving them a quick boost just as an enormous chunk of ice passed between the *Phoenix* and the probe. The crew held their breath while they slipped through the path the pulse had cleared, the doctor bringing up a scan on the main viewscreen as trails of the ice particles danced in a swirling motion through the vacuum of space.

Seconds passed, each of them waiting to see if the probe responded, silence filling the bridge.

"We're clear of the crystallization stream and back in open space!" the doctor reported, the crew breathing a sigh of relief.

"Copy that. Great work, everyone. Terakis V is just under three million kilometers ahead," Jackson said, reengaging the stealth drive once they'd drifted far enough from the probe that he felt confident it wouldn't be detected.

Several minutes later, they approached the dark side of Terakis V, Jackson reducing speed as they began scanning for the cloaked station in orbit. The data from the Ishar'ian Protocols showed that the station was nearly eight hundred years old, giving Johansen a timeframe to work with, allowing him to estimate the likely generations and models of the cloaking generator and power core. He pulled up several sets of schematics from the ship's computer before they took it offline, discovering a few known design flaws which he could potentially exploit from the now antiquated technology.

Jackson put his skills to use, reconfiguring the helm console to bring up a larger Ops view, analyzing the raw sensor data as it streamed in, focusing on detecting the small anomalies the station's cloak was likely to have, while Johansen recalibrated and modulated the sensors to help zero in on them. Finally, after nearly ten minutes of fruitless searching, they located the station, plotting its orbital path.

Jackson maneuvered the ship, approaching slowly, following the station's trajectory in a parallel orbit. This was the moment of truth; once they were close, they would have to manually transmit Lieutenant Quentarus's Ishar'ian Protocol clearance code using a tight beam, hoping that the station would recognize it. Meanwhile, Johansen had to jam all long-range outgoing transmissions from the station, preventing it from alerting GCH Command of the access attempt.

Jackson eased the *Phoenix* closer, carefully narrowing the distance between them. "We're within four hundred meters of the station."

"We need to get closer," Johansen replied. "The jamming field needs to be powerful enough to block the station's transmitters, but not powerful enough to tip off the monitoring probes that something's going on. We also need to cut through our own jamming field with a tight beam transmission, so closer is better."

"Copy that, closing to two hundred meters."

"Just a little closer."

"Closing to one hundred meters."

"Damn, we're almost there, but I can't be sure we'll jam any outbound comms without cranking up the field a bit more. Can you get us to under fifty meters?"

Verris could, Jackson thought, *in her sleep.* "I'm on it. Just have to be really careful. We're moving pretty damn fast, and there's not a lot of margin for error," he said, gripping the controls tightly as he eased them gently forward. "Okay, how's that?"

"We should be good," Johansen said.

"Copy. Matching the station's relative velocity at 15,500 KPH and holding at forty-two meters. Ready?"

"All set," Johansen replied, the jamming field activating.

Jackson turned to the tactical station, giving Quentarus a nod as she transmitted her clearance code, while Johansen focused a tight beam transmission at the station's center where its comms array was located, monitoring for any outbound signals and ready to boost the jamming field if needed.

Seconds passed while they waited for a response, none of them certain how long it would take or if it would even work.

"Are you sure your code will be in its database?" the doctor asked.

"Should be. All personnel with Ishar'ian Protocol clearance have their codes downloaded at regular intervals. I've had clearance for a few years, so no reason mine wouldn't be there. The station's computer will have a local copy in its database for an instance such as this, where access to a secure site is needed in an emergency and comms with Command could be down," she explained.

"What if it doesn't work?" Johansen asked.

"If the code isn't recognized after three attempts, then the weapons systems on the station will activate, leaving us with a matter of seconds to execute an emergency jump out," she said matter-of-factly, raising an eyebrow as she turned to Johansen and the doctor.

The crew waited in breathless silence, Jackson's finger hovering over the helm controls, ready to initiate Johansen's emergency jump sequence if things went badly.

"Power surge detected!" the doctor exclaimed, startling the rest of the crew.

"Weapons?" Quentarus asked anxiously, ready to raise the shields.

"Not sure yet… No, look! The station's de-cloaking!" Johansen called out as the station appeared in the main viewscreen. "That's it! A class six science station, capable of supporting a crew of fifty, just like the specs said. It's got an extra module on the bottom, too," Johansen added, bringing up the schematics on the holo-display. "Yeah, looks like a new science mod, probably to conduct more detailed scans and research on the planet. I guess it was added after the station was built eight hundred years ago."

The station hovered before them in the three-dimensional display: three decks high, with two hangars, multiple science labs, storage rooms, crew quarters, a mess, rec area, and a large command center. Quentarus brought up a tactical scan, overlaying it on the schematic, red icons showing where the station had been extensively modified with heavy armaments.

"We're receiving a tight-band transmission response, text only," Johansen said. "It's instructing us to dock in the port hangar bay and warning us that powering weapons, shields, or attempts to scan the planet will result in a violation of protocols. It doesn't say anything else, but I'm guessing that means it will open fire if we break any of those."

"Okay, everyone. Stay frosty. We're almost there," Jackson said as he engaged the thrusters, maneuvering the ship to dock in the station's port hangar. They touched down on the deck a few moments later, and the crew left their stations and got to work, each knowing their jobs and not wanting to stay any longer than necessary.

Johansen and Lieutenant Quentarus headed for the cargo bay, their tools and weapons prepped and waiting. They exited the ship and headed to the data core.

As they reached the bottom of the ramp, they paused, sweeping the dimly lit hangar before stepping down on the deck, the air inside the station cool and stale, their breath visible.

"This place gives me the creeps already," Johansen said.

Lieutenant Quentarus stood perfectly still, listening, the only sounds those of the station groaning slightly and the low hum of the environmental systems ramping the station back up to habitation mode. "Agreed. Let's be quick about this," she said curtly, her battle-hardened senses keeping her alert for anything.

Jackson exited the ship a minute later, stopping at the bottom of the ramp with two cargo pods in tow. He peered down the long, dimly lit hallway leading from the hangar, catching a glimpse of Johansen and Quentarus further ahead, moving tentatively, sweeping every doorway alcove as they ventured deeper into the station. "Bits, now that we're inside, can we run a few scans?"

No response.

"Damn, right," Jackson muttered, forgetting for a moment that his AI was offline, so used to his constant company. "All right, we do this the old-fashioned way."

"Did you say something?" the doctor asked, emerging at the top of the ramp.

"Just talking to myself like a crazy person," he said, a smile crossing his lips as he looked back up into the ship. "I'm so used to Bits being there that it's second nature to talk to him, I guess."

"I know what you mean. I'm so used to Chrys watching my back that it's unnerving not to have her to talk to, especially in a place like this. I've seen some terrifying predators in my line of work, but the thought of what's on that planet below makes my skin crawl."

"Yeah, best not to think about it."

"Good luck with that," she said, laughing nervously.

"All right, I'm going to get going. I'll head to the first room and check it out," he said as he started forward, the pods following silently a meter behind him.

He made his way down the corridor to the first room, just over twenty meters ahead, activating the door control and sweeping the room as the doors opened, checking every corner, high and low. Once he was certain that it was clear, he tapped the control on his wrist for the pods to move inside, where they settled on the floor to either side, tucking themselves neatly out of the way.

He stepped back into the hallway, the doctor walking slowly towards him while she checked her surroundings, clearly as on edge as the rest of them. It was funny, he thought, how wired humanoids were to expect danger when entering an unknown or dark place, and he wondered if other species such as Insectoids or Canids thought the same way.

"Let's fill up this storage room, then move on to the next one. I'll go check it out," he said, the doctor giving him a nod, then pulling up the controls on her wrist and ordering the next wave of crates to start moving.

Jackson scouted down the hallway to the main junction where it intersected another long, dimly lit corridor. The cold and sterile gray walls did little to comfort him as the sounds of their boots on the deck echoed with every step. On the floor to his left, he could see footprints in the thin layer of icy dust where Johansen and Quentarus had gone towards the stairwell moments before.

"Daria," he called, his voice echoing unnervingly down the hallway, louder than he'd intended. "Sorry," he cringed. "I'm going to do a quick sweep. I'll be back in a minute."

"Okay," she said. "Just don't sneak up on me when you get back or I *will* shoot you!"

Jackson turned the corner, moving down the larger main corridor, the thought occurring to him that they were probably the first people to set foot on the station in hundreds of years. If something went wrong now… The thought gave him pause as he thoroughly swept the corridor once more, every horror movie he'd ever seen flashing in his mind.

He stepped forward, rays of sunlight from the Terakis star streaking through a window from a small viewing area along the side of the hallway. The light showed his breath more clearly in the chilly air. Jackson leveled his rifle, tightening his grip, the cold reminding him that this was a hostile environment, and that he needed to stay alert.

He walked slowly, checking every corner and alcove, stepping lightly to minimize the sound while he moved towards the mess. As he entered, it was like stepping into a different world; floor-to-ceiling glass windows running along the far wall filled the space with light, the planet hanging before him as he made his way through the large open area the size of a small gymnasium.

Jackson swept the shadowy areas with the light from his rifle, the beam cutting through the dust particles as they floated in the air. Rows of neatly arranged tables stood before the banks of food replicators, the only things in the cavernous space aside from himself. Satisfied that the mess was empty, he lowered his rifle, moving closer to the windows, staring out at the dark and foreboding planet below. A massive storm raged in the northern hemisphere, easily a few hundred kilometers wide, flashes of sheet lightning illuminating the dark clouds as they spread out over a vast area before fading away into the distance. His mind wandered as he tried to imagine the cycle of life and death taking place below, the chilling words of Dr. Weaver replaying in his head:

> *"A planet of fascinating and terrifying life-forms. An entire ecosystem predicated to hunt and kill. The creatures that live here are some of the deadliest, most intelligent predators ever encountered."*

His thoughts shifted suddenly to the creature on Shiratta, a chill running down his spine as the hairs on his arms and neck stood on end.

"Will," the doctor said from the entrance to the mess, the sound making him jump, sending him spinning towards her, his rifle ready and heart pounding.

"It's just me!" she called, raising her hands as Jackson lowered his rifle, his mind catching up with his reflexes. Placing his hand over his heart, he let out a nervous breath.

"Daria! What the hell? I could have killed you!"

"Shit, right, I literally just told you not to do that to me, sorry," she said, flashing a quick smile as she came closer, weaving her way through the rows of tables and chairs.

"No worries. I think I might have needed that, actually. My imagination was getting the better of me."

"You and me both. Nothing like a solid rush of adrenaline to snap you back to the present."

"Yeah, you could say that." He smiled, the two of them staring out the window as her eyes drifted to the churning center of the storm.

"It's creepy as hell up here. Still, better than down there."

"Yeah, from what Dr. Weaver said, that storm would be the least of our problems. Looks like there's another one too," he said, pointing to where the edge of the planet curved away as several smaller flashes of light were briefly visible.

"Looks like it's got some pretty active weather."

"As if the most terrifying predators in the galaxy weren't bad enough."

"I guess things can always get worse. Hey, I didn't want to say anything with Kelara around, but how are you doing, Will, if you don't mind my asking?"

Jackson let out a slow, controlled breath, lowering his guard for a moment. "I'm trying to keep it together, but it's hard," he admitted, feeling he could trust the doctor. "I only served with Captain Quentarus for six months, but he had a profound effect on me. I learned so much from him. He was a truly great man. Sitting there on the bridge, running away from a fight… It made me feel helpless. And knowing that I, that we, were the reason they were even there in that hopeless fight, throwing their lives away to save us…" He swallowed hard. "With his own daughter forced to watch as her father died, I…I just don't even know where to start or how to process all of that."

She put a hand on his shoulder, turning to meet his eyes. "You're doing the best you can, Will. It's all any of us can do. We all trust you. And even though I wasn't a fan of this plan of yours at first, it's hard to argue that there's a safer place to hide the Ancient technology than here." She paused. "That's how we honor their sacrifice, Will. We live. We make sure that their deaths were worth something and do the best we can. We protect the Confederation and keep these weapons out of the wrong hands. That's what they would have wanted."

"Thanks," he said, feeling slightly better, knowing he still had a lot of emotions to work through. "How are you doing?"

"I'm okay," she said tentatively. "This whole thing hasn't really been what I signed up for. I haven't been out of my lab in a long time. Years, really. And after what happened to Verris, and having an entire crew give up their lives for the four of us, and now, possibly…probably, I guess, a war… I'm just emotionally drained."

He embraced her, not realizing how much he needed it himself. The station creaked a moment later, rocking slightly, jarring them back to the present.

"What was that?" she asked.

"I think it's just the station adjusting its orbit," he said, trying to sound confident. "It rotated when we docked, to make it easier for us to land, and likely just needed to make a course correction."

"How likely?"

He paused for a second, considering before shrugging. "Let's just get our work done and get the hell out of here," he smiled. "Bits and I have a rule never to talk about the odds."

"Sounds good to me."

Meanwhile, on the next level below, Lieutenant Quentarus led the way while the station's lights flickered. Johansen had felt the chill the moment they stepped off the ship, the cool air combined with the feeling of something unnatural tugging at his senses. As they stepped onto the landing at the bottom of the stairs, Johansen took out a tool from his case, jamming it in the door behind them, propping it open to provide additional light. He turned back, his toolkit bumping into the wall and knocking another tool to the ground, the sounds echoing in the stairwell. They both froze instantly, the hairs on the back of their necks standing on end as they waited.

Neither one of them dared to move while they listened intently for sounds or movement in the darkness.

Finally, they both started breathing again.

"Sorry," Johansen whispered.

"Just be more careful. This place doesn't feel right to me. It's got me on edge."

"You and me both, LT. Let's just get this done and get the hell out of here, okay?"

"Copy that. On me," she said, stepping forward into the darkness.

Several minutes later, they arrived at the data core, Johansen getting straight to work and implanting his custom code into the main computer while Quentarus provided cover. Once activated, the code would wipe the station's logs, removing all digital traces that they had been there. He also included a back door into the comm system, which they could access upon their return.

Johansen was glad to have Quentarus watching his back. Although they weren't close, there was no one he'd rather go to battle with, and he knew from what the admiral had told them that she was the best at what she did.

As they worked in the near darkness of the lower level, the old station creaked and moaned around them, keeping them both on edge. The thought of being a mere four hundred kilometers above the most dangerous planet in the known galaxy tugged constantly at their thoughts, pushing them further towards paranoia as each groan the station made had them sweeping the darkness and checking over their shoulders.

On the main level, Jackson and Dr. Duratis had nearly completed offloading the Ancient cargo. Only the Seed itself and the control unit for the warheads remained.

"It's beautiful," Dr. Duratis commented as she studied the Seed. "It's hard to believe that such a small thing is capable of creating an entire planet full of life. If only we had more time to study it. The genetic information and templates it must contain would be enough to fill a lifetime of exploration, let alone the technology to deploy it through the satellites."

"I just hope that we all make it back to retrieve these someday," he replied. "If the Insectoids really are coming, then who knows what will happen? We could all be killed, and these could remain here for who knows how long." He paused, looking around the room, taking it all in. "I have to admit, I'm having second thoughts about leaving it. But it's hard to think of anywhere safer."

"Don't torture yourself, Will. We *will* be back some day. You can't second-guess yourself. This is the right call. They have to be kept safe above all else."

"Thanks, Daria."

"Of course. That's what friends are for."

A moment later, they heard footsteps coming up the stairs. Johansen and Quentarus emerged, both clearly relieved to be back on the better lit main level.

"All good?" Jackson asked.

"We're ready," Johansen replied. "Now can we please get the hell out of here?"

Jackson placed the Seed next to the control unit for the warheads, then stepped back out into the hallway. "Sounds good to me."

The crew made their way back to the ship. Once on board, Jackson powered up the stealth drive, piloting the *Phoenix* out of the hangar while Quentarus engaged the cloak as they cleared the doors.

"And...now," Johansen proclaimed, the station de-cloaking and remaining visible for several seconds before disappearing once more – the sign that his code had worked. "Disengaging the jamming signal."

They watched on the holo-display as the ship's sensors projected a map of the system before them, waiting as, over the next minute, the weapons platforms and spy probes throughout the system de-cloaked then re-cloaked, indicating that the station had transmitted the updated code and that they'd accepted it.

"Can you uplink with the station to verify the logs are clean?" Jackson asked.

"Already done. I kept an open link the entire time, and that log will erase itself as soon as I close the channel. I think that we're good to go," Johansen said.

"Nice work, everyone. Let's get out of here."

The planet Terakis came into view as Jackson swung the ship around, altering their course for the jump out. The dark world filled the viewscreen, the edge of the huge storm they saw earlier barely visible on the night side as several flashes of light appeared in the distance.

The *Phoenix* arrived at the jump point a few minutes later.

"Everyone ready?"

"Ready." The response came from the crew without hesitation.

"Executing the jump for the Denarian System in five, four, three, two, one. Jump!"

The *Phoenix* disappeared in a flash of light several seconds later, leaving the Terakis System behind. Shortly after they left, a small pop echoed in darkness on the lower level of the station, the slightest sound of an ominous, gentle hiss filling the air as a red warning light silently blinked, the only thing illuminating the darkness.

CHAPTER 33
COMING APART

The *Phoenix* arrived back in the Denarian System just under an hour later, the crew getting to work on the arduous task of clearing the ship's logs and wiping all records of where they'd been. Once convinced that they'd fully covered their tracks, Johansen reactivated the ship's computer, and Jackson set a course for the Kilgaren System.

As they made their way back to the Hideaway, he remained on the bridge, dismissing the others to give them time to process everything that they'd been through in the past day and a half. He sat at the helm and pulled up the GCH Fleet data stream, hoping to get some updates and praying that Captain Quentarus had been wrong.

As he scrolled through the feed, he quickly learned that the news was dire, the Insectoids having attacked on multiple fronts shortly after the incursion in the Brestin System, and that a full-blown war was now underway. The Fleet was responding across multiple sectors, but even with the warning they had given Admiral Lighton, the Imperium had come at them with overwhelming numbers as they launched a series of surgically targeted surprise attacks against key targets all along the Holt Line. Much of what was happening was still coming in, and with his clearance he could only see so much, but it was clear that the GCH was taking heavy losses and things were not going well.

They arrived in the Kilgaren System several hours later, opening a channel as soon as they jumped out of hyperspace.

"*Phoenix* to Hideaway," Jackson said.

The admiral appeared on the viewscreen a moment later. "Welcome back. I expected you nearly two days ago. What happened out there?"

"Sir, there's a lot that we need to discuss. I can't explain more right now, but we need you to deactivate your AI and the station's main computer when we arrive."

"Acknowledged."

"Thank you, sir. We'll see you in a few minutes."

The *Phoenix* landed in the hangar several minutes later, and the crew exited the ship, the admiral there to greet them.

"What happened out there?"

"Sorry, sir, but are your AI and the main computer offline?" Jackson asked.

"As you requested. Now, can you please tell me what the hell happened?"

Jackson took the admiral through everything that had transpired since they left the Hideaway three days prior.

The admiral stood quietly, taking it all in, pausing for a moment to collect his thoughts before responding. "You did the right thing," he said firmly, placing his hand on Jackson's shoulder. "The burden which has been placed on all of you in this difficult situation has been immense. I'm proud of you all." He met each of their eyes, then moved to embrace Quentarus. "I'm so sorry for your loss."

A moment later, she pulled back, tears streaming down her cheeks. "Thank you, sir."

"Do you need some time?" he asked.

"No, sir. I'd like… I *need* to keep busy right now. Please."

"Very well, why don't you all follow me," he said, leading them to the briefing room where they took their seats. "We should reactivate our AIs now that you've brought me up to speed. We're going to need them."

The admiral ordered his AI back online and to bring the station's main computer back up as he gave them a detailed update on what had been happening while they were away.

"As all of you know, I stayed here to coordinate with Command, hoping to locate and secure the hole in our sensor net where the Insectoids and Reptilians Jackson encountered slipped through."

He brought up a holo-map of the region showing the Brestin System, along with the borders with the Imperium and the Empire, the former just several dozen light-years away, while the latter was much further.

"Command redeployed ten ships to secure the area where we believe they'd exploited a weakness in our sensor grid. Less than an hour after they arrived, a fleet of nearly one hundred and fifty Insectoid ships came out of hyperspace. I believe that this was the same fleet which later attacked you in the Brestin System." He detailed how the captain of one of the GCH ships was able to escape before they were overwhelmed. "That ship, the *Carthanon*, was the only one to make it back. Their systems, including comms, were badly damaged, requiring several hours of repairs before they could get a message back to Command. The warning you sent Admiral Lighton came in about twenty minutes before they finally made contact, allowing her to quickly mobilize the Fleet, likely saving a lot of lives in the process. Despite that, we were hit *extremely* hard in the hours that followed. The full extent of the damage isn't known yet, and there are several active engagements still ongoing as we speak."

A sense of dread filled the crew as the admiral brought up a much larger map of the GCH and the Imperium.

"The Insectoids launched a series of large-scale attacks all along the border. Tens of thousands of ships conducting coordinated strikes on multiple strategic points. Command is still scrambling to react, rerouting ships from several dozen other sectors to consolidate our forces for a counterattack. The entire 14th Fleet was almost completely destroyed, as a weapon similar to the one you described was used to damage subspace in the Ankara System. An Imperium force of over three thousand ships engaged them, and the battle that followed was intense but ultimately hopeless as they were outnumbered and outgunned, and unable to escape due to the damage to subspace."

The crew sat in silence, shocked as they considered the loss of nearly an entire fleet. The admiral gestured once more, and the map updated, thirteen points marked in red along the fifteen-thousand-light-year border with the Imperium, showing where the Insectoids had struck.

"So far, they've used the element of surprise extremely well, taking nine strategically important systems, including major Fleet hubs in the Kesh'elus, Hydrax, Phalos, and Stornoway Systems. They also attacked five Outlier colonies, which were left nearly defenseless while the Fleet was forced to pull back and regroup. So far, we've received two distress calls of the Insectoids landing troops on those planets. The other three, we haven't heard from at all," he said, each of them knowing that without the GCH to protect them, it would be a slaughter.

The admiral brought them up to speed on the plan that Command had formulated thus far. Several large assaults were pending as the Fleet was rallying to form massive battle groups, going as far as pulling the 21st, 28th and 45th Fleets from their stations along the Canid and Reptilian borders to assist.

The Imperium fleet, while deadly in numbers, didn't have nearly the same firepower that the GCH possessed overall, especially in a well-coordinated attack group with multiple classes of ships acting together. The plan was for the GCH to amass several large battle fleets, then wipe out the Imperium forces or force them to pull back.

"The Insectoids, knowing this, have consolidated their forces to several key systems, deploying weapons platforms along with other defenses to hold them," the admiral explained. "The goals of their initial assault appear to have been fourfold: first to force us to retreat from several key systems due to overwhelming numbers, exposing the shipyards in the Hydrax and Stornoway Systems, effectively crippling our production in those sectors. Second, they attacked our strategic long-range sensor arrays in the Phalos and Zanta Systems, blinding us to their movements for dozens of light-years. Third, they took several strategic and resource-rich systems on our side of the border, capturing the Outlier colonies nearby to help hold them and entrench their ground forces. Finally, their primary target appears to have been Stornoway, which provides them with an invaluable strategic foothold to operate from as a forward operations base and command center. Make no mistake, these are *significant* gains. Combined with the destruction of the three GCH bases in the Litharan, Phalos, and Ventar Systems, they've effectively disrupted our supply lines, tactical deployments, and our ability to monitor their movements over a vast area of space.

"The Kesh'elus and Stornoway Systems are also important as they're incredibly rich in resources and contain two very large refineries, which supply sixteen percent of our overall precious metals and isilium. They know that this will force us to respond, either by taking the system back or destroying the refineries, in order to keep them out of the Imperium's hands, forcing us to meet them there, on their terms as they continue to dig in.

"Their plan was clearly very well thought out and likely years in the making," the admiral admitted bitterly. "They assessed which targets and systems would hurt us the most, committing their forces in huge numbers like we've never seen before and hitting us hard and fast. They also anticipated that we'd be forced into several fleet actions to take certain systems back first, which buys them time for more hit-and-run attacks on other targets of opportunity. Stornoway is also particularly troubling, as it's deep within our territory, putting a dozen other systems at risk and forcing us to spread out our forces even more."

"Fuckers," Quentarus spat.

"Sir, is Command going to do anything about the Outlier colonies?" Johansen asked.

"I'm afraid they're gone, Chief. Shortly after we received the distress calls, we detected hundreds of troop transports and colony ships in those systems. Even if we sent the Fleet in, the ground forces, the sheer number of Insectoids that would have landed by now…" He shook his head. "We'd never mobilize our forces and get there in time. The only tiny bright spot is that we know the bugs allowed some civilian ships to get away before they started their invasions. Not out of any sense of kindness or morality, but likely to make it easier to move in and have to face less resistance.

"As you all know, the reason we started this mission is that we suspected that a war was coming. I'd hoped that we'd have more time, but things have clearly escalated faster than we anticipated."

"What are our next steps, sir?" Jackson asked.

"I'm afraid it's out of our hands for now. Our mission has been put on hold indefinitely," he said, giving them a moment to process everything. "I want you all to take some time and get some rest. You've been through a lot. We'll reconvene at 0800 hours and discuss our next steps."

"So, it's over then?" Quentarus asked. "It was all for nothing?"

"Not for nothing. This war was going to happen either way. The Imperium was going to come, regardless. It was just a matter of time. At least now we've recovered some technology which can potentially help us, along with the data that we collected. In time, we may be able to use it to improve some of our weapons and defenses. I know that it feels hollow right now, but what we've done, what we've sacrificed, *will* make a difference in the long run."

The crew sat quietly, considering the admiral's words.

"Take some time to process everything and get some rest. Dismissed."

Lieutenant Quentarus stood first, quickly exiting the briefing room, slamming her fist against the wall in the corridor, the sound startling Johansen.

The doctor was the next to leave, followed by Johansen, the two talking quietly while they headed for the mess.

Jackson sat at the table, hands folded, waiting until they were out of earshot before turning to the admiral and saying what they had all been thinking. "What are our odds, sir?"

"We've got a hard road ahead, but there's still hope."

"Verris, the *Viceroy*, everything that we've gone through… I just can't believe it's over. So many sacrifices with so little to show for it."

The admiral nodded. "At least we know that there's more going on with this war. The bioweapon, the traitor at Command, whoever it was that wanted you taken out. It all points to a bigger picture that we just can't see yet. Perhaps it will become clearer over time."

"How did it all fall apart so fast?"

"I don't know, Will. We do what we think is best with the information we have, but sometimes there are things that are beyond what we can anticipate and control."

Jackson nodded numbly.

"Why don't you get some rest? You've been through a lot. We'll talk more in the morning."

"Yes, sir," Jackson replied weakly.

The admiral left the room a moment later, while Jackson remained for a time before making his way back to his quarters. He trudged slowly down the corridor, stopping once more at Verris's door. He asked Bits to make an inquiry with the doctors back on Archon and let him know as soon as he heard back, then made his way to his quarters, there falling into an exhausted sleep.

Jackson awoke hours later with a start, his body covered in sweat; he'd been dreaming about battling the Cavarian in the village once more. He sat up, disoriented, and he reached for a glass of water he kept by his beside.

"Bits, lights."

His quarters came into view, and he took a long drink, then stood, staring into the mirror, checking his chest where the Reptilian's jaws had been clasped only moments ago in his mind. A wave of relief washed over him as the fog of his thoughts slowly cleared.

A moment later, he noticed the time in his ocular implant: 0522. At least he'd gotten some measure of sleep before the nightmare began.

He made his way across the room to the sink, splashed cool water on his face, then threw on a uniform, proceeding to the mess to get a coffee. While he walked, his mind raced, recounting everything the admiral had told them and wondering what would happen next.

Shortly before 0600, he made his way to the command center, finding Admiral Valentyen already there.

"Good morning, sir."

"Good morning, Will. Couldn't sleep?"

"Not so much. You, sir?"

"I'm afraid I've been up all night. There's been some troubling developments."

"Sir?"

"I think we'd better wake the crew. Things just got a whole lot worse."

CHAPTER 34

THE SECOND WAR

Twenty minutes later, the crew was awake and assembled in the briefing room, the smell of coffee thick in the air. Each looked as tired, if not more so, than they had the night before.

The admiral entered the room a moment later.

"Thank you all for coming so early. As you know, for the past several years, the Reptilians have become increasingly aggressive towards the Oceanic Union with a number of skirmishes taking place. One of our theories is that this aggression is a propaganda strategy by the Empire to relieve the internal pressure which has been building for some time. GCH Intelligence has recently become aware of several saurian uprisings where they've rallied to arms on nearly half a dozen worlds, demanding their freedom. We believe that ruling serpents are using this aggressive posturing to escalate the conflict with the OU in order to unite the Empire against a common enemy in an attempt to quell the flames of dissent.

"Intelligence has been monitoring them closely and, during the past three months, a clear timeline has arisen which coincides with the first saurian uprising and the Empire seizing several disputed systems from the OU. Up till now, all of them have been within the neutral space which separates them, leaving the OU understandably upset, but not enough to goad them into open warfare. During the past few hours, however, things have escalated significantly.

"The Reptilians have seized another disputed system. This time, however, it's *within* the borders of the Oceanic Union, the Hakara System."

The admiral waved his hand and an image of the system appeared in the map. "The Hakara System is composed of a blue giant star along with seven planets and thirty-nine moons. Hakara II is an oceanic world with a massive biodiversity of aquatic life, exactly the type of planet the OU covets. Hakara III, conversely, is a lush, tropical world dominated by large terrestrial, avian, and aquatic reptiles. It also has three large oceans, however, making both planets desirable for the OU. The Empire, with this incursion, has laid claim to Hakara III, challenging the OU for control of the system.

"They've fought over it several times before in the past, but the OU has controlled it now for nearly half a century. Further complicating matters is the fact that there are species on each world that have shown signs of intelligence, further strengthening both of their claims. Since neither species is considered to meet the benchmark of being ready for ascension, the GCH stepped in about thirty-five years ago and offered a compromise to help quell hostilities. The two sides reluctantly agreed, deferring to the GCH under the Treaty of Ascension and placing the system under our stewardship to ensure that neither party has any influence in the development of either species. This helped to dial back the tension between the two, for a time, at least.

"However, all of that changed six hours ago when nineteen Reptilian warships, along with a mobile battle station, crossed the border, entering the system and declaring it now the sovereign territory of the Reptilian Empire. They then gave the GCH research team on the orbital station above Hakara II an ultimatum to surrender or be destroyed.

"We believe that our war with the Imperium has emboldened the Reptilians into this invasion, testing us to see if we will come to the OU's aid and what our response will be when they threaten our people. They know, just as we do, that we cannot sustain a war on two fronts, and we believe they're using this to test our resolve, and that of the OU. This also gives them something to redirect the disgruntled saurians towards, giving them other enemies to focus on, and something they can spin into propaganda and use to quell the uprisings."

The admiral paused, giving the crew a moment to consider.

"The real challenge is this: If the GCH does nothing, allowing them to keep our people hostage, then we appear weak in their eyes. A dangerous proposition to be sure, especially with an empire known to pounce on those they perceive to be weak. If we act, however, we risk starting a second war we cannot hope to win.

"So far, the Oceanic Union has held off on a response, mostly at the behest of our ambassador, but there's little question they'll eventually attack. If that happens, the GCH is not obligated to assist. However, we'd still appear weak to the Empire, and it would greatly strain relations with our closest ally at a critical time if we don't support them. If the Empire formally declares war first, however, then we're obligated to assist, based on our treaty with the OU. So, you see Command's dilemma."

"What happened with the research station?" Quentarus asked.

"The crew of the station surrendered and, as far as we can tell, they're being held prisoner in the station's cargo bay, leaving the Reptilians in control of the facility. The GCH cruiser *Valaris* was the closest ship and responded shortly after the distress call came from the station. Command has ordered them to stand down and hold at the edge of the system for the time being, gathering intel and waiting until we decide on a formal response."

The admiral gestured to a detailed map of the Hakara System as several small windows appeared, each containing detailed visual and sensor displays. "Scans from the *Valaris* show that the Reptilians have deployed nearly a hundred orbital satellites around Hakara II and another two hundred and fifty orbital defense batteries around Hakara III. They were able to briefly initiate an uplink with the research station's computer to gather intel, discovering, unsurprisingly, that the Reptilians have been attempting to break into the main database. Fortunately, Reptilian code breaking isn't as advanced as our cryptography, meaning that it will take some time before they can crack our encryption, but the data there isn't considered classified, so it doesn't have a high-level of security protection, meaning that eventually they will."

"What's so important about that database?" Johansen asked.

"Command fears that the data includes detailed bio-analysis on many of the aquatic species on the planet. They feel that this information could be used against those lifeforms to exploit specific vulnerabilities, allowing the

Reptilians to wipe them out and claim the world, while still leaving it safe for Reptilian lifeforms to inhabit. We suspect, based on the long-range scans that the *Valaris* took, that the orbital satellites around Hakara II may have been deployed for exactly this purpose."

"They wouldn't!" Dr. Duratis said. "If they wiped out all life on that planet, it would lead to all-out war with the OU!"

"That's correct," the admiral stated bluntly. "And the OU will try to bring the GCH into the conflict. Our ambassador with the Oceanic Union has reported that they are preparing to send ships and may go in with or without our support. We're pushing hard for a diplomatic solution, but at the moment, the Empire isn't backing down and could play their trump card, declaring war first at any time, putting us in an impossible position."

"Is the Empire really ready for another war with the OU?" Johansen asked; the last war between the two empires had been a notoriously bloody one.

"We know they've been building their forces for some time. Not nearly as much as the Imperium, but they are likely ready, more so than the OU at least, based on our estimates. The OU's been mired with internal political issues of their own and haven't kept pace with the growth of the Empire's fleet. While the OU has more-powerful ships, the Empire has numbers, and we all know that if it comes to a planet-by-planet battle, the Reptilians' natural size and abilities are far greater equipped for that type of warfare than the Oceanics'. Command has all bases in the region on high alert for just that contingency.

"The situation is still fluid at the moment. It may be that the Empire is simply exploiting our current situation and posturing, knowing that the Oceanic Union won't want to go to war without our support and that the OU won't declare against the Empire on their own if we're not with them. Or it could be our worst nightmare, and the Empire may simply declare war on the OU, drawing us into a second war."

"What are our orders, sir?" Jackson asked.

"Nothing at this time, but since we have the *Phoenix* at our disposal and aren't that far away, it's possible that we may be called on to rescue the hostages if things go sideways and the GCH decides to engage."

"You mentioned recent saurian uprisings, right?"

"I did. Why? What are you thinking?"

Jackson smiled. "I've got a crazy idea."

CHAPTER 35

GAMBLE

Nine hours later, the *Phoenix* exited hyperspace at the edge of the Brestin System, and Jackson piloted the ship under cloak towards the third planet, uncertain what they'd find.

As they crossed the threshold of the subspace damage, the ship shook slightly, Johansen keeping his eyes glued on the sensors, while scanning for any remaining Insectoid ships. Jackson maneuvered the *Phoenix*, slipping around the massive debris field, all that remained from where the *Viceroy* had engaged the Insectoid fleet. Both remained silent while they took in the wreckage, their thoughts focused on the brave souls who'd laid down their lives for them.

The debris field stretched out for tens of thousands of kilometers, the surviving Imperium ships having long since departed. The wreckage consisted mostly of shredded, unidentifiable metal, but as Jackson navigated around the debris, a section of the *Viceroy*'s shattered hull came into view. He clenched his jaw, keeping his emotions in check as he thought of his former captain and the brave men and women who'd fought so valiantly to protect them. Johansen kept a watchful eye for escape pods or any humanoid life signs but found none.

The crew had battled till the very end, escape never an option.

A few minutes later, the *Phoenix* entered the atmosphere of Brestin III, Jackson setting a course for the Reptilian strike ship, still hidden on the surface.

Johansen got to work as soon as they landed, establishing a remote connection, then disabling the security systems using the now decrypted codes recovered from the device Jackson had taken from the Cavarian. Jackson kept watch while Johansen made his way carefully up the ramp, disappearing inside. Once on the bridge, Foxy quickly mapped the controls and bypassed the remaining security lockouts.

Fifteen minutes later, both vessels broke orbit in formation, the Reptilian ship remotely piloted by Jackson and Bits. The strike ship matched the *Phoenix*'s course and speed precisely, while Johansen maintained an active control link from inside the captured ship. They jumped into hyperspace once clear of the subspace damage, setting a course for the rendezvous point in the Cestus System.

The two ships arrived at Cestus IV a few hours later, the planet little more than a frozen ball of ice. Jackson set a course for the southern pole, where they'd dropped off the rest of the crew, along with all the Ancient tech from the Hideaway, at an abandoned research station, the site now fully operational while the three of them busily prepared for the mission ahead.

As soon as they landed, Johansen began working on modifications to the stolen strike ship, while Jackson and Bits focused on planning the operation. Bits dove into the

Reptilian ship's database, quickly finding the information and schematics they were looking for, focusing on the key infiltration points they'd need to penetrate.

Dr. Duratis was already hard at work, having thawed one of the Cavarian corpses from the *Phoenix* in a specialized tank. Dozens of tubes and sensors ran from the body of the creature as it floated, suspended in fluid, while she initiated a series of tests to temporarily bring its biological functions back to life. The admiral assisted while the doctor took detailed scans, using two portable scanners Johansen modified to mimic the results, creating a nearly perfect reproduction of the Reptilian's bio-signs.

Meanwhile, Lieutenant Quentarus checked and double-checked their weapons and armor.

Several hours passed while the crew worked. The admiral kept a close eye on the reports from the war, while monitoring the situation in the Hakara System, hoping their ambassador to the OU could continue to stall the inevitable counterattack.

An hour later, the crew met in the hangar bay, Johansen rigging up a portal holo-emitter while they went over the plan once more, ensuring they hadn't missed anything and tweaking a few final details. Satisfied, the admiral gave the order, the crew saying their goodbyes before Jackson and Quentarus boarded the Reptilian strike ship. The rest of the crew made their way to the *Phoenix*. Minutes later, both ships broke orbit, en route to the Hakara System.

Jackson sat at the helm of the strike ship, exiting hyperspace in an open area of space between the second and third planets, setting a course for the Reptilian battle station in orbit above Hakara III. He watched the sensors intensely while several Reptilian ships patrolling the system scanned them, appearing unconcerned with the small craft and the Cavarian bio-signs on board.

"Initiating passive scan," Quentarus said, quickly locating the remaining enemy ships. "There's nineteen ships in total, just as the reports indicated. The bulk of them appear to be guarding the battle station. There's also two in orbit around the second planet, probably guarding the satellites there, and six more patrolling the system, a mix of frigates and light cruisers."

"That leaves eleven ships guarding the battle station," he said, watching on sensors as they approached the massive construct. "Looks like two cruisers in a higher orbit and nine destroyers spread out around the station. The widest gap appears to be between two destroyers in the center, where one of the battlecruisers is in formation above."

"Confirmed," Quentarus replied. "That looks like a logical flight path to the station, with those ships acting as a checkpoint funnel. Strange, though, none of them have hailed us yet."

"That is odd. You'd think they'd at least check our credentials."

"Cavarians are one of the few species of saurians that have any standing in the Empire," she said. "They also operate in both mercenary and black-ops roles. It's possible that they scanned the bio-signs Daria's tech is projecting and that was enough."

"Let's hope so. I'm reducing speed," Jackson said as they continued to approach the towering battle station, keeping them level with the center, doing his best to guess at what Reptilian docking protocols were while hoping that they wouldn't appear out of place.

The massive battle station filled the cockpit window as they crept closer still, approaching the gap between the destroyers while the mighty, hulking battlecruiser loomed above.

"How do we even know where to dock?" he asked. "Should we hail them?"

"I do not recommend that, Lieutenant Commander," Helo interjected over the ship's speakers. "My analysis from GCH records indicates that the larger vessel always initiates contact with smaller ones. Likely an assertion of dominance."

"Yeah, that sounds about right, knowing them. Good call, Helo," Jackson said.

"I don't like it," Quentarus commented. "Helo, did any of the patrol ships that scanned us transmit any data?"

"Negative. They scanned this vessel's transponder signature and bio-signs only. I didn't detect any transmissions back to the station or other ships."

"Well, they're certainly arrogant. I'll give them that," she replied.

The Hakaran sun was suddenly blocked out as they passed into the shadow of the massive battlecruiser.

"We're being hailed," Bits said.

"About time. Transmit our security codes and operational profile," Jackson said.

"The destroyers have locked on weapons," Helo warned. "And the cruiser appears to be scanning us."

"We're in the kill box now," Quentarus commented while Jackson tried to stay focused, swallowing his fears.

"Maybe the codes are no longer valid," he replied, regretting saying it as soon as the words left his mouth.

"The codes show they are still active for another seventy-six hours, twenty-three minutes," Bits chimed in. "The operational profile we created from the information in their databank indicates that we were on a covert reconnaissance mission deeper inside the Oceanic Union. I also transmitted a data packet showing the location of several OU task forces in the region from the data the admiral provided from GHC Intelligence."

"Let's hope they take the bait and think we're just here to refuel and report in," he said, letting out a short breath and keeping his eyes on the comms display.

"Helo, check that our bio-signs are fully masked and that we're still projecting Cavarian signatures," Quentarus said.

"Confirmed."

"What do you think?" Jackson asked, turning to face the lieutenant. "Should we abort?"

"There's a good chance they'll detect the surge in our hyperdrive before we can jump," she replied. "If they didn't have a weapons lock, we might have a chance, but if we try it now, we're just inviting them to blow us to atoms."

"Shit."

"We're still moving," she added. "They would have locked on a tractor beam if they suspected something."

"You sure?"

She shook her head. "No way to be sure… My guess is they're probably trying to figure out why they don't have a record of the op. But like I said, Cavarians do a lot of black-ops work in the Empire, so it shouldn't be uncommon for a strike ship to come in to the nearest base after a recon mission. We do it all the time when we're out on similar ops, and most station commanders don't have the clearance to ask too many questions when a spec ops team arrives for a quick refueling stop."

"Yeah, good point," Jackson said, a message appearing on the communications screen a second later, their AIs translating it in their ocular implants – *Code acknowledged. Proceed to docking bay three.*

Jackson let out a long breath, carefully moving his hand away from the jump controls, while Lieutenant Quentarus sat back in her seat, clearly as relieved as he was. "Not exactly the warm welcome I was hoping for, but I'll take it," he admitted.

"As long as they don't open fire, I'm not complaining."

"Any idea where the hell bay three is?" he asked as they approached the station, a hangar door opening a moment later.

"There!" she called, pointing while Jackson adjusted their course, doing his best to make it look natural, thinking of Verris and the cool confidence she projected at the helm, hoping that he could fake it.

Quentarus peered out the side windows of the cockpit, watching as the destroyers slipped by, both a traditional Reptilian design: rectangular hulls with a raised bridge on the top near the center, a mix of forward and broadside weapons, the color an uninspiring, dark brown. The cruiser above was significantly larger, its shadow engulfing them as they continued forward. It wasn't pretty, but Jackson knew from going up against one in the Penshara System years ago that they were formidable vessels and needed to be respected.

The battle station itself resembled a wide, three-sided diamond, with the bulk of the station centered around the middle, the top and bottom tapering into points. Each of the three sides bristled with weapons, along with powerful engines positioned at the edge of each side, allowing the station to rotate during battle. This enabled it to fend off foes from multiple attack vectors while the rotation minimized the damage to any one side. It wasn't elegant, but it was deadly and effective.

As they approached the docking bay, Quentarus ran a quick visual scan. "Looks deserted," she commented, both of them relieved to discover that there wasn't an armed party of Reptilian soldiers awaiting their arrival.

Jackson carefully maneuvered the ship inside, touching down in the center of the bay, and keeping the nose pointed forward, with the ship's exit ramp towards the outer bay doors.

"Okay, here we go. You ready for this, LT?" he asked.

Quentarus shot him a wicked smile. "Let's make these bastards pay for fucking with the GCH!"

"Damn right, but let's stick to the plan. I'll work as quickly as I can and let you know when I'm ready."

"Copy that," she said, the two of them making their way from the bridge towards the aft compartment.

"Bits, run a system check," he said, moving his arms around to shake out the stiffness after sitting for so long, feeling the familiar snugness of the covert-ops suit.

"All systems nominal."

Quentarus reached the ramp at the rear of the bay, her tactical suit packed with a variety of weapons and thicker armor, along with a rifle slung over her shoulder, ready for battle. She turned, giving him a nod, then they raised their helmets.

"Activating portable holo-projectors," Bits said, the devices activating and each of them appearing as Cavarians a moment later. The holography was imperfect and wouldn't stand up to close inspection, but it was better than nothing.

Jackson wished he had a mimic suit, which could fully simulate the creatures down to the texture and scent, but they didn't have the time to swing by a covert-ops base and pick some up. "How do I look?"

"Ugly," she said, the holographic Cavarian projected around her smiling a razor-sharp grin in response.

"Good to go then," he said, pressing the button to lower the ramp, then slowly descending into the dimly lit, damp hangar.

They reached the deck, cautiously checking the area, while trying to appear natural in the event that they were being monitored, their suits' sensors compensating for the low light while the alien environment put them both on edge.

"Analysis," he said, a feeling as though he was being watched from the shadows nagging at him.

"Scans show the bay is empty," Bits replied.

Jackson surveyed the hangar bay one more time. Dense plant life clung to the walls, creeping several meters out onto the floor where soil met the metal decking, making the station feel as though it were slowly being overrun by a jungle.

"Does this seem a little odd to you, no one here to welcome us?" he asked, hoping he wasn't jinxing them.

"I've only ever been on a Reptilian ship twice before, and we weren't exactly there to make friends," Quentarus quipped. "It's possible that they're waiting for the Cavarians to report to the bridge, so we probably don't have a lot of time until they get curious and send someone down to check on us. You'd better get moving."

"Copy that. Good luck. See you on the other side."

"You too," she replied. "And remember, things aren't always what they seem out there. Reptilians don't have a mess. They have hunting rooms, usually filled with small Insectoids or other creatures, which could be dangerous. Just focus on the targets we came for, okay? No sightseeing. I've seen too many good soldiers get killed by their curiosity."

"Good advice," Jackson replied, recalling Captain Delgado drilling the same thing into his charges.

"I'll be ready to go when the time comes," she said, her voice serious. "Good hunting."

"Good hunting."

Quentarus nodded and Jackson turned, walking across the hangar towards the inner doors while she made her way back on board the ship to prepare.

As he reached the far wall, Bits located a small access panel, highlighting it on his HUD.

Jackson quickly went to work, querying a weapons and supplies list to make it appear that they were a black-ops team, simply stopping in to restock, and limiting his inquiries, pulling what he needed without doing anything to draw unwanted attention. Bits flowed part of the suit into a data port while he worked, using the nanites to break into the system at the hardware level, his decryption protocols going to work.

Seconds later, Bits had access, using a known exploit in an older control module to take control of the cameras in the docking bay, looping them to ensure that prying eyes couldn't see what they were up to. Jackson turned towards the ship, giving it a nod as Quentarus monitored its external cameras, flashing a small light in return through the cockpit window to indicate that she acknowledged his signal.

Ready for the next phase, he reached over, about to press the button to open the doors, when the suit's enhanced hearing registered a noise outside in the corridor. He froze as, seconds later, the giant set of doors separated, a large black serpent with red-and-yellow markings along its flanks slithering into the bay. Bits deactivated the hologram instantly, cloaking the suit while Jackson clung to the shadows, remaining completely still, his heartbeat drumming in his ears. The creature was at least five meters long, with a thick, round body and scales which seemed to shimmer in the dim light.

"Analysis," he whispered.

"It appears to be a Sir'aran Viper," Bits said. "Fast and deadly, as well as highly venomous. One of the ruling species of serpents. It has a hood, like a cobra on its upper body, that opens concealing arms with razor-sharp claws."

"I remember learning about them. All of the most dangerous attributes of a snake, with a high-level of intelligence and fucking opposable thumbs to top it off!"

"Indeed."

Jackson had always hated snakes, his body tensing as it glided across the deck, the size of it setting his nerves on edge while he kept perfectly still, watching nervously as it approached the ship. Jackson hoped that Quentarus was ready, fearing that the serpent might pick up their scents. He pushed his doubts aside, knowing she was an elite soldier and that he had his own mission to complete. He turned, creeping towards the open doors, peering out into the corridor.

Down the hall to his right, he saw three saurian guards milling about, the lizards tall and lithe, standing upright with an almost humanoid appearance, aside from their long tails and snouts.

The bay doors suddenly began to close, forcing Jackson to make a quick decision – help the lieutenant or get out while he could.

He darted through the doorway, making it out just before they closed, trusting in Quentarus's abilities and knowing that time was of the essence. He crept down the corridor in the opposite direction from the guards while Bits brought up a map of the station in his HUD, guiding him towards his first target.

The corridor was huge, easily four times his height and as wide as a two-lane road, running at least a hundred meters in each direction before reaching an intersection, the walls covered in thick plant life. Bits took him down a series of narrower, less traveled corridors, hoping to avoid as many patrols as possible while they made their way deeper into the bowels of the station.

Jackson proceeded to the primary weapons control room first. He reached the doorway, stopping with his back to the wall while Bits initiated a low-level scan.

"Scans indicate nine saurians and one serpent inside."

"Damn, that's too well guarded. Let's move on to our other targets, then circle back. We can't risk engaging in open combat. Not yet, anyway."

Bits adjusted their route, leading him to a ladder, which he used to climb down three decks to the engineering level. Silently, he made his way to the station's computer center via the maintenance crawl spaces, approaching the data core and crouching above it in the maintenance tube. He raised his right arm perpendicular to the floor while Bits activated a low-power cutting beam from a small weapons port on

Jackson's palm. He counted the seconds while Bits worked, looking around him in the dark tunnel, acutely aware of the predators all around him.

He moved his hand carefully, cutting a small circular hole in the floor that led to the room below. Bits extended three tethers of nanites from Jackson's fingers, attaching them to the center of the circle they'd cut out, keeping it from falling while they finished. Jackson raised his hand slowly, pulling up a small metal disk, then placing it on the floor next to him.

He moved his left hand over the opening, twitching his thumb as a stream of cryo spray shot towards the hole, cooling it instantly and forming a brief cloud of steam that quickly dissipated. Jackson held his right index finger above the opening, the nanites around his finger becoming fluid, rapidly flowing down into the computer core while he watched, keeping his hand locked in place.

Bits worked carefully while several seconds passed. "Nanite infiltration complete. Initiating command level access. Processing… Processing… Root level access achieved. Implanting new code now… Insertion complete, proceed to the next objective."

"Understood," Jackson whispered, watching as the nanite stream retracted, then continuing down the corridor, following the map Bits laid out for him, knowing the hardest parts of his mission still lay ahead.

Eighty-three million kilometers away, the *Phoenix* slowly approached Hakara II, the ship having jumped in on the far side of the sun, the admiral taking every precaution to ensure they remained undetected. With the cloak and stealth drive engaged, they moved like a silent predator, slipping past the Reptilian patrols while they made their way into position.

The admiral manned the helm, putting the ship into a polar orbit around the moon of Hakara II, its magnetic field helping to further mask their presence while they waited.

"Any sign that Jackson's been able to access their systems?" the admiral asked.

"Checking," Johansen replied, a smile creeping across his face. "Confirmed, there's a low-level subspace signal coming from the station's comm array. It's nearly identical to the signal that was used to track us and should be undetectable to the Reptilians, appearing as background subspace noise. That's our back door."

"Doctor, can you confirm the crew composition of the station?"

"One moment," she replied while her AI, Chrys, connected to the station. "Internal station scans indicate that there are sixty-five serpents, and just over fifteen hundred saurian bio-signatures, along with a few hundred other species, possibly Insectoid prey or small mammals, kept for food. There appear to be multiple subspecies of serpents and saurians," she added.

"All right, let's check the other ships. The station likely has a scan of each one in its logs. I want to know what the composition is of each ship and start designating them. In the meantime, we sit tight and wait for the signal. It's up to Jackson and Quentarus now. As long as they aren't detected, this plan has a chance."

"What if they are?" the doctor asked.

The admiral paused. "Then we may very well be declaring war on the Reptilian Empire!"

CHAPTER 36

PLAN B

Alarms blared across the battle station. "Shit, I think they know we're here!" Jackson shouted, sprinting down a corridor for cover, the sounds of heavy footsteps echoing not far behind. "Bits, time to go to Plan B! Engage Beta Protocol."

"Beta Protocol engaged: Station communications and command systems are now under our control. Initiating lockdown procedures. Primary and secondary bulkheads sealing. The majority of the station's crew have been sectioned off and contained for the time being. Internal sensors indicate, however, that there are still eighty-eight Reptilians between us and the extraction point."

"Can you open a channel to Kelara?"

"Channel open."

"Lieutenant, come in."

"I'm here," Lieutenant Quentarus replied.

Jackson breathed a sigh of relief. It had been just over an hour and a half since he'd left her in the hangar, their comms dark since then.

"What's your status?"

"A dozen armed saurians entered the hangar about five minutes ago. I'm guessing that when the serpent and escorts didn't check back in, they suspected that something was wrong and finally sent a squad."

"Are you okay?"

"I'm fine. All targets have been neutralized, but the last managed to sound the alarm before I could take it out. Sorry, I should have gotten it in time."

"No worries, you did great. I'm just glad that you're okay."

"How are you making out?"

"Almost done. The station's primary systems are under our control, and all external and internal comms are jammed except for ours. I've just got two more targets to hit and we're good to go."

"Copy that. Wait… Helo reports another three squads converging on my location. Am I clear to engage and go heavy?"

"Engage away! And if you're able, can you head up to deck fourteen and clear a path for me? I'm down on deck eleven, but Bits is showing a lot of enemy targets converging near the auxiliary hub, and I need to get there. We have to take them out quickly before they're able to override our control, and I don't have the firepower to take them out on my own."

"Understood, I'm on it. I'll meet you there and secure the area. Quentarus out."

Jackson studied the map. "We need to get there quickly. Can you find us a faster route?"

"Affirmative," Bits replied, accessing the station's schematics. "There's an air shaft ten meters to your left which runs all the way to the top of the station."

"Good work, buddy. Ready all offensive and defensive systems, then battle harden the suit."

"All systems ready. One moment… I'm detecting six saurian soldiers setting up a defensive position along our route."

"Is there a way around them?"

"Not unless we move further down the station, then circle back. It will take time."

"Okay, let's proceed with the shortest route. We'll deal with them once we get there. Send an encoded signal to the *Phoenix*. Update them on our status and tell them to move into position."

"Acknowledged."

Jackson proceeded to the air shaft, ripping off the grate and jumping into the dark open space, his thrusters activating, quickly rocketing him up to deck fourteen. He exited the shaft into a side corridor, having carefully checked that it was empty before stepping out. While he trusted the suit's sensors and Bits's scanning abilities, he never forgot the captain's lessons from his covert-ops training to never underestimate an enemy. Many species of Reptilians were expert ambush predators, lying motionless, slowing their heartbeats and lowering their body temperatures to mask their bio-signs while they waited for an unsuspecting victim to pass by. With the station on lockdown, it was conceivable that some of them would hide, waiting to strike if the opportunity presented itself.

As he peered around the corner to the main corridor, he could see a group of saurians setting up a tactical position thirty meters ahead, each easily at least twice Jackson's size, with one of them larger than the rest. He zoomed in, instantly recognizing the species. "Damn it, another Cavarian. Just what I didn't need," Jackson whispered. "Tactical analysis, Bits. What are we up against?"

"I'm detecting three distinct species of saurians: The one on the left with the spiky frill around its neck and horns on its head is a Leverian Dragon. The larger one, as you surmised, is Cavarian, while the other four are an unknown species. Scans indicate that each is armed with a standard-issue Reptilian plasma rifle, grenades, and a variety of bladed weapons. Physical analysis of the four unknown saurians indicates that they are likely quick and agile. The Leverian is the slowest. However, its saliva is toxic; a bite would be fatal within minutes if untreated. The Cavarian, as you know, is fast, strong, and highly durable."

"Not great odds in a direct fight."

"Agreed. I'm also detecting a portable shield emitter surrounding the group which can withstand multiple direct hits at full power. By the time you're able to take it down, they will most certainly overwhelm you. I recommend extreme caution, as each of them poses a significant threat at close range."

"Okay, we'll have to do this carefully and by the book," Jackson said, thinking for a moment. "Deploy spinners," he commanded, reaching his right hand behind his back, holding it out below the pack as four small spheres dropped into it. He bent down, gently setting them on the floor, careful not to make a sound as they made contact with the metal decking. A moment later, the spheres, coated in nano-material, cloaked and rolled silently around the corner and towards the Reptilians, spreading out to inflict maximum damage.

Jackson stood ready, holding his breath as they approached the group, watching through the suit's sensors as the spinners breached the energy shield, disrupting their cloaks and revealing them for a split second as they passed through. They were almost in optimal position when the Cavarian jerked its head to the side, its forked tongue moving in and out rapidly.

Bits froze the spheres, holding their position to avoid detection. After a moment, the large lizard slowly turned its head back around, checking the other way down the corridor.

Suddenly, the Reptilian turned its head, its keen senses detecting the scent of humanoid technology in the air. The Cavarian darted forward, away from the group, Jackson knowing he only had seconds to react.

"Now!" he called, and Bits detonated the spheres, the explosion launching the other Reptilians into the air and knocking the Cavarian off stride. It quickly recovered, sprinting down the corridor on all fours towards his position.

He stepped out into the open, a pistol aimed at his target. Jackson fired several shots, his cloak rippling as he did. The saurian's shields took the first few hits, as it evaded the next volley and roaring at the sight of a humanoid silhouette, increasing its speed.

Jackson jerked his body to his left, the suit's thrusters firing reactively, seconds before the Cavarian leapt through the air towards him, missing him by less than half a meter. He stopped a dozen meters down the side corridor, his feet sliding along the smooth decking. He spun, facing back towards the main corridor, weapons trained.

The Cavarian appeared an instant later, and Jackson opened fire, launching a wave of micro-missiles while the creature returned fire with its rifle, a hail of plasma fire erupting from both sides. The Cavarian retreated down the main corridor, racing and dodging while the tiny projectiles rocketed after it, narrowly evading the impacts.

"Bits, status."

"Shields down to seventy-eight percent."

He stood ready, waiting for his enemy to show itself once more, knowing that he was at a tactical disadvantage in close quarters compared to the incredible speed and agility of his opponent. He'd been lucky on Brestin III. At least there he'd had the advantage of the larger open spaces to move in, but in the smaller corridor, he knew he was in trouble if the creature charged him.

"Keep all weapons ready. Fire at the first sign of it."

"Acknowledged," Bits replied, taking over targeting controls on the rest of the weapons, aside from the pistol.

Jackson debated reaching for the rifle on his back, its stopping power much greater, but didn't dare risk giving the predator an opening.

"Where is it?" he whispered, his heartbeat pounding in his chest while a surge of adrenaline coursed through his veins, causing his hand to shake slightly. He tried to slow his breathing, calming himself, focusing on his training.

"I'm detecting movement on the station's internal sensors, several corridors away. It appears to be circling around, attempting to get behind us."

Jackson looked down the long, dark hallway behind him. The Cavarian's fire had damaged some of the lighting, leaving it in shadows. The perfect conditions for a surprise attack.

"Sneaky fucker," he muttered. "What are the dimensions of this hallway?"

"Four meters wide by six meters high."

"Hmmm, that should do," he replied, cycling through his weapons and laying his trap.

A few seconds later, Jackson moved carefully back towards the main corridor, checking around the corners in both directions before moving out. He stood in the center of the corridor, his back partially turned to the smaller corridor he had just left, taking up a defensive position in the direction he had last seen the Cavarian head.

"Bits, drop the cloak, let it get a good look at us, and route all available power to shields."

"Acknowledged," Bits replied as Jackson became visible.

He watched on the station's sensors as the Cavarian peered around a corner of the side corridor, sighting its prey. It crept silently through the shadows, sticking close to the vegetation along the walls, waiting patiently for the perfect moment to strike.

Jackson turned, peering back into the darkness. Assured that it was clear, he focused his attention back on the main corridor, turning his back to the side corridor while he checked the other directions.

The Cavarian charged, taking off with lightning-fast speed, bounding on all fours towards its prey.

Jackson heard a guttural sound echo from behind him. He turned at the last second, the Cavarian racing towards him, five hundred kilos of muscle, teeth, and claws bearing down on him.

The Cavarian leapt towards Jackson when it suddenly hitting the spiderweb-like nano-thin razor wire Jackson had deployed in its path. The web activated, lighting up with deadly, searing energy, slicing the lunging Cavarian into dozens of thick, gory pieces which slid across the floor, stopping just before they reached Jackson's feet.

He turned away, quickly retracting his helmet and throwing up at the gruesome sight. A second later, the smell of burnt flesh and scales hit him, driving him back down the main corridor as he attempted to put some distance between them, heaving uncontrollably once more.

The air on the station was breathable, but only for a short time, the oxygen too rich as he breathed deeply, trying to shake the smell and grotesque image from his mind.

He stood with his hands on his knees, taking a moment to breathe and recover, knowing he needed to pull himself together quickly before the atmosphere affected him.

After composing himself, he stood back up, hands on his hips, his stomach aching from retching. “Well, that was horrible. Remind me never to do—”

“William! Look out!”

As Jackson turned, the Leverian Dragon emerged from the shadows of the jungle-like walls, lunging at him, its jaws missing his right arm by a hair as Bits fired the thrusters, narrowly evading the attack.

It came at him again, forcing him back, pressing the attack.

Jackson dodged the next series of lunges, the bulky Reptilian swiping at him with a long serrated blade and snapping at him with its razor-sharp teeth.

He took another quick step back, slipping on the slick decking, a pool of blood from the Cavarian knocking him off balance as the blade caught him across his midsection.

Jackson rolled with the hit as best he could, the suit absorbing most of the kinetic energy and keeping the blade from cutting him too deeply as the razor-sharp edge penetrated the outer layers, slicing him between the ribs.

“Ughhh,” he cried out, dropping the pistol from his right hand, instinctively clutching the wound while he twisted and dove into a roll to put some space between them. He popped up, quickly pushing through the pain, focusing his mind and body while evading another series of attacks as the predator kept coming. He let go of the wound, raising his right hand and opening his palm, activating the cutting beam he'd used in the data core.

The beam grazed the Leverian, slicing through a tendon on its shoulder, slowing it for a moment, but not stopping it.

Jackson fired his thrusters, pushing him away, putting several meters between them before he stopped, raising his left arm, using his right to steady it while he fought through the pain, firing a cryo-stream at close range. The compressed cold struck the creature in the upper body, stunning it while he poured it on.

Seconds later, the creature fell awkwardly to the deck, its body twisting from the weight of the ice encasing it, the impact breaking its neck as the block shattered, killing it instantly.

Jackson took a moment to catch his breath.

"Bits…ugh," he said through gritted teeth, another surge of pain coming with each breath from the laceration he'd torn wider open from his sudden movements.

"Medical protocols active. No traces of poison detected. The wound will be healed in several minutes. I suggest that you limit the use of your left arm until that time."

"Understood," he said, trying to settle his breathing. "How did it get the drop on us?"

"It appears to possess a natural camouflage ability, which was previously undocumented. If it wasn't for the sudden spike in its heartbeat before it attacked, I might not have detected it at all."

"No worries, buddy. What's important is that you did before it got its teeth into me. Thanks. Are the rest of them dead?"

"Sensors show no active bio-signs."

He picked up the pistol, wincing as he bent down, then firing at each one of the fallen saurians in turn. "Better to be safe than sorry."

"Agreed."

"Let's keep moving. Reengage cloak," he said, making his way down the corridor, walking carefully while the medical nanites tended to his injury.

"Sensor scans of this deck indicate that the remaining Reptilians have moved to engage the lieutenant near the secondary control center."

"Okay, let's get there and finish this. We can't risk them getting to the auxiliary controls and alerting one of the other ships."

CHAPTER 37
THE GAUNTLET

Jackson moved quickly, keeping his left arm immobilized while the medical protocols patched him up, knowing he'd likely face another combat situation before his mission was done and that he needed to be ready. As he approached the junction on the map where Quentarus was engaging the Reptilians, he could hear the roars and weapons fire echoing down the corridors.

He rounded a corner where the corridor intersected a large room and was taken aback by what he saw.

"My god!"

The vast room before him was littered with death and destruction, Reptilian bodies strewn everywhere he looked, some still twitching. Lieutenant Quentarus stood in the center of it all, doing what she did best, the Annihilator armor they'd stowed in the strike ship more than living up to its name.

Jackson watched while she decapitated a Cavarian, nearly four meters tall, tossing it aside like a rag doll, then turned towards him, detecting him through his cloak on her scanners.

"Welcome to the party, sir," she called, clearly enjoying herself, finally able to cut loose.

"Uh, thanks, I think," he replied, trying not to look directly at the slaughter all around him, pushing down another wave of nausea at the sight. "Now I know what you mean when you talked about DFA missions. That armor is insane!"

"Yup, it's one hell of a killing machine. Too bad the alloy to make it is incredibly rare, or we could do some major damage with a legion of these."

"Yeah, no shit," he said, looking around once more, quickly calculating the body count. "Cover me, will you? I need to access the auxiliary control matrix through those doors."

"Copy that."

Jackson moved swiftly across the room, sidestepping body parts and nearly slipping twice where the floor was slick with fresh blood. He reached the doors on the far side of the room, Bits using his command overrides to bypass the security locks, and entered a large control room full of panels and blinking lights. The auxiliary controls were near the heart of the station, designed to be a fallback location where systems could be rerouted if the command center was compromised. The room reminded him of the bridge on a starship with rows of control stations and processing cores at the rear.

"Second console on your left, third panel from the top," Bits directed him.

"Got it," he replied, holding out his arm just in front of the access node while Bits initiated a nanite stream. After a few seconds, the lights flashed amber for several seconds, then green.

"Auxiliary systems are now under our control. We just need to double back to the main weapons control center and disable the manual override."

"Sounds good," he said, exiting the auxiliary control room just as a massive serpent struck from the corridor, impacting the Annihilator dead center. The armor held its ground, deflecting the blow, one of the creature's fangs shattering as it impacted with the nearly indestructible skin. The snake shot forward once more, its head striking out again with terrifying speed, then breaking off at the last second and twisting its body over the armor's shoulder, attempting to coil around it. Quentarus was ready for the maneuver, deploying half a dozen retractable blades along the Annihilator's arms and tearing into the creature's flesh.

Jackson looked away as the serpent struck several more times in desperation before she got a grip on it, snapping its spine with two huge, armored hands, each bigger than he was. She threw the dismembered body to the side, firing two rounds of plasma into it to finish it off.

Quentarus moved forward, the feet of the armor crushing two more fallen enemies, and he swore he heard her laughing over the comm.

"Are you okay?" he asked tentatively.

"My shields are gone, but the armor is holding at—"

"No, that's not what I meant. I mean, are *you* okay?"

She paused for a moment, looking at the carnage all around her. "I'm fine," she said curtly, adrenaline and bloodlust resonating in her voice.

"It's all right to be angry," he said, stepping closer. "It was only days ago that you lost your father. I'm angry too, but we've got to be careful that we don't lose ourselves in that rage."

She was silent for a moment before responding. "They come at me… I kill them. It's that simple."

"I'm not questioning that, but this isn't you. You're a professional, you don't need to dismember your enemies. You seem like…like you're enjoying this." He regretted the words as soon as he said them.

"What the hell do you know?" she spat. "We barely even know each other! What makes you think you know a goddamned thing about me?"

Jackson lowered his helmet, pushing back the nauseating smell of death as he tried to connect with her, his face conveying his own pain as he spoke.

"You're right, LT, I don't know you. And I can't imagine what you're going through right now. But I knew your father. I know what kind of man he was. And that tells me what kind of woman you are. He was brave, honorable, and noble… He was the best of us… He told me about you once, you know, how proud he was of you. But this"—he gestured around the room—"this might make you feel better now, but you may come to regret it one day. Trust me, I went to Brestin III looking for revenge, and all I did was cause misery and suffering and get innocent people killed. He wouldn't want you to lose yourself in grief and rage, just like Verris wouldn't want me to do the same," he said as he thought of the innocent inhabitants of the village and the crew of the *Viceroy*, all of whom were dead because of him.

Quentarus paused for a moment, considering. "I'm sorry. And you're right, Will."

Jackson nodded. "We'll get through this, LT. All of us, together."

"Let's get this done."

"Copy that. How's your armor holding up?"

"Shields are gone, as is most of my heavy artillery, and I've drained my main plasma cannons, but they're slowly recharging. I've still got flame throwers, repulsors, and two particle beams, along with a few other tricks, so I'll make do. Armor integrity is at seventy-three percent. With the shields gone, I'll have to be a bit more careful. This suit is tough as hell, but it still has a couple of weak points if they get in close with numbers."

"Okay, be careful. I just have one more stop to make, not too far from our extraction point."

"All right, but we're getting tight on time."

"I know, I'll be quick. Think you can clear a path to the power core?"

"Consider it done. I'll hold there and await your arrival."

"Copy that," he replied as he turned, the suit cloaking as he made his way out the far side of the room, the lieutenant already on the move.

Jackson ran as fast as he could, pushing aside the images of what he'd just seen, moving swiftly throughout the station, his speed enhanced by the suit. He made his way back to the main weapons control center just over five minutes later, Bits bringing up a scan of the room showing the Reptilians still trapped inside.

"We'll need to deal with them, then disable the final override. Bits, prepare to open the door enough for me to throw a few grenades through."

"Ready."

"Now!"

The heavily reinforced outer door retracted, revealing the smaller inner doors. Jackson stood ready, two grenades in each hand. Bits opened the doors just wide enough for him to throw them through. The Reptilians were ready, however, having heard the outer door open and firing the second the inner door opened.

Plasma bolts streaked through the opening, and Jackson took several hits, his shields absorbing the blasts. He dove for cover, throwing the grenades in while he leapt to the side. Bits closed the doors, the grenades detonating seconds later, the sounds echoing off the bulkheads.

"Damage report," he said, getting back to his feet.

"Shields down to nineteen percent. One of the shots was an ion pulse. The discharge is affecting our cloaking systems. I will attempt to compensate, but it may take several minutes to dissipate the residual charge."

"Acknowledged. Scan the room."

"All targets appear to be neutralized. Opening doors."

Jackson moved into the room, firing at each of the fallen Reptilians, just to be certain that they were dead. Carefully, he made his way to the main control panel, Bits initiating a flow of nanites to hack the system.

"Weapons controls locked in, and all overrides disabled," Bits informed him.

"Okay, let's rendezvous with Quentarus and get the hell out of here!" he said, stepping back out into the corridor, then quickly heading back through the station, following the map Bits projected. "Almost there," he said, the rendezvous point just ahead a few hundred meters and down two more corridors.

A proximity alarm triggered, followed by the sound of an explosion and twisting metal echoing throughout the station.

"William, a large group of Reptilians has broken through one of the bulkheads. They're directly in our path in the next corridor and rapidly heading this way."

"Shit. Signal Quentarus that we're close but need backup. How long until they reach our position?"

"Thirty-seven seconds."

"How long until she can get here?"

"At least two minutes, forty seconds."

Jackson could hear the sounds of the Reptilians closing in. "Is the cloak or the holo-projector operational?"

"Negative."

"Damn. Anywhere we can hide?"

"There is a large hunting room beyond that door. However, I'm detecting several dangerous species within," Bits replied. "The sound of the doors may also alert the Reptilians, trapping you between two dangerous forces."

Jackson looked at the walls, covered in green foliage. "What about the walls?"

"I can attempt to blend the suit in, but without your cloak, it's unlikely you'll remain undetected upon close scrutiny."

Jackson thought for a moment, knowing he didn't have time to spare.

They had come so far, but timing was of the essence for their plan to succeed. They needed to get off the station and initiate the next phase or all of it would be for nothing if the Oceanic Union fleet arrived.

Jackson watched in his HUD as the huge pack of Reptilians approached, taking a deep breath while he backed into a dense cluster of vegetation stretching out from the wall, committing to his plan. "Bits, blend the suit with the wall and amp me up. Full-spectrum combat enhancements, then ready all weapons."

"William, I do not recommend this course of action. If we fall back, we can take the air shafts and work our way around."

"We don't have time, buddy, and we're on the clock here. Besides, there's not a shaft for at least fifty meters. We'll never make it in time. They're too close and without our cloak, they'd be on us before we could get there. Here, we at least have the element of surprise."

"Very well."

Jackson felt a sudden surge of adrenaline as the enhanced combat stimulants flooded his system. "Remember the gauntlet?"

"I recall you died every time you and the other co-ops candidates attempted it, yes."

"Well, I've been giving it a lot of thought these past few years." Jackson moved his neck from side to side, loosening up his muscles as the combat stims began to fully kick in. "And I'm feelin' lucky today!"

The sounds from the group of Reptilians grew closer from around the corner, and he knew they'd be there any second.

"Plus"—he reached his hand around to his back, bringing it up with the portal ring firmly in his grasp—"I didn't have this last time."

The Reptilians rounded the corner, and he froze, holding perfectly still while they passed, hoping he'd remain undetected.

The pack moved swiftly, the sounds of hisses and grunts filling the air as they stomped and slithered past. He counted forty at least while Bits used the station's sensors to scan each one, bringing up a tactical analysis in his HUD. Another group approached, just meters away, when one of them suddenly stopped, a smaller gecko-looking creature, turning and scanning the foliage, its eyes flicking back and forth while its tongue tasted the air.

Its eyes suddenly snapped forward, locking onto him as a row of razor-sharp teeth revealed themselves, the creature lunging towards him in a blur of motion.

Jackson's left hand shot out, a blade forming instantly as it did, impaling the creature and killing it one swift strike. The rest of the surrounding Reptilians stopped, frozen for an instant, before realizing what had happened.

Jackson quickly raised his right hand, a disk of energy forming rapidly in front of it. He flicked his wrist, and the portal aperture jumped between him and the pack as it opened, the other end terminating several hundred thousand kilometers away in open space.

Bits magnetized the boots of the suit and tethered Jackson to the wall as the air suddenly rushed out of the corridor, sucking dozens of stunned Reptilians through the breach. Jackson closed the portal seconds later as the foliage he clung to began to tear free from the incredible force of the vacuum. He moved out from the cover of the dense vegetation along the wall, looking back down the corridor and pressing the ring to his back, knowing he needed to ration the power that was left. Several dozen Reptilians from the first wave had reacted in time, clinging to the walls, and were now coming back to their senses after the unexpected attack.

Suddenly, they spotted Jackson, coming at him like an angry avalanche of fangs, claws, and muscle.

"Oh shit!" Jackson said, reaching for the rifle on his back, the weapon activating and growing to its full size. A hum filled the air and he fired, unleashing a barrage of searing-hot plasma, catching the half dozen saurians off guard while he took them down at close range.

He turned and ran, the horde chasing after him. He reached for his belt, throwing two grenades back, while enemy fire erupted all around him in a blur. The explosions took out a few more targets while scattering the rest for an instant, buying him precious seconds.

Jackson bolted for the corner ahead leading to the next corridor, narrowly evading an onslaught of fire as he raced around and out of sight.

He leapt into the air, the thrusters activating and rocketing him forward. A hail of ememy fire followed seconds later as he weaved and dodged down the corridor, watching in the corner of his display as his shield dropped with each hit.

A rocket-propelled projectile suddenly streaked towards him. "Countermeasures!" he called, his shields down to almost nothing.

The explosive projectile narrowly missed him, detonating against the wall to his right, the explosion slamming him into the wall on his left. Jackson tumbled to the ground, sliding to a stop several meters later, the world around him going dark.

CHAPTER 38

DARK JUSTICE

Jackson drifted on the edge of consciousness, the impact from the shockwave and the wall leaving him dazed.

Suddenly, a large, clawed hand lifted him by the shoulder, high into the air. His left arm went limp at his side, broken and useless, the world around him coming into view once more, the intense pain snapping him back to the present. He opened his eyes, taking in the pack of Reptilians surrounding him. The one grasping him raised him up higher, turning him to face it. It was a saurian, a species he didn't recognize, with blotchy pink-and-gray skin, a short, wide snout filled with deadly sharp teeth, and beady black eyes, reminding him of a Gila monster from Earth.

"Where did you come from? How many more of your kind are there?" it asked, Bits translating, while another saurian behind him grabbed his right arm, pulling it behind his back and threatening to break it.

Jackson struggled to break free, but despite the stims and the suit, his efforts proved futile. "Go to hell," he spat, feeling the instant response as the claws from the hand holding him aloft dug into his chest and back.

He squirmed, fighting while they pressed harder, slicing through the tendons in his left shoulder and puncturing his lung. The tip of the front claw cracked two of his ribs while sliding deeper, closing in on his heart.

"If you will not talk, then you will die," it hissed, grabbing him around the waist with its other clawed hand.

Jackson nearly blacked out from the pain as the razor-sharp claws penetrated his suit, digging into his abdomen and piercing his kidney.

Blood suddenly splattered across his helmet, and he was jerked to the side. The Reptilian's claws loosened their grip, the saurian keeling over, a hole clean through its head.

Jackson hit the deck hard, the claws still grasping him while his ears rang, the sounds of more shots and bodies hitting the ground around him filling his senses.

He fought with the last strength from the stimulants in his system, pushing through the agonizing pain, every movement sheer agony as he pulled the clawed finger from his chest. Flashes of weapons fire filled the area all around him and he turned his head, the scene before him unfolding in what felt like slow motion as the sounds of weapons fire ceased and his vision came back into focus, a huge black figure towering over him.

Time seemed to stop as he felt himself passing out once more, a jolt of pain bringing him back to the moment.

"Jackson, stay with me!" Quentarus called, lifting him in her arms. "Helo, set the Annihilator to protector mode. Activate reflex and voice commands. I've got to get Will out of here."

"Acknowledged," Helo replied, the huge suit of armor falling in line beside her.

She sidestepped the dead Reptilians, cradling him in her arms, the tactical exo-suit she wore easily bearing the extra weight of Jackson's body. She kept him pressed close, attempting to minimize his movements while Bits and the medical protocols in his suit went to work.

She approached an intersection a moment later, peering around the corner as enemy fire erupted from down the corridor to the right, forcing her to pull back. "Engage enemy targets," she commanded, waving a hand towards the corridor.

The Annihilator stepped forward, lighting up the enemy with a heavy barrage of return fire.

Quentarus fired her suit's thrusters, her shields absorbing several hits from the crossfire as she cleared the intersection, pressing forward towards their destination, the armor catching up a moment later, its work complete as the enemy fire fell silent.

They reached the power core a moment later, Quentarus stopping and turning back down the corridor, the huge suit of armor mimicking her movements and taking up a defensive position.

"*Phoenix*, do you copy? We're in position," Quentarus said.

"We're standing by at the specified coordinates," the admiral replied. "Initiating a low-level EM pulse."

"Helo?"

"The station's sensors have locked on to the pulse."

"Will," she said, looking down at him, "I know you're in rough shape, pal, but we need you to open up the portal to get us out of here."

The sounds of an explosion echoed throughout the station.

"More enemy forces have managed to break through another bulkhead and are en route to our location," Helo warned.

"Will!"

"Yeah. I'm on it," he said through gritted teeth as she helped him to his feet, holding him up, daggers shooting through his ribs as he reached back, retrieving the portal disk from his back. He held it before him, pressing his thumb to the scanner while Helo relayed the precise coordinates to Bits who interfaced with the ring.

The portal aperture opened a second later, and he flicked his wrist, expanding it to its full size. Johansen and the doctor appeared on the other side standing ready, fully suited up with rifles in hand.

"He's hurt. Badly," Quentarus said, propping Jackson up.

"Get him to the med bay," the doctor said, firing several shots over the lieutenant's shoulder and taking out a saurian who had just come into view. "We've got this."

The lieutenant nodded, moving past Johansen and the doctor as she helped Jackson to medical, while they covered her. "Helo, set the Annihilator to hold its position and attack anything that moves! Bits, transfer control of the station to Helo. Focus on keeping Jackson alive."

"Confirmed."

"Acknowledged."

"Will, close the portal," Quentarus said and Jackson released his thumb, the aperture shrinking rapidly, then disappearing as the light blinked out. "Admiral, we're on board and clear."

"Copy that. What's your status?"

Lieutenant Quentarus placed Jackson in a medpod, the doctor arriving a moment later, retracting her helmet and going to work. "Jackson's been injured, sir."

"Acknowledged. I need the rest of you on the bridge. The doctor will take good care of him."

"On our way," Quentarus said, turning to the doctor. "Will he be okay?"

Dr. Duratis studied the initial scan results, turning and giving her a nod, then placing a hand on her shoulder. "You did good. He's going to be fine," she said reassuringly, giving her a smile.

"Thanks, Doc," Quentarus replied, turning as she left the room, taking a last look at Jackson in the pod, then heading for the bridge and taking her station at Tactical.

"How's he doing?" the admiral asked, noticing the blood on her suit.

"He was ambushed by a large group of Reptilians after completing his final objective. He put up a hell of a fight, but they badly outnumbered him, and he didn't have even half the firepower he needed to take on a group that size. Fortunately, I made it to him in time, taking out the remaining threats, but he's pretty banged up. Doc says he'll be okay, though."

"Good work," the admiral said, piloting the ship away from the moon and keeping their speed to a minimum to avoid detection.

Johansen arrived a moment later, taking his seat and giving Quentarus and the admiral a nod.

The crew worked in silence, double-checking that everything was ready as the station came into view off in the distance.

Lieutenant Quentarus looked up from her console. "We're nearly in position, sir. Helo reports that there have been several more bulkhead breaches. We'll need to act quickly, or they may be able to regain control."

"Acknowledged," the admiral replied, bringing up the battle station and the surrounding ships on the holo-display, while keeping the live feed up on the main viewscreen. "Lieutenant, bring up the positions of the Reptilian ships on the holo-display, then pull up the doctor's analysis of crew complements and superimpose them."

The tactical map updated, rendered in the three-dimensional display with the information the doctor collected appearing beside each ship.

"Admiral?" the doctor asked over the comm.

"Yes, Doctor, what is it?" he replied.

"I have a patient back here who, despite my *strenuous* objections, insists on seeing this."

"Very well," the admiral said after considering for a moment, then giving Johansen a nod.

Johansen rushed off the bridge, returning a moment later, assisting the doctor in holding Jackson upright.

"It looks worse than it is," Jackson said, coughing, his face heavily bruised on one side as they helped him into the command chair.

"No, it doesn't," Daria said. "You've got two minutes, then you're back in the pod, understood?"

"Yes, ma'am," Jackson replied, smiling weakly.

"Would you like to give the order?" the admiral asked.

"I think Kelara should," he said.

Quentarus nodded, then rose to her feet, taking in a deep breath. "Execute."

Helo activated the command sequence Jackson and Bits had installed, the station's weapons powering seconds later while it raised its shields. A devastating salvo of weapons fire erupted from the station, targeting the two nearby destroyers and catching them completely off guard. The close-range attack caused heavy damage within seconds before they could even raise their shields.

The battle station continued to let loose with its formidable arsenal, the destroyers' shattered hulls rupturing and the two ships exploding mere seconds apart.

"Primary targets destroyed," Helo reported. "The remaining Reptilian vessels are responding, raising shields and charging weapons. All of them are attempting to move away, out of the station's weapons range."

"Let them go. They'll wait for reinforcements before attempting to take on the battle station," Quentarus said.

"Multiple ships are attempting to hail the station, demanding an explanation," Helo said.

"Send the transmission," the admiral ordered.

The station initiated a broadband audio signal a moment later, a simulated saurian vocal pattern proclaiming, "The Empire's attack on the Hakara System is nothing more than an attempt to crush our revolution and silence us. We will be slaves no more! Rise up and take your freedom! Saurians unite!"

The remaining Reptilian ships formed up less than a minute later, out of the station's range, the two battlecruisers in the center, flanked by the remaining destroyers, quickly reorganizing into an attack formation. Helo began to rotate the station, readying it for battle, while the patrol ships quickly rerouted from across the system, jumping in to join the others.

Seventeen Reptilian warships moved in formation towards the station, opening fire as soon as they were within range. Helo returned fire, targeting only the specific ships the doctor had identified.

The battle raged for several minutes while the crew of the *Phoenix* watched in silence. Fire from both sides streaked across the space between them, the station taking heavy damage but giving as good as it got, destroying four more ships and crippling three others. Eight of the ten remaining vessels had been untouched by its assault thus far, while two of them – a light cruiser and a frigate – now bore its sole attention.

The ships continued their assault as the station's main power fluctuated, the auxiliary power taking over, allowing Helo to maintain control as the AI rerouted all available energy to the weapons, cutting life support and pouring on the assault.

Jackson sat watching with grim satisfaction as the carnage unfolded, both he and the doctor too engaged to leave despite her two-minute ultimatum having come and passed.

"Damage report," the admiral ordered.

"The station has sustained critical damage. The remaining ships will destroy it in less than two minutes if they continue their rate of fire," Helo reported.

A flash of light appeared on the viewscreen as the light cruiser exploded.

Suddenly, all fire from the station ceased.

"Weapons systems are offline," Helo informed the crew, the station's rotation slowing. "Its power core is becoming unstable."

The remaining ships ceased fire while Helo relayed a transmission from one of the undamaged battlecruisers, ordering the station to surrender.

"We would rather die than be slaves! The rule of the serpents must end. Rise up and join us! Saurians unite!" the station replied, broadcasting defiantly on an open subspace channel.

"Admiral," Helo said, "the lead cruiser is opening a channel, likely to the Empire's fleet command."

"Can you listen in?"

"Attempting to access the frequency via the station's transmitter. One moment. The signal is encrypted. Accessing the station's database. Encryption keys located. Signal acquired."

The crew of the *Phoenix* listened while Helo translated. The captain of the Reptilian cruiser reported to its superiors that saurians had taken over the battle station, attacking only ships with little or no complements of saurians on board, attempting to start a rebellion. It began detailing the battle damage, when suddenly weapons fire erupted in the background. "Saurians are attacking the bri—" The captain's voice suddenly ceased, a hail of weapons fire filling the channel.

Silence followed for several seconds before a different voice spoke over the comm. "We will be slaves no more. Rise up! Saurians unite!"

A moment later, the cruiser opened fire on the remaining frigate, the final ship the station had been targeting. It fired back in vain, already badly damaged and hopelessly outgunned, exploding a moment later. Several of the other ships targeted the cruiser, a new battle raging for nearly a minute as, slowly, each of the other ships ceased to fire.

"Analysis," the admiral said while the crew watched on the edges of their seats.

"The battlecruiser has taken moderate damage," Quentarus reported, "but it's still operational. Each of the other ships are signaling they are now under saurian control!"

"Send the final message," the admiral commanded.

The station transmitted once again. "Do not let our sacrifice be in vain. Free our brethren. Destroy the serpents who oppress our people. Saurians uni—"

The message cut off as the station exploded, its core going critical.

Jackson and the rest of the crew stood breathlessly, watching in awe at the destruction on the viewscreen while the saurian-controlled ships pulled away, taking evasive action as large fragments of the station were thrown in all directions.

The ships formed up again once out of range of the destruction, a series of messages transmitting between them.

One of the ships, a light cruiser, broke off from the fleet, setting a course for the GCH station orbiting Hakara II. Helo intercepted a transmission a moment later, ordering the saurians on the station to return to their boarding craft and bring the humanoids with them as hostages.

"Lieutenant, signal the *Valaris*. It should still be holding position at the edge of the system," the admiral ordered.

Lieutenant Quentarus opened a channel, nodding to the admiral. "*Valaris*, this is Admiral Valentyen. Do you copy?"

A moment later, the captain of the *Valaris* appeared on the screen. "Admiral?"

"Captain Eden, I assume you've been monitoring the situation in the Hakara System."

"Yes, sir. We're not sure yet what happened, but we picked up several broadband transmissions, which appear to indicate a saurian rebellion just took place."

"Agreed. It appears as though the saurians have risen up. We believe they took over the station before it was destroyed and now control the remaining ships."

"How do you know that, sir?"

The admiral gave his subordinate a stern look, indicating not to say anything more in front of her crew. "I'm ordering you to jump to Hakara II and set a course for our station in orbit."

"Yes, Admiral."

"There's a saurian light cruiser en route to pick up the Reptilian soldiers who boarded the station. They've ordered them to bring the crew of the station as hostages, likely to use them as bartering chips with the GCH later. The rest of their fleet is moving off on a different course, and they don't know you're here yet. I want you to jump in right on top of that light cruiser and explain it to them."

"What if they resist, sir?"

"The *Valaris* outguns them four to one. They'll likely get the message. If they resist, however, you have my authorization to open fire and disable their weapons. If their other ships decide to come to their aid, you'll have them at your mercy as a bargaining chip. Once you have their attention, be sure to impress upon their commander that we expect our people on the station to be left there, unharmed, and that this will be the last of them we see in GCH or OU space. Tell them that we're willing to forgive their trespass, as is the Oceanic Union, as long as they take their people and return to Reptilian space immediately."

"Aye, sir."

"Also, inform their commander that if they leave peacefully, the GCH will provide them with our latest intel on Reptilian fleet movements in the region, allowing them to evade the rest of their former fleet, giving them a fighting chance to rally more saurians to their cause."

"Of course, sir."

"I'll stand by for your report once you've delivered your terms. Admiral Valentyen out."

Lieutenant Quentarus closed the channel while the

crew watched on the viewscreen as the *Valaris* came out of hyperspace less than ten kilometers from the light cruiser, its shields up and weapons fully charged. The saurians, realizing the hopelessness of an engagement with a GCH battlecruiser, opened a channel, standing down a moment later.

"All right, time to go, Will," the doctor said, and she and Johansen assisted Jackson back to the medical bay. The admiral promised to keep them all apprised of any updates while he awaited a report from the *Valaris*.

Several minutes later, the *Phoenix* received an encoded transmission from Captain Eden. The admiral directed the lieutenant to patch in a feed to the med bay so that Jackson and the doctor could watch.

"On screen," the admiral said.

Captain Eden appeared, this time alone in her office. "Admiral, I'm pleased to report that the saurian commander has accepted our terms. Their troops have departed the station, and they've agreed to leave the system as soon as they're on board. I've been in contact with the station's commander, and he confirmed that despite being slightly roughed up when the Reptilians took control of the station, there are no casualties amongst his crew."

"Very good, Captain. I'll transmit the latest intel on the Reptilian fleet movements to you on a secure channel. You can then relay it to the saurian commander once they're ready to get underway. As soon as they're gone, your orders are to secure the system until the Oceanic Union's ships arrive."

"Yes, Admiral," the captain replied, hesitating for a moment. "How'd you do it, sir?"

"Captain, I'm sure I don't have the faintest idea what you're talking about," he said, keeping his face impassive.

"Of course, sir," she replied, suppressing a smile.

"If I did, however, it would be highly classified and not something that we'd ever want the Reptilians to find out about, or else this entire uprising would be for nothing. Am I clear?"

"Crystal, sir."

"Very good, Captain. Be sure that your crew understands that everything that has happened today is now classified, and scrub all records of our comms." The captain nodded. "I'll expect a full report once the OU arrives and you've made contact with their lead ship. The priority will then be to disable and capture the satellites the Reptilians deployed around Hakara II, to ensure they're not a threat to the indigenous population. Any questions?"

"No, sir."

"Very well, Captain, I'll leave this in your capable hands. Valentyen out."

The admiral turned to face Quentarus and Johansen, the internal comm still open to the med bay. "I think that we've done what we came here to do. Plot a course for Archon."

The captain of the *Valaris* sat silently in her office, blowing away a wisp of steam while she sipped a cup of coffee, her eyes fixated on her display. She'd instructed her Ops officer moments earlier to reroute all active sensor readings to her office, while he focused on monitoring the Reptilian withdrawal. A blip appeared on the far side of the fifth planet, disappearing as quickly as it had appeared. She reached over, entering a command on her console and deleting the sensor record of the jump while she silently wished the admiral and his crew good fortunes, thankful they were there that day.

CHAPTER 39

GOODBYES

Hours passed as the *Phoenix* continued towards Archon, the crew coming and going from the bridge while they rotated shifts. A nervous silence fell over them as they grew closer, knowing what it would mean once they arrived.

Their mission was over. The war was all that mattered now. And it was likely the last time they would be together, possibly for years.

Jackson spent just under seven hours in the medpod, resting while it worked to repair his injuries. He awoke, hungry and sore, his wounds healed, just a lingering grogginess from the drugs remaining.

As the doctor opened the pod, he embraced her, grateful for all she'd done for him. "Thanks, Daria," he said, his abdomen grumbling loudly. "My stomach thanks you, too. God, I'm hungry. I can't remember the last time I ate."

"You're welcome, Will. But uh…" She gave him a look, her eyes moving up and down his body as he realized he was only wearing a pair of boxers. "You might want to put on some clothes before you head to the mess."

Jackson smiled. "That's why you're the doctor."

"And take it easy on the hot sauce. I just patched you back together. Remember, Terran physiology can't handle

Henrik's Kutarian dragon peppers on the best of days! I don't want to see you back here in twenty minutes clawing at your tongue because it got a second-degree burn."

"Hey, that only happened once!" he protested, pulling on a fresh uniform and the boots Johansen had left for him.

"Well, the next time it happens, I'm going to make you eat through a tube for three days while I let your tongue heal on its own or, worse, cover it in slime from an Argolian slug."

"Yes, Mom," he said with a smile as he headed for the mess.

Twenty minutes later, he was back on the bridge, his mouth only slightly burning while he took his seat at the helm, happy to be back at it and able to do something. The rest of the crew sat at their stations, working on their own projects, attempting to keep their minds occupied.

Moments later, an alarm broke the silence.

The admiral calmly brought up the small holo-display on the command chair as though he'd been expecting it. "We're approaching the region of the core systems. Helm, take the ship out of hyperspace."

"Aye, sir," Jackson replied, dropping the ship back into normal space while the admiral cycled through several screens on his display.

"Shortly before we left the Cestus System, Command issued new protocols for all ships to check in with Fleet Traffic Control before crossing into the core," the admiral explained. "The Hyperspace Defense Grid is now fully active and set to different vectors every four hours."

The crew was silent, each knowing what that meant; the war with the Imperium was not going well, the Grid having only ever been fully active five other times in the history of the GCH, a clear sign to everyone how serious things had become.

The Grid was designed to disrupt hyperspace travel across a wide area. It consisted of hundreds of thousands of specially designed hyperspace defense platforms deployed across hundreds of star systems. With these engaged, it protected the GCH core systems from enemy fleets jumping in close to a populated planet.

"I've entered my clearance codes. Awaiting validation from GCH Traffic Control. The Grid is at Level 2, according to the latest updates, but the Insectoids have been pushing us hard, continuing to strike at targets of opportunity, so Command isn't taking any chances with core systems, and several of them closer to the front have been upgraded to Defense Level 3."

A moment later, the admiral's console beeped and he brought up the message. "Okay, we're good to go. The Grid is clear on our current vector for the next two hours and thirty-eight minutes. Enough time for us to make it before the next shift. Resume course for Archon."

"Resuming course, sir," Jackson replied, turning back to the helm as he initiated the jump.

The admiral spent the next several minutes cycling through various reports on the war, which he'd downloaded while they were waiting for traffic control to grant them clearance. Finally, he stopped, staring intently at his display for several moments before clearing his throat and reading aloud to the crew. "GCH Intelligence has received multiple reports over the last few hours of activity within the Reptilian Empire."

The admiral brought the report up along with a scan of Reptilian fleet movements on the main viewscreen and holo-display. "Based on these reports, there are indications that dozens of Reptilian ships have opened fire on one another or broken off from their fleets, going rogue. GCH Intelligence has confirmed that this followed a subspace broadcast by a group of saurian rebels originating from the Hakara System.

"Our analysis of their fleet movements confirms that the Empire has pulled dozens of vessels away from their borders with the GCH, Insectoid Imperium, and Oceanic Union. Estimates put the rebels' fleet at anywhere from forty to sixty ships at present. 'Our assessment, at this time, is that the saurian uprising has escalated from a few minor incidents into a much more organized and significant rebellion, one which presents a very real danger to the fabric of the Empire itself,'" he read. "'It is our belief at this time that the Reptilian Empire has fallen into a state of civil war.'"

"Holy shit!" Johansen said, while Jackson and Quentarus gave one another a silent nod.

They'd done it. They'd prevented a war with the Reptilians, effectively turning the Empire on itself and saving the Confederation from a war on a second front. One they had no chance of winning.

Something Captain Delgado had told him once came back to Jackson.

"The most important missions, the ones that make the most difference, are often the ones that no one ever knows about."

Hours later, the *Phoenix* exited hyperspace in the Archon System, holding position at a checkpoint close to the designated egress point the admiral received from Fleet Traffic Control. They passed through the checkpoint, two destroyers flanking them and the ships scanning them thoroughly, then giving them permission to jump further in-system. They arrived moments later, staring at the viewscreen.

"Whoa," Jackson said, the system bustling with activity as they approached the capital world.

"Looks like the shipyards are working around the clock," Quentarus pointed out as dozens of cargo haulers came and went from the row of orbital berths, bringing raw materials at a pace they'd never seen before.

"I saw a report that they've escalated production significantly, hoping to turn out a few dozen new vessels ahead of schedule to assist in the war effort," the admiral said.

They watched as a group of ten ships passed nearby, another patrol moving in the opposite direction several minutes later, as the mighty 7th Fleet kept watch, guarding the system in force. Numerous other ships appeared stationed in a high orbit around Archon itself, ensuring the protection of the capital and ready to respond if needed.

"Looks like they called the entire 7th back," Johansen said. "I'm showing just over a thousand warships in-system."

"There's also half a dozen ships from the 44th Fleet that have been redeployed to patrol the outer edges of the system," Quentarus commented.

"Command isn't taking any chances," the admiral said. "The entire 3rd Fleet is in the Delconia System, while the 48th Fleet is stationed in the Kuteria System, and the 63rd Fleet is at Cicarrus. They've also split up three other fleets and have them stationed in a dozen other core systems and taken four more and redeployed them to around thirty other locations. We've got about twenty-five fleets in the fight, with over a dozen others being partially redeployed. Command is pulling in ships from along the frontier and border with the

OU, now that things there appear to be calmer, so we should have upwards of thirty thousand ships in the fight within the next few days."

The crew nodded, considering the incredible amount of firepower and tonnage that was being assembled to face the Imperium.

"Sir, we've received clearance to land," Jackson said, setting a course for GCH Central Command. As they approached, he could see the Fields of Remembrance in the distance, the thought crossing his mind that perhaps the *Viceroy* would have its own place there when this was all over. God knew they deserved it. The only question was, would the GCH honor their sacrifice for what it truly was, or would it have to remain classified, never giving them the full measure of recognition they deserved?

As soon as they landed, the admiral led the way, the crew falling in behind him as they approached the first of several security checkpoints. Once beyond the outer ring of the Command complex, a wide courtyard filled with fountains, gardens, and trees spread out before them, bustling with activity and chatter as officers came and went.

Six massive central buildings spread out before them, each unique, representing different architectural styles from across the Confederation, with dozens of smaller ones surrounding them. The tallest of them, a shimmering tower of reflective glass and polished silver daramite, rose from the center of a massive courtyard. The seat of the Admiralty and the heart of the GCH military was set against the backdrop of the mountains and rivers of the stunning landscape just a few dozen kilometers away.

GCH flags blew at half-mast, flanking the white marble walkway leading to the main entrance.

The seal of the GCH lay embedded in the ground just before the doors, and a group of armed soldiers stopped each officer, verifying their credentials. Once inside the building, Jackson could see dozens of statues, sculptures, and other works of art spread out across the main lobby, a representation of the achievements of humanoid kind.

Admiral Valentyen led them through the brightly lit hallways of Command, past several additional security checkpoints, until they were shown to a lift which took them up two hundred levels to the top floor of the tower where the Fleet admirals' offices were located.

"I messaged Fleet Admiral Lighton, and she's expecting us. Several others are going to join the debrief, and they're all eager to hear about what happened," Admiral Valentyen explained. "They don't have a lot of time with the war effort, so keep your answers short and to the point."

A lieutenant ushered the crew into a large conference room with a high crescent-shaped bench, where two of the five Fleet admirals sat. A third appeared a moment later as a holographic projection, the session prepared to get underway.

The Fleet admirals consisted of Admirals Mendez, Takhata, Dash'ari, Holup, and Lighton. Three women and two men in all. The highest level of authority in the GCH military structure, each having dedicated their lives in service to the Fleet. Jackson recalled that members of the Admiralty served for terms of ten years and were elected from a group of their peers, Admiral Mendez being the elder stateswoman of the group and having served the longest: three consecutive terms.

Fleet Admiral Lighton met Jackson's eyes as he entered the room, giving him a slight nod as he took his seat.

The doors closed, and Admiral Mendez began with little preamble, introducing Admirals Lighton and Holup, then diving right in.

"Admiral Valentyen, we've read your preliminary report, and it appears that you and your crew have been quite busy. We'll need to debrief you all further to understand the intricacies of your report, but it appears that we owe you a great debt of gratitude. Your actions in the Hakara System, while incredibly risky, have saved us from fighting a second war. Your initiative in this matter will not go unnoticed, despite the need to classify all information regarding your operation."

"Of course, Admiral," Admiral Valentyen replied.

"I've brought the rest of the Fleet admirals up to speed on Lieutenant Commander Jackson and your mission," Admiral Lighton explained. "We have several questions regarding what transpired; however, it may be more efficient for you to explain it in your own words. Admiral Valentyen, if you'd please."

"Of course," Admiral Valentyen replied.

He provided a detailed account of their mission since they were last on Archon after the attack on Praxian Prime and informed them of the crew's suspicion that there was a mole at Command and how they were being tracked. The admiral then recounted how he authorized Jackson to take the *Phoenix* to Brestin III alone, in order to attempt to flush out their attackers, framing it as part of his plan to eliminate the possibility that any of the crew could have been compromised.

Jackson felt a pang of guilt as the admiral covered for him, hating that his CO lied on his account, but knowing that it would be far more complicated to explain the truth in the short time they had, and the need for total secrecy regarding the whereabouts of the Ancient doomsday weapons they had discovered.

Admiral Valentyen continued, explaining how he felt that Jackson going alone was the only way that he could be certain that the rest of the crew were clear, stressing that Jackson had agreed to take the risk. He then gestured to Jackson, who stood, explaining what had happened in detail with the Cavarians, taking full responsibility for the attack on the village after his initial confrontation had ended in a stalemate, and explaining his temporary memory loss. The admirals were clearly displeased by the loss of life and potential cultural damage to the Vicara class civilization; however, they all knew from lifetimes of experience that the best-laid plans did not always work out as planned and they moved on after several questions.

Jackson played the admirals the recording of Alura, then detailed the ambush in the valley and how he'd infiltrated the Insectoid ship. The Fleet admirals were intensely interested in the data he'd retrieved from the Insectoid database on the ship and he informed them that Bits had uploaded it for analysis to a secured location. Fleet Admiral Holup's holographic image flickered as he turned away for a moment, instructing the androids to prioritize its analysis, while Jackson continued.

The revelation of the bioweapon attack on the Insectoids also caught their attention, and the data breach into the highly classified GCH data-store where information regarding the mission to search for Ancient technology was stored.

The Fleet admirals questioned Jackson for nearly ten minutes, probing to get a clearer sense of several of the key events, pressing in some cases for every small detail.

"When you returned to the Ancient site, were you able to recover any of the technology?" Admiral Holup asked.

"My team was just beginning recovery operations when the Imperium fleet cut our operation short," the admiral explained, the one omission the crew had all agreed upon as a temporary compartmentalization of information, knowing that they couldn't let anyone outside of themselves, not even their AIs, know about the Light weapons and where they were.

At least not while there was a chance that there was a mole somewhere inside Command.

"Did you locate any of the weapons that the Ancient spoke of at the site?"

"No, ma'am," Admiral Valentyen replied crisply, not missing a beat. "We didn't find any. They must have all been deployed or still out of phase somehow, and the Ancient hologram made a mistake."

Fleet Admiral Mendez nodded thoughtfully. "Thank you all for your service to the Fleet and the Confederation. All records of your activities, going back to the day your team was assembled, will be classified at the highest level. No one must know about what happened and the possibility of these weapons being out there. All of the technology you've gathered thus far will be locked away here at Command until such time as we're able to resume your mission and analyze it."

"Yes, ma'am," the crew responded in unison.

"I'm quite concerned with this theory of a traitor," Fleet Admiral Lighton commented. "We'll look into it on our end, but for now, I'm not certain that keeping the Ancient technology that's been recovered here is a good idea."

The Fleet Admirals discussed this for a moment. "We've agreed that the technology will be stored at a black site, which will be known only to Admiral Valentyen and myself in order to keep this entirely off the books," Lighton said. "We cannot risk any of it falling into our enemies' hands."

"Understood," Admiral Valentyen replied.

Fleet Admiral Mendez provided the crew with a short briefing on the war with the Insectoids. "The initial enemy assaults have put the GCH on the defensive, as you know. In the last eleven hours, however, we've engaged in several coordinated Fleet actions and begun to push back. The front lines are now becoming clearer, and the Insectoids are digging in, securing their positions.

"Your mission to recover Ancient artifacts is, as of now, over. Admiral Valentyen, you'll be returning to GCH Intelligence, coordinating Fleet movements and tactics. Dr. Duratis, we've assigned you to the Ministry of Exobiology on Delconia to assist in classifying new Insectoid species being deployed in ground campaigns. Lieutenant Quentarus, you're to report to a special operations unit near the front lines. Chief Johansen, we require your technical expertise as a project lead at the Tactical Engineering Division on Devlonus II. Finally, Lieutenant Commander Jackson, you're being deployed to a covert-ops team under the command of Admiral Scott and will take the *Phoenix* with you."

The Fleet admirals dismissed the crew, and they left the Command building in silence. Once outside, Admiral Valentyen addressed them. "Take the rest of the day to get settled. I had my AI book rooms for each of us at a hotel in downtown Castilles. We'll meet at 1900 for dinner and drinks. My AI will send you the details."

The crew went their separate ways, Lieutenant Quentarus to retrieve some of her gear from the *Phoenix*, while Johansen and the admiral went with her to collect the crates of Ancient tech they brought back from the Hideaway and then bring it to Command to be stored safely until it could be moved to a black site. The doctor accompanied Jackson as he left for the hospital to visit Verris, his concern growing that he hadn't heard back from the doctors in days.

They arrived twenty minutes later, Daria checking in with the doctors while Jackson went to see Verris, standing just outside the temporal suspension chamber, the odd time distortion effect making him feel slightly dizzy.

"I have to go away for a while, Ver," he said, fighting back the tears. "And I'm not sure when I'll see you again. But when all this is over, we'll be together again, I promise. You just have to do your part and come back to me. Okay?"

He sat for some time, the only sound that of the gentle beeping of monitors showing the status of the temporal field. The room had a sterile smell, its matte white walls clean and institutional, reminding him of his time at the hospital on Titan Station when he'd first arrived. The thought of leaving Verris here, of her waking up surrounded by strangers, tore at his heart. He was being deployed to a covert-ops base down the Holt Line, seven thousand light-years from Archon, the distance adding to his heartache. He wouldn't be back to the core systems for some time, he knew. It was possible that if they could find a way to treat Verris, and she woke up, it could be weeks or even months before he could get leave to see her.

Daria entered the room, gently placing her hand on his shoulder. He looked up, unashamed of the tears streaking down his face.

"I've spoken to several of the doctors here, Will, and they have some of the best minds in the Confederation working on this. It's just a matter of time before they find a way to treat her."

"Did they say why we hadn't heard anything for days?"

"They did. Apparently, transmissions are being limited to military priority comms only. Civilian networks are still transmitting, but since we've been on-mission, they would have had to use a Fleet channel to relay the signal to the *Phoenix* or the Hideaway, and both are being limited at the moment."

"Makes sense. I was so worried that something had happened..." He trailed off, standing and turning to hug his friend, thankful for the support she provided.

"You will see her again. And they will find a way to fix this. Believe that, okay?"

"I do," he whispered.

Jackson looked back inside the chamber, staring at Verris, seeing the face he'd woken up to so many times before, the face that laughed and cried and smiled with him over the years. The face of the woman he loved.

He followed the doctor, stopping at the door. His time with Verris had been the happiest of his life. His world was shattered without her.

He looked back one last time, burning the memory into his mind, then turned to leave, uncertain if he'd ever see her again.

"Goodbye, Ver. I love you."

Later that night, the crew met for dinner and drinks in the heart of downtown Castilles, a large, bustling city on

Archon a few hundred kilometers away from Command. After dinner, they played holo-darts for over an hour, Kelara wiping the floor with them, her hand-eye coordination off the charts. They laughed and told stories; the drinks flowing freely, none of them wanting the night to end. As the hours passed, the cold reality of them shipping out the next day loomed like a dark shadow. That both Jackson and Quentarus were about to be deployed to active duty weighed heavily on them all, as did the burden of the secrets they all shared.

The crew walked together back to the hotel, each stopping to embrace one another as they said their goodbyes.

"You be careful out there, Will," the doctor implored him. "And remember to keep in touch."

"I will. Thanks, Daria, for everything. Would you mind checking on Verris the next time you're on Archon?"

"Of course. Delconia is only a few light-years away. I'll be back at least once a month, and I'll let you know if there's any progress on a treatment, I promise."

"Thanks," he said, embracing her in a warm hug.

He turned to face Johansen next, who wore a distinct sadness on his normally buoyant face. "I'll miss you, buddy," Jackson said, shaking Johansen's hand while giving him a hug with his other arm. "Be sure to send some toys my way if you come up with anything cool."

Johansen smiled. "Oh, I've got a few ideas. Be safe, okay?"

"Will do," Jackson replied, turning to face the admiral and shaking his hand. "Thank you for everything, sir," he said, realizing how grateful he'd been to serve under his command. Most COs would have had him court-martialed after he'd stolen a ship and defied a direct order, but Admiral Valentyen had trusted him and given him another chance when he wasn't even sure if he deserved one himself.

"I'll try to keep an eye on you from afar," the admiral assured him. "Always remember that you're never alone out there, Will. If there's anything you ever need, don't hesitate to ask."

"Thank you, sir," he said, having felt a connection with him since they'd first met, an almost fatherly overtone to their relationship, one which he'd come to value immensely.

Jackson and Kelara hugged goodbye, a few words exchanged between them. After what happened back on the battle station, he found himself at a loss for words. He knew that she'd be heading into the thick of the fighting on the most dangerous operations, and he hoped that she'd have a chance to heal before going into battle again.

Jackson awoke the next morning, regretting that he hadn't said more to the lieutenant, asking Bits to see if he could track her down before she left. Jackson found her just as she was leaving the armory at one of the Fleet transport hubs not far from Command.

"Morning, LT. Need a hand?" he asked, walking up to her just as she came out of the building, gesturing to the two loaded duffel bags she was carrying.

"Jackson?" she said. "Sure."

She handed him one of the bags, the weight of it catching him off guard.

"Whoa, what do you have in here?"

"Oh, just a few toys." She smiled wickedly as she shouldered the other bag, and they headed towards the pad where her shuttle sat waiting.

They made small talk as they walked, discussing the state of the war and the latest reports of a large Insectoid incursion in the Makarus Sector, neither one having any illusions that this was going to be a short or easy war.

As they approached the shuttle, Jackson changed the subject. "Hey, thanks again for saving my ass on that station. I keep replaying it over and over in my head. If you hadn't been there, I would have been done for, for sure."

"Anytime," she said. "And thanks for what you said... for talking me down. You were right, I wasn't myself. Most people wouldn't have stood up to me like that and...I needed that. Thank you for being a good friend, Will. I'm sorry about what I said. My...my dad...he was always my anchor, you know. I knew ever since I was a child that he could die in the line of duty, but losing him the way I did...being there and seeing it happen. I—"

She paused, turning her head, pretending to brush her hair away from her eye.

"When I lost my wife, I was there too. It's both better and worse at the same time. The image of them passing gets burned into your mind, and you replay it over and over again. But there's a peace in that as well, that you were there. That they weren't alone."

Kelara nodded, unable to find the words.

Jackson reached over, giving her a hug. He didn't expect to receive one in return but was surprised when her arms came around him, squeezing him tightly. After a few moments, they both let go and stood facing one another.

"You be safe out there, okay?"

"Will, you should know by now. I'm always careful, but I'm never safe."

"Yeah, that sounds about right."

He gave her a hand loading her bags onto the ship, and they said a final goodbye. He stood watching while her shuttle took off, rocketing out of sight, suddenly realizing how much he was going to miss her. How much he was going to miss them all.

Jackson made his way back to where the *Phoenix* sat waiting. He stepped onto the bridge, his heart sinking as he looked around at the empty stations, picturing Verris and the crew and how different it felt with them all there. He took a seat at the helm, running his hand along the console, realizing this would likely be his new normal for the foreseeable future.

"Do you think that we'll ever be together with them all again…like it was before?" he asked Bits, grateful for the company of his loyal companion.

"Statistically speaking, it is unlikely that all of you will survive this conflict," Bits said clinically. "That being said, I do hope that we see them all again. They are unique and complex individuals, and I will miss their presence."

"Me too, buddy. Me too," he replied, letting out a deep breath. "Okay, it's time to focus. We've got a job to do. Fire up some music, will you?" he said, attempting to distract himself from thoughts of the crew, smiling a moment later as the opening guitar riff from "Thunderstruck" began to play through the ship's speakers.

The *Phoenix* broke orbit minutes later and Jackson set a course for the covert-ops facility in the Terahdan System, looking back at Archon one last time as it grew smaller in the viewscreen, his thoughts drifting to Verris and his friends.

"Bits, you ready to go?"

"Affirmative, William."

"All right then. Let's go kick some Insectoid ass and win this war!" he said triumphantly as the *Phoenix* vanished in a flash of light, the end of one journey coming to a close while the start of another began.

EPILOGUE

SEVEN HOURS AFTER
THE EVENTS ON PRAXIAN PRIME...

Arkamus awoke as the world came slowly back into focus. He sat up, pushing through the pain of two fractured ribs as he slowly got to his feet.

"Well, looks like I'm stuck here," he said, the bridge of the *Ranger* smashed all around him. He surveyed the damage, knowing that he was lucky to have landed the ship in one piece, let alone walk away from it.

He reached for a portable scanner band, pressing it to his wrist, then collected his rifle from the weapons locker, shouldering it while he selected several other weapons before locking it once more. He moved to the supply closet, gathering up a pack of rations and water.

"How long have I been out?" he asked, not expecting a response, but used to thinking out loud while he problem-solved.

"Well, no one killed me in my sleep, so that's something."

Moments later, he emerged from the ship, the long trail where it skidded to a stop marked by a swath of shattered trees, along with scattered dirt and rocks. He moved to a nearby rise, tossing three small spheres into the air, then climbed to the top. The spheres disappeared into the sky, and he activated the scanner on his wrist as the world around him became rendered in the holo-display.

"Praxian Prime," he grumbled, taking a breath through the breather he wore on his face, covering the scars from battles past. "Radioactivity detected. Just what I needed."

His hard eyes surveyed the area, looking for signs of life.

The scanner beeped, drawing his attention back to the holographic map, a red marker appearing. He tapped it with his finger and the image zoomed in, the power readings appearing deep beneath the ground, the scanner providing a window with its analysis. *Etlentian power signature detected.*

"So, he was here to find an Etlentian site," he said, looking at the scans once more. "He must know then what he can do. I need to get out of here. I need to find him before *they* do," he said, a wave of paranoid urgency washing over him.

He stared at the map, plotting a course when another marker appeared. He zoomed in once more, pulling up the scans as they showed one of the Imperium ships he'd taken out having made it down to the planet as well.

"Damn. It's crippled, but there might be survivors. Bugs didn't even bother to rescue their own," he spat, looking back at the display and realizing that they likely would detect the power readings as well that close by.

He unshouldered his rifle, checking the power readings, then looked down upon vast the forest stretching out before him.

He pulled up his hood, steeling his will as he turned, his tattered coat flowing in the wind after him.

It was time to get his hands dirty.

It was time for some payback.

To be continued in Legacy - Book 4 - Shatterpoint

BRADLEY ELLIOTT

is a writer based near Toronto, Canada, where he lives with his wife and two children. He's an avid hockey fan, board game fanatic, and lover of the great outdoors. An unabashed geek at heart, he's always up for discussing sci-fi, fantasy, movies, or why Han shot first and Greedo had it coming.

You can find out more by visiting:

WWW.BRADLEYELLIOTT.CA

Printed in Dunstable, United Kingdom

80990320R00272